Helen

SAVAGE SLEEP . . .

"may well stir up savage controversy . . . IT IS AS GRIPPING AND AS HYPNOTIC A PIECE OF READING AS YOU ARE GOING TO DO ALL SEASON."
—The New York Times

MILLEN BRAND

is "one of the very few American novelists with the ability and qualification to write about such a serious subject and to present it so engrossingly that the reader cannot keep from becoming personally involved."
—Erskine Caldwell

"A TERRIFYINGLY BEAUTIFUL BOOK!"
—Ann Fairbairn,
author of "FIVE SMOOTH STONES"

D0048034

SAVAGE SLEEP

BY MILLEN BRAND

A NOVEL

"... in every one there are certain species of desires that are terrible, savage, and irregular, even in some whom we think of as obviously well balanced, and this indeed becomes evident even in sleep."

PLATO, The Republic

This low-priced Bantam Book
has been completely reset in a type face
designed for easy reading, and was printed
from new plates. It contains the complete
text of the original hard-cover edition.
NOT ONE WORD HAS BEEN OMITTED.

SAVAGE SLEEP

A Bantam Book / published by arrangement with
Crown Publishers, Inc.

PRINTING HISTORY

Crown edition published October 1968
2nd printing ..... October 1968
Literary Guild Alternate Selection March 1969
Bantam edition published October 1969

Quotations for Dr. Marks's article, "Resolving Acute Catatonic
Excitement," are adapted from an article by John N. Rosen, M.D., in
Direct Analysis: Early Papers, *published by Grune & Stratton, Inc.*

Bantam Books are published by Bantam Books, Inc., a National
General company. Its trade-mark, consisting of the words "Bantam
Books" and the portrayal of a bantam, is registered in the United
States Patent Office and in other countries. Marca Registrada.
Bantam Books, Inc., 666 Fifth Avenue, New York, N.Y. 10019.

To My Father

NOTE

When I was working as coauthor of the screenplay of *The Snake Pit* over twenty years ago, as part of my research I talked among others with John N. Rosen, M.D., who was then just in the process of developing direct psychoanalysis. In *The Outward Room*, I had described the effort of a hospital doctor to bring Freudian insights to a psychotic, but a psychotic who was still in complete verbal contact and in other ways accessible. Even so, what I wrote was considered a pioneering novel. Now I was introduced to a psychiatrist who had found a way to talk with the mentally ill in their full state of disorientation and unreality, those whose very language was unintelligible in the ordinary sense. I began to watch Dr. Rosen work (for such psychotics have no self-consciousness) and I felt that this was the fulfillment of a promise hardly more than hinted at in *The Outward Room*. It was a therapy evidencing strong identification with the abandoned and rejected of our "sane" world, and I felt that it ought to be written about.

What I wrote, however, was again a novel. Cases would have to be imaginary (as in *The Outward Room*): no literal facts exist that adequately convey the sense of an immediate reality that is the essence of fictional form. *Savage Sleep* is not a nonfiction novel. It is a creation in its own right. For that reason, other than where persons are publicly known and so named, all other characters and their situations are fictional, and any similarity to an actual person or event is purely accidental.

The action takes place from 1943 to 1946.

Many friends in the profession helped me, particularly by giving me access to all parts of state hospitals (a large number of which I visited). My first-hand knowledge of psychotics includes extensive work as a psychiatric aide.

My particular thanks go to my son Jonathan for his devoted editing.

SAVAGE SLEEP

Part 1

1

The driver was leaning against his ambulance, talking with a Building Two attendant: "You got the commitment papers. They got to come. You just settle for that and you got it made, right?

"But it ain't always easy, like this pickup this morning. Let me tell you. This resident that goes with me, Dr. John Marks, is in his forties. Now why would a doctor in his forties be a resident at New State Hospital? That got me wondering from the start.

"It's a simple pickup on Bushwick Avenue. On the way, a truck ahead of us gets stalled and we can't go. It's no big thing, I clang the bell, but this Marks sticks his head out the window and starts yelling. I mean yelling. Well, the truck driver passes some remark, and here's Marks out the ambulance and walking towards the truck, taking off his coat. Anyhow that gets the truck going, and I swing in quick and pick Marks up and go on about our business. That's the beginning.

"So then we come to this tenement and go up, and already there's four cops there. This Mrs. Blumstein we're getting is quite a case, they got her in a straitjacket. One of the cops says her son got killed the second day of the Sicily landings.

"Well, here's this Marks, he starts talking to her—he talks a good five minutes whenever he can get a word in with all the screaming around. Finally he says, 'Mama, I just heard. They're not after you right now. They told me as long as you're with me, you're safe.'

" 'What do you mean, "they" told you?' I ask him.

"He says, 'The fiends,' yeah, and now the woman calms down, so he wants to take off the straitjacket, but the cops won't let him, and lucky because right away she's scream-

3

ing again. The cops want to get going. Why wait, you know? I thought we'd never get that woman out of there.

"Well, I'll see you."

Beating at his thigh with his gloves, the driver walked down toward Garage 22.

After Dr. Marks had arrived at the hospital, in the downstairs hall of Reception he took off Mrs. Blumstein's straitjacket. She remained quiet. She followed him to the elevator.

Did she know now she was in a hospital? He felt a quick tide of sympathy for her. It started from picking her up on Bushwick Avenue, the neighborhood where he grew up. And she had a motherly look, a look incompatible with her insanity. He might not be experienced, but he felt this woman could be reached.

She was examined by Staff and diagnosed and assigned to one of the electroshock wards, out of his charge. He kept thinking about her.

He went to see her.

As he came toward her outside the shock-treatment room, she walked out of line. Her hair was graying, and the corners of her eyes were withered. Indentations beside her mouth quivered as if they knew more than other parts of her body. A nurse caught her. "Stay in line, please."

She saw him clearly. Five radiant gold rods shone from his head, and she knew he was Moses because he was much larger than an ordinary man and had spoken with God. Being God's chosen, he would have a message for her that would undo the damage and restore the loss. He said, "How is it, Mama?" She was blinded by tears that slipped out and rolled down her cheeks and left her lashes wet.

Moses disintegrated and disappeared. The corridor was vacant. He was aware that now she didn't see him.

The nurse led her into a small room and told her to lie down on a leather-covered table like an operating table. She had difficulty understanding, and so one of the attendants indicated with motions what she was to do. The nurse put a wedge under the middle of her back, and the attendants grouped themselves around her and put their hands out to her chorically. She tried to say something, but a septic white cloth wad was put into her mouth. Dr.

Wellman adjusted the Shock Duration setting for two fifths of a second. The nurse smeared salve on her temples, a soft, lemon-colored jelly. She looked aside as Dr. Wellman grasped the electrodes. The electrodes closed their goring clamp on her temples, a switch was snapped, and she moaned or the outrush of her breath sounded of itself. Her eyeballs turned back. As her convulsions began, her body rose in the middle and jerked in rhythmic spasms. At the same time, her arms tried to lift, but the attendants thrust them down. The visit to death was brief, then the journey back began. For this, the attendants gathered her, still unconscious, into a blanket.

They wheeled her to an adjacent ward where seven beds were filled and placed her in the eighth, turning her body face down. A girl in the first bed lifted her head, staring at the attendants. "Grandpa," she said. "I just seen him in the other planet." She shook her head slowly. "I just seen him. Now my body's here. Here! It's here." She sobbed. "Where's my child?"

An attendant laughed.

That afternoon he went to Mrs. Blumstein's ward and found her sitting on the side of her cot. Complete silence. No, a slight murmur as if she wanted to say something, but had been reprimanded. It went on and stopped. "Mama?" No answer. He put his hand on her shoulder and with a quick movement, she rubbed her chin against his wrist. As if she knew him. As if she was calling to him. He found himself uncontrollably moved. Inside there she's lost. She's a human being and lost.

He found an excuse for visiting at Dr. Wellman's office. He said, "This Mrs. Blumstein—you know, a new case you have for shock—"

"Yes."

"I brought her in, I mean I made the pickup, and I have this feeling for her. I have the feeling that it would be possible to talk with her, get through to her, find out what's the trouble with her. It would mean stopping shock because you can't reach her in this amnestic daze she's in. But couldn't we stop shock and then I could try to talk with her? Try to get her aware there's somebody outside interested in her?"

"But even if Staff agreed to stop shock now, she

wouldn't be in contact," Dr. Wellman said. "And so you couldn't talk. The shock is to try to bring her into contact."

"Is everything out of contact?"

"What do you mean?" A suspicious look.

"When we dream at night, what's the part of us that remembers the dream?"

"If you're thinking of psychotherapy, you know that isn't feasible until you *have* contact. Just try talking with them the way they are now. See where you get."

Always when Dr. Marks reached home, he needed an interval to cleanse the hospital out of him, stop living there. Begin to be a husband and father. He needed it tonight particularly.

Margaret always helped. She at least was totally responsive and alive. After three children she showed no sign of childbearing, none of the sagging look of the multipara. She was nearly his own height. She was lithe and had good legs, something particularly attractive in a woman. She was self-confident, and flashes of mockery lay in wait in her deep hazel eyes. With her self-assurance, you would never suspect she had a few funny insecurities (they seemed funny): afraid of having any debt outstanding, for example, and afraid of leaving Brooklyn.

"How was it?" she said. "You look kind of beat."

"It was a day. How're the kids?"

"Your daughter's been chasing Murray."

"I'll fix that."

Nancy was nearly four and was the last child, a girl after two boys. He thought, What more could you want? But she *was* more—she had high spirits, strenuousness, sadness, and insidious talents of adoration. Naturally she adored him and he encouraged it. Wasn't it good for her?

She came running now, with her blond hair. She had a habit of pushing one strand steadily away from over her left eye, staring through it as she moved it. "Daddy!"

"Yes?"

"Is Uncle Robert coming?"

He glanced at Margaret. "Is he?"

"No, he's not coming."

Dr. Marks's brother usually brought a present for Nancy. That *could* be why they got this question from her. She said now, "I love him, don't I?"

"You like him, you love me. Remember it." And Dr. Marks took her up in his arms. "But you could phone him. You want to talk to him on the phone?"

Shyly: "No."

He kissed her and put her down and walked back to the boys' room. Bob (named after Uncle Robert) you might know was studying. "You got nine hours of homework again tonight?"

"No, only eight hours," Bob said, smiling. He was fifteen, in second-year high. He had always had a thing about his schoolwork. When he was just starting school, he used to cry over his homework, he'd get an ink blot on it, cry, start again, get another ink blot, cry, start again, and keep on till he had it right. He had his mind made up to go to medical school.

Johnny was three years younger, interests just beginning to define themselves. Music, maybe? Trumpet?

Both had Margaret's chestnut hair. And luckily neither looked like him. Going back up the hall, he glanced in the mirror at his own darker hair. Is it true I look like a gangster? Well, possibly. Something about the face, gangster or immigrant (one generation from Russia)—something about that look of layers of clay pasted down and not too well smoothed over. Five years ago he had been coming out of a tenement on a routine call to a miserable old woman; he'd been carrying his bag—what the hell, could it be mistaken for burglar's tools?—and somebody opened fire on him. One bullet went through his cheeks, another creased his head, and he fell down. Later he picked various bullets out of his clothing. He wasn't seriously hurt, and two days later he got a note at the office: "Dear Dr. Marks, sorry we mistook you for somebody else. It wasn't you we were after and we don't want you to worry."

Kindness, pure human kindness.

Nancy tagged after him to the living room to his habitual chair, and he held her awhile, putting a cigarette in his cigarette holder and blowing smoke rings for her. She giggled. When Margaret came in to take her to bed, she pouted. "You go on to bed," Dr. Marks said, "and I'll be in to kiss you good-night."

He remained in his chair, smoking. He thought of working out his next chess move (by mail) with his cousin Steve in Denver, but it wasn't the night for it.

Margaret, he thought, had some reason to be concerned about money. (He couldn't help a constant awareness of his whole situation just now, try as he would to repress it.) He was getting twenty-four hundred a year as resident after being one of the top—and top-paid—internists in private practice in Brooklyn. The hospital had offered him eighteen hundred, but he had pushed them up to twenty-four hundred because of his qualifications. Big deal for a family of five. He had a fair reserve in the bank, but it wouldn't last indefinitely.

His father "knew" he was crazy. Only Robert had any understanding of what was going on. And sometimes he asked himself, What *was* going on? What started all this?

In private practice, he had patients from time to time who were nervous, who had unexplained pains ("Oh, Doctor, my kidneys are killing me"), whom the usual medication didn't help. He gave them placebos, but wasn't satisfied. He had that feeling—you have to help anybody you agree to help. With the greatest reluctance, he came to the conclusion that these people must be having some mental thing: the mind influences the body. That meant he had to find out about the mind and two years ago he had decided he could get the insight he wanted with a Freudian training analysis. He was referred to Dr. Erich Naumann and Dr. Naumann had accepted him.

He had then gone on a limited basis to The Psychoanalytic Institute (he was now taking the full course) and had found he had to have clinical psychiatry. He tried a shortcut. Instead of going to a State Hospital, he got a job at The Vansittart Clinic in Manhattan, a leading clinic treating psychoneuroses. That way he figured to keep on with his medical practice on the side. The only trouble with that was he had still no knowledge of any serious mental disorder, and one day a woman came in and said people were spying on her from upstairs through the ceiling. . . .

"How do they do it? Is there a hole in the ceiling?"

"No, no," she said, "they can see through the ceiling. The people upstairs. They know my every move." She said it eagerly and he had the definite impression that she needed these people seeing her. "They're spies."

"You know this is a mental clinic here?" he asked her.

"I know."

"Why did you come here?"

Unembarrassed: "To get help against the spies. I called the police and when the policeman came, he raped me."

"What was his name?"

"I don't know his name."

"Did you get his badge number?"

"Certainly not," she said haughtily.

"Why do you say, 'Certainly not'?"

"I don't take numbers."

"Oh. Those people upstairs. Did they see you get raped?" he asked.

"No, they weren't looking just then."

He had gone to the Clinic head and told him about this woman and said, "She must be crazy."

The Clinic head had considered this classic remark and said, "To be useful in this clinic or anywhere else, you've got to learn more about insanity," and had sent him to New State Hospital.

"Nancy's ready for her kiss," Margaret said. He went back and found his daughter lying on her pillow waiting for him. She knew he would bend down and give her a hug, enfolding her in the love that would carry her through the night.

He hugged and kissed her. "Sleep well. Happy dreams," he said.

"How do you know I'll have happy dreams?"

"I'll see to it. I'll make them happy."

She laughed.

He came back into the living room and, unappeased by this love, told Margaret about Mrs. Blumstein. "I'm going to take a hammer to Dr. Wellman's shock machine."

"Yes," dubiously.

The first thing he had heard when he had arrived at New State was that there was a great cure for insanity there—electricity, Metrazol intravenous, and hypodermics of insulin. He was told published papers showed you got better than ninety percent cures. One paper said ninety-eight percent. Thousands of patients were going home. By then he had passionate feelings of commitment (instantaneous commitment) to the patients. Time after time it was like Mrs. Blumstein, something calling to him, appealing to him. Something had to be done.

He volunteered to give shock. Giving it violated the

deepest feelings he had against making people unconscious, but if they said it cured, he would do it.

In two weeks, he found out that shock simply wasn't doing what they said it would do. One of his shocked patients got into a nice amnestic daze for about a week and they sent her home. The next day she was rushed back to the hospital in violent excitement. Another young woman was discharged and a week later she climbed out on a fire escape where she lived and started taking her clothes off. Case after case was back on the wards until he asked himself: If this is such a great cure, why is the hospital still thirty percent overcrowded?

He also asked, Why are patients I'm shocking developing full-blown psychosis? Or going mute? He heard of deaths from shock. He read on the charts: "Spinal fracture . . . finger broken . . . leg broken."

One day he got himself transferred to other duties and that was the last of his giving shock.

Echoing in his mind, a patient's voice: "Something terrible is going to happen to me."

Another voice: "They told me I'd just feel the needle and then I'd go to sleep and the needle'd bring me out and I wouldn't mind, but they lied! It hurts. It aches my heart somehow, I can't explain it, it just runs and runs. I feel it like I'm going to die." Hysterically: "I can't stand it to have sixty insulins. I can't. I can't. They told me I'd sleep deep, but it's just catnaps. I'm so mis'able. It's such an awful feeling. I can't stand it. I can't stand it."

Margaret said, "I don't blame you for how you feel. You know that. But you have to be careful. Did you tell Dr. Naumann about Mrs. Blumstein?"

"Yes, I told him. And he calmed me, as usual. An interesting thing—he tied it back with Bushwick Avenue. . . ."

Out of a swirl of mist appeared a building. Three stories, of white stucco dead against a bland sky. On the ground floor of this building, a shoemaker's shop extended back from narrow windows, and, to the side, a door and stairs gave access to the upper-story flats.

SOCIETÀ MUTUO SUCCORSO in the corner of a nearby window.

In a side street off Bushwick Avenue congregated storefronts of verdigrised copper, and houses with rot pouring from the windows. Many funeral parlors. The trolley tracks hummed down the hill and off through the avenues. The smell of garbage hung in the air, always. Across Bushwick, a brewery raised a brass metal dome like a church cupola, and on Meserole Street, St. Catherine's Hospital flung up its sharp-pitched roofs and the red lines of its towers.

The canal. From upstairs in the house, it seemed as if you could look out to a shimmering tongue of water. Was it a canal?

Three houses from his, on a brick doorway, a flood of names was written, one on each brick: Mattio, Carlo, Leo, Joe C, Johnny, Zito, Buzza, Eddie, Bobby, Rocco, Sammy, Marian, Angelo, Elly, Molly, Rosie, Honey, Verna, Mielo, Tommy, Tony.

It was an alien world, unusually fearful for a child. It had seemed to him as if everything around him was unintelligible. Strange figures talking in an unknown language. He was strictly forbidden by his mother and father to cross the street, even to go away from the immediate house front by himself, and this prohibition was extended to Robert (at that time his sisters, Dora and Babe, were babies). "Don't cross the street." "Stay away from the wops." The "wops" were particularly fearful because they were not explained to him and he couldn't talk to them. Nothing was ever explained to him. This was what he was most conscious of, out of the years of his childhood. Nothing was ever explained.

He grew older and the ruling against crossing the street was lifted. Again without explanation.

His grandmother. His father's mother. The matriarch of the family, and now he had a memory of her on a particular Friday evening. She was devoutly religious. Some meat hadn't been delivered, and he said he knew where to go, he'd get some, so he ran down and brought back a steak, but it was from a Christian shop. His grandmother recognized it apparently from the butcher paper—he could only guess now how she had known, but she had known. And she poured out on him such contempt, she scourged him so with words in the presence of the entire family, that it was as if he had been physically beaten. But no word about what his sin was. No explanation. Never an explanation. Nothing explained so that he could know what he had done wrong, so that he could avoid his sinful folly another time.

At about that same time, he heard a couple of girls in the street referred to as "whores." They seemed to him like nice girls as they walked along, so he took occasion at home to refer to his growing sisters as "whores." His father unloosed his belt and beat him black and blue. No explanation. And later as his mother bathed his bruised buttocks and made some pitying remark, she too failed to tell him what he had done wrong.

It seemed to him now an unparalleled cruelty. A beating itself was supposed to convey the meaning of the word "whore." A tongue-lashing was supposed to explain non-kosher meat. Something inside him had cried out bitterly at this continual contempt expressed for him.

Once he had had a useless tantrum, with nobody around, beating on the floor with his fists (he wouldn't have dared in his father's presence). But it made him think of some of the patients at the hospital pounding on the floor or walls. Could it be that they too were secretly pleading for explanations? Was that what it meant, that they (old or young) needed parents who would explain to them what they were unable to understand themselves? One had said: "What the parents teach us in the night is in the night."

It was so much in the night. A pathology of asking to understand.

Mrs. Blumstein rubbing her chin against his wrist.

He kept thinking of his (evidently) insane appeal to Dr. Wellman to try to talk with Mrs. Blumstein. He thought of the files of women you walked through, their voices running after you like pleas ("Please"). These were not persons inherently different from himself or Margaret, nor were they different, either, from children. Something was the same.

He said to Margaret, "You know this analytic rule of free association. It's been going through my head: Isn't it something like psychotics? I mean, isn't that what psychotics do like that? You know the rule, you say whatever comes into your mind even if you think it's disagreeable or unimportant, you try to let one thing lead to another." (No self-criticism.) Freud told his patients to close their eyes. He told them to have "the mimic tranquillity of the man observing himself," a psychic state like the way the mind is before falling asleep—a borderline of attention. Dr. Marks thought, Isn't this the moment when your thoughts turn into visual or auditory substitutes, equivalents? He expressed this to Margaret and said, "What it comes down to is you're close to dreaming while you're awake. But isn't that the way a psychotic is? His hallucinations mean dreaming while he's awake. It's a kind of waking sleep. His productions then, the things he says, are certainly free enough. There's only the loosest kind of connection sometimes. I keep thinking these productions are like the analytic hour. You can listen to them. You can get some idea of the Unconscious from them."

"It's interesting," she said. She knew a good deal about Freudian theory by now.

"If I just knew more. If I could just stay steadily with a patient, and listen. I do try. But if I got caught, I'd practically be reported to the Superintendent. It means breaking the hospital code or something. All that doctors seem to want there is to get away from the patients, hike themselves up into top-level jobs, and leave the patients for the nurses and attendants. I mean it. It's as if the patients were dehumanized."

James Cady was standing motionless in a corner of a sixth-floor men's dayroom, a seventeen-year-old boy wearing denim pants and a blue shirt with two buttons unfastened. His hands were straight down and flat at his sides as if he were standing at attention.

Dr. Wellman motioned the visitor to follow. "You asked how 'withdrawn' they were. Watch." He lit a cigarette and blew smoke toward Jimmy's eyes. The eyes did not blink. Dr. Wellman brought his cigarette toward the right eye. The eye did not move or vary in expression although the burning end of the cigarette seemed about to plunge into it.

"Catatonic stupor. His eyes don't close."

Immobile and staring, Jimmy saw not the cigarette but an instrument pointed at him to examine him for a rare disease. The framework and knobs of the instrument and its long tube ended in an enormous eye. He was very small and this was a giant's eye. The large examining eye had a single word written across it: EMPEROR. The letters sprang apart, came together: REEROMP. The word REEROMP sounded in the air. His joints sprang apart like the letters and came together again. He would have to be very quiet now, very quiet. It all depended on keeping quiet. If he moved in the least now, it would be dangerous. Particularly if he moved his jaw muscles.

The elevator off the dayroom dropped with a sighing sound. That sound of breathing. Near. It was near and threatening. Something was breathing fire. He should be moving this way and that way, to avoid the fire. But if he moved, everything would come to an end. Move. Move. I cannot. He cannot. There was fire coming down. That tongue was working under the fire, everything was getting terrifying and contorted. "Move, save yourself." The voices: "You cannot save yourself. You're no good—filth, filth, filth."

He screamed soundlessly: "I'll have torture. No. No—"

"Filth—"

"No."

Dr. Marks finally figured out his chess move with Steve, using the small board on which he kept one of his several games-by-mail. Margaret watched him, but knew better than to advise. He stretched and said, "I wish I could stop thinking about the hospital. Maybe it'll let up."

"Likely," she said.

"Bed?"

They got up together and went to look in on the sleeping children. Nancy seemed peaceful, but Bob had his head buried in his pillow and was breathing uncomfortably. Margaret rearranged his head so that his breathing eased. Dr. Marks thought, Did Ma ever do that for me when I was a kid? Then he thought, Well, how would you know if you're asleep?

But wouldn't part of your mind know? You know these things.

2

At the hospital the next morning, Dr. Marks received a note from Dr. Steiner: "Please call at my office at your convenience." When he entered the Superintendent's office, Dr. Steiner said, "Please sit down." He had a whorl of hair like a bird crest, and his eyes had a strongly focused look. The look was hard to define—menacing? But his tone was pleasant. "I just wanted to mention to you that I hear good things about you. Several doctors called. Dr. Favario." What they had called about apparently was to mention to him several successes of their new colleague. Dr. Marks had spotted an intestinal cancer. Dr. Marks had diagnosed a renal colic and saved an appendectomy. "I don't need to tell you I'm glad to see a man like you here. We're short of doctors, desperately short with the war, and to have a good doctor like you—"

His phone rang and he excused himself. Dr. Marks heard: "Yes, they said I wouldn't get them, but the engineer and I drove up early—" When he hung up, he said, "I hear you're discouraged about shock treatment and I thought it might be useful to have a talk with you. I sometimes find with doctors who've just come in, there's an initial disappointment. They don't know that sometimes they stop too soon. Sometimes it takes a second or third series of shocks before there's any improvement. Of course that's something the more experienced doctors know, but I thought I'd mention it. We're doing everything we can here to make an outstanding contribution to therapy. We're getting results: few hospitals have the percentage of discharges we have and we're getting very favorable notice. We've even given shock to some child patients and to some senile cases."

Children and seniles!

"I wanted to have this talk with you. Of course, I wanted you to know how much your good work is appreciated. That comes first. But it's also important to speak to you and a few other residents about shock because we seem to be having a good deal of trouble just now getting consent signatures. I want you to be able to convince relatives that they should sign consents—this is as important as giving shock itself."

'They lied. It hurts. I feel it like I'm going to die.'
'Don't kill me, Doctor. Please don't kill me.'

"We just can't take any chances on giving shock without consents. We've already had four suits brought against the hospital, and I've had to warn the staff to be extremely careful. Now what might help is to show the relatives some of these tables." He passed Dr. Marks several mimeographed tables of statistics. "Of course I know this is only part of your work. But it is a very important part." When he saw that Dr. Marks had the tables actually in his hand, the Superintendent seemed to relax, and in a different, in a pleasant and interested tone, he asked, "Incidentally, maybe you'd tell me—how did you make that diagnosis of renal colic?"

Later in the morning, as Dr. Marks was going through the dayroom of Ward H, he saw two muscular nurses feeding a patient ice cream. They held the woman by her arms, which she raised distraughtly in something between a threat and a plea. "Eat, eat." "No, ahhhhhhh! I'm afraid—" "Eat." "Black. It's—" One of the nurses swabbed a spoonful of ice cream into the woman's mouth as she opened it to speak. "Swallow! Swallow!" "Ohhhhhhh." Somehow the woman sobbed and swallowed, and gazed wildly and questioningly from one nurse to the other. "The sign says north. Is it—?" "Eat." "Where am I? Won't the conductor or trainman or somebody tell me where I am?" The nurses forced another mouthful into her mouth and what she refused to swallow ran down over her chin. A doctor appeared from an alcove. "You, sir, I want to talk to you," the woman said. "Please, Florence—" "But I have to talk to you, conductor. May I?" "If you eat your ice cream, I'll talk to you." Wildly she said, "He won't. He won't. Bastard, he breaks everything."

Dr. Marks sensed her frustration. Always that desperate need to communicate. He felt its agony with this patient. Ward H, one of the shock wards. When he went to the door on the far side, he found that a patient had scribbled *ell* after the H on the door and nobody had yet cleaned it off. The paint behind the writing was like the oval of a soft blind eye as if the same letters had been written there and cleaned off again and again. Shock. *Hell*. On the male insulin ward, moist heat floated above the men going into coma, attendants sometimes with knees on the patients' naked chests to hold them down until they "went under."

This is what a *mental* hospital had become.

Fourteen, fifteen years before, he had visited Saint Elizabeth's Hospital in Washington as part of his medical training. He could recall the wards of the insane there. There had been an essential difference. The difference was that patients there had not been resigned to a torture beyond the torture they deserved as mentally ill, beyond the torture of insanity. Electricity, Metrazol, insulin.

(Progress notes in James Cady's folder—Case No. 17244:)

7/31/43. Insulin shock treatment completed. Continues mute and withdrawn. No appreciable change.

8/2/43. Approved for electric shock.

When he lay down on the couch in Dr. Naumann's office at five o'clock, the time of his daily session, he felt a mild block. Sometimes you resist sleep, the sleep of self-examination. Naumann of course would notice it. He was tenacious and unfailing in noticing everything. He was a genius.

In articles and clinical reports and in several books, Erich Naumann had made contributions to theory that had been recognized by Freud. He had studied in Vienna and at Burgholtzli under Bleuler (in the later days), had practiced and written in Berlin, and ten years ago, escaping Nazism, he had come to New York. He was now in his sixties, small, thin, and slightly bald. He took no care for dress or possessions, and he had no outward interests beyond his work, so much so that his colleagues said that he was "all Unconscious." He spoke English comprehensively. He thought in German. He had one unusual element in his background that he shared with a close friend, Dr. Paul Federn, another emigrant: an interest in the psychoses. In his younger days, when he had had the physical stamina, he had been on the staff of a Berlin mental hospital, and with courage and great natural absorption, he had investigated the psychotic process. It was a matter of regret to him that with advancing years he had not been able to continue this, for he felt that the new insights he gained helped him as an analyst. He was modest. At times he could be sharp, even sarcastic, but as Dr. Marks was well aware, he was always his patient's friend and maintained an unchanging therapeutic loyalty. This along with the profession's technical reserve.

Just as Dr. Marks had read Freud, he read Naumann, summarizing and even memorizing. Many of Naumann's papers had been translated into English, but where not, Dr. Marks painfully read them in German. It could not be just part of his transference to think that Naumann's understanding was little less than God's. What that man knew! It was almost too much to have that omniscience breathing at the head of the couch.

As his start-of-the-session block continued, he thought, If I talk about the hospital, that may get me into it. He told Dr. Naumann about his interview with Dr. Steiner. "So what he really wanted was for me to get consents. Strange, isn't it, that there is more and more difficulty for doctors to persuade families they are doing something good for the patient?" He went on to tell about a woman who broke a tooth during shock treatment yesterday and whom Dr. Wellman had had to send to the dentist, and this woman had had a kind of hysterical fit at the dentist's office. "The reason shock treatment was developed, they told me, was because epileptics aren't supposed to be schizophrenic so you produce artificial convulsions and that's supposed to be antipathetic to schizophrenia. But this woman apparently had seizures anyway. Well, that's like the whole thing there."

He was reminded now of an epileptic he had brought to the hospital, and he told about it in detail because of the light it could conceivably throw on insanity—at any rate on the working of the mind. Also because the woman with the tooth fracture yesterday had reminded him of this epileptic and this reminder had entered into a dream he had had last night. He described how he and an ambulance driver had arrived at a rooming house for a pickup, and

the landlady told him it was "always the same thing with
this fella. His brother keeps him, pays his room and comes
to look after him. So first it's, 'Call my brother. I'm not
feelin' well.' Then a few days and he has a fit. He has a fit
now. And locks his room. He'll be layin' on the floor now
with the door locked." The driver said, "If the door's
locked, how we gonna get in?" "We'll get in," the landlady
said. "Come on up." They went up to the room and the
door was locked and the room was silent. "Harry, unlock
the door," the landlady called. No answer. "Harry, unlock
the door," she said in a confident voice. "How's he gonna
unlock the door if he's got a fit?" the driver said. "He'll
unlock it. Harry," she called again, insinuatingly, "unlock
the door." There was a little click, the faintest sound of a
click, and the landlady's face cleared. "There, the door's
open," she said. The driver said, "It's open!" "Yes, open
it." He opened the door and went in and a young man in
pajamas lay in an epileptic coma on the floor. "Who
opened the door?" the driver said. "He did," the landlady
said. "How could he? He's got a fit." "Just the same, he
did it." The driver went stubbornly around the room,
looking for somebody else. He looked in a kitchen alcove
and in a closet. "It's no use looking for nobody, he did it,"
the landlady said.

The strange fact that a person in coma, in an unques-
tionable coma, got up and unlocked the door.

"I told you about this because it has something to do
with a dream I had last night. I had a nightmare. A real
one—something I haven't had in a long time."

No sound from the chair at the head of the couch. That
meant, Go on. Dr. Naumann in listening was loose, non-
defining, explorative. He did not set the "watchers at the
threshold," but tried to let everything come in, from everywhere—past experience, present, the conscious, the unconscious.

"It wasn't just this epileptic," Dr. Marks said. "I better
give you the whole background." The classic Freudian
briefing, for it all entered into the dream. He told Dr.
Naumann how he had been talking with Margaret about
free association and psychosis—Naumann let him talk
without comment. "I also mentioned to her that I had
been thinking about my childhood lately. At one time I
had a low opinion of anybody who kept looking back to

the past. But that seems to be my main job in my analysis."

"I would not say that."

"It's a good part of it anyway. It gets so when I go to sleep, I feel like I'm working for you."

Dr. Naumann noted the usual ambivalence toward one's analysis in this remark. But now Dr. Marks was beginning to tell about the actual dream. The nightmare:

"I dreamed I was looking back over my shoulder, and somebody was pointing at me and saying, 'That's a symbol for thinking of the past. He must be crazy.' Two men appeared in a doorway. One was tall and definite-looking and the other was indefinite. I knew they had come to take me to a mental hospital. The tall man said, 'All right,' with a good deal of authority, and said to get ready to come with him. I put up my foot to try to shove him away and got scared and woke up. I found that my right arm had gone completely to sleep."

Dr. Marks turned his head and body, still feeling that complete numbness of the right side, and he wondered whether it had been the dream or the physical discomfort that had awakened him. A nightmare presumably means that the dream disguise is breaking down; that's the terror. He had not felt the terror too vividly. It was merely like something second-hand, something experienced out of courtesy—nothing like the panic he felt when he used to have nightmares as a boy. But he had better go on: "The looking back over my shoulder obviously refers to what I said to Margaret. Oh, and here's something—the tall man. My car developed some trouble with the differential yesterday, and I have it at the garage, so Dr. Wellman offered to pick me up this morning and take me in to the hospital with him. He's tall. He must be the tall man taking me to a mental hospital."

"Well, what do you think that means?"

"I don't like Wellman. He believes in shock. He's shocking Mrs. Blumstein. And I told you how I tried to get him to stop shocking her so I could talk to her—"

Dr. Naumann: "Haven't you often said your father is tall?"

Dr. Marks moved his arm. "Yes, he's tall. But this man in the dream didn't look anything like my father."

"Whom did he look like?"

"I can't think, yet I seemed to know him."

"Perhaps you will talk about this man," Dr. Naumann said. ("Perhaps" had a faint sound of "perhahbs" behind it, and many other words of Dr. Naumann's had German sounds behind them: and, und; also, ahlzo; is, iss.)

"He seemed to be—to have more authority than an attendant. He was clean-shaven, very pleasant, distinct features. My father's clean-shaven, although he had a beard at one time, but he shaved the beard off about the time he gave up the seltzer route."

The seltzer route—Dr. Naumann had these points of reference about it: that Dr. Marks's father was an emigrant from Siberia who came over with an older sister when he was eight; that he worked in a sweatshop, sometimes as errand boy, sometimes on the machines, until he saved enough money to buy a seltzer route; that when he got himself a horse and wagon and boxes of seltzer, he made a bare living at it for some years, then changed his business and began to do better. Substantially better.

"Well, perhaps there was some resemblance to my father," Dr. Marks went on. "Now I think of something else. Recently I told you you'd better come down to the hospital with a straitjacket for me. I was insane. I wanted to get rid of the shock machines and needles. So you're the man in the dream, too. But that isn't all." After a delay: "When I was thinking about my childhood, I thought about Bushwick Avenue and how my mother and father made me stay right around in front of the house. I couldn't cross the street. The other kids made fun of me, but I never disobeyed because with my father, you didn't disobey—it just wasn't in the cards. When I've been sore about that, thinking back to it, I've sometimes thought, 'My father put a halter on me.' "

Yes, Dr. Naumann thought, I substitute for the father. And not pleasantly. But there was another side to the dream. The tall man telling Dr. Marks to "come with him," and Dr. Marks putting out his foot.

Dr. Marks said, "It seems with this straitjacket-halter business, I've identified you with my father who beat me up and with Dr. Wellman whose main job is giving shock, knocking out patients as surely as if he were slugging them in the jaw. So you must be like them in some way."

"In what way?"

"I don't know in what way." After a silence: "But *you* know in what way, don't you?"

Continued silence.

Dr. Marks had been a shade embarrassed telling Dr. Naumann that he identified him with his father and Dr. Wellman, but in the analytic hour you tell everything. And he had made the identification, and not only that, he had felt it too. There was something the same about them. But what, what?

"It seems to me you push this analytic reserve too far. Once in a while when I ask you something, you could answer it." So, Dr. Marks thought, I've made a challenge of it.

And the silence continued.

"I believe you could answer this one question for me. I noticed you did something for one of your other patients. Just as I was coming in, I heard you calling the telephone answering service and giving him a new hour. You don't change my hour."

"What's in your mind now, while you're angry with me?" Dr. Naumann said quietly.

"I'm not angry."

Silence.

The tall green walls above him seemed to slide apart and an associative thought precipitated itself—*kelev*. And he remembered: "My first Hebrew lesson. I learned four words—'bottle, room, dog, and book.' When I came home, I wanted to show off my Hebrew to my father by using one of the words. The one I used was *kelev*. 'Hello, *kelev*,' I said. 'Hello, dog.' My father was so mad he almost beat me."

"But whether you meant it or not, you were disrespectful. Why?"

"My Unconscious must have had some reason to be mad at him."

"Why?"

"Why, why? He beat me. He kept me tied down. Like I said."

Persistent: "What else?"

"What else?"

Dr. Naumann: "What is in your mind now?"

"*Kelev*. 'Whore,' another word that made my father mad. I was thinking last night about patients at the hospital pounding on the floor or on the walls, and I thought, Could it be they were secretly asking for explanations? Is there a pathology of wanting to understand?"

"From whom did *you* want explanations?"

"My father."

"And why were you angry with him?"

"He didn't give me explanations."

"And why are you angry with me?"

Now the soreness went out of him, about Dr. Naumann and his silence. For there was that one difference. Dr. Naumann didn't use the belt (didn't strap him), didn't use the electric switch like Dr. Wellman. And thinking of that, Dr. Marks began to undo the transference, to lift it, veil-like, off Dr. Naumann. For there was a difference in his refusal of explanation. It wasn't unfeeling or punishing. It wasn't cruel. It didn't hurt him. It asked him to grow up, to become an equal. It allowed him to join the figure of a father in a father's knowledge.

He tried to speak and was unable to. His emotion stopped him.

Later in the session, he said, "I'm thinking about that epileptic in the rooming house. It reminds me of a story about Bleuler before he was at Burgholtzli, about when he was at Rheinau, and most of the hospital nursing staff there came down with typhoid. You know that story?"

"Even so, you will please tell it."

"The staff couldn't work, so patients, even those diagnosed as completely deteriorated dementia praecoxes, did nursing, they even did staff work, and that work couldn't have been simple. They were like the epileptic who unlocked the door. Bleuler said that meant their brains were unchanged, hadn't really deteriorated. As a matter of fact, as you know, that's why he invented the term schizophrenia, to show that even if they had this problem of dissociation, their brains were unimpaired."

"What makes this so interesting to you?"

"I keep thinking about the patients at the hospital. Many—maybe most of them—the brain is still all right, if Bleuler is right."

"The brain is all right if they haven't had shock."

"Just the same, I've been so used to finding pathology all my life," Dr. Marks said.

"There is a very simple answer," Dr. Naumann said.

"Yes? What is it?"

"Go to the hospital morgue."

"This Naumann's something." He sat in the living room with his arm laid across the back of the sofa, feeling good (a not infrequent result of an analytic session).

Margaret: "What's he done now?"

In her eyes he read jealousy. I shouldn't like Naumann more than her. I shouldn't like anybody or anything more than her.

He told her about unraveling his dream (the nightmare) and then undoing his transference. "I always get a little more each time, a little more of the truth—what come through the resistances. It *is* the truth. That Naumann, he knows—he checks and crosschecks. And if he can know what he knows about me, why can't I know more about patients in the hospital?"

"But you're accessible, aren't you?"

He smiled. "You think I'm accessible? You should tell Naumann that. In a way they're more accessible. Their defenses are down, their Unconscious flooding all over the place. One woman patient says, 'Up and down, up and down. Open the gate, Richard.' And then, 'Up and down, up and down,' and then, 'Fuck.' "

"Well, yes."

"One of them says, 'I have an abnegation medal.' And she looks like she has, too."

"If you tried to make that up, it would be hard," she said.

"You couldn't. Their Unconscious is in a torment all the time. They'll ask you a question that hurts so you almost can't stand it. There was this Florence—" He told her about Florence and the ice cream.

'Won't somebody tell me where I am?'

"How about some music?" he said, getting up. "I have to get away from this." He went to a small upright Lerner piano on the rack of which stood a book in which he had made pencil notations of melodies of old songs (he had a thing for blues) and current popular hits. He had never had lessons, but played the piano by a system of his own —the left hand for single notes and the right for chords so the right, logically, would do the most work.

Margaret said, "Nancy's in bed. Maybe she's asleep."

"If she's asleep, she won't wake up—you know her. If

she's awake, she can come." The boys would come. The piano always meant singing. He pumped hard and rhythmically, measuring with his foot the groupings of the bars.

Johnny came in first, followed by Bob. Nancy trotted in in her nightie, blinking and pleased. "Okay," Dr. Marks said. "Ready? 'Walk into Jerusalem just like John.'"

Margaret sang with a pure alto, like a finer version of her speaking voice. Johnny's voice was clear and exact, and Bob's was clear. Nancy sometimes had trouble with the words, but sang "mmm mmm mmm" if she forgot them, and was always on the beat.

He felt supported by all these voices to which he lent his own rough bass.

"Walk into Jerusalem just like John."

Nancy touched his arm.

"Yes?"

"Did you walk into Jerusalem, Daddy?"

How did you explain to a child the thing of the Apostles; still worse, the heaven of Jerusalem and hell of slavery? "It was a different John," he said. "This song is a song some unhappy people sang who wanted to walk into a better land."

"Did they?"

"No, they're still walking, but they'll get there. All right, are we with this?" Hitting a chord with all the strength of his right hand, he said, " 'Mule Walk.' "

3

On Dr. Marks's next day off, he drove to the hospital at his usual time, but did not park in his usual place in front of Women's Reception. He went around to a side parking lot behind Building Ten. The day was clear and fine, nothing unreal about this day, and nothing unreal about these grounds except, around certain tree trunks, an accumulation of windblown pieces of paper—toilet paper, newspapers, candy wrappers—patients' messages to the outside world, dropped from various windows.

Leaving his car, he went to an entrance with a white-lettered sign—MORTUARY. It was in an old brick building, so old it seemed like a red rock filmed over with lichen. He could see, as he entered, the heavy square doors of the refrigerators, each with a small white identifying slip riffling in the moving air.

He found the morgue-keeper's office down a lateral corridor and found the keeper clutching a form and shouting into a telephone: "Get it to us. It's no good without the signature. The signature! Right away!" When this crisis passed, Dr. Marks asked if there were some posts scheduled and the keeper answered, "Three." "I'm a doctor in Reception—" An elderly man interrupted, asking to see a body—"See the man outside. Outside." "I'm Dr. Marks, in Reception. If I may, I'd like to watch one of the postmortems." "Of course, Dr. Marks. The doctors will be right down." The telephone rang, and again the keeper took up the receiver, excusing himself. Across the corridor outside, three bodies shrouded in canvas were wheeled into the dissecting room and transferred to tables there. The attendants unwrapped them hurriedly. The odor of disinfectant fanned outward from the room's swinging doors.

The preparations for a dissection, why did they always seem like a drama about to begin? When he was a boy, an aunt sometimes took him to the movies. In the movies of those days, a tinkling piano began to play, and on the white screen, streaks of a hypnotic, rainy light began to fall. His heart quickened with anticipation: What will it be? What will I see? At every postmortem, he had that same feeling: What will it be? What will I see?

A doctor entered the morgue-keeper's office and went to a locker, to the left of the door. The keeper called across to him, "The undertaker's in a rush for Brown, if you could do that one first."

"All right."

"This is Dr. Marks, from the hospital here. He's asked to watch you, if you don't mind. Dr. Marks, this is Dr. Pirosh."

They shook hands. "I haven't seen you around," Dr. Pirosh said. "Where are you?"

"In Reception. I've only been here at New State a few weeks."

"Come along."

Dr. Pirosh walked quickly into the dissecting room where the three posts lay waiting. The two nearer ones were men, the further one a woman with an abdomen swollen with fat. In her dead gray hair, two small red ribbons. Perhaps she herself had tied those ribbons before she died; they looked girlish and her face too had a girlish look. Was that part of the insanity? for Dr. Marks reminded himself that this was the corpse of an insane person. It just as well might not be. Many women of her age refused to grow old and tried to preserve a similar girlish look. It was even a pleasant look on many women, and went with good nature and a tendency to corpulence.

Dr. Pirosh was reading the tags on the toes of the two men. Brown was the second one, a man in his twenties, his flesh flattened until it clung to the bones. He looked as if he had starved to death. "This is a case of acute catatonic excitement. I still think it should be possible to keep these people from dying."

"I guess I'd better explain," Dr. Marks said. "I'm not a psychiatrist. I've just begun my residency. What do you mean, acute catatonic excitement?"

Dr. Pirosh was putting a wooden platform down on the floor. "I guess you are new, aren't you?"

"I'm afraid I am."

"Nobody mentioned this? You haven't seen any of them?"

"No." He stared at the starved body.

"Well, acute catatonic excitement is what it sounds like, a severe excitement. Just excitement alone won't kill anybody, but sometimes it gets out of control, and fever and exhaustion set in—the patient can't rest, can't absorb food. It gets very bad. Once exhaust status sets in, the patient's done for. They usually die in one to two weeks." Dr. Pirosh adjusted a small wooden bench over the right leg of the corpse and began to put on a pair of rubber gloves. "Small," he complained about the gloves.

"With this patient, there must have been a very high fever," Dr. Marks said.

"Yes, it goes very high sometimes, and sometimes in a matter of minutes—jumps up. Then you have shock—and good-by. Or when it persists at temperatures over a hundred six, seven? For a week?"

A hundred six, seven. Infection. "Don't you treat them for infection?"

"No, there's no infection."

"No infection?"

"No, none at all."

"You mean you won't find any infection here? In this body?"

"Certainly not."

"Then how do you explain the fever?"

Dr. Pirosh shrugged. "You're welcome to watch." Taking a knife in his gloved hand, he quickly made a Y incision in the breast and worked back the skin. He energetically cut down the rib cage on either side. With the sureness of long practice he lifted the plate of bone and reached in his hands and took the heart and cut it loose and laid it on the wooden table. With slicing strokes he opened it, his cuts following the auricles and ventricles as the blood flowed in life. Indicating the exposed tissue: "No dilation. Everything clean and normal."

He threw the heart on the scales and weighed it. Three hundred grams. Well, Dr. Marks thought, there could be a normal heart. It wasn't here that he expected the pathology. Possibly it would show up in the lungs, a terminal pneumonia. Or it would be a hidden tuberculosis, or a swollen kidney.

Dr. Pirosh cut a small piece from the heart and dropped it into the sections bottle where it floated downward, exuding streamers of blood. Two other doctors entered the room. "Dr. Edwards, Dr. Bellona——" Dr. Edwards, first in, chose the corpse of the woman. "I want to see what's in this belly."

"Here," Dr. Pirosh said to Dr. Marks, holding up the dark mauve lungs of the catatonic, which were almost black. "Anthracotic pigment, but perfectly normal." Dr. Marks examined them. It was in these lungs there should have been a terminal pneumonia. But there was no pneumonia and no least sign of tuberculosis—nothing at all.

Dr. Pirosh slit the belly wall and felt in for the kidneys. He brought out their normal, unswollen circlets shining like huge earrings. He sliced them. They were clean, showing no trace of infection, no trace of tuberculosis.

"I don't understand it," Dr. Marks said, noting the clean texture of the organs.

There was a flutter at the door—twelve student nurses in blue striped blouses, their young faces flushed from the outside air, drifted past the corpses of the men, which looked like pictures from the Vesalian anatomy, the skin folded back in ragged edges. The exposed penis of one man lay straight, that of the other, bluish at the tip, was unnaturally bent. The girls with their two supervisors shied away from the men and gathered at the corpse of the woman, almost completely surrounding it. Dr. Edwards took a light tone with them: "Now here you see evidence of necrobiosis." He asked what necrobiosis was. "None of you know? Really? Well, I won't embarrass the supervisors by asking them."

"Bladder normal," Dr. Pirosh said to Dr. Marks, showing him the thin bladder of the acute catatonic. The final urine, artificially passed, poured down the center drain, flushed by the steadily running hose. "You'll notice the gall bladder's bursting with bile. Starvation."

There was a stir among the student nurses: "Lipoma." Out of the oversized dead woman's belly, Dr. Edwards had just produced a large lump of yellow fat, like a nugget of gold. "Lipoma of the mesentery." Dr. Marks thought, Then that was the reason for the distended belly. Beyond the ordinary layers of fat, that ball of benign fat had been growing, and it was quite a sample, he noticed. But his attention had been only momentarily taken from Dr. Pirosh and he now watched him carefully section the liver. The liver was a nutmegy brown, as normal as any healthy liver he had ever seen. The pancreas was whitish and healthy.

"All right so far?"

The spleen, always swollen in infection, was normal size.

"All right?"

Dr. Pirosh cut through the thirty feet of intestine, washing out the content and making the wall visible. No inflammation or ulceration.

"Still all right?"

Still all right, and now Dr. Marks's emotions were in revolt against this uniform evidence. He was confused. He was angry. Pirosh was too smart. There *was* infection somewhere, and he would find it before they were through. There had to be a somatic explanation for that kind of fever.

All the glands were in order—adrenal, thyroid. The lymph glands were a healthy red, and spongy.

Possibly the prostate gland, possibly the testicles—there would be a hidden testicular tuberculosis.

Nothing.

When Dr. Pirosh had made the final exploration of the anal passage and had torn at the passages to the head, he stood back. "Well, there it is," he said. All the vital organs lay exposed now in their brilliant colors, filling the table's enamel tray. It was all exposed, it was all there. And no infection, no disease, no cause of death. There was no reason to die, and nothing in the sections would change the fact. It was irrational and it was impossible.

It must be in the brain. That was all that was left. That was where the lethal pathology must be. For this was not just the mental illness that he had told Dr. Naumann he wanted to find in the brain cells—this was a killing fever. You cannot die of a prolonged fever without a visible pathology.

Dr. Pirosh put a small wooden block under the cadaver's head and, grasping the hair, he cut loose the scalp and laid its flap over the white face. When he cut the temporal muscles, they folded down like unhooked garters, exposing the dome of the skull divided by its perfect stitching. Taking the saw, he drew it back and forth carefully, lifting the skull off at last like a cup. Uncovered, the brain sagged toward its base. Under the vanishing net of the arachnoid, its corrugations trembled and became still.

"All right," Dr. Pirosh said, "it's all yours."

Dr. Marks examined the dura and the whole brain surface. There was evidence of congestion, but it was only such as would be produced by fever. No congestion that could cause fever. No areas of softening or hardening with their familiar visual evidence like the defects of a drying plum, no least reddish track of hemorrhage, no inflammatory exudate so characteristic of bacterial infection (meningitis or encephalitis), no graying tumor or beginning of tumor, no widening of any of the sulci, no atrophy. When he shrugged his shoulders, Dr. Pirosh reached in with the knife and cut the rope of the medulla deeply, and cut the thin strands of cranial nerves, and the brain came out easily into his hand. Its sphere, the softest and most delicate of all the body tissues, was without lesion or defect. It was a perfect brain.

"Now what do you say?"

"I don't find anything," Dr. Marks said.

Dr. Pirosh lowered the brain into a jar of formalin.

Dr. Marks added, "And yet, I'd like to see the sections of this brain."

"All right, come back a month from now, when it's hardened."

"I will."

"Or I'll tell you. Convince yourself now. There are plenty of these cases. In the laboratory right now are sets of slides of acute catatonics who died just like this one, just the same. You won't find anything more than you've seen here grossly, but you're welcome to look at them if you want to."

"I'd like to look at them," Dr. Marks said.

Dr. Pirosh went with him to the laboratory and got out a set of slides. Dr. Marks picked up one of them with its carefully prepared center and put it under the eye of the microscope. As he stared down, the characteristic bright colors appeared. He looked for sickly staining, for pus cells, for congested blood vessels. For dilation. He took his time, because he had an excellent, complete, carefully prepared set of slides. He looked for any irregularity, any absence of the ganglion cells. He looked for any possible evidence of a cause for fever. Slowly, slide by slide, cerebrum, cerebellum, pons, and medulla, he worked through the set. No least scar tissue. Nothing anywhere but a normal and unblemished brain, regular in its structure and pure and wholesome in its cells.

"Do you see anything?" Dr. Pirosh asked quietly.

"Nothing!"

"This patient had no shock treatment. You would find damage if there had been shock."

"I would?"

"Yes, there's always more or less damage from shock whether they died of the insanity or something else. I've mentioned it in Staff but they don't seem to want to hear me."

Brain damage from shock! That was something to follow up later, but he was interested now in something else. Before him lay the slides of the brain of a man who had died of a continuous high fever and no pathology.

How could such a thing be possible? How did this man die?

"Hello—what brings you in? Sit down, make yourself comfortable. . . . Yes?" Dr. Wellman said, answering a ring of the telephone. "No. Specks in the glucose. I know. . . . Let the bottles settle. Don't shake them up, let them settle." He put the receiver back and turned to Dr. Marks. "Well," he said, "you're the last person I expected to see today."

"I'm tracking something down. Tell me, are there any cases of acute catatonic excitement in the hospital right now?"

"Yes, there are several."

"I'd like to see one."

"What's your sudden interest?" Dr. Wellman seemed amused. The novice trying to learn the facts of his profession, his tone said.

Dr. Marks told him about the postmortem and his wanting to see such a case alive.

"Well, there's no problem about that. They're over in Building Seven, in the Medical Ward. As a matter of fact, one of them is a case I've handled," and now a lacing of dark lines deepened under his eyes. "You want to hear about it?"

Dr. Marks said he would be glad to hear about this case.

"This boy, his name is Jimmy Cady and he's only seventeen, was first admitted last November. I remember it because his father made trouble. He drinks. Quite different from the boy, and I think he likes the boy. I never met the mother. The boy is bright and did well at school. He has an older brother and a younger brother and baby sister. When he was admitted here, he was moody. Heard voices, the usual thing: 'Do this, do that. You're filth, you're a genius.' The paranoid pattern. We tried a month of insulin shock and that did no good at all, so we decided to try electric shock. After five electric shocks, he went into excitement. The excitement got worse until we had to send him to Medical."

How casual Dr. Wellman was about this report of shock failure! "Can I see him?" Dr. Marks lit a cigarette.

"Well, it's just about lunchtime now. Why don't I make an appointment for you for right after lunch?"

"That would be good."

"I'll call Linscomb, Dr. Marvin Linscomb in Medical, and he'll set it up for you. Building Seven, fourth floor." Dr. Wellman took up the phone. The call was slow being put through and Dr. Marks noted Dr. Wellman's firm grasp of the phone. It was like his grip on the shock-machine electrodes. The day was clear. The office was silent —only the sound of a woman's raw scream came distantly through the door. Dr. Wellman was saying, "I've made arrangements for you to go over. Any time after one, Miss Davis, the nurse in charge, will be expecting you."

"Thank you very much."

Jokingly: "Well, all you have to worry about now is that he doesn't die before you get there."

It was one thirty when he reached Medical. Miss Davis met him in the corridor, a pleasant, middle-aged woman. "You're Dr. Marks, aren't you?"

"Yes."

"And you want to see Jimmy." Impulsively: "Oh, I wish they could do something for that kid. It's such a shame!"

"But don't they—don't you do things for him?" he said.

"Just physical procedures—you know. Temperatures. Tube-feed him. Give him sedations. Maybe put him in continuous bath." Despairingly: "Nothing does any good. He just gets worse. I don't know—"

He remained silent.

"If something—I have the feeling—"

"Yes?"

"Oh, he's such a nice kid, Dr. Marks."

She took him to Jimmy's room and he went to the foot of the bed, to the foot of the tough white canvas restraint sheet. From an opening in it, a head thrust out. Thrust back, pulling against the sheet, becoming purple as if it were strangling, and the whole thin body thrashed.

Then the skeletal head stilled a moment and stared.

Looking into those eyes, Dr. Marks had a profound shock. Why didn't anybody tell me?

The kid was dying of fear. Not "excitement," just plain fear.

The eyes protruded. Jimmy tried to whisper—"Wh wh wh wh." The sound was unintelligible. His eyes desperately strained to see, but see what? He doesn't see me. Wh Wh. His mouth choked shut, then he whispered, "No no no no no," and tried to focus and center his eyes. "No no no—don't."

"Don't what?"

"Don't—"(whispered but stronger)

"Don't what?"

"Anzel . . . Mike, Mike . . . Zzzzzzzzz." He whispered the "zzzzz" through his teeth as if imitating a motor and when he had made this motor sound, he let his head drop back and stared upward and from side to side. "Monsters." He shoved the sheet desperately and turned and tried to reach the side of the bed.

"Who's there?" Dr. Marks called sharply.

"Anzel, anzel trap. They're coming . . . Zzzzzzz." Wilder: "I don't, I won't . . . Help! Help! Did he yell?"

"Did who yell?"

"He says no." Softer and in despair: "He says no."

The drying, cracked lips were again whispering inaudibly. "Ah . . . Oh." Strangled but imploring: "Help! Help!" I'm dying. I'm afraid. I'm afraid. I'm dying.

Nobody with him. No doctor. How can you not be with someone who's dying?

"Who yelled?"

'Help! Help!'

He went around the bed and put his hand on the boy's burning, bone-dry face. "It's all right," he said.

No inflammation, nothing but a terrified brain. It was as if everything since Dr. Marks had entered the hospital, all his frustration, his involvement, his feeling of unbearable concern for Mrs. Blumstein, all the cry of the halls, the eyes, the walls, all the animal appeal in the human and the human in the animal-like silences, all the need to help and do for these helpless creatures—it was as if it all centered down now into this starved boy. This was the one he would listen to. No time for presumptive further training. No time to question, worry about authority, delay.

This boy was dying.

4

But he did have to be this much concerned about authority. To be with Jimmy he would have to have permission, obviously.

This Dr. Linscomb that Wellman had been phoning. He would be the one to ask.

As he went to Dr. Linscomb's office, he told himself, Be careful. Cool. The worst thing is to show a passionate concern for a dying boy.

His first look at Dr. Linscomb confirmed this. It was a bald, anonymous head. If a light was placed over it, the features on it would disappear and it would become an egg.

Dr. Wellman looked warmhearted compared to this.

"I'm Dr. Marks. Dr. Wellman, I guess, phoned you about me."

"Oh, yes, Dr. Marks."

"I guess he told you I'm new at the hospital, and this is my day off so I thought I'd go down to the Morgue. I thought I'd take a look at the physical pathology of insanity." No response so far. "I happened to see Raymond Brown's post, and I was amazed that there wasn't any sign of infection."

"There never is any."

"Not seeing any infection, naturally I wanted to take a look at a living case, and I've just seen Jimmy. I believe it's clear to me now what these cases die of. It's just fright."

"Yes, the fright is so evident, isn't it?"

"Isn't there some way to reassure them?" Dr. Marks said.

"That's the strange thing about it. No, you can't reassure them. I suppose it's the condition they're in—"

"But isn't there even a remote chance that a doctor being with them could make them feel less frightened?"

Dr. Linscomb's smooth head lifted to this challenge. "Just hypothetically, suppose we take your point of view.

There are three excited catatonics on the ward right now. Do you propose that nine doctors stay with them—that's counting three shifts around the clock? That would tie up a considerable part of our staff."

"But if they're dying—"

Dr. Linscomb now looked annoyed. "We use every physical precaution—tube-feeding, sedatives, baths. But I can tell you, when they go into exhaust status, they just don't get well, Doctor. I wish there was some answer to this."

"I have today off as I said, so I'm free. Could *I* stay with Jimmy?" Dr. Marks asked.

"By all means. It will give you a chance to verify what any experienced psychiatrist knows, so by all means stay with him."

"Perhaps I could read his chart?"

Dr. Linscomb handed him the chart and said with a trace of sarcasm, "The case is yours."

Dr. Marks got the following picture from the chart:

James's father was Patrick Cady, a Catholic who had stopped going to mass regularly although he had not broken with the Church. James's mother, Mary, was a devout Catholic. The parents fought, the main issue being Patrick's drinking. Patrick had a brother, Michael ("Mike, Mike") who had lived with them for some years (possible father substitute?). Last year the uncle left them, and that was about the time things got worse for Jimmy. The sibling situation: there were three boys fairly close together—Joseph (two years older than Jimmy) now in the Army, Jimmy, and Henry who was three years younger. Then there was a jump of over twelve years and a sister, Frances, was born, who was now fourteen months old. That made a surprisingly long gap between the boys and the girl.

Jimmy grew up during the Depression thirties. His health was delicate until he was ten, so much so that at one time he had been thought tubercular. His mother often kept him home "for his health" and because he had night terrors. He was passive and quiet. Still he skipped two grades in school. When he was thirteen, he had a painful boil at the edge of his right eye, which was lanced. After that, he became moody and irritable and quarreled with his father and hardly noticed his mother, this being behavior that was entirely unlike him. Just before he entered the hospital, he sketched a number of strange-looking pictures.

One picture had an eye in it, pierced by what looked like a railroad track. The caption of this was *Friendship* and when he was asked what it meant, he said, "I like boats." First he drew these unusual pictures, then he stopped talking and for two days refused to eat, then he developed a fever sore on his lip and became excited and said, "The world is evaporating." The hospital record, following admission, showed that he suffered from auditory hallucinations. He reacted badly to visits from his father, who came to complain that not enough was being done for him. His mother did not visit him, for some reason not explained. The rest of the hospital facts followed the summary Dr. Wellman had given. The patient's last temperature reading was 106.4.

The way Dr. Wellman had summarized this in telling him about the case: you would have thought even a hospital psychiatrist would mention some of the details of the case record, which were suggestive, to say the least. The boy being passive—that showed a feminine trend and probably was compliant to a need in the mother, or the father. No girl in the family until the belated arrival of Frances— maybe one or both of the parents had wanted a girl. The passive streak ended after the lancing of the boil near Jimmy's eye, a castration symbol. Evidently he had then revolted.

He had been reading the chart at Miss Davis's desk. As he finished, she came up through the shadow of the corridor, her hair fresh-brushed and burnished, and her eyes warm. "Are you going to do something for Jimmy?" she said.

He answered, "I'm told nothing can be done. However, I'm going to stay with him."

He entered Jimmy's cell, aseptic in the afternoon sunlight, and approached the bed. Jimmy again lifted his head and stared.

He was trembling. At any moment the frantic thrashing might begin.

"It's all right, Jimmy. I'm going to be with you now."

Jimmy's eyes expanded. They tried to focus. He gave himself one overall shake, undulating the sheet. Under that sheet he was in a straitjacket, part of being "in restraint." By now Dr. Marks had only too many times seen the whole process of "putting a patient in restraint." The attendants, as many as were needed, held the patient down. His arms were put in the straitjacket's long envelopes and drawn over his chest and laced fast. In this position he appeared to hug himself. The jacket itself was then fastened firmly to the sides of the bed, stopping most of his body movement. His legs were trussed together and tied to the foot of the bed. When the heavy canvas restraint sheet was fitted over his head and stretched down over his body, it held him relentlessly in a grip that was like the unrelaxing grip of the psychosis itself.

"No no no no . . . zzzzzzzz." Jimmy's voice was the barest whisper. His eyes stared out.

Dr. Marks had asked Miss Davis if Jimmy talked much and she had said he did when the excitement "worked him up." "But it's just crazy talk."

The thing was to listen. He had told Margaret his belief that the productions were conceivably understandable, that they were the productions of a waking dream, and Dr. Naumann had once told him not to be anxious if he failed to get the meaning of one of his dreams. "It will appear again—again and again."

There had been glimpses of meaning in the case history in the chart. The indications of fear after the lancing of the boil near the eye. No fear is unrelated fear. There is something or someone the boy is afraid of.

Jimmy's whispering continued for several minutes while his eyes roved. Then he began to speak more clearly: "Help! Help! He's tough. Does he know? Anzel." Louder: "Nothing. Gone. Spread it around, you. Cannons. Guns." His voice faded back to its whisper and his eyes dilated. "Torture!"

A long silence followed in which he trembled. His hair was dry and dull, his skin like paper. He thrust up with his full strength against the restraint sheet, and its collar caught his neck. His face became suffused. He flung his head from side to side as if he were dodging shadows. "Nothing there? Gone. Zzzzzzzzz. He says no." His voice became more distinct. "Trap. Zzzzzzzz." He said again, "Trap," and tried to reach the side of the bed. He shouted, "The bastard. Where is he? Should I die? (screaming) I'll die. Why that American torture?"

"Who wants to torture you?"

"He says no. Shove over, Joe. Guns. Combinations again."

Guns, cannons—penis?

Jimmy: "He pitched that slow ball in the stomach. Zzzzzzzz."

Something to do with his mother's pregnancy? Frances?

"Help. Where's Daniel Kyle? Help!" A long silence. A shiver. Then: "Torture! Where's Joe? Did he die?"

Dr. Linscomb had insisted you couldn't reassure him. But here he was calling for help. Didn't you have to try? "You won't die, Jimmy. You're going to live."

"Shove it. He kills them all dead."

"You're safe now. You won't die."

"Help! Did he yell? That German-American Empire. Fight. Baby Mike. Zzzzzzzzz."

"I'm going to save you. You're—"

"Torture! You know that bastard? My brain says so, but I don't say so. Help! Did he yell?"

Dr. Marks continued his steady reassurances, but with no evident effect. Not the slightest. As far as he could see, Linscomb was right.

"He knows everything, he's nosy. I love him. Let's murder that bastard." Opposites: *'I love him. Let's murder that bastard.'* "Zzzzzz. When's he coming? Did they catch him? Where?" Shouted wildly: "Zzzzzzzzz. They can if you say so. No." Slower: "Take it away and give it away. Scram, bud. Torture! I'll have torture!"

Silence. Then whispering again, disconnected, discontinuous, and fearful. Dr. Marks looked at his watch and realized that almost an hour had gone by. "Oh, how I love her! I hate him every day. Zzzzzzzzz."

And no change at all. I do get things: at times he seems to be saying, I'm a man. That surge of maleness. Then panic. That schizoid hate/love thing. Other things. But as for contact—if anything it was in the reverse direction. He's affecting me. I'm beginning to be more aware of him and fond of him behind that starved face. Miss Davis was right, you do like him.

But what was the kid afraid of? That was what mattered. *'Torture! I'll have torture!'*

Listen—

Miss Davis came in. "Dr. Linscomb has asked me to tube-feed him some milk. He does need it."

"Of course." He stood at the window to avoid the repellent sight of that rubber tube plunged down through the nose. A large clump of red flowers was growing inside the hospital fence. He stared fixedly at it and heard a rustling sound, the rustling continued, then the tube was removed and Jimmy's voice came up after it in a gulp: "I'll have torture. Angel trap!" And he began to scream. His outburst had incredible strength.

"There, there," Miss Davis said and put her hand on the thin shoulder through the sheet. The screams continued.

Dr. Linscomb entered the room with an attendant who quickly untied the restraint sheet and bared one of Jimmy's legs. Dr. Linscomb plunged a hypodermic into it, and almost at once silence fell.

But as Dr. Marks watched:

"He doesn't seem to go to sleep," he said.

"Sedatives don't have too much effect," Dr. Linscomb said. "This won't last too long, but I do feel he needs this much rest."

"Isn't there something more that can be done?"

Dr. Linscomb looked up. "I can assure you there's nothing we know of to do that we don't do. We do everything I've told you, everything you see. On every case we do a urine and blood count every day even though nothing shows up. Perhaps you have a suggestion, Doctor?"

"I only wish I did."

"We do everything we can, everything known that can be done."

At five o'clock he was in Dr. Naumann's office, on the couch. The room slowly reversed itself to the horizontal as he gazed open-eyed at the ceiling. It felt good, for the time being, to be prone and to be in the Master's presence. And I have to let Jimmy "rest."

He told everything that had happened connected with Jimmy, including his talks with Dr. Linscomb and the final sedation. The complete account took some fifteen minutes.

When he was finished, Dr. Naumann said, "This autopsy of Brown, you were surprised at not finding a pathology."

"Of course."

"I wonder if you should have been so surprised. Let me just ask: do you think you can track the smelling of a rose through the brain? Do you think you can detect under the microscope how one man desired another man's wife?"

"I get what you mean."

"What is fantastic is the general ignorance of these people in psychiatry. This Dr. Linscomb—as soon as you started to talk to him, he should have been able to tell you that there is already a literature, an important literature, concerned with the evidence or nonevidence of pathology in Bell's mania. The weight of evidence, as in your instance, is that there is no pathology. Any hospital psychiatrist like this Dr. Linscomb should be completely up on it."

"Bell's mania?"

"That's what they used to call it. It used to be thought of as a separate clinical entity. Now it's recognized as one terminal stage of the psychotic process."

"Have you seen it yourself?"

"I have seen a few cases in the hospitals."

Then Dr. Naumann knew. Knew that terrible fear. He mentioned it again and Dr. Naumann corroborated it: "Yes, that is the essential thing—fear, *Angst, triebmassige-Angst*. That is what they die of."

"It's unimaginable to me that these hospital doctors can leave cases like that, leave a kid like Jimmy. I only came here for my hour because he's sedated. Even so I hated to leave him. Shouldn't somebody be with him? Just to put their hand on him? Do something? If there's the least chance of reassuring him—"

"How did you feel toward this boy Jimmy when you were beside him?"

"I told you."

"Yes." Silence.

"Such a wonderful kid. You can feel it even with all the insanity. Even Miss Davis, the nurse there, she felt it. Anybody would."

"Any particular thoughts as you stood beside him?"

He remembered, he had had a particular thought. As Dr. Naumann waited: "I did have this thought, that my father didn't stay by me. You know, he closed himself away."

Interesting expression, Dr. Naumann thought: ". . . closed himself away." He remained silent.

In Dr. Marks's mind now, a thought came in spite of his not wanting it, in spite of his resisting any thought that led inward. I don't want to remember a dream just now, he almost said to himself, but he had remembered one, or a fragment of one. It was the damned habit of analysis, and you have to tell it. So, though reluctantly, he said: "I had a dream last night and I lay awake for a minute or two this morning, thinking about it. It was about my father. He seemed to live in the middle of the country—of the United States—somewhere. Then he was in New York on his way abroad. He was going to take a ship or something. It seems he wasn't going to see me. Hadn't planned to see me. But I telephoned him and although I was eager to see him, I was relieved that he couldn't make it."

He wasn't going to see me. He had closed himself away.

Could that be why I had that thought standing beside Jimmy? But I would have had it anyway. It was a natural thought to have had.

"Can you remember any more of the dream?" Dr. Naumann said.

"I know there was more, but I can't remember."

"In your dream, did you feel you had seen your father recently?"

"No, I hadn't seen him in a long time."

Silence.

Dr. Marks said, "The way you put that, that I had seen my father. He hadn't seen *me* in a long time. He's the one who was in the middle of the country."

"What do you suppose 'the middle of the country' is?"

"My association is Memphis—Momphis—" Embarrassed: "Obviously my mother."

"Where was your mother in the dream?"

"I didn't know."

"Isn't she usually with your father?"

"Yes, she would be with my father."

"So neither your mother nor your father was with you. They had left you alone."

After a moment's silence, Dr. Marks said, "I don't know that my parents have ever actually been away like that. They've always lived around here."

Silence.

"But I do have a feeling that my father goes to see Robert, he's the big success, and he doesn't come as much to see me. Oh, he comes. But he likes that big place where Robert lives."

Silence.

"I guess that's 'the middle of the country' too? Robert has this six-foot-wide bed where he can send a telegram to his wife, and the family lace cover—that's a kind of beige bedcover that my grandmother brought from the old country. My folks had it for a while, and they didn't think it was so classy so they gave it to Robert. He knew the value of it all right. They didn't give it to me, but I didn't have a big enough bed for it."

A lot of associations to the family bed, Dr. Naumann thought. Dr. Marks puts his father in the middle of the country. He has the unconscious wish to put his father with his mother. "So you telephoned your father."

"Yes, *I* had to telephone him. He doesn't telephone me. How true a dream is! You know how a dream gives you a feeling of truth. It touches something—something you've felt when you're awake. It's true my father 'closed himself away.' Yes, we've been over that, and you've shown me that my father was concerned for me, but this other feeling of his being closed away is still there. I can't shake it. I just can't do anything about it. Maybe it goes back too far."

"Were there some specific occasions when you felt shut away from him?"

"I don't know."

"Any time when you had that particular feeling, that your father was not with you when he should have been, or you were not with him when you should have been?"

"Well, there was the time when he got the place on Eastern Parkway. Where we lived, you know. He took one of the girls with him that day, Babe I guess it was, so he came back and he doesn't say a damn thing. I guess he told Mama that night. But he didn't even tell Babe or any of us kids that he was getting this place. Then he did get it, and gradually we found out. You know, the way we found out all these things. By ourselves. Never get the kids together and tell them anything."

Silence.

"I can't think of anything else."

Still silence.

"Well, of course he didn't tell me anything sexual. He kept me out on any of that information. Sometimes I would want to ask him a question about that—I'd get scared about masturbation or something—but you can't talk about anything like that. You can't talk about anything at all."

A brief stirring in the chair. "What other thoughts did you have as you were beside Jimmy?"

"Well, there was a moment I thought, Thank God that isn't me lying there."

"Didn't you tell me Jimmy was considered tubercular?"

"Yes."

Silence.

"You're thinking of that business of my having been suspected of having tuberculosis when I was a kid. I thought of it too as I read his chart. Identification. 'Thank God that isn't me lying there,' but maybe he is me."

Dr. Naumann thought, No wonder he wants to be a parent to this child Jimmy, and a good parent. A psychotic anyway has such an attraction, for those who are not afraid. He had felt it himself. He thought of one of his own patients of the early days—his steady, slightly enlarged humid eyes, his fast-beating pulse, his anxiety. How it drew you! In spite of the barriers—Freud's "organ speech," words momentarily decomposing, the eyes turning away, turning inward. With all their turning away, they provoked your deepest feelings.

"This identification," Dr. Marks said. "This will help me understand him—all I've been learning about myself here—"

"Identification can help, but it is not everything. What you want to know is the patient himself—"

"I felt I was beginning to. I felt his productions had meaning—just as I was telling Margaret. 'Take it away and give it away,' he said. 'Take the temptation of my penis away. Take the temptation of my maleness away.' So I won't be tempted by Mother."

Dr. Naumann thought, Yes, strange how few psychiatrists—even analysts—wanted to try to understand psychotic productions. He remembered those of his own former psychotic patients. Certain phrases about eating. About killing. Silences. You could almost see the Unconscious threading its way among the dream defenses.

But he was allowing Dr. Marks to evade him with this conscious talk. And he had the feeling that this might be an important session, there had been hints—

"The sounds he makes," Dr. Marks was saying. "That whisper. Wh wh wh wh. And that zzzzzzzz sound. They must have meaning, too."

"Let's return to your dream." Press the associations to the family bed. "You mentioned this cover from the family bed. Can you describe it in more detail?"

In discomfort, Dr. Marks tried to put his hand in his pocket, then he eased it out again on the couch. "Well, it was lace—had this kind of design."

"What design?"

"Well, I can't exactly describe it. It was just squares, no particular design. I can't just remember. Something in the middle, something at the corners. The rest was more like transparent."

"When you see it, do you think of it at your brother's, or at home?"

Complete silence.

Countersilence.

"At home," Dr. Marks said at last.

Why that long silence? "Would you describe the bed at home?" Dr. Naumann asked.

"Well, I never saw it much."

"Why?"

"Well, you didn't go in the bedroom." Having said that, Dr. Marks was silent again.

"You easily described your brother's bedroom."

"Well, that's now."

"Why didn't you go in the bedroom at home?"

Dr. Marks seemed uneasy. "I'm thinking—I don't know why—of that story I told you about the brother that came to the rooming-house room for the epileptic."

"Perhaps you will associate to that."

"I don't understand. What part of it?" Dr. Marks asked.

"Any part you like."

"Well, the door was locked. This key the epileptic used was in the door on the inside. A big key like a skeleton key, what we used to call a skeleton key when I was a kid, a key that we used to think would open any door. I used to see keys like that in the five-and-dime and I'd think if you had it, you could open any door."

"What door?"

"Well, I don't know."

(Father was "closed away.") "What door?"

Now Dr. Marks put his hand to his face nervously.

"What door?" Dr. Naumann persisted.

"I can't understand it."

"What?"

"That I could have forgotten all this time. How could I—"

Silence.

"When I was smaller—I don't know how long—for a while—my father kept the door to his and my mother's bedroom locked."

Silence.

"Yes. Yes, that was probably it. I wanted to go in that room." Dr. Marks's breathing seemed to be deepening. "I did once. I remember it was a Saturday afternoon, I remember that. I was scared as hell about going in."

Silence.

"I ought to be able to remember. Something terrible must have happened to make me violate that prohibition." What was it? What was it? He did remember going into the room. Again in memory he went in and stared at it, at a bulky mahogany-veneer dresser, at a stand by the bed, at the bed. The bed had been carefully made up. Yes, it had the lace cover on it, the same one. There it was spread out. I stood there and I was looking at it. I was looking at it because I had never seen it. Everything hidden. Hidden. I was looking through that transparent lace cover at a red cover or blanket under it, carefully smoothed out.

"What are you thinking?"

Dr. Marks was aware of trembling. He said, "Red, the blanket under the lace cover was red."

"Yes?"

"In Jimmy's room this afternoon I looked down out the window while he was getting tube-fed, and there were some red flowers. Blood. Ah—"

"It was Saturday afternoon," Dr. Naumann suggested.

"You have to heat the meat. But it's a sin to light the fire on shabbas, so we got a Christian neighbor, a boy named Willie, to come in and light the fire. So I watched Willie because it was a sin—he was taking the sin on himself—so I thought, God sees him. What would God do to him? Would God allow him to do that sin without doing anything to him? The kid went out in our stairway, it had a carpet, and on that carpet—it must have been loose somewhere—he tripped and fell. Blood, he was streaming blood! I saw it and yelled. Ma came running out and right away she turned and said, 'Get a sheet from the bed. Here, here's the key. Go in the bedroom and get a sheet,' and she threw me the key." The key to the forbidden bedroom. It was as if the whole city with its forbidden secrets of filth and terror screamed at him in that one moment. ('Whore,' the strap rising and falling, shadow, rot, verdigris, and dust.)

His forehead damp. What will be done to me for seeing my parents' bed?

Pavor nocturnus. A phantasmal self separates from the

real self and stands ready for the approach of punishers. They have guns. They shoot in the dust, bullets that can kill. A strange light flows down the canyons, that keeps changing. I'm guilty. I'm lost. Bullets. I'm trying to hide. The child screams and wakes.

"Why are you so disturbed?"
Silence.

Driving home.
The hood of his maroon car shimmered in the sun. His shirt collar felt tight, swelled by some force of blood. The hood of the moving car had a bloodlike tone.

He felt strange, getting estranged, strange.

It came again. It was like nothing he ordinarily felt after a session—never before. He suffered a jet of fear that left him shivering. Fear. Watch. Hold it, hold it down, watch it. He looked at the street. It was neutral, reality was going out of it like color. Color was draining out of it. His fear increased. Under a compulsion he couldn't understand, he stopped the car and walked to a privet hedge and touched it.

At the touch of this ordinary thing he was all right, as if cooling from a great heat. He was himself again, normal, and he wondered if what had just happened had not been some momentary physical disorder. No, the experience had not been physical, it had not been that.

Face it.
It had been something like insanity.

Driving home, he began to feel better, but he came in preoccupied and asked Margaret to hurry dinner. "I'm sorry," she said, "it'll be a while yet. You hungry?"

"Not particularly. In fact, I shouldn't be taking time for dinner."

"Why, is it some emergency?"

It was an emergency all right. He told her about Jimmy in some detail, so he believed she began to feel it. "I used the sedation for a chance to leave him and have my hour with Naumann and that bastard decides to push me, picks this time to push me to the limit."

Should I go on, should I tell her the rest? That vivid and sensitive face quick with its sympathies—with its angers too—waiting. Let her know, tell her. The experience had been brief, it almost wanted to drop away from him as if it hadn't happened, but it had happened.

"On my way home—" He described the momentary alienation, and she was immediately alarmed.

"But, darling, that's—that's like insanity."

"I know. I know it is."

"I'm worried about all this."

"I'm not. I'm all right."

She stared at him.

"It could even help me. I give Naumann credit."

"Naumann!" she said angrily.

"I may be closer to Jimmy now. Which could help."

Still angry: "Naumann only cares about his own work."

"No, you don't know this man. He had—he worked with the insane too."

"But if this does *this* to you." She was quieter.

"I know how you feel. Don't think I don't feel funny. But I think it's just a momentary thing, maybe good. It doesn't feel as if it would come back. And I had quite a session, I went through quite a thing as a kid. It makes me feel for this kid."

Nancy had had her dinner early, in the kitchen. He went into her bedroom where she was sitting up in bed, and kissed her. "Stay with me, Daddy."

"I'm afraid I can't, sweetie. Tomorrow maybe."

The boys noticed at dinner that he had nothing much to say. He attacked his food ravenously though somehow inattentively, and cleared his plate even before they did.

"You leaving us?" Bob asked as his father got up.

Dr. Marks said, "With your permission," and went down to his car.

When he reached the Medical Ward, the early dark had begun to flow in, across the city roofs where it underlined an occasional cornice. It would soon be night.

He found Miss Davis sitting at her desk, her hair frozen above her white gown. "Dr. Marks," she said, getting up quickly.

"How is he? Is he awake?"

"Oh, yes. The sedatives hardly affect him. He was making that zzzzzzz sound not a half hour after you left. Yes, he's awake."

Is he awake? Dr. Marks thought. Miss Davis said, "His temperature's gone up half a degree."

"Almost a hundred seven, then."

"One of the others was a hundred seven and four-tenths yesterday afternoon—Ethel. It's down a little now."

The egg of Dr. Linscomb's face seemed to appear before him, saying, "We have three on the ward right now."

He made an unconscious rotation of his shoulders (relief of tension) and went on down the corridor. As he approached Jimmy's room, he heard the "zzzzzzz" and the creaking of the bed. That bed creaking. When Nancy was just a baby, less than a year old, he'd hear her bed creak as he approached it. The bed would sway as she moved, then it would be still, then it would creak sharply, and before his vision would burst one of those ecstatic thrusts of her baby legs. Like a laugh. But the creaking of this iron bed was not such a laugh. It was terror, it communicated terror. From its sounds, he could tell the bodily plunge and the way it was suppressed, cut off. Then a listening pause. Then the plunge repeated, and the listening. Listening to what?

He went into the room in the dark and went to the foot of the bed. The bed now was completely silent. He saw the sheet as an unvarying plane as his eyes adjusted themselves to the darkness.

"Zzzzzzzz. That was the green paint he took, huh?" Again silence and a slow movement of the head began.

Now the whole body jerked and the bed creaked loudly. Dr. Marks felt power in it, power that continued in spite of the boy's fever and exhaustion. "That bridge, that bitch. I saw him go in there. Help!" Whispering: "I'll take torture."

Angst. Anxiety. Terror.

"Zzzzzzzz. Pitch that slow one, Murph. Help! He says help!" The walls became clearer. The room was pure in its bare frame. It was a pure stage for fright, with only the night-light from the corridor vaguely showing. "He was blind that time, he sneaked down DeKalb. Zzzzzzz. You seen him, Joe?" A wild scream dying into a dull moan, then a whisper. "I know he's invisible. They put the pot sideways. She knew it. Zzzzzzzzzzz." The voice was thin and choked off. Even the breath seemed hoarded.

He felt as if he almost got meanings. The secrecy of his

parents had increased his cunning, maximizing the nonverbal "process," making him know things he shouldn't know. Like that time with Lena—Lena who did the wash on Bushwick Avenue—that time he came down the cellar and she was leaning over the tub and rubbing rhythmically, and just then he knew she was having sexual thoughts. He knew. He himself got excited. She asked, "What are you thinking?" and when he refused to answer, she flipped water at him. And laughed.

He listened to a long string of fragmentary productions. Phrases. Whispers. Screams. "Monsters. That was the wrong screw, bud. They went up another street that time. Torture!" He put his hand quietly on the kid's crossed arms. "I'm here with you, Jimmy."

"Torture! Help!" Silence, a frantic scream, then silence again.

"I'm going to stay with you." Does he know my hand is touching him? Is it the pressure of my hand, or is it some delusion, some horror? He withdrew his hand and again stood listening.

Listening until his mind drifted to its own thoughts.

Naumann had called it *Angst.* There was a commoner name for it, a vulgar name:

"Unholy terror."

And it was unholy. Yet human. Animals never knew it. Animals never got out of contact. At Ted Rutledge's summer place at Lake George, he'd seen rabbits and pheasants —none of them got out of contact. If one of them didn't keep raising its head out of the field grass, watching for enemies—dead.

An animal dropped its young and then ran. Man lay helpless for months. And when he had to go back to the crib, okay—the hospital provided it. True, Jimmy's pathologic infancy wasn't being too well cared for here, but in principle Jimmy could live.

"Zzzzzzzzzz." A convulsive shake of the bed. "Mmmmmmmmmm—zzzzzzzzz." Desolately: "Where's his tongue?"

The rigid, spasmodic breathing continued. Breath after breath raised up the straitjacket and the heavy shroud of the canvas. "Wh wh wh wh wh. The long one's the one to watch. Help! Zzzzzzzzz." *'The long one's the one to watch.'* Penis, the penis directed at the mother.

More and more a pattern became evident behind the flow of disjointed phrases, the terror, the screams. *'Torture!' 'Where's his tongue?' 'The long one's the one to watch.'* It came again and again, the revealing flash of hysteric light, the flash of meaning.

At midnight, he was still listening. A new nurse had come on and Miss Davis had evidently told her what was happening, for she had merely tiptoed to the door once, and as he said nothing, had gone away. The deep night brought up the few sounds that remained during sleep. Sleep? He remembered the impression he had had of non-sleeping when Jimmy was given the sedative. At least the level of sound quieted, coughs were lowered, screams died down.

"Zzzzzzzz. I wish I had a fucking Messerschmitt." He wants to be a boy, then the fear of incest: *'Torture.' 'Take it away and give it away.' 'That was the wrong screw, bud.' 'Where's his tongue?'*

The flood of words rolled on: "Help! Did he yell? That German-American Empire. That—Zzzzzzzzz." *'German-American Empire'* and *'British-American Empire.'* Fusion. The fusion of two powers. Parental intercourse? "Don't take nothing, bud. Help! Scram. Regiments." The kid was shuddering and thrashing from side to side. He vaulted from whispers to screams.

At last Dr. Marks went out into the corridor, blinking tiredly. The new nurse, sitting at the desk, was a young woman, competent-looking.

"I'm Dr. Marks."

"I'm Miss Tait. Is there anything I can do for you, Doctor?"

"Have you a cigarette?" She gave him one. "I'm getting tired. Could I borrow a chair?"

"Do you want me to bring it to Jimmy's room?"

"Thanks."

When the chair came, he put it against the white catafalque of the bed. He *was* getting tired. When he sat down, his head almost at once leaned against the canvas. Each breath he took dulled his consciousness.

"Help! Where did he go? The bastard."

He had to stand up. That was the only way to keep awake. He again got to his feet.

The boy's eyes were open, and, in the dark, seemed

swollen to an unearthly size. "Zzzzzzzzz. Patriots. The second one's the one to kill. Complete torture. Help! Help! Where's that . . . Guns!"

The fatigue Dr. Marks felt seemed to be loosening him. Making him receptive. It was as if images were roused in his mind to meet the words that came in the unchangeable turnstile of the boy's mouth. *The second one's the one to kill.* Wasn't Jimmy the second child? Why killed? Why should he be killed? Willie on the stairs. Was that me? Was I the one who sinned? Sin. "Torture. Help!" Screams. Screams of fear. Who knows what happened to this kid? Does he even know? What do I know of all that happened to me? I didn't know I was kept out of my parents' bedroom. If anybody asked me, I would have said, Who remembers his parents' bedroom? Who goes into it? You just black out. Don't remember. Who knows what else is in me I don't remember? How can you not remember? *How can you be insane?* "He's crazy. Where is she? Where is that bitch? No. Put it there, bud." The kid turned his head slowly to one side, staring in terror. "Zzzzzzz. How we doin', Mike? Zzzzzzzzzz." Then continuous screaming. The screaming wore on into a whisper, then started again and Dr. Marks felt a momentary impulse to strangle it, to stop it. It was so relentless. It hit that nerve response, that nerve that said, Do something. How many parents have an impulse to stop the baby's screaming? After trying this and trying that, and it doesn't stop—stop! Can the parent hate the child? Jimmy's glinting eyes searched here and there. He held his breath, he began thrusting fearfully under the sheet. This lonely fear—"Help! Help!" He screamed, "Where is she? What's she picking up her leg for?" A woman. And a sexual movement. Who? Who was *picking up her leg?* "She's the one. Where is she? My mother! (a sobbing scream) I'll have torture!" The first time he had said it—"Mother." "He's coming at me. He spits teeth every day. If only I had—" He rolled to one side, shuddering, and the shuddering increased. "Help! I got none. I got none. Go somewheres else. Knives. It's terrible. The British-American Empire. Who wants anybody else to do that? He says yes? He says no. No! No! Zzzzzzzzzz. Ahhhhhhhhh." A long scream, then: "Please don't—Mmmmmmmmmm. No! Papa, don't cut off my balls!"

The listening, the long waiting, the exhaustion, the non-knowing—it was over. The kid had said it.

What do you do now? Quick: "I won't. I won't," Dr. Marks said.

"Thanks. He suffers torture."

Tell him you understand him, know his secrets, get them out in the open.

"Zzzzzzz. She's got her leg up. Zzzzzzzz."

"That means you want to fuck your mother. I know your secrets."

"Knives. Zzzzzzzzzzz—"

"You're afraid of Papa. I know what the knife is—"
The boy screamed at him.

"You're afraid your prick will be cut off."

"—where's that one-crack bastard? Wise cracks, hey? Get him a gun."

"You want a prick."

"Torture! He peed straight down. Help!"

"You're a boy, Jimmy. Only girls pee straight down. You can't be a girl. It's no use. You have a prick."

"Mmmmmmmm—zzzzzzz. Where's that trap? Keep your leg in, bud. Joe's the one."

"You think Joe fucked your mother so you didn't. But you wanted to."

In the frenzy that followed, Dr. Marks was afraid Jimmy would tear the restraint sheet loose. The boy thrust and gasped for air. He lifted the great hollow of his chest with all his strength and screamed.

Miss Tait came running. Dr. Marks felt a humming in his head, like a distant motor.

"What's the matter?"

"Don't touch him."

"But what happened?"

"Come out here in the corridor where I can hear you."

She said, "Don't you think he ought to have a sedative?"

"No. No, no sedative." The corridor rocked and hummed. "I was talking with him." But he was too tired to tell her, to explain.

As he drove home, he kept thinking, How is he? The further he got from the hospital, the more he thought, What am I doing, driving away?

He passed an all-night diner and saw a telephone sign.

At the phone, he got a connection through to Miss Tait. "Hello?" he heard her distant voice.

"Hello. This is Dr. Marks."

"Oh, hello, Doctor. Yes?"

"How is he?"

"He's much quieter."

"No sedative."

"No, no sedative," she said.

"And you're sure he's really quiet? He quieted down on his own?"

"That's right, Doctor."

I knew his secrets, I didn't castrate him. "What's his temperature?"

"It's down to a hundred five nine."

"Did he say anything?"

"He said, 'I drank a drop. I'm a baby.' "

No, you'll pass out if you try to do anything more tonight.

"I almost think he's sleeping now," the nurse said.

He looked at his watch. Two thirty, going for three. "Let him sleep. I'll be back about five thirty. Tell the relief nurse at four not to disturb him. No sedation no matter what he does."

"Yes, Doctor."

"You'll remember that."

"I'll remember, Doctor. I'll tell her."

5

He went into the bedroom and as soon as the door creaked, Margaret called from the bed, "Darling?"

"Haven't you been sleeping?" he said. He put on a reading light by the bed. He felt restored merely by the presence of the familiar room.

"Yes, I slept. But I kept listening for you in my sleep."

He thought, Jimmy. Even sleeping, part is not asleep.

"What happened?" she said.

"Something terrific, I think. I don't know." Undressing, he started telling her. "Fantastic, isn't it, that he said clearly, 'Papa don't cut off my balls'? After all the disguises, just out and said it. It seems to prove all you have to do is listen." He was torn between tiredness and enthusiasm as he took off his clothes. "It was some feeling when he said that. God."

She gazed up at him, half smiling. He said, "You know, maybe he wanted to tell me." He described what had happened at the end, how he had interpreted. "When I told him what things meant, there, it certainly got a reaction. We communicated, I know that. That's something, isn't it?" He told her about his phone call, that the kid was quieter and his temperature was down a degree. "Maybe it means something."

"Now you better get some rest."

"Am I going to rest, till five o'clock!"

"You're getting up at five?" She said it as if he was out of his mind.

"Remember a few years ago before we were married I used to neck with you till five thirty and start practice at nine?"

"But—" She thought of his hospital routine. "You're on duty tomorrow."

He got into bed. "I can't help it. I'll just let the blood tests go or get somebody else to do them. Maybe even skip rounds." How good the bed felt, and yet, as he was over-tired, the humming of fatigue began to sound again. "I can manage for a day. I've got to. No, I can do it." As if talking to himself: "You know the last thing he said, 'I drank a drop. I'm a baby.'"

"Yes?"

"What do you suppose that means?"

"How should I know?" she said, curving against him.

"It's regression. The kid is trying to get out of this Oedipal trap, so maybe he's saying he can't do anything wrong because he's a baby. 'I didn't commit that sin, I didn't commit incest, I didn't hurt anybody. I couldn't.'"

He put out the light by the bed, and the city beyond the windows became visible. He felt, to the east, the long, flat avenues out of which Jimmy had come, and he himself had come. A baby in those streets. A child. Was there something in the common background he had with the kid—St. Catherine's spires, the brass dome of the brewery?—that helped him? Increased his understanding? Something was helping him.

'I drank a drop.'

That girl Lena he had thought of as he was standing by Jimmy—he remembered something else that had happened with her, a year or two later. By then she had had a baby and she was there again doing the wash and again he had gone down into the cellar. That same mischievous, sexual look and she picked up the baby and began nursing it, baring her breast in his presence. She called him over to her and suddenly rounded her breast and offered it to him. He refused. She insisted. He took her nipple in his mouth and sucked it, and the milk that he got from it didn't taste good—

Tasting that milk, he plunged toward dream. He dreamed of a room in which steam was escaping from a small spigot. He felt that he ought to turn it off, and his sleep swung deeper and soon there was nothing but blackness.

He felt as though only the moment after he went to sleep, the alarm crashed him awake. Breathing hard, he felt a rush of soft hair across his face and Margaret's lips moved to his. "Darling." The nightlong-deepened warmth of her body opened under him, taking him as she came out of slumber.

Afterward, the bed spoke not with love, but with Jimmy's remembered fear.

Driving to the hospital, he thought of his plunge from breast to sleep, and from sleep to love. But then his thought went back to Jimmy. Thinking of Jimmy, he was only half aware of the eternal low Brooklyn house steps flowing backward along the sides of his car moving fast in the early morning light.

He began to go over Jimmy's productions again in his mind, fitting them to Freud. He knew Freud and Freudian theory by the memorized book. But is the book enough? It's one thing to know the text, another—

Okay, begin by the text. What's the theory of psychosis, what's this thing with Jimmy?

In health, the ego, the conscious part of the mind, is in contact with reality and not in contact with the Unconscious. In psychosis, this same conscious part of the mind, the nuclear core or whatever you want to call it, is in contact with the Unconscious and not in contact with reality. Neurosis is an ego-Unconscious sickness. Psychosis is an ego-environment (outer world) sickness. In this sickness, the world goes away and instead, the psychotic creates himself a new world, a wish-fulfillment.

A cat walked out from the curb and returned dilatorily to a garbage can. He didn't see it. He went on thinking.

This idea of wish-fulfillment. You fulfill a wish in a dream and if it's a forbidden wish, it makes you afraid of punishment. I want Mama, but Papa will cut off my balls.

But there's a counterwish in Jimmy's psychosis—I don't want Mama. *'I peed straight down.'* If I'm a girl, I can't do anything to Mama, and Papa won't hate me. But the fear comes with that too because to be a girl means castration, biologic death.

His mind jumped to another example—Florence—the one they were feeding ice cream. She'd tried to kill her daughter—that was reality. But she had repressed that reality (as Jimmy had repressed his male sex) and now she was on a train trip somewhere. On the train trip she wouldn't be home, and in comparison with being home, the train was just heavenly. But the trouble was there was a fear hidden in this too. I do not hate my daughter, I do not want to kill her. On the contrary, somebody outside (undesignated) wants to kill me. *'Something terrible will happen if I eat.'*

Fear. Terror.

Terror and the repression of reality. The neurotic represses reality too, but he represses only part of it. He sets a limit to what he'll repress. The psychotic, no. He represses everything—the world is dying, all reality. Now the Unconscious has no boundary, and the terrorizing goes on while you're awake. Didn't I just have a glimpse of that?

And yet even in this total irruption of the Unconscious, part of the sane mind is left. Breuer's Anna O. case: Breuer said that even when Anna was at the worst, in the psychosis, "there sat a keen and quiet observer somewhere in a little corner of the brain," who watched her being crazy. Dr. Marks could recall the passage in *Studien über Hysterie* word for word, it said that Anna had been so aware of the sanity within the insanity that when she recovered, she felt depressed and believed the whole psychotic experience had been simulated. Freud had often noted the same thing, and I'm sure in Jimmy too there's an observer in "a little corner of the brain." A baffled watcher, a terrified watcher. If I hadn't felt that, I wouldn't have interpreted to him, wouldn't have told him what things meant.

As my father never told me.

It was that watcher I must have reached when I spoke to him:

'Papa, don't cut off my balls.'

'I won't. I won't.'

When the kid said, "Papa," he was introducing me into the psychosis (a new thought). And I answered for Papa. I had to. I had to say, "I won't," when he said, "Don't cut off my balls." But that means I *was* Papa.

I *was* Papa?

Maybe that's what reassured him really. It had seemed to do him more good than any of the general reassurance. Maybe that's just what I should keep on doing.

Be Papa.

A milk truck held him up. He sounded his horn and the truck moved over. Now he wanted to get there, to be at the hospital—how was that kid with his straining eyes and pulse? Was he alive, had he made it through these hours? Was he waiting for "Papa"?

Why did I leave him? (But I had to.)

A traffic light stopped him, the red light like an inflamed eye. Danger, danger—he glanced up the side street and went through the light. He raced the car two more blocks and entered an avenue and now ahead he saw the hospital fence and the first row of tall, familiar porched buildings. Had the kid lasted? Was there enough life yet in that draped skeleton of his?

There had to be—

Then he felt a strange calm.

A new nurse was on duty, her whiteness gleaming in the morning light.

"How's Jimmy?"

"Weak. Awful-looking. Temperature's been around a hundred five." She said what he was thinking: "He won't last much longer."

"They don't all die?" he said.

"But they do, Doctor. You know."

He looked at his watch. Quarter to six.

"Will you need me, Dr. Marks? I'm Miss Alston."

"I'll call you. I want to see him alone."

The room was overbright with morning sun as he came in. A cry of "Angel" greeted him and the hollow-eyed head was trembling. The tremor made it seem stiff. But he was alive.

"Hi, kid. I'm here."

His emaciation was as if a spoon had been put to his cheeks. What he said was in a whisper of terror. "Monsters. Where? Zzzzzzzz. Mortar fire! Dracula!" Now moaning: "No, he says no." The apron of the sheet bellied wildly, shuddering and plunging.

"Son." Last night he called me. Now I'm calling him. "Son, I'm your father—"

"Zzzzzzzzz," desperately.

"I'm Papa. Papa who loves you."

The sunken eyes stared and swelled. "He didn't say he loves her. I love who? Gorillas. You're right, I robbed a world. Proud of it. I spent it on a BB gun. Patrick Cady, the dirtiest bitch that ever lived. Zzzzzzzzzz."

"I'm Patrick Cady. I'm your father." Tell him what I believe helped him last night. "I know all your secrets, son, but I'm not going to hurt you. Nothing could make me hurt you. Even when I know what you want to do with Mama, I forgive you for all that."

"He's begging." Screams. "Please, please! Oh, trouble. Patriot. Where did he wander? I'm caught inside."

"You're not caught. You can come out now. You can have a prick now."

"Help!"

"Your prick's safe, son."

"Zzzzzzzz. Don't be invisible. What's that one-two for? Long live the German-American Empire. Who is he? He's Mike. I— Don't let me, don't let me!"

"You mean don't let you fuck Mama. Of course I won't let you fuck Mama. Don't worry, you can't do it now."

"Where is he? I'm a puzzle. It's awful. It's—"

"Sure if you fucked Mama, it would be a dreadful thing, but you only thought about it. You never did it."

"Thank you, Mike," the boy said in a low tone. He's still evading Papa—now he won't call me Papa. Dr. Marks leaned over and took Jimmy's face in his hands. "Listen, Jimmy." Making the kid look at him: "I'm your father."

"Who am I?"

"James Cady."

"My name ain't James Cady. He said he ain't James Cady."

"You are Jimmy Cady."

"He says no."

"Not he. You."

Silence. The first silence, the first appearance of listening. "They got all those guns. It's terrible. That bastard, he's the one who did it. Who am I?"

"You're Jimmy Cady, and I'm Papa and I love you."

"Mike says he loves me. All that torture." Shyly: "Patrick?"

The first response. "Yes, I'm Papa. You can know it now."

"I'm Ponce de Leon, junior. I restore youth. Zzzzzzzz." Wildly: "Where is he?"

"You. You. You're right here, right by me. Safe."

Jimmy jerked his head violently. "Traps. All that juice. Squirt it around fast."

"Good boy. Use your squirter. It's a nice big one and you can be proud of it."

"Zzzzzzzz. Help! Throw that bitch out. I make fires."

"Keep your prick."

"Kill that bastard."

"That means you don't want to be afraid of me, son."

Jimmy began to laugh hysterically. Waves of laughter shook him. When this hysteria subsided, he said softly: "She was a girl. She's a man now. The richest guy in the world." He made the motor noise.

"You *are* a man now, Jimmy. You don't need to pretend to be a plane. You can let everybody see you're a man."

"Zzzzzzzzzz."

"I love you. You don't have to beg me to love you. I love you anyway."

"Papa."

"Yes, I'm Papa."

With anguish: "I don't want Frances in me."

The wonderful kid. All mixed up. All that killing stuff in him. Having to be Mama— "Son, you're a boy. I only want a boy. You don't have to be Mama for me to love you."

"Zzzzzzzz. Zzzzzzzzz."

"All I want's a boy."

"Zzzzzzzz. No. Patrick Cady, my father. Oh, Ma, what trouble!"

"It is difficult, son, but you'll manage it." It seemed to Dr. Marks that the sheet rippled in answer. He felt the boy's effort. He had a rush of feeling as if he would somehow bodily lift the boy, carry him by force away from his terror somewhere into a better place.

Just so he knows I'll be here. He put his hand on him. "I'm here, son."

"Somebody said she's gone."

"I'm the only one can help you now."

"Zzzzzzzzzz. That's the fast ball, bud. That bastard, Joseph. Wipe him out."

"I know you hate your brother. Mother loved him more. She didn't love you enough. But I'll make it up to you, son."

"That snake—"

"Yes?"

"So many tongues. Mike. He's the one had the stick."

"You have one too."

"That American kid. If he just walked in. I walked out. Zzzzzzzz."

"You're my kid."

"Mmmmmmm—wh wh wh wh."

"You can believe me now. I'm Papa. I know everything you're thinking. I'm the one who understands everything."

"Mmmmmmmmm."

"I'm with you."

"Let's fly that P-Four. What do you say? Zzzzzzz."

"Good!"

Wildly: "I'm climbing. Where's that stick?"

"Here it is. Take it. I want you to have it."

"Horrors."

"I love you, son."

A long scream and then a catch of breath. Then in a very quiet voice: "Oh, he calls me son." The boy moved his head from side to side and began to smile. He was looking at Dr. Marks, and on his face came something like the breaking smile of a small child. It was also a silly smile, Dr. Marks thought, but he felt like calling the whole hospital in to see this smile of a child coming back to life. But immediately, as if in desperate fear of this smile, Jimmy began to scream. "Zzzzzzzz. Where's Mike? Joe, the fucking bastard. I'll kill him." Softer: "It's something funny here. Convulsions." Louder: "He's going to die." Softer: "I still got time to live."

'He'll die, I'll live—' "Why try to escape from me, son? I love you."

"Where is she?"

"Who?" Dr. Marks asked.

Softly and with desperate hope: "She called me the freshest. I'm a baby."

"You are a fresh little kid, but I love you anyway."

"Yes, Ma." He started screaming again. "Joe, Joe, help! I don't like the way my eyes see him!" Agonizingly: "Don't do it, please don't do it!" He madly made the motor noise, which choked off in his throat.

"You're dreaming now, son. But I'll wake you up."

"Zzzzzzzz. Thank you. I restored her life by being a genius. He's the one. I grew up slowly."

"You *can* grow up now because I love you." Dr. Marks leaned down and stroked Jimmy's head.

"My mother's hand. She says I'm handsome. Certainly I'm dead. I'm a disgrace to East New York. I was never dead, Ma." The tone softening: "Where am I?"

"New State Hospital, a mental hospital."

Jimmy's eyes tried to focus. "A mental case? Who are you?"

"Dr. Marks."

"Oh, Dr. Marks. Patrick Cady."

"Your doctor." Dr. Marks's heart was quite overwhelmed. A response and answer.

"I wish he'd take a walk." Bitingly: "Set up the greatest torture, the greatest in the world."

"That's all over now, that torture."

"Yes." The kid's eyes seemed to be seeing.

"Who am I?"

"That bastard is gone now."

"Who am I?"

"Scram, bud. They're all over in the other lot."

"Who am I?"

After a long silence: "Dr. Marks." The exhausted head sank back.

I did it. I did it. Dr. Marks wanted to run to the door and scream: This kid knows who I am. An insane, dying kid answered a question. You say they can't be reached. They can be reached.

He was filled with love. With gratitude for the child who had acknowledged him, acknowledged his fatherhood.

He noticed Jimmy's extreme emaciation. He ought to eat. Could he eat? He *looks* like somebody who can eat. If I feed him.

'I drank a drop. I'm a baby.'

He called Miss Alston and said, "There's something I'd appreciate if you'd do for me. I want to get some food right away from the kitchen, some milk, some bread, maybe some warm soup and mashed potatoes. Anything like that they have. Anything soft." Gently he said, "Will you do that?" In answer to the question in her eyes, he added, "I'm going to try to feed him. You know the kitchen is slow sometimes. It's very important to get this right up. Will you see to it? And bring a spoon?"

"Yes, Doctor. I'll do it right away."

Not as motherly as Miss Davis, but willing.

He went back to Jimmy. The kid's eyes were still trying to focus as if he hadn't quite got the knack yet.

Babies' eyes focus that way. But what's psychosis anyway? Regression. But what's regression? He's a baby maybe—he says he's a baby. But he talked about his sister Frances who's now only a little over a year old. *'I don't want Frances in me.'* So everything's there. What's happening now is there: *'Where am I?'* And the Oedipal fear: *'Don't cut off my balls.'* And *'She called me the freshest. I'm a baby.'* All in the mind at the same time.

And that awful split. The collapsed ego shouting with pride: *'Set up the greatest torture, the greatest in the world.'* *'Genius.'* *'Richest guy.'* And that other split: hate and love—*'Kill that bastard.'* *'I restore youth.'*

"Jimmy."

The eyes jumped. Alarm. "Where did he go? I change empires. Good night."

Firmly: "You can't change anything, Jimmy. You can't be anything but what you are, a boy."

"I robbed continents! I knocked her over?"

"You just imagined you did. But even if I'd caught you doing it, I'd have forgiven you. I love you so."

"Ma, I got my eyes back." The exhausted breath sighed and became calm.

"That's right. No secrets between us. I'm going to let you in on everything, kid."

"He says yes."

And again the eyes were focusing.

Miss Alston came into the room, carrying a tray of food which she put on a stand. He thought, How am I going to feed the kid? There in the restraint sheet? With that coldness, that grip on his arms like the psychosis itself? That's no way to feed a child.

"Please help me," he said to Miss Alston. He went to the bed and started unfastening the sheet.

The nurse did not move forward. He realized the state of mind she was in. She seemed to know that something extraordinary was happening—there was probably something about Jimmy that indicated it. Her bringing the food indicated it. But I'm breaking the rules.

"This is all right, Miss Alston. I assure you there's no danger."

No danger! her eyes said. How can you take a patient in full-blown acute catatonic excitement out of restraint? They have maniacal strength.

"If you're worried, I'll do it alone. Stand back if you want."

He untied the heavy cords and loosened the thick canvas sheet, and the boy's starved legs came into view—little more than sticks. Like the cadaver Brown's legs. He flopped the boy over like a bundle and undid the strait-jacket lacings down his back. He jerked off the long sleeves and threw the empty jacket to the footrail of the bed. "Okay, you're free now, Jimmy."

The boy slowly put his hands on the bed. "Monster." But like a feeble echo: "Zzzzzzzzz."

"Come on, stand up to the world! Doesn't it feel good to be out of the straitjacket?"

The spindling legs shivered and under the nightgown, the ribs swelled in their faint corrugation.

"Sit up now."

Actually he helped Jimmy sit up and propped him against a pillow. "All right now, Miss Alston, would you please bring me that bowl of soup?"

The nurse still wasn't acting as if she believed what she saw. But how could she? The kid had been assaultive, he had been tube-fed, he had been thrashing, screaming, straining against his restraint sheet—but mainly he had been dying. This was a condition neither she nor any other previous human being had seen reversed. If it *was* reversed.

Dr. Marks rested the bowl of soup in his lap. Putting one arm around Jimmy, with his free hand he raised a spoonful of warm soup to the boy's lips. "Eat," he said. The boy opened his gaunt, wasted lips and Dr. Marks tipped the spoon in. "Swallow." Jimmy swallowed.

Now Dr. Marks began to bring the soup up in the rhythm one uses for a child, the authoritative rhythm that establishes a pattern of eating.

"What happened?" Miss Alston said. "What did you do?"

"I'll explain it to you later."

After the soup, Jimmy ate some potatoes. He showed a little confusion at the soft solid, as a baby might, but chewed a little and swallowed. Eating is instinctive. Eating is basic. When Jimmy faltered in drinking some milk, Dr. Marks said, "All right, that's enough. You did fine, son. You ate and drank fine." To Miss Alston he said, "I don't want to overdo this. Take this," handing her the glass, "so I can lay him down again."

He slid Jimmy gently to a lying-down position on the bed, and put the pillow under his head.

"Thanks, you bastard. You can't make me change my mind." So, Dr. Marks thought, he's not going to let a little food win him over. "I don't let them live. I'm creating the end of the world. I'm a billionaire."

The important thing was to bring the world back again. "You see how much I'm caring for you, son."

"Wipe out all those goddamn bastards. Zzzzzzzzzz."

"You're not a bastard, I feed you. You figure that one out, kid." Jimmy seemed to be listening with close attention. "That means just one thing. That means you matter to me. That means I love you."

Complete silence.

"Nobody can love you more than I do. I'd do anything for you."

"Mike."

"I'm Papa."

Jimmy broke into tears. He wept loudly, his body torn with release. Screams filtered among the sobs, and he cried as if he could never stop. Then gradually he did stop, like a baby catching his breath. Dr. Marks searched for words to comfort him. "It's all right now, kid. It must be good to know somebody understands you, isn't it? Understands how you feel?" A subsiding shiver. "You've been scared to death, haven't you?"

"Zzzzzzzzz." Dr. Marks noted this feeble defiance and yielded to the temptation to smile. Jimmy said, "I'll kill you," and staggered up to his feet, his hospital nightgown hanging as if from a hanger. His legs buckled but steadied. "You—" He swung his fist and the inaccurate blow carried him off balance. Dr. Marks caught him and like a parent with a baby stretched him again at full length on the bed.

"Miss Alston," he said, "I guess we'd better put him back in the straitjacket for his own good. Would you like to help me now?"

Without hesitation: "Yes, Doctor."

He watched Jimmy's reaction. It was noncombative. His breathing was sustained and regular. Once or twice he sighed deeply. After he was back in restraint, he seemed reassured.

"What's this, son?" Dr. Marks held up his watch.

"A watch," the boy answered.

"Correct. Do you still know me?"

The boy was silent. Resistant?

"Who am I?"

Slowly: "Ten thousand armies—"

"Who am I?"

"The doctor."

"What's my name?"

"He says yes."

"You say yes."

"Zzzzzzzzz."

Okay, Dr. Marks thought. You can't expect him to come out of it all at once. He had to learn to trust you. "You're better, Jimmy. You'll stay better. You understand? I'll be right here with you now until you're all right."

After a pause: "Yes."

"Good. That's the way to talk." A good, clean "yes."

Jimmy smiled from the straitjacket, a likable smile, nothing silly about it.

That smile does it. He doesn't need a straitjacket. That smile is well enough for me. All the kid's hidden normality, all the natural realness that had been hiding behind the psychosis, came out in the smile.

Dr. Marks again undid the fastenings. The sun blazed behind the shade, it was full daylight, and sounds of the wakened hospital wards came from the distance.

And Jimmy sat up and trembled.

That shiver wasn't fear. Dr. Marks took the kid's hands and felt them. Fever. He had forgotten the fever. The trembling was a thin fever-trembling. That high fever. But now he noticed something. Yes, it was moisture. As he held Jimmy's hands, they began to get wet. The wetness seemed to extend. Definite beads formed on the kid's forehead and then a single drop formed and rolled like a tear down his cheek.

The moisture increased and almost as if he was secretly laughing, the boy shook and pressed his head into Dr. Marks's white coat.

He was pouring sweat.

6

Miss Alston stared at the rectal thermometer. "It's normal," she said.

Dr. Linscomb was on the phone when Dr. Marks appeared in the door of his office. "Yes, I heard about that. I heard about it. It's good. Well, I'll speak to you later." He hung up the phone and turned to Dr. Marks. "Yes?"

"Dr. Linscomb, Jimmy's temperature is normal. He's out of the excitement, completely out of it, out of the fear. He's in partial contact—please come and see him."

"His temperature's normal?" Instead of showing any impulse to get up, Dr. Linscomb kept his hand on the phone. "The temperature, you know, fluctuates wildly sometimes. I wouldn't go too much by the temperature."

"No, no, it isn't any fluctuation. The kid is really out of it. When he got over his fear, he broke out into a natural sweat. He's been eating. He's wonderful. If you'd just come and see him."

Dr. Linscomb still had his hand on the phone. "Eating?"

"Yes, he's eating. Soup, mashed potatoes—"

"Well, this certainly is one that fooled us." He lifted the telephone and put it down and folded his hands. "You're sure he had this sweat? Temperature holding normal?"

"No question about it."

"I would have asked anybody to diagnose that case. It certainly looked like acute excitement if I ever saw it."

Dr. Marks stared at this man and said, "You mean it wasn't acute excitement?"

"It couldn't have been. Once they're in exhaust status, they just don't get well."

"But you don't know what's happened. This recovery is something new. It's never happened before. I found a way to treat Jimmy."

69

"Yes?" A cold "yes."

"Yes. Last night—" He had hardly started on his story when Dr. Linscomb said, "Dr. Marks, you can spare yourself the detail. I'm sure you're convinced that what you did had something to do with this recovery, but we know here what we're dealing with. They do *not* get well if this is really acute excitement, and we were premature in diagnosing this particular case. I'd like to listen to you, but—"

"But, Doctor—"

"I'm sorry, I'm busy. I have several calls to make." Dr. Linscomb was lifting the telephone again.

"Will you talk with me later?"

"Now really, Doctor."

In a fury Dr. Marks said, "What's the matter with you? Don't you want to know that something important happened here? Is there something about this that you're afraid to look at?"

Now Eggshell was staring a cold and implacable stare. We will settle with you later, the stare said.

Dr. Marks turned and left the office.

He phoned home. When Margaret answered, he said, "Do you feel like being happy about something?"

"I do."

"I'm glad somebody does. Jimmy just had a great sweat, just hung onto me and sweated, and his temperature came down to normal. He's in partial contact. If he keeps on like this, he's going to make it."

"Darling!"

"But Dr. Linscomb isn't interested. He says it was a wrong diagnosis because if the kid could come out of this, obviously he was never in it. He won't even look at him."

"Darling, never mind. You did it. You did it. And Jimmy's going to live, isn't he?"

"I can't see why not. Yes, he's going to live."

He determined to stay with Jimmy until night or at least until the kid fell into a natural sleep. He called Reception and left his location with one of the nurses there whom he asked to take calls for him. "Please don't transfer them over here unless they're really urgent." He went on back to the kid's room and found him quietly resting under the covers. He wasn't sleeping. His eyes were open, but without any staring or terror. All that terror seemed cut off at the source. At any rate, it was not in evidence. And its disappearance left him curiously serene the way people look after great pain.

Dr. Marks thought, Imagine not wanting to come and see this.

This Miss Alston—she had responded well. Well, she had seen it. She was so far the only one who had seen it.

He settled himself for a long stay with the kid. Somewhere a bell was ringing, and outside the window a pigeon beat its wings. The bell stopped. He thought how the kid had screamed. He thought, Will he stay like this? Will it last?

But the peaceful breathing went on and on.

His watch ticked toward noon. The staff dining room— in that room there would be human beings. This Eggshell must be a special case of noninterest (or of vested interest, vested in being right). Nobody else could be like him. Here was news, news that gave hope, news of a possible regenerative happiness. What if it *was* just one case? What if it *was* only an uncertain and merely possible beginning? Here there must be those who wanted to listen. Here there must be some like himself who wanted to help the sick.

The staff dining room was a long room with soft green walls and tall white fluted columns. It made him think of the word *sanctuary*. All the noise of the working hospital was shut off behind its walls. The tables were covered with linen and there were a few flowers.

He had noticed how early many of the doctors came to eat and how slow they were to leave this room. Some of them played blackjack after lunch.

When he came in, at one of the larger tables sat Dr. Wellman, Dr. Parker, an intern named Savelli who was under Dr. Wellman's supervision, Dr. Spencer, and a young doctor named Rossman. As there was an empty place, he asked, "May I join you?"

"Certainly," Dr. Wellman said. "How did you make out over at Medical? See this Cady kid?" To the others: "Yesterday Dr. Marks told me he'd never seen a case of acute catatonic excitement and I referred him to one I sent to Medical—Jimmy Cady." To Dr. Marks: "You see him all right?"

"I saw him—"

Joking: "Is he dead yet?"

"He's not going to die."

Sharply: "What do you mean?"

As the waitress (who had just taken his order) walked away, into the sound of her steps Dr. Marks said, unable any longer to keep radiance out of his voice, "It's true, he won't die. His temperature's normal and he's eating, he's even in partial contact. Listen—let me tell you about this." Tell it careful, remember Dr. Linscomb. He held his blunt hands in front of him as if metaphorically he were holding a head, as if he were addressing both Jimmy Cady and this group of doctors. "There's this total terror, you could see it in production after production. 'Help! Help! I'll have torture!'" and he cited the productions, he cited a whole series of them. The waitress brought his soup, but he left it untouched. He spoke without stopping and without break. He told how he listened, how he believed he understood, how he interpreted, how he took the father's role in the psychosis, continuing, not letting up, and at last how the kid had come into partial contact. (There had been some apparent restlessness as he talked.) "They can be reached. Isn't it true that up to now nobody has believed they can't be reached? But this kid was reached. He answered questions. He began to differentiate me from his father in the psychosis and he finally knew me as his doctor."

Dr. Wellman, who had been the most restless and had not been eating for several minutes, said, "He knows you as a doctor? Knows you by name?"

"Yes."

"Temperature normal? Been holding normal?"

"Since he had that heavy sweat, yes, it's been normal."

"I did think when I sent Jimmy over, he might not be so bad, but the reports from Medical were certainly misleading. It certainly sounded like exhaust status."

"You mean you don't think it was?"

"But it couldn't have been if he recovered."

"You mean you don't think Jimmy really had those temperatures?"

"Oh, he may have had temperature, but, Doctor, they just do not recover."

Dr. Marks was looking again at Dr. Linscomb. But this man in front of him he had told the explanatory details to. This man had heard step by step what he had done. "You don't think that what I've told you makes sense? That you can get into the psychosis—"

Dr. Spencer said, "If I were you, I wouldn't continue talking around about this. You've just come in—I understand this is the first time you've been in a mental hospital —and it's understandable that with your particular frame of reference, I mean, believing what you believe—"

"Doctor," Dr. Parker said, "Dr. Spencer just means you don't want to get the staff laughing at you. Let's face it."

"But I'm right."

"I understand you believe you are."

"But do you want to come and see this patient? See his physical condition, look over his chart? Dr. Wellman?"

"Jimmy'll be back on the ward soon and I'll see him then."

"You're under analysis yourself, Dr. Marks?" Dr. Parker said.

"I am."

There was a commiserating silence following this statement.

Dr. Marks said, "Is there anybody here who wants to see this kid?"

Dr. Rossman, a small doctor with a long straight nose, said, "I do."

"Rossman, you think there's something in this?" Dr. Spencer said.

"I want to see it."

One of the doctors at the table next to them said, "I couldn't help overhearing what you were saying. This must be the patient Dr. Linscomb telephoned me about."

"He telephoned you about Jimmy Cady?" Dr. Wellman said.

"What did he say, Red?" Dr. Parker said.

"He mentioned the patient had improved and he had an idea. He thought, take this patient who it's assumed was dying and give him a coma of a thousand units and see if it wouldn't maybe pull him right out. It's certainly an idea, but the insulin ward is full right now and we can't take him."

Bastard, Dr. Marks thought. No word of protest that that bastard wants to give Jimmy insulin. Later—

Walking across in the noon heat between the buildings, he tried to calm himself, to tell himself these doctors were understandable. To them nothing the patient says makes sense: if they have any interest in him, it's to define his illness, give it a name. From then on the psychosis (and the terror) might as well not exist.

All that shuffling of feet when he began telling them about the kid's productions: *'I don't want Frances in me.'* *'She's a man now.'* That's to make the psychotic content not exist. They have something simple and mechanical to do, and they can do it to everybody and keep out of trouble.

But now he thought with a return of anger, Linscomb was saying push the kid as near death as possible. And Wellman and company agreed. Beat down and deaden the kid's spirit and nobody will have to know what the hell is in him. Shock—

He had been looking up medical papers on shock, items in the technical journals proving brain damage, tissue damage throughout the body: Pirosh knows it. They could know it. But that isn't what they want to know.

Bastards.

When he came back to the infirmary, Miss Davis was on duty. She met him in the corridor. "Doctor." Her face was glowing under her spectral hair. "Doctor, Miss Alston told me— You saved Jimmy. You saved his life."

I saved his life. He said, "Have you spoken to Dr. Linscomb?"

"No. He phoned up when Miss Alston was here."

"Oh, he phoned?" She seemed to find his tone odd. "What did he say?"

"Well, she said he asked how Jimmy was and said to put him on a convalescent diet."

"That's all?"

"I believe so."

"No mention of me?"

"I don't believe so."

"No mention of insulin for Jimmy?"

"Insulin for Jimmy!" she said.

"I know. I'd like to ask you—you, Miss Tait, Miss Alston—not to send him to insulin without letting me know." And why don't I speak to Linscomb? he thought. No, I can't. I simply can't. "I'd better warn you, Miss Davis. This hospital isn't going to like what I did with Jimmy.

I'm finding out. They don't want to know a psychosis has to do with sexual things, perversions, other horrors—"

Sunlight from a distant lighted end of the corridor struck toward her, illuminating the response of her face. "I know what you mean—"

He took her arm and walked along with her. "There's going to be an official line about Jimmy. That line will be that he never was in exhaust status and, in fact, never had anything but a mild excitement that was mistaken for a medical case. If he had been in exhaust status, he obviously couldn't have recovered. 'They always die,' you know?"

"But if they'd just see him—"

"They don't want to see him until he's better, until he eats for a while and so on. No, there's one doctor who's going to come up, a Dr. Rossman. He was at my table at lunch, and he doesn't seem to block like the others."

They were close to Jimmy's room now and Miss Davis said, "Doctor, no matter what anybody else says or doesn't say, I was on this case and I know that you did save Jimmy. That's all. I know."

"Thank you." He found he could hardly speak. When you get a little credit, he thought, do you have to crack up?

Jimmy glanced toward him as he entered the room. That was something new. An awareness that you're in the room. You and not the imaginations of insanity. "Hello," Dr. Marks said.

The boy tried to speak.

"I came back and I'm going to stay with you now." Smiling: "I love you as much as ever."

"He said yes."

At least "yes" now, and not "no." "*You* say yes, son. Tell me, are you hungry?"

"They brought me some—some—"

"You want to eat?"

Slowly and clearly: "No."

"That's the way to talk. I thought maybe you'd be hungry again. You're sure you're not?"

Jimmy seemed confused and tried to smile.

"I'm taking good care of you today, son. Even if it isn't long since you ate, you can eat again if you want to."

"Zzzzzzzzzz."

"No zzzzzzzzzzz."

"Okay," the boy said.

"Okay what? You want to eat?"

"No."

Did this mean the kid really didn't want to eat or was it some kind of negativism? It didn't feel like negativism. He seemed to be resting, and perhaps eating could wait a while.

"Thirsty? Want something to drink?"

"No."

He sat down by the bed and took Jimmy's hand. The kid held it. It was actual holding. And there was no more fever vibration. If I feel this pulse, I believe it won't be racing. But it's funny the kid doesn't go to sleep. Sleep. The word was soporific. The hand he was holding was holding him. No more need to struggle—the guardian hand was carefully holding his. Before he knew it, the world around him had become unreal: it had simply stopped being there. He was breathing deeply, then he no longer heard his breathing.

He was starting his car. But it had a floor shift, not a steering-wheel shift, and he was pulling, pulling on this kind of shift.

"Zzzzzzzz."

He opened his eyes and the kid wasn't looking at him. Then he became aware that the kid had made the "zzzzz" at somebody else. Dr. Rossman was standing in the door with the hesitance of an intruder. "Dr. Rossman. I'm afraid I was asleep."

Dr. Rossman came forward. "I'm sure you must be tired, Doctor."

"I didn't get much sleep last night. But it's all right." Dr. Marks released his hand from Jimmy's—Jimmy was still holding him—and yawned and stood up.

Dr. Rossman: "Hello, Jimmy."

"Zzzzzzzzzz."

"All right if I touch his forehead?"

I can trust this guy, Dr. Marks thought. "Go ahead."

His colleague put his hand on Jimmy's forehead. "Cool," he said.

"The last reading we had before his temperature broke was a hundred five. It dropped over six degrees."

"Remarkable."

"Those fucking bayonets," Jimmy muttered, raising his head after Dr. Rossman had withdrawn his hand.

Bayonets. "Yes, all that trouble," Dr Marks said. "But I'm going to keep you from doing anything wrong now. You're safe now, you know."

Jimmy let his head fall back and was quiet again.

Dr. Marks (to Dr. Rossman): "Take out your watch and show it to him."

Dr. Rossman took out his watch.

"What's this, Jimmy?" Dr. Marks said.

"Requirements . . . necessary facts."

"What is this, Jimmy? I want you to think and answer right. What is this?"

"A watch."

Dr. Marks said to Dr. Rossman, "You'll notice that what he answered before wasn't really incorrect. Jimmy." Jimmy looked up. "Where are you?"

"Mmmmmmmmmm."

"Speak up now when I ask you something. Where are you?"

"I guess—"

"Where are you?"

"In a hospital."

"Who am I?"

"Doctor Marks."

"Where were you born?"

Answering more clearly, as if coming into reality: "East New York."

"What street?"

"Sutter Avenue."

"What number?"

"That one—"

"What number?"

"Three seventy-one."

"What floor?"

"Scram, bud. They still throw that slow ball."

"What kind of crazy talk is that?" Dr. Marks said.

"They called me the freshest."

"Yes, you're a fresh kid, and I love you. I'm proud of the way you're doing here, Jimmy. I'm protecting you every minute."

"He says he loves me."

Dr. Marks took his hand again and pressed it. "I don't say it. I do love you very much, kid."

Dr. Rossman was standing soberly watching. "This certainly is remarkable," he said.

"He knows the number of the street where he was born. Do you know the number of the street where you were born?"

"As it happens, I do. But if you move much, I guess you could forget."

"Look at this kid. Just look at the condition he's in."

Dr. Rossman examined the sunken face, the bonelike, infantile-looking arms. The fingers with their joints exaggerated.

Dr. Marks: "What do you say?"

"I'm sure this was acute excitement. I'm sure all you said at lunch was true."

"May I ask something?" As Dr. Rossman nodded: "Are you under analysis?"

"I've been thinking of it."

Dr. Marks beckoned with his head. "Come out in the corridor a minute. Jimmy, I'll be right back." Their feet made a curious unison on the linoleum, and caught by that beat, he thought, Two, not one. Two, not one.

Outside, he said, "What's to be done in a place like this?"

"I don't think you'll get very far, with this. I hate to say it."

"Are there others like you here?" Dr. Marks asked.

"I'd better speak only for myself."

"If I even thought there were others."

"What would you do?"

"It isn't what I'd do," Dr. Marks said. "It's how I'd feel. I can't bear to think I'm alone here and can't reach anybody."

"You've reached me."

He touched Dr. Rossman on the arm. "Thank you."

At two thirty, although it was not a regular mealtime, Dr. Marks decided to feed Jimmy again. He went looking for Miss Davis who was not at her desk. He found her tube-feeding a woman. (Why was it always the nurse who did the tube-feeding? Why not a doctor occasionally? Why shouldn't a doctor take over this parental duty?)

The woman Miss Davis was feeding seemed to hang animal-like from the tube. As he came in, she jerked her head, making the tube tear at her nostrils. She gave a whine that sounded as if it were muffled behind heavy glass.

"Yes, Doctor?"

He indicated the patient. "Who is this?"

"Ethel Simpson."

Emaciated. "Exhaust status?"

"Yes. Yes, this is another one."

For an instant Ethel's gaze leaped to him, streaked with terror, and returned to the tube from which she hung in her animal- or fetus-like dependence.

"Did you want something, Doctor?"

"Well, when you're through."

"I'm just about through now." He waited and as the tube slid up and out, involuntarily he readied himself for that gulp of air and that probable scream. There was no scream, but there was another whine. "I kill graves. Bastard. Graves." Then silence.

"I came to ask if you'd like to get some food up from the kitchen for Jimmy." He told her what he wanted. "You might bring along something for me too. I didn't eat much for lunch." He was hungry.

"Help!"

Help.

Goddamn it, he said, let me alone. Right away, crying into your mind.

Getting you with that terror.

He said, "Is this one dying too?"

"The temperature's over a hundred seven in the past two weeks in spite of everything we've done. You see her. What do you think?"

What do you think? he thought as he walked back to Jimmy.

When Miss Davis arrived with the food, he decided to try something. He arranged pillows behind Jimmy and put a spoon in his hand and a bowl of oatmeal in his lap. Jimmy held the spoon correctly.

"I guess you're well enough to eat alone now, son. That's a good warm bowl of oatmeal you've got there."

He went out into the corridor with Miss Davis. "What sort of person is this Ethel Simpson?" he said. He looked down the corridor toward the room where she was.

"Much different from Jimmy."

"I get that."

"Jimmy," she said, "he's sweet. But there's something angry and—and even provoking about Ethel. Of course, how can anybody like that be provoking, when they don't know what they're doing? But still—"

"I know what you mean. Maybe you'll tell me what her history is."

"She's thirty-two. She just had her first baby."

A postpartum. "Married long?"

"Three or four years—to a nice man. I've seen him. Willard. Willard's mother lives with them . . ."

"You seem to hesitate," he said.

"Ethel talks about her—if you can call it talking. She doesn't seem to like her."

So the nurse listens to the patient. He said, "Any more about her history? The breakdown?"

"Yes, she was all right during the pregnancy, but right after the baby was born, she didn't seem to feel as if it belonged to her. It seems her mother-in-law took care of it. Ethel wouldn't. Or couldn't. One day she said there was no baby—that was the start. Then she stopped talking and wouldn't do any work around the house, then she got suicidal."

Fear. *'I didn't do it.' 'Monsters!' 'Help!'*

"What's this business of having babies?" he said. "Why is that so hard on a woman? Why should a woman go off the deep end from having a baby?"

"Well, it's quite a physical experience, isn't it?"

"Not that bad. I've seen it hundreds of times and I don't think it's that bad."

Miss Davis seemed to search her mind. "Some of these young women with a first baby, they worry or can't take the responsibility. Worry about money."

"But is that enough to drive them insane?"

She said "no" and shook her head.

"To produce all that terror? Don't you think there's something strange about it?"

"Yes." She seemed to be thinking about it. "She certainly says strange things, Doctor."

He had turned back toward Jimmy's room. He motioned to her and said, "Take a look."

Jimmy's bowl of cereal was empty.

Knowing about Ethel seemed to have badly increased his fatigue. His nerves were in a state today. He was unable to get out of his mind that reaction in the dining room. And now to have seen another one dying here. One who would inevitably die. And there was a third one he was afraid to look at.

He went back and sat down by Jimmy. Exhausted as he was, he was unable to fall asleep again. Jimmy too lay unsleeping. Once he muttered, "American Empire," and looked embarrassed. "What's the American Empire?" Dr. Marks asked, but the kid could not tell him. "Something you have to fight?" No answer. "You don't have to fight those things anymore—"

"All those bitches."

"What bitches?"

"Yes."

"What bitches?"

But the kid wouldn't answer. He just lay in the gradually darkening room, in the afternoon shade, and a little nervousness seemed to be appearing in his eyes.

Evening, crossing the roofs of the city, brought a change. Jimmy began to mutter. He moved restlessly and apprehensively as the dark made its gradual presence felt.

He hasn't slept in weeks. Not real sleep. The dulling by sedatives was never real sleep. He must be more tired than I am. He must be dead. But he just lies there with his eyes open. Why? Is he afraid to sleep? Afraid of something?

Sleep, the eight-hour psychosis. "To sleep, perchance to dream."

All he left in waking from his waking dream waits in sleep. 'Monsters.' 'Torture.' Son, it *is* torture. But you have to face it. You have to sink down into that dangerous sleep and accept it and know it and know that you're safe.

He took Jimmy's hand again. The darkness increased in the room like thicknesses of gauze, and shapes and outlines grew indistinct. Through the frame of the door, the night-light in the hall appeared. "Papa," the boy whispered.

"I'm here."

"I never meant to do it."

"I know you didn't. It's just a crazy imagination you had in your mind. That's all there was to it."

"Yes."

"Yes. Relax now."

The city's lights came on, below. Alive. They lightened

the room. "Jimmy." The head turned toward him, alert and listening.

"Jimmy, before long your father will come to the hospital again. It's just a misunderstanding in your mind about him—all that fear you had. Of course you know better now. You know that he loves you very much."

"Papa loves me?"

"He loves you very much."

Outside, the patients in other rooms began calling their irrational, worn, and desperate calls, now lower, now louder.

"Papa loves me?"

"If he was here, he'd tell you he loves you. You know he does just like I do."

"He loves me?"

"He loves you."

The voice came lower. "Ma?"

"Ma too."

Tenseness seemed to go out of the hand holding his. Jimmy said nothing more. His breathing changed and became shallower. It sounded in his mouth, then the rhythm became regular and deeper.

Dr. Marks said softly, "Jimmy?"

There was no answer.

7

Dr. Marks partially woke that night and sank back, aware that his sleep was disturbed: A flash of lightning stopped in midair like a halted motion picture. It became a chromium-plated sign over a tunnel. He was walking through the tunnel with somebody at his side. The tunnel became a country road and he had to get through a gateway that had two flexible barriers coming out from either side. The barriers read J on one side and C on the other. The letters bent themselves around until they made almost complete circles, and as he tried to step through them, they threatened to come together and stop him. He sank into a deeper sleep. There seemed to be something standing in front of him. A child laughed and said, "Are you going to hurt me?" He wanted to say, "No," but was unable to, and the child's face became less distinct. He was touching a tree that grew out of a hole in the ground. . . .

"Near the house on Bushwick Avenue," he told Dr. Naumann, "there was a cellar window with a small sunken space in front of it, in the sidewalk, and a tree grew out of this space. That seems to be the tree. When it rained, it poured in there and made a pool, and another kid and I used to put matchboxes in the pool and float them. The tree was maybe fifteen feet tall. It went up to about the second story of the house, just one thin trunk. After a while it died and we broke it off by shinnying on it. The inside was a whitish wood. It stayed that way, broken off, for a long time, then somebody cut it down."

As he associated to the dream, Dr. Marks was not entirely happy. Couldn't this damn Naumann let up on him for one session? He had come here filled with Jimmy, rested after a good night's sleep and reassured because Jimmy had been holding his gains through the day. The seductive pulse of egoism was singing in him. Naumann was the one person he could tell this to who would fully understand him and who would rejoice with him—the hell with the hospital.

He had started to tell Naumann.

"You say this Jimmy is out of danger? How do you know he's out of danger? Did you take his temperature?"

Did I take his temperature! He described to Dr. Naumann how the temperature broke, he told him the whole course of the "treatment." Dr. Naumann listened in silence. "Today I had to catch up on my blood tests, but I visited him twice." Each time the kid was sitting up in bed, wearing a hospital robe that he adjusted a little. Quiet, but his eyes alive, and he talked with a definite interest in talking, blundering, fading out of contact, but coming back fast.

"Yes? Yes?" Dr. Naumann said. He seemed now to be listening attentively. But no elation, the bastard. "And so now there has been this recovered case, as you say. How do they take this at the hospital? You've brought it to the attention of some of the doctors?"

Dr. Marks first described what had happened with Dr. Linscomb. Dr. Naumann made him go over this in detail, even to exactly what he had said to him. "This asking him if there was something about the patient that made him afraid—that was an interpretation. It was ill-advised and you have made yourself an enemy." Dr. Marks felt checked after the easy rein he had been giving himself. It was true that that had been a mistake—he had recognized it immediately afterward. But he said, "Do you think he'd have reacted any differently no matter how I handled him?"

"It's advisable to proceed with every possible assumption of winning the other person over."

Winning Eggshell. And how about the doctors at lunch? He had proceeded with every possible assumption of winning them over. And what had happened?

Dr. Naumann: "You did interest one doctor."

"One doctor!"

"One doctor is a help. This is a difficult project."

Dr. Naumann did not then discuss Jimmy any further. He seemed to turn with an automatic interest to work. If anything, he seemed more eager than usual to get to the analytic hour proper.

The dream, Dr. Naumann thought. The initials, J C—the "flexible barriers." J C—Jimmy Cady. But why had those initials been so attractive? Both had shapes that lent themselves to rounding into "almost complete circles." Breasts. But why Jimmy? Jimmy had opposed him. Jimmy for a long time hadn't been responsive. But breasts? And was it just Jimmy? Always screens, disguises. And there had been Oedipal as well as oral content. Testicles? Balls?

"Whitish wood," Dr. Marks said. He half snickered. "Easy to see what that is."

Silence.

"Semen."

Or milk? How oral material is resisted! Even I resist it.

"I was thinking about Jimmy the night before last, I thought that he and I came from about the same neighborhood. I thought maybe that might help me understand him. No, I didn't really think that. I know it takes more than that to understand somebody. But this kid I used to float matchboxes with, in that pool, or puddle, by the tree —his name was Gus. I once had a fight with him and licked him, and after that he seemed to like me. Imagine liking a sissy who can't go off the block, who has to be taken to school. But at least he found out I could fight."

All this talk about a fight. "How did this fight start?"

"Well, he said something to the older of my two sisters."

Silence.

"He said maybe, 'Hello, beautiful,' or what we used to say in those days, 'Hello, luscious.' "

Continued silence.

"So I had to go to work on him."

"Defend your sister—that was Dora."

"Yes, Dora."

"You've said she somewhat resembles your mother?"

"I suppose you mean Gus is my father if Dora was my mother. You mean I was fighting my father."

"Or, who fights for Mother?"

Doubtfully: "You mean I wanted to be Father too?"

"Dr. Marks, who do you suppose was this child in your dream? This child who said, 'Are you going to hurt me?' "

"What I think of immediately is Jimmy. There were those initials in the dream, J and C. That's Jimmy Cady, and I guess 'Are you going to hurt me?' means 'Are you going to help me?'—dreams often go by opposites. And the child was laughing, I guess was happy. I made Jimmy happy. Oh, another thing. The initials turning into circles. That was Jimmy's balls—'Papa, don't cut off my balls.' The whole thing was about Jimmy. Well, you'd expect that, after what I went through."

Silence.

Dr. Marks too remained silent.

"Do you have further associations to the initials becoming 'flexible circles'?" Dr. Naumann said quietly.

After a moment: "No."

"Such dramatic material and you cannot find any further associations?"

"But isn't the meaning clear? What could be more definite than their turning into balls?"

"Try to tell me something more about this child in your dream."

Dr. Marks was silent.

"Was the child a boy?"

Confused: "I think so."

"You mean it might not be a boy?"

"Perhaps."

Jimmy: *'I peed straight down.' 'She's a man now.'*

"What are you thinking?" Dr. Naumann said.

"What I'm thinking is embarrassing, but I suppose I have to tell it. When I was about seventeen, when we were living at Eastern Parkway, one hot morning I was asleep in bed without my pajama top on and a kitten crawled up on the bed—we had several at the time—and woke me up. It began crawling on me and stepped on my nipple. So I thought, I wonder if it wouldn't suck at my nipple and I wondered what that would feel like. So I put the kitten's mouth right to my nipple and it began to suck. It was a funny feeling, like a deep tickling or even like a vibration of some kind. I didn't like it and pushed the kitten away."

"Why were you reluctant to tell me this?"

Dr. Marks shrugged.

"You don't suppose this is so unusual? Every boy and man has moments of thinking what it might be like to be a woman. A woman thinks the same way what it would be like to be a man." I can say this to him, but I can't say, "Dr. Marks, you're the child of ambiguous sex in your dream." Dr. Naumann continued: "Under rather unusual circumstances you've begun treating a patient. That increases the importance of not having blocks in yourself."

"What blocks?"

"One is you've found it hard to feel fear of castration."

"Conscious fear."

"I bring it to your attention because you had trouble seeing that such fear existed in Jimmy—you took a long time to find it in the productions, and Jimmy even had to tell you in so many words. I believe he did understand that he had to tell you. Then you blocked on something else, that Jimmy had an unconscious wish to be a girl."

Silence.

"Should ambiguity of sex in the Unconscious surprise you? Men and women exist in each other. Woman has a clitoris and experiments with it as you experimented with your tiny breast-points. The two sexes exist in each other's bodies, and don't you suppose the Unconscious is still more bisexual?"

Dr. Marks felt disturbed. Why? Why should this disturb him?

"What are you thinking now?" Dr. Naumann asked.

"I remember something."

"Yes?"

"Something about my father. Something I heard—I don't know just how old I was." And he could not now remember who had told it. He had an indistinct image of a woman, some relative, and of his mother. His mother he could recall clearly, the other woman not. It was in the kitchen, for he could remember the scrollwork of the elaborate metal stove they had. He was sitting there, staring as he used to in those days at the bright metal of the stove, and listening. "It was something they told about what happened to my father in Siberia. My father's mother wanted him to go to Hebrew School in the town there, and he didn't want to go. I think they said something about his being an agnostic—he is an agnostic now, which is something I respect him for—and maybe they said that 'even then' he was 'that way.' But I don't see how he could have been, for he must have been only about eight at the time—not more than eight. Anyway they said that to avoid Hebrew School, he ran away from home and went to a neighboring town nine miles away. His mother found out where he was, and they say she came after him with a horsewhip. She lashed him all the way back home, all that nine miles."

"You just remembered this?"

"Yes. Perhaps it's one of the blocks you mention."

Silence.

Dr. Marks seemed roused. "This was my grandmother. It was the same one that gave me that tongue-lashing when I got the meat from the Christian butcher. The great matriarch—the bitch."

"She made your father passive," Dr. Naumann said.

"Yes."

"With a whip, a masculine instrument. An instrument of assault," Dr. Naumann added.

"How I hate her! How I hate the very thought of her!"

"You were beaten as a child too, weren't you?"

"I was. But I feel it now for him."

"You're sure? Perhaps you yourself weren't beaten hard enough."

"No? Let me tell you then. Father sometimes beat me with a whip specially made of five or six leather thongs. Beat me naked. I'd manage to stand it until the fifth or sixth lash, then I'd cry. Father never let up on me till I cried. Why do you suppose I told you it wasn't in the cards not to obey my father?"

"Why haven't you told me about this before?"

Furiously: "I was embarrassed. Embarrassed. To tell you my own father beat me like that. But I've told you why, and that's why I could tell you."

"You've defended your father."

"All right, so I have. And I've defended myself."

Silence. Dr. Naumann said, "So your father became your grandmother." The man became the woman. He went on, "What about your own will, with these inhuman beatings? Was it broken?"

"Never."

"But you were affected. You admit you were passive."

Dr. Marks's voice was hoarse. "I fought it. I always fought it. If I had the least chance, I asserted my own will."

"How?"

"Once my father put me in a corner and told me I had to stand there until I apologized. I stood there for hours. I finally fell asleep on my feet. I didn't apologize. I reversed the law of my family and turned it back on them: 'Never give in to an adult.'"

"Jimmy. You must feel so much for him. Perhaps you

want to be a new father to him, the father who does not change the sex of his child?"

True, Dr. Marks thought. A deep well in him seemed to stir.

"You're also paternal to yourself. Is it not possibly you who don't want your sex changed?"

Dr. Marks said, "I seem to know so much that I didn't know before. I never knew, I never thought that I might have been defending my father when I refused to give in to him. All my lifelong hatred of anything that hurts the will, anything that hurts consciousness. Anesthesia—'Be dead.' All those needless appendectomies—all that cutting. 'Never give in to a child.' 'Never give in to an adult.' And at the hospital, all those doctors clubbing their children with electricity."

Defending your father's sex. Defending your own sex, Dr. Naumann thought.

Notation on Ethel Simpson's chart: "Patient's temperature held at 106.3 for an hour. 7 P.M."

Dr. Marks returned from his session with Naumann and stayed with Jimmy again until he went to sleep. The kid dropped off earlier than the night before. Making up for the weeks of exhaustion, Dr. Marks thought; finding in sleep a restorative something that Freud had more than hinted at. For there was another side to the Unconscious and to unconsciousness. There was the side that went past the archaic dangers to the safety of inorganic quiet and reposed there in a slumberous simulacrum of the state from which life had emerged. The death instinct. Sleep without monsters. True rest.

But down the hall Ethel whined and said "strange things" and, unresting, sank toward actual death.

He had seen how dry her forehead was, wrinkled and prematurely aged-looking in its emaciation. She had blue eyes and chestnut hair like Margaret's. The child in her had darted momentarily out at him in that look of terror (Help, I'm dying—like Jimmy). He could not put it from his mind, that she would have to die.

But did she have to?

Stop thinking that way. And yet he thought, All I would have to do is go down there and begin again. Begin the listening.

Suppose this time it didn't work and he wasn't able to find out "what she was afraid of." Suppose Jimmy was an exception, accessible in some way other patients were not. But didn't you have to take that chance?

Again he heard the muffled whine.

Seated at the nurse's desk, he opened Ethel Simpson's chart. Hospital facts: she had been in Medical eight days. She had entered the hospital March seventh and had been mute until the outbreak of the excitement, seventeen days ago. The outbreak started after her mother-in-law came to see her. No report on that visit. On other previous occasions her husband had come to see her, apparently without any effect one way or the other.

Personal history: the first important fact—given—was that her father died when she was six.

Looking up from the chart, he thought about that single fact. Her father dies. That's an abandonment, to make up for which she would need a great deal of understanding and love from her mother.

But her mother is now hard-pressed financially and goes to work and has little time for her. Furthermore there is an older brother of Ethel's, Herman, a responsible boy who also has to go to work and who is the mother's favorite, practically her substitute for the lost "man."

The chart: at eighteen, Ethel married Willard Simpson and the same year her mother died. (Abandoned her for good.) But now, Dr. Marks noted, there was a new chance. The mother-in-law, Cora Simpson, came to live with them (a new mother who might be more loving, who might make up for the unloving real mother). But "Mrs. Simpson seems to have been wrapped up in her son. In her conversations with this interviewer, she expressed only concern for 'Willard,' how good he was and so on." Ethel began to "hate her husband" and to be miserable. Then a child was conceived, and the immediate effect was unexpectedly pleasant. Willard was pleased and the mother-in-law began to show some consideration to Ethel as the prospective mother of her grandchild. Ethel was in the best of health during the pregnancy and seemed in better spirits. The birth of the baby, Aline, was normal. But postpartum came a strange attitude of Ethel toward the baby, as if this were "something not really connected with her." Example: Ethel's brother Herman was high Episcopalian and wanted the baby baptized in his church (which had formerly been Ethel's too). Willard and Cora Simpson were Baptists and objected to this request. Oddly enough, Ethel took no interest in what developed into a family row, being willing to have the baby baptized "wherever it was decided." Willard reported to the interviewer that Ethel acted "as if the child did not belong to her."

Before she became mute, Ethel complained of hearing voices that "commanded her to kill."

Whom might she have wanted to kill? Dr. Marks thought. She hated everybody: her mother and by transference, her mother-in-law, Cora. Her father and Herman (her mother's favorite) and by transference, her husband, Willard. The child?

But under hate, from his experience with Jimmy (and with himself), he would be led to assume love.

Love or fear? For he thought of that sight he had had of her hanging frightened from the feeding-tube. Dependent. Here was this woman who couldn't care for her baby and has to be cared for like a baby. Fed like a baby. Even worse. A baby can suck. This regression was to the umbilical cord.

How can it happen? Again, as he had weeks ago when he first entered the hospital, he thought, How can it happen? What can possibly drive the mind to this point of derangement?

He sat staring at the corridor wall behind the desk, aware of that soft level of sound, like a stroke of plush, that brought to him the presence of the insane in the rooms around him.

"Ethel?" He stood in the door of the dark room. The bed had its head against the wall opposite the door, and momentarily in the dark, it took on the look of a coffin suspended over a grave. (Enough in my mind to provoke that illusion.) Slowly from the coffin, in the space allowed by the restraint sheet, Ethel raised her head. "Hello," he said. In answer she screamed, startling him in spite of himself. The scream faded off into an up-and-down note like an infant's wail. Then: "Who? Comes wholly. Wholly. Wholly." (Was it "wholly" or "holy"?) This was followed by the whine that he had heard before.

He thought, All I'm going to be here for now is to listen. Would it be better for her to see me clearly or not? But what does it mean for her to see me? Did Jimmy see me, or did he see his father or his Uncle Mike? Or his brother or mother? Possibly there may be less fear if she can see me. Light has an element of reality.

He turned the light switch, Ethel blinked, and he saw the fear, even more terrible than Jimmy's. That darting glance from the tube had not misled him. But the moment he saw it, it was replaced in some inexplicably deliberate way by hate.

"Willard. Step aside. Yes, wholly. Wholly. Storms again. I hate her bitchy face."

He said, "I'm going to help you."

She pushed violently against the sheet. As her body pressed upward, her jacketed arms looked like magnified breasts. Grotesque and gigantic. She yelled, "The murderer is Cora. Kill that bitch. That dope. I killed her with my eyes to relieve my mother, Cora." It was all there, he thought. And a double hate. Mother-in-law and mother. She stared at some point near him in the air, her hate concentrated there. "Cement them all. Fix everything. My mother-in-law is a dope fiend. Those cemeteries. Jealously? I ignore everyone. I tear up everything. I pick up graveyards easily." Her tone gradually became even more provokingly arrogant, supremely confident. "Guardians of the hose. Not one, not two, but wholly, wholly. Holy God, do Thou protect and— I raise the dead. I command everything. I know that bitch Cora destroys them." A scream. "Go down there and stab her."

"Stab whom?"

"Infinite power. That bitch."

"Who is she?"

"Not one, not two, but all in all," she cried, her neck rigid.

"Where are you, Ethel?"

"She says—" (muttering).

"Do you want me to help you?"

The head raised, hate and fear blazed: "Murder-in-law!"

That was it. He was not distracted by a scream that now wailed like an ambulance siren, going steadily up and down. 'Murder-in-law.' And behind the mother-in-law was concealed the mother from whom this woman had to defend herself. But why? Why did she have to? What was she afraid of? He continued listening.

Two hours later he began to interpret tentatively.

Ethel, almost as arrogantly as if she were Cora: "Cora put Willard in hell."

"Your mother hates your father because he loves you."

Listening: "No."

She might be right. Her father died when she was young. Was it Herman who loved her?

"Throw that small basket into the river—"

"You want Herman to love you," he said.

"A few mistakes? He has a spike?" A plaintive scream.

"He has a penis. And you want him to give you a penis." Should he say "prick"? Somehow it seemed not right for Ethel. She was pouring productions now: "Mabel caught that last flyer there. Push everything off. I give the orders around here. Murder. Stop signs. She cleans the streets every time—"

"Why do you have to feel so big?"

"In the lower regions?"

"You want a baby in you—"

"That was the real mistake. Murder crawling around. Cora grabs them." Writhing.

"Cora's your mother."

The sheet rose violently and she screamed not with the babyish note so at odds with her arrogance, but with all-out panic. "Killer!" The sheet sank down and revealed her flat, sunken stomach and small starved thighs. *Cora's your mother.* That frightened her. She saw I saw something just as Jimmy did. She saw I saw her longing. Abandoned by the mother-in-law who had no love to spare for her. And no mother to turn to. No wonder Cora kills everybody. And Ethel kills them back.

He felt no sureness about his understanding of Ethel. The sole thing about her that was like Jimmy was that he was getting fond of her. But this one wasn't trying to reach through to him, or if she was, it was very faintly. This one trusted only herself. This one was resigned to being alone.

Yet in a few minutes more, she was resting more calmly, and he noted the structural likeness of this to the result of his first interpretations with Jimmy. Did she too feel he knew her secrets, but didn't punish her? He doubted it. Still, he began to sense a new quality that changed her face. The second person that existed in her.

Was it this that had sent him that first blue-eyed glance of terror? The glance that had called to him as a father? But this was not terror, but resting. Was he mistaken to think the resting had anything to do with him? At this stage of exhaustion, they had to have some muted kind of rest, if only a momentary fogging. And now, out of nowhere again, came the scream. The defiance, the pride.

As soon as it moderated, he said firmly, "Good night, Ethel. I'll be back in the morning. I'm not going to let you die."

In the morning he would see her, but he was going to keep the main treatment for tomorrow night. He had his day's work to do, which he had better not miss again, and he wanted a long, uninterrupted period of time for listening, for trying to get at this "child." Would he succeed? This was "murder," hate, this was a wall. But there was a kind of irrepressible happiness in him. What if he *could* do it?

Going down the corridor, he stopped at Jimmy's room. He had heard nothing as he approached, not the least sound, so that this room was conspicuous for its real stillness. Like an island. When he went in, it was to find the islanded stillness even more profound than he expected. The boy lay on his side, his hands unfolded and loose. His eyelashes made a faint line below his closed eyes, in the dim light. That line, curving and merging softly into the cheek, seemed the sign of his inward peace. So children sleep when they are safe. When they are reassured and comforted. Safe.

The men's insulin ward, he knew, was still filled. He had checked on it, to be sure Jimmy wouldn't be sent down. The nurses had promised to call him if any new order came through. But somehow he believed Linscomb would now forget his "experimental" project.

The next morning from the laboratory he phoned Dr. Rossman. After they had chatted a moment, he said, "What I called you about: I've begun work with another catatonic in exhaust status and I'm wondering whether you'd like to see it. I'm not sure what I can do, but I'm trying. I wonder if you'd be free this evening to come over to Medical."

"Why, yes, I would. I'd be very much interested."

"This seems like a harder case than Jimmy—a woman, a postpartum. I did some interpretations last night like I did with Jimmy and it seemed to have an effect. I don't know. Anyway tonight I'm going to make an all-out try."

"It would be a privilege to see it."

With warmth: "I think somebody ought to see this thing. If there's any meaning in it at all, there would be meaning for somebody else."

"What time do you want me to be there?"

"Suppose we make it eight o'clock and I'll brief you on the case before we start in."

"I'll be there."

At lunch, as he walked among the dining-room tables, he noticed Dr. Pirosh. Dr. Pirosh indicated an empty chair and said, "Are you still trying to find the pathology of acute catatonic excitement in the brain?"

"Yes, but not with the microscope." It was a wonderful opening to talk, and he told Dr. Pirosh everything that had happened since he had seen him. "I'd been meaning to call you up and tell you about it." He recalled that Pirosh had said, "I still think it should be possible to keep these people from dying."

Dr. Pirosh listened interestedly and finally said, "I don't know. I don't know what to think. I'll agree psychoanalysis does give clues to the gross dynamics. I'll go as far as that, but I'd be cautious in the way I evaluated this thing with Jimmy."

This thing with Jimmy. "But he was dying, and now his temperature's back to normal and has been for two days."

"It is remarkable. But it may be an exception of some kind. Perhaps there can be an accidental recovery. What will tell more about it is this Ethel you're starting with now. Two in a row would be hard to argue away as an accident."

"I'm not too confident what I can do with Ethel. She almost scares me, the way she fights everything. Very hard, very—" He found it difficult to express that unyielding defiance.

"I know the kind."

"It might be helpful if you came to watch tonight."

Dr. Pirosh seemed hesitant. "Can you watch something like that?"

"How do you mean?"

"Don't you have to be alone when you treat a patient like that?"

"I don't think it would matter. The nurse was in and out of the room while I was treating Jimmy." Dr. Marks was thinking of how indifferent the patient really seemed to be to everything. "I think the only people that matter to her are the ones in her own nightmare."

"Interesting. Yes, I would like to see it if you think it's all right."

"Another doctor is coming to watch, Dr. Rossman—do you know him?"

"Yes, one of the younger men."

"Then you'll join us." He made arrangements with Dr. Pirosh for their meeting.

Drs. Wellman, Parker, and Spencer were coming in. That look of entering the sanctuary. Now, safe from any thought of patients, they would have an hour or more to eat and relax. He gave his order to the waitress and turned to Dr. Pirosh. "At the Morgue the other day, I don't think I mentioned how much I was impressed by your saying you weren't too happy about shock."

"I'm not. I'm certainly not."

"Do you say that out loud here?"

"Oh we're not all shock enthusiasts here. By no means."

"No?" No?

"Some of us take a damn dim view. When you do a lot of posts and see the hemorrhaging—a hemorrhage in the cardiac controls in the brain, and good-by. There's always some brain damage. I've mentioned that in Staff as I believe I told you." Dr. Marks nodded, eager for this man to go on. "But the important thing is, shock isn't helping patients. Oh, I know about the statistics. I suppose they showed you statistics when you came in."

"They did."

"Meaningless. You know the reason the statistics looked good at first was that they were interested in the patient."

"I don't follow you. Isn't shock a way of not being interested in the patient?"

"It certainly is now," Dr. Pirosh said. "But go back to when shock treatment came in, say the late thirties. Then they didn't do anything for patients unless you can call going up on the ward with a basket of embroidery doing something. So shock represented doing something, it represented being interested. They'd open a small shock ward, the first one, and put the best doctors, nurses, and attendants on it, and of course everybody watched closely to see what would happen. Patients seemed to respond to this interest, and for a while there was some improvement in spite of the shock. But then they began giving more and more shock, and it got to be routine and that was the end. Originally the figures for insulin shock, with Sakel and others, were supposed to be about thirty percent better than average. Not now."

"But what about these hospital statistics of Dr. Steiner's?"

"Statistics of discharge. But you know as well as anybody else here that this hospital is still jammed to capacity. Why? Well, the main reason is that hemorrhaging of the brain makes the patients forget, and they seem better and are sent home, but then the hemorrhaging is absorbed and the patient relapses and he's right back in the hospital. That nice routine—discharge-return, discharge-return—can go on for some time, and then maybe you have a patient who just won't respond."

"Respond to what?"

"To shock, to interest, to anything." Dr. Pirosh added, "What you're doing with patients yourself is showing an interest in them. And maybe that's what's working for you. Maybe that's why you succeeded with Jimmy."

"You mean the specificity of the treatment doesn't matter?"

Dr. Pirosh agreed that that was what he meant.

"You mean it *does* matter if you're treating a physical disease, but not if it's a mental illness?" Dr. Marks pressed him. "Would you say you could treat diphtheria and typhoid with some unknown factor X, some common factor?"

"That's different. The germs are different." Dr. Pirosh seemed unaffected. "No, I do believe something happens when you show an interest in a case."

"Nurses show interest and compassion, some of them."

"Yes, I'll admit that. And it helps."

"But no exhaust status cases have recovered."

Dr. Pirosh was silent. Finally he said, "Well, I'll be seeing it tonight, and maybe then I'll have a better idea about it."

Dr. Marks told Dr. Naumann that Jimmy had been holding his own and that he had begun working with Ethel. He told him about the Ethel case.

Dr. Naumann listened with interest, but made no comment. Except: "You must be getting exhausted."

"Don't mention that," Dr. Marks said.

Then silence. That meant you were to begin the work of the session (tired or not). Dr. Marks said, "I wasn't too exhausted to have a dream last night, and I can remember part of it at least. I dreamed there was this woman, and I was going somewhere with her in an open trolley, maybe to some summer resort. We sat in seats facing forward, four in a seat. Then some man had me by the arm, he was guiding me and I was walking somewhere. I saw a summer hotel ahead of me. Several buildings, the main one in the center. It had a flat roof, and a chimney went up that had four struts holding it, like heavy guy wires running out to the corners of the building. I walked toward this building, and the earth began to shake and I was afraid the chimney was going to break. It was made of bricks and if it fell, it would probably kill me. The chimney did break. First the top began to fall, then the middle burst and everything came crashing down. I was alone. The man with me was gone. I was under the bricks." He moved on the couch, which gave off a sound of leather and metal. "The chimney looked like one at New State. It was the same color brick. The place was New State. The woman had a small mole on the side of her jaw like my mother, but she seemed not to be my mother." A pause. "She seemed like Mrs. Blumstein, now that I think about it. I called Mrs. Blumstein 'Mama.' I told you she looks like a mama. I even thought it would be nice if I had a mother like that. Like what she must be normally—she's steadily getting worse—Wellman's increasing the strength of the shock treatment, probably because of what I said to him about her. Anyway in the dream, the trolley was crowded and I was glad that it made me sit close to this woman, whoever she was. Then this man was grasping me. My father sometimes held me like that when I was a boy, when he would go upstairs with me at the house on Bushwick Avenue. I can still feel him holding my elbow like that, and feel myself going up. Your legs feel light like your feet hardly touch the ground. My father is tall. I'm not tall like him. Another thing about the stairs: yesterday at the hospital just outside the dining room, a woman patient told me very confidentially about going up the stairs in the Eiffel Tower in Paris. It seems these stairs take you up to an eating place, a restaurant." He added, "That's the chimney, isn't it?" He stopped. He felt a vague discomfort, and could not think of anything more to say.

"Please continue."

"Well, I felt small, under the chimney, and then I was afraid. I was afraid I was going to die."

"And what does that mean?"

"The chimney's my penis. I'm being castrated."

A suspicious willingness, Dr. Naumann thought, to give this interpretation. This woman in the trolley. Dr. Marks's closeness to her might well mean being her. Identification. But he was also close to his father—in this double closeness was more of this confusion of sex that had been troubling him lately. Jimmy's confusion echoed in himself. In the course of Dr. Marks's analysis many clues had showed an association of New State Hospital with his father—even this dream had showed it. So the phallus, the penis, might well be not his own, but his father's. In that case it was a different crushing he experienced under the chimney. There were still further possibilities. A phallus (penis) has a likeness to a breast: both give out a milky substance at the tip. And Dr. Marks identified the chimney with the Eiffel Tower that has a restaurant at the top.

But Dr. Marks still seemed strongly to resist any oral understanding of the Unconscious. Well, you must not push the analysand (the person being analyzed). You must let him find his own way. All Dr. Marks saw was castration and even that was with an air of compliance. Dr. Naumann said, "You do not sound as if you are convinced by this thought of castration."

"Oh, I guess I am. The shaking of the chimney could be incestuous desire for intercourse with my mother and in punishment, my member withers. The chimney falls."

Silence.

"But I don't have any conscious anxiety about it. You've pointed it out. I don't quite understand it and I'm concerned about it because it's part of my evident block with Jimmy."

"Could you tell me, please—have you conscious anxiety about anything?"

"What do you mean?" Dr. Marks asked.

"I'll express it differently. Do you sometimes fear some- thing in ordinary life?"

"Yes, at times."

"Objectively speaking, do you really have cause for anx- iety?"

"I could have. I might lose control of myself at the hos- pital, these doctors giving shock, and then I'd be the hell out of there."

"Are you really afraid of that?"

"Perhaps not. I'm under analysis."

Dr. Naumann noted the slight animus in this, but let it pass. "Yes. Now suppose you were dismissed from the hospital—what would that mean?"

Dr. Marks answered with some heat, "Castration, but taking things that way, you can make almost anything into castration."

It was right that a threat to one's security was not a threat of castration. Castration is always specifically a physical threat, a threat to the body. "I don't wish," Dr. Naumann went on, "to 'make almost anything into castration.'"

"You're like these doctors who want to make everything into chronic appendicitis. The least bellyache and rush them to the hospital. Operate."

"You don't exaggerate, perhaps?"

"No, maybe ten percent are really necessary. In all my years of practice, I never did an appendectomy on a pa- tient who hadn't developed the classical symptoms of ap- pendicitis. I don't know how many hundreds I saved from the ordeal of surgery."

"Ordeal?"

"Yes, it is an ordeal. All that fear——"

Dr. Naumann asked him what fear.

"Fear of dying." (Castration is always equated in the Unconscious with physical death. Here it comes out, Dr. Naumann thought, just where he does not mean to reveal it.) "You know what it is—you've been a doctor. I mean the patient's fear. Fear of the surgical procedures. The feeling everybody is against him: surgeons, doctors, nurses."

Silence.

"You think I don't know what I'm talking about? How about when I was a kid and broke my arm and was taken to a hospital in Brooklyn, and the admissions officer sent me up to Surgery? I asked some nurse what 'surgery' meant and she said, 'Oh, that means they'll cut your arm off.' How is that?"

That was physical enough, Dr. Naumann thought.

"Doctors are warped, sick. They like to cut—that's why they go into that profession. You think I don't know? I dislike them, all of them. And that includes my Uncle John. Dr. John. I've told you. Coming around, and the family bowing down to him. But he was no better than the rest. He loved to cut. Cut, cut. Get the knife in his hand. He performed that operation on me for the so-called tubercular glands of my neck. And then for the hernia. Any excuse. Anything to get some exercise with the knife."

Dr. Naumann: If he felt this way, logically why was he himself a doctor? But a doctor is masculine and he himself will not be castrative. He will on the contrary be good, reparative: "I don't know how many hundreds I saved."

He will not unduly use the knife—

The knife used for cutting, for cutting out, for cutting off.

And there was an added determinant—"My family bowed down to the doctor."

"These doctors at the hospital," Dr. Marks went on. "Giving shock. The knife you do have to use sometimes. On legitimate appendectomies. On legitimate tonsils. But shock." These patients being laid out on the shock-treatment table and jerking in convulsions.

When he had had his arm set, he had fought madly against the ether. In a frenzy. He could not tolerate the thought of being made unconscious. He said it aloud: "I hate anesthesia. When I had my arm set, I screamed and fought and pleaded I'd stand any pain—"

"Why?"

"Well, how did I know what they were really going to do to me? That nurse that said they were going to cut my arm off, and— The ether makes you helpless and they can do anything to you, I thought. Even kill you."

Silence.

"I wonder what it's like to die. Why do we fear it so, fear anything about death? I do. I've heard of people who don't—lucky them. But I don't understand them. Because I want to live. I remember the first time I saw a death, on Bushwick Avenue. The tailor's son was run over when he stepped off the curb to catch a ball. His father ran downstairs and picked him up all bleeding, probably dead right then, and carried him to the next corner, to a drugstore. And I looked through the window and saw him on a bench, motionless and bloody. Later the ambulance came and carried him away.

"But that wasn't the first death I knew about. The first one was in the country one summer, a woman gave birth. I didn't know the woman, and I didn't know till later why the baby died. It bled to death from circumcision. But the night it died, I happened to look through a door and saw a man with a long beard watching, that the baby shouldn't come to life. It was eerie. That was all I felt. It had no meaning for me. But the tailor's son had meaning. He was my friend, he had just begun to play the fiddle and he could play 'My country, 'tis of thee'—that was wonderful. So his death meant something to me."

"You felt it," Dr. Naumann said.

"I felt it. It got to me."

"What does it mean, to play the fiddle?" he said casually.

"I don't know—"

"Say what you think of."

"Oh, you make music."

"How?" Dr. Naumann asked.

"You play, you run your fingers along the neck, you finger it— Masturbation."

"Exactly. Please, what happens if you play with your fiddle?"

They cut it off.

'Papa, don't cut off my balls.'

That kid with his suffering and I took so long to see it. Castration is death.

It *is* death.

"Wholly, wholly dead."

Drs. Rossman and Pirosh stood to the side, and Dr. Marks stood directly in front of Ethel, as before, facing her at the foot of the bed. The light was on, reflected in her large eyes. She seemed not to notice the other two doctors, but it did seem to him that she was aware of him. It was nerve-racking to feel that her hate might be focusing on him.

Well, he could succeed only if he tried. He rolled his

shoulders and saw himself reflected in the levered window behind the bed, levered like modern prison windows—the whole place was like a prison.

"Wholly, wholly— Are you a policeman?"

The question echoed his thought the way so many of these patients seemed able to do. There was a flicker on Dr. Pirosh's face. "No, I'm not a policeman. I'm your—"

A scream.

He leaned forward, gazing into the burning eyes. You'll have to listen to me, he thought. Scream or not.

"I'm disgusted," she cried, stretching back her head and elongating her body under the sheet. "Let's kill Grace or somebody. My name is Ethel Samson."

"Are you bragging? You're not as strong as Samson."

Defiant: "I've been in Gay Paree living on water."

"You don't have to live on water. I'm Mother. I'll give you food."

"She says no. Where is Herman, my brother?"

"You want me. Not Herman. I love you."

Violently: "Graves." She had lifted her bony head and was glaring at him with naked hate. "I hope my brother is General Washington. That's my husband. He crawls around five times, the bastard." She spit violently upward. "Cora. Murder her. She's my murderer."

"I'm Cora. I'm not your murderer." She spit again, straight into the air. She thrust wildly up under the sheet as if to tear it loose. She screamed, "No meal today. You better hold onto Papa's money."

"I know you want Papa's penis. I know all your secrets, but that doesn't make any difference to me. I forgive you for everything."

"Kill that bitch! She controlled the world. I wish that fucking bitch was dead."

"You don't have to kill me to save yourself. I love you so I would protect you from anybody."

Proudly: "It's that dead grave. I know her dopey thoughts. Kill Herman."

"You think Herman's my favorite. What a mistake!"

"I don't want dope or cigarettes. That basket's gone."

"You're afraid to have a baby. You're afraid I won't like it. But I will. It'll be Willard's baby, not Herman's. I know you have those thoughts about Herman—" A quick whining. "But I'll keep you from doing anything wrong."

"Willard, stubborn as always. He did it with a knife."

"I love you so, you can even have what belongs to me."

A momentary gleam of fear. Then: "He has lots of money, but I don't want it. Bitchy Cora loves money."

"I'm Cora and I know your secrets. You can have the baby. I'll keep you safe and protected."

"Bitch!" Furiously: "Drop dead, you. Murderer."

It was not going to be easy to be tender with this one, to convince her he had a maternal feeling for her. "I think of you all day and you know you're my favorite." Gently: "Wasn't I here this morning?"

Suspiciously glaring: "My mommy lives across the hall from me."

"She's right here. She's me. I'm your mommy."

"There's been a robbery around here. Who drops dead all the time?"

Robbed of the penis she wanted? Of the baby? Kill, rob — "Let's tell the police and get it back," he said.

"All that dope! I'm Miss America. How I hate that bitch!" She made several lunges at the sheet. "My crazy mother-in-law." Almost screaming: "I'll outwit her. Who wants that bitch?"

"Nobody! I love you—"

"I'm the wise one who travels this whole world over."

That pattern beginning again, of self-exaltation. *'Miss America.' 'I'm the wise one who travels this whole world over.' 'My brother is General Washington.'* Believing they're the worst, they have to be the best in order to have any hope of being valued.

"You don't have to be that great for me to love you," he said.

Proudly: "This is a dead grave. I keep it clean. Monuments."

"You can be alive now. Anybody I want to live can live."

The answer was arrogance. No screams for help, or if there were any, they were hushed and inaudible, stopped by the need to be strong enough to overcome Cora and her mother. Which should he be, Mommy or Cora?

Drs. Rossman and Pirosh were leaning against the wall. They were quiet. They were like the doctors who gather in an operating theatre, silent and absorbed.

"There are killers loose around here."

"I'll stop them—"

"A few twenty-five-cent pieces. That goofy bitch. Just a little swelling or two and she'll make it."

"You want to nurse Aline. You want your baby." This was the first time he had mentioned Aline by name. Loud screams. "She says she hates her. She murders everything! Nobody wants her!" He sensed that this outpouring of rage was to conceal fear. Her dark hair whipped around her head, dry and disordered. Her productions were shrieking, *Listen! Listen! I'm hated and I hate, hate, hate. Nothing can stop me from hating.* He came around and pressed his hands on her arms as he had with Jimmy. He caught her shoulders through the sheet. "Daughter, I love you. I'm Mommy and I love you."

"Murderer! Bitch!" With horror: "I know her slick ways. You can't trust her. Tell Herman not to trust her. She steals everything."

Steals the baby?

"Kill her dead. She wants all those pots, the bitch."

"You can have your baby. Nobody else can have her but you, Ethel."

Wild screams. When they stopped, she was silent for a while, staring into the air. Resting? Withdrawn? He felt hope, as if this might be a good sign, but immediately the productions began again, first clear, then muttering. "Who set that tent over there? She breaks a few bones, I guess." And before he could speak, she screamed.

Dr. Pirosh said, "It's getting late. I have a heavy day tomorrow."

Dr. Rossman said too, reluctantly, that he had better go. Dr. Marks went with them out into the corridor. "I'm staying," he said. "This is a tough one. I'll give it all night at least."

Dr. Rossman said, "I see what you're after, what you're trying to do."

"I'd hoped there'd be more movement, so you could get the feeling of it. But this is rough—"

"There's a kind of sense."

"This one isn't like Jimmy. Well, maybe it is, but it's harder to get through. Do either of you have any thoughts?"

Dr. Pirosh smiled. "I'm afraid we don't have your insight, or your nerve. But good luck."

"Thank you both for coming."

Dr. Rossman pressed his hand as he said good-night.

They were sympathetic, but probably I looked foolish. Who wouldn't think you're crazy, trying to talk to an insane person? And no visible result, absolutely none.

He went to the men's room to relieve his bladder, and felt as if strength drained out of him. When as usual he shook his penis, he thought, You're the cause of all this trouble! Ethel wanting it, Jimmy not wanting it.

Did she want it? Would that be the approach?

Or was there some other approach?

As the night lengthened, he still had no effect whatsoever on her, on that screaming pride that could spit, so violent were some of its haughtier productions.

Miss Tait, now on duty, came and tube-fed Ethel and wanted to give her a sedative, but he told her to wait till he left. Sometime between three and four in the morning, he said, "Ethel, I won't be here for a while. But don't think you won't still be close to me. I'll think about you every moment I'm gone. You're my favorite child."

And she was his child. He had become fonder and fonder of her during these hard hours, even though his therapeutic attempt to adopt the role of parent seemed so ineffective.

There must be an answer. He wouldn't give up. He couldn't, for her body, that body that screamed bloody murder, was steadily burning away with a fever that would bring doctors running to any ordinary patient.

During the following day he worked ten hours with her, not always actively, at times just listening, but intervening when he felt it might help. There did seem to be increasing communication between them, but he had no idea what it meant. What had happened to the method of reassurance that had worked with Jimmy?

In the late afternoon, he went to one of the beds available to the doctors on night rounds and slept deeply for several hours. At nine, he was back with Ethel.

It was the same arrogant hate, though perhaps with less physical strength behind it. Toward midnight, she hissed, "Don't trust her. She murders even God."

'She murders even God.' This recurrence of God: *'Holy God, do Thou protect and—' 'Wholly—holy.'* Suppose instead of being Mommy, he became the strongest possible power, the power that, as she herself implied, had the

strength to deal with Cora and Mommy. It was worth a try. "I'm God," he said.

Loud shrieks.

"Cora can't murder me," he said. "Nothing can hurt God or kill God."

"What fakes, the poor child!"

"I'm all-powerful." Give her something fancy now, to match her own craziness. "Cora didn't murder me or I couldn't talk to you. I'm the one who kills. I killed all your enemies. There they are, all dissolved now."

The eyes staring at him. "Where's that electric chair?"

"I put everybody who hurt you in it."

A single loud scream.

"God can do anything."

"So much money gone."

"Yes, they were trying to steal from you. I stopped all that, of course."

"Kill Cora and put her to death."

That meant, Save me. "Of course I will. God can stop anybody from hurting you, and he can protect you and love you."

Silence. For the first time she seemed to be listening.

"Everything has to obey my power. I'll be your mother."

"I love her dopey ways."

"I love you," he said.

Her head dropped. She said like a child: "I like you when you're standing up. Mama has blue eyes."

"You can let me help you."

"Yes." Quietly: "I'm fighting her. It's very hard."

"Of course I'll help you fight her, you know."

"All right, thank you. Somebody is robbing my clothes."

She wants to be naked in my presence. She wants to do that for me. He said, "I love you even if you are a woman."

"No. That's the confusion, the difficulty. My mother-in-law loves money so much. You're Willard."

"I'm not Willard. I'm God. Remember that."

"Thank you. You have to kill that killer-diller Cora. That bitch. What a job! I hate her."

"Who?"

"My mother. I'd like to kill her. She's a fucking murderer. By the way, is there still a World War on?"

A rational question. "Yes. It's still on."

"Monuments." In a low voice: "Today is the Angel of Mercy Day."

'Today is the Angel of Mercy Day.' The way she said it seemed like a message. And it was a reasonable message. Just as her question about the war was a reasonable question. And if this was a message, what a message! *'Today is the Angel of Mercy Day.'*

Surely there had been some progress. The tone was different. The productions now were not as aggressive, not as charged with inordinate hate. The air was calmer.

He said, "This *is* the Angel of Mercy Day." The Angel of Mercy, the ministry of God. He waited to see if the quiet would continue. It did. Up until now he had been afraid to take her out of restraint. Too much threat, hate. You get a sense of what an interaction is, even with an insane person. Of what you can expect from them.

Now it might work. And if it worked, it might do a lot. It might give her confidence in his love: mightn't she respond to the feeling of being released, symbolically at least, from everything that rendered her powerless?

"I'm taking you out of restraint."

"Are they large graves today? Thank you. Still waters. Where is that bitch?"

How he hated restraint! "I'm untying you, Ethel. Does it feel good?" He loosened the lacings of the straitjacket and pulled it off.

"So much work. I know she must be watching."

She raised her head. Her arms were down along her sides and now, slowly, she lifted one arm. She tested its freedom. With her arm again at her side, she looked down along her body, seeing (actually seeing?) her freedom from physical restraint. "I guess they went out today," she said.

"You're out of all those things that tied you up," he said. "You can move your arms a little if you want to." Gently: "Isn't this better than being in that crazy restraint?"

She stared up at him.

"You know what restraint is, don't you?"

"That fucking bitch."

I guess that's as good an answer as she could make, he thought.

"Ethel, I'm going to get some food for you. What kind of food would you like?"

"Powerful people, I always say. What did you say?"

"I'm going to get some food for you. What kind would you like?"

"Let's fight her today."

"What would you like to eat?"

"Eat?" The first real contact. The first direct response.

"Yes, eat," he said.

She glanced around the room fearfully.

"Ethel, nobody, absolutely nobody, will hurt you."

"I outwitted her."

"Pay attention to me. What do you want to eat?"

Her eyes steadied and their haunted gaze settled upon him. "Dreams," she said. "Something like water."

He went outside and asked Miss Tait (who was now on duty) to order up some warm milk and a bowl of cereal. When he came back, Ethel had closed her eyes like a sleeper, and her whole body lay rigidly outstretched. He thought, What does this mean? Are we going to have trouble? But he remembered Jimmy's resistances, his erratic swinging of his fist.

"Everything's all right, Ethel. I'm taking good care of you."

Not opening her eyes, she said, "That killer diller."

"How she wants to hurt people! But she can't, you know."

"Thank you." Her eyes jumped open. "That Gay Paree again. All that stuff."

"Yes, you can give up all that dream stuff now. You won't have to try to live on water anymore. I'm here now."

Now she remained quiet until Miss Tait came in with a bowl of cereal and a glass of milk. As soon as this appeared, Ethel screamed, the bed shaking noticeably with the violence of her breath. He said, "Ethel, this is Miss Tait, your nurse. It's not your mother or Cora. Miss Tait, please give me that glass of milk." He had slipped his free arm under Ethel and lifted her up. Now her screaming changed to a whining like a baby's. How many times in practice he had gone into houses to hear that baby's protesting whine! Anh, anh. He clasped his hand over Ethel's shoulder, holding her, and brought the full glass of milk to her lips. He tipped it into the whine and there came a muffled choking, a scream, and then the surprised silence of a baby being fed.

Miss Tait watched from under her neat white cap. In the unaccustomed silence, Dr. Marks heard a patient cough in another room. The drinking continued.

When he had fed Ethel the last of the cereal, he said, "It's good to get a meal inside you, isn't it? You can sleep after this." She slashed her arm in the air, almost knocking the empty cereal bowl from his hands. "My mother-in-law has a brawl or two. She's a killer, isn't she?"

As he lowered her down on the bed, he said, "You don't have to be afraid of her anymore. I'm much stronger than she is."

"That's swell. I threw out my husband and brother. You have to be my husband. I'm getting knife stabs all over." She seemed exhilarated.

"I'll protect you," he said. "You can depend on that."

"I know I was floating in air."

"You were, but you're back again now."

"Cora, that murderer!"

"Try to forget Cora, child. Now that I'm here, you don't have to worry about anything."

Both her arms were resting quietly on the bed now. "Somebody's gypping my secret things from me." As she stared up with a not exactly frightened look on her face, he said, "Where do you live?" Her temperature must still be high, he thought. She must still feel the disturbance of body as well as of mind. To his astonishment, she said, "On President Street."

He remembered from the chart that that was, in fact, where she lived.

"And what is this place where you are now?" The questions you asked were standard and limited.

"Such dopey ways."

"Where are you now?"

"In a bed?"

"I know you're in a bed, but where is this bed? In what kind of place are you, Ethel?"

"No monuments anymore, the bitch." She began muttering.

"Ethel, listen to me." Quietly: "Think now. Think carefully. I want you to tell me where you are."

She looked around the room, at the walls, the bedside stand, at Miss Tait attentive in her white cap. Tears sprang into her eyes and she said, "I had a baby."

He took her hand and pressed it. "You still have a baby, Ethel. You're going to get well and go home and have that baby again."

"My mother-in-law lies a good deal, the bitch."

Firmly: "I don't lie to you, daughter. You're my daughter and I tell you the truth."

"You have blue eyes."

"Thank you for letting me be your mother."

"All those graves."

"Yes. By the way, what's your name?" It was worth a try.

"What's Ethel's name?"

"What's your name?"

"There is this Ethel Simpson."

"Thank you. That's you, all right."

"No money on Tuesdays. I hate Mommy. Go away, please."

"I can't go away till you're well."

"Yes, thank you."

"Wholly well."

With a breaking smile: "Wholly, wholly well."

He had to talk with somebody, tell them what had happened. Dr. Rossman, he had watched it earlier, he would understand, he would know what the exultance was. That Ethel was even this much in communication, that Jimmy wasn't the only one, that it could happen a second time, that he could bring that hard, proud, euphoric Ethel into dialog. He looked at his watch. Quarter of two in the morning. Well, Rossman was a doctor. Doctors get night calls, don't they? And Rossman lived in one of the hospital apartments—that seemed to make it more excusable. Without waiting to let his good sense get the better of him, he put through the call.

"Hello," a sleepy voice answered.

"Dr. Rossman?"

"Yes."

"This is Dr. Marks. Kill me if you want to. I had to call."

"What's happened?" Dr. Rossman now seemed fully awake and his voice was excited.

"Ethel just drank a glass of milk and gave me a few answers to questions."

"My God, she didn't!"

"I don't say she's out of trouble yet, but she's coming out."

Dr. Rossman said, "I wouldn't have believed it."

"I didn't believe it myself till it happened and it doesn't feel real even now."

"What did she say?"

"Well, she knew she lived on President Street and she made several remarks that showed she was getting things, that I was getting through to her."

"Man! I'll come over."

"No, better wait till morning. I'm going home myself."

"You *must* be tired."

"No, I'm God."

Dr. Rossman laughed. "I'll tell Pirosh. You get home and get some sleep. Even God rested, you know."

He didn't go home. He stayed by Ethel. He thought about how she had referred to her baby. '*I had a baby.*' That really got to him, that maternal breakthrough. A whole new side of her had been revealed: even flashes of humor. And now she was glancing sideways at him like a child unsure she will be liked.

'*You have blue eyes—*' My eyes are gray, but her mother had blue eyes.

He felt her forehead. Still warm, still dry, but perhaps not quite as warm or quite as bone-dry.

He asked Miss Tait to take her temperature, and it was down almost two degrees.

What would help her relax? he thought. Perhaps a warm bath?

"Is there any way we could give Ethel a bath?"

"Well, I could bathe her in bed," Miss Tait said.

"I was thinking of how it might help her to lie in a warm bath."

"I'm afraid there's only the women's showers."

Showers. "Even that might be good for her."

Miss Tait was uncertain.

He thought of that arm slashing through the air. There was strength there. "She could stand a shower. I'll take her myself if you'll show me where it is. There are no other women there now, I guess."

"Oh, no."

"All right, let's get some slippers for her."

Miss Tait got the slippers and a bathrobe, and he said, "All right, Ethel, you're going to have a bath. Sit up now."

To his surprise, she sat up, though a little unsteadily, and extended her gaunt legs over the side of the bed. He put the slippers on and said, "There, you can stand, can't you? And we'll put this robe on. All right. Good. Now can you walk a little?" She walked. "That's right." Casting alarmed glances right and left, she went with him down the hall, a night choir of whispers and moans following them. How natural all the fear in this corridor would seem, he thought, if you knew the punishment and hurt that were behind it!

When they came to the shower room, he said, "You're going to have a warm shower in here. Do you understand?"

He made her sit on a stool while he ran the water in one of the stalls and adjusted it. He wanted it the right temperature so that there would be no shock as she got under it. "All right now, you have to take this off." As he helped her take off her robe and nightgown, she showed no more resistance than a child might and when she was naked, he guided her into the stall. Her body accepted the water, that pleasing flow, but as she became aware of her skeletal gauntness, she seemed frightened. He said, "You're pretty thin just now, but you'll soon fill out again, don't worry." The warm water rained down her, and she made some pointless random movements with her hands. "You don't have to wash yourself," he said. "I just want you to be in the warm water." The warm, healing drench of water flowed over her and down her.

At last he said, "All right, come out now." He said again, "Come out," and she stepped forward into the large towel he held for her, and let him rub and dry her.

Come out. She'll come out, he thought. He recalled one of the pontifical sayings of his Uncle John: "We bind the wound. God heals."

After he got home, he phoned Miss Tait. Ethel's temperature had gone down another degree and she was sleeping.

He had set the alarm for five the following morning, and as sometimes happened, he woke up before it went off. Dawn was expanding beyond the windows with a special pure blackness and he thought, Another day. Then he remembered the day before. Ethel. That change in her arrogance. Her wavering contact with him. *'You have blue eyes.' 'I had a baby.' 'Yes, God.'*

He'd felt so sure with Jimmy. It had been clear-cut with him. He was not so sure with Ethel. God had helped her, yes, but God only as a transference. After he left and she was alone and lapsed into dream (psychosis), would she, like Jimmy, come back to the real world? Would she look for him? Had that contact and that partial dissipating of her confusion yesterday been enough to hold?

He sat up and Margaret stirred. In sleep she was not as proud as awake. Her lips softened with the sleeper's vulnerability. He thought, she had been gratifyingly happy, when he came home, at his results with Ethel, listening as he told her about it in detail, and he wondered if he had oversold himself. How is she (Ethel)? was all his mind said now. How is she?

He dressed rapidly. He seemed not aware of any intervening time until he was parking in the parking lot near Medical.

On the ward, he went, a little after six, directly to Ethel's room. Entering, he felt disoriented. He looked to see if he was in the right room. It was the right room. But Ethel's bed was made up and empty.

He hurried into the corridor to find Miss Alston. He found her several rooms away, giving a woman a bedpan.

"Where's Ethel Simpson?"

Distressed: "She's been sent to insulin."

"To insulin! Why didn't you call me?"

"I did as soon as I had a chance, but you'd left home. She's only been gone a half hour or so."

Linscomb—

How had he heard? Miss Alston might have spoken to somebody, not meaning anything, or Rossman could have said something. It goes through the very air in a hospital.

At the nurse's desk, he picked up the phone (it can't be so), got the hospital switchboard, and asked for an extension. He heard a receiver lifted and a voice said, "Yes?"

"This is Dr. Marks. Has Ethel Simpson reached the ward yet?"

"She has, Doctor."

"Has she been injected?"

"Yes, she has been—"

He hung up.

* * *

He heard himself saying, *'I can't go away till you're well.'*

Linscomb: *'Take this patient who it's assumed was dying and give him a coma of a thousand units.'*

Who would believe a human being really capable of it? But Linscomb had wanted to do it with Jimmy. He had wanted to do it. And he would have done it if the men's ward hadn't been filled.

How could Linscomb? How could *any* doctor send a recovering child back to the fear and stillness and sweat of insulin? How could he do it?

On the fifth floor of Building Nine, Dr. Marks went to the door of the women's insulin ward. As soon as he knocked, a nurse answered and let him in. He stood in the wide entrance to the ward, with a stand of glucose bottles on one side and the nurse's desk on the other. The beds stretched off past this vestibule.

"I'm Dr. Marks who just called. I'd like to see Ethel."

"Yes, Doctor. This way."

She showed him Ethel lying on the bed in a straitjacket. Even with her arms crossed over her breast and with the full lines of the loose bed sheet over her, even with the faint heat of the incipient coma, she seemed weightless. She was conscious. She looked at him and knew him and said, "Doctor."

"Yes?"

She said, her low voice in despair, "You said you wouldn't go away." What, he thought, gave her that clarity? "Bitch. Those damn monuments." Her eyes became dull and she did not speak again.

He waited beside the bed. An unnatural quiet fell. Some of the injected ones screamed and fought. But only briefly. A young doctor came over and spoke to him. "I'm Dr. Harmon. Did you want something?"

"I just want to stay with this patient until I can see Dr. Linscomb."

"I see. But the patient is in stupor now. She had a thousand units."

"Even so."

"Dr. Linscomb is going to come here?"

"I'll ask him to before he leaves home," Dr. Marks said.

"Is there anything I can do?"

Nothing—only Linscomb had the authority to do what had to be done here. "I'm sorry, no." He watched Ethel's shallow breathing, and waited.

At eight o'clock, he asked the nurse to telephone Dr. Linscomb at home to say that Dr. Marks urgently asked him to come to the women's insulin ward before he went on duty. The nurse said that Dr. Linscomb said he would be there.

A half hour later Linscomb arrived. "Yes?" he said to Dr. Marks. "You wanted me?"

"Please order glucose for Ethel immediately."

"I don't understand, Doctor—"

"Doctor Linscomb, please let me bring her out of coma. She said something before she went under—I was here— that showed she felt I had abandoned her. I expect you know I've been treating her. Let me reassure her. Let me do the one thing she needs now, prove to her she isn't abandoned by her doctor."

With sarcasm: "Her doctor."

"Yes, I am her doctor. She's felt betrayed so far by everybody in her life and she mustn't feel betrayed by me. She *must* have glucose."

"No."

"Please, Doctor."

"No."

"It's in her interest. You know that Jimmy's getting better. And now she's getting better, without insulin, just with what you may wish to call human understanding, of a special kind."

"Of a special kind—just what do you mean by that? Let's speak frankly."

"This is a mental case, Doctor. I'm treating her with what the hospital loosely calls psychotherapy."

The scorn became open. "Psychotherapy," Dr. Linscomb said. "And you're a resident? An almost completely untrained resident? Who gave you authority to treat this case with psychotherapy?"

"But Ethel is obviously coming out of psychosis, out of excitement. Isn't that why you gave her insulin?" A frown from Dr. Linscomb. Dr. Marks: "Why not let her come out naturally, let her continue with what was clearly doing her good? Why take a chance with that? I don't know what will happen unless I can give her some reassurance now."

"I have a reason for what I'm doing. I want to let the insulin clear everything out of her."

"But the insulin—"

"She's insulint!" a woman cried. Another woman screamed. A rush of hysteria swept over the beds as the lesser-dosage cases woke up.

"I think we'd better go outside," Dr. Linscomb said.

Outside the ward was a dimly lit interior dayroom and corridor.

Dr. Marks asked, "Did you *see* Ethel before you sent her to insulin?"

"This patient never had real excitement—there was some other intervening condition—"

"Did you see her?"

"I didn't have to see her and she couldn't have been in exhaust status—"

"Must you prove yourself right? Can't you conceive that you could be wrong?"

"*You* speak to *me*—"

"I do. I know what's really behind this, it's a motive you're not admitting—"

"Dr. Marks!"

"A personal grudge. A plain, simple personal grudge—"

"Dr. Marks, you'll apologize for this!"

"If it's not a grudge, give her glucose!"

Dr. Linscomb stared at him in silence.

"You have to be right. Because she didn't die, now you want her to die." He grasped Dr. Linscomb's shirt and drew back his fist. "You want to kill her."

"Dr. Harmon! Dr. Harmon!"

He heard steps running from the ward. He said, dropping his fist, "You'll never know what keeps me from beating you senseless, the way you're beating her."

8

He found he could not see Ethel. He went back to the ward at ten thirty when he figured she would be out of coma, and the nurse told him that Dr. Linscomb had left an order for him not to be admitted. It was written in the book. She offered to show him.

"Never mind. How is Ethel at least?"

"I don't believe I ought to say anything, Doctor."

"WBC 9,500," he wrote. As his pen scratched along, the lens of his microscope faded. He felt empty.

He went to his office window. He wondered if he had eaten lunch and was surprised that he could not remember.

The small, bare cube of the room contained only a clothes tree, his desk, and two chairs. One chair for himself and one for the visitor. The wire-webbed window faced the central lawns. He had no telephone (but he could be signaled to answer a phone outside).

This was the office rated by an experienced pathologist in this hospital.

He sat down facing the door, the window light behind him. He noted the stillness. Past several turns of corridor, the faint screams of women patients were sometimes audible, but they were now resting. Sedated. The women who so constantly wandered in the corridor from a nearby day-room were silent too. No "Please" (delivered to some power in the air), no "Where am I?", no muttering about "needles" or "being electrocuted."

Silent.

His head throbbed in rhythm with his pulse.

Ethel. He still saw her looking at him as she had when she spoke to him before entering coma. Another figure joined her in his mind, a woman he had noticed on a second-floor porch standing behind the netting with her back to him, a shawl pulled over her head—she had struck him

118

with a particular horror. She or her posture seemed to say, I'm not living.

His thoughts were interrupted as a shadow showed on the wire-webbed window in his door (the corner of the pane was cracked where it had been hit by a violent patient). A hand knocked on the door.

"Come in."

To his surprise, it was Dr. Harmon. "I was going by—"

"Don't apologize."

"I wanted to speak to you," Dr. Harmon said. He was young-looking in spite of a large moustache. "You must be feeling very bad."

"Tell me how Ethel is. Then maybe I'll know how I feel."

"She came out of coma, but she's in complete withdrawal. Completely mute. No contact with the environment at all."

Dr. Marks said under his breath, "I should have slugged him."

"And she was doing so well, I understand," Dr. Harmon said.

"What do you mean, 'I understand'?"

"Well, I heard Dr. Pirosh knew something about it and I phoned him and he said yes, she was in partial contact with you. He thinks it's possible you were responsible for two cases in exhaust status improving."

"I'm sorry—neither case was correctly diagnosed. Neither one *was* in exhaust status. They couldn't have been or they wouldn't have improved. That's obvious."

"You mean that's the official position. But I saw Ethel." Dr. Harmon's face clouded. He opened the office door. "I'm due back on the ward. I just came by to say I'm sorry."

"Thank you. Thank you for stopping by."

("Please," a voice now said in the corridor. "Please.")

When he was alone in his office, Dr. Marks thought back to his first days at the hospital: that aching empathy with the ill, that compulsive fury he had felt to do something for them. There had been at the back of his mind then a conviction that there were doctors at the hospital who understood analysis. Trained analysts. Men who would be working with this knowledge, who would be treating patients. Men who healed.

There had to be such men—how could there not be?

How could there not be?

One day when he was at the Van Sittart Clinic, he had been walking down Fifth Avenue with a colleague, a doctor, when they met a line of children, orphans from a nearby asylum being guided along by middle-aged women attendants. A little girl in the line caught his friend's eye. She began to smile. Her smile, attractive to begin with, became staggeringly charged with sweetness. It was luminous. His friend stared at the child and at last said, "How happy the mother of that child must be!" "But the child's an orphan," Dr. Marks said. "Of course not," his friend said. "That woman behind there, she's the mother." "I'm sorry. The children are from an orphan asylum. The woman's an attendant." His friend argued. The child did have a mother. That woman was the mother.

There had to be a mother.

There had to be doctors at the hospital here who treated the mind as a mind, who used the great dynamisms and skills of healing that modern psychology made available to them.

He was called to the ward telephone. "This is Dr. Rossman. I just want to say—I'm intensely sorry for what's happened."

"How much do you know? Do you know what the coma did to Ethel?"

"It's generally known. But I know something else. It's mainly why I called you. Have you been speaking with anybody?"

"Just Dr. Harmon. He came by—"

"Dr. Linscomb has seen Dr. Steiner and there's likely to be quite a blowup. You're probably to be called in. If it turns out you need anybody to speak for you, I mean I could tell what I saw—"

"Thank you. May I say something completely foolish?" Dr. Rossman waited. "Ethel was doing fine before insulin. Now she's a mute catatonic. Wouldn't it seem Dr. Linscomb should be called in rather than I?"

"I know." With a change of tone: "But think of the brave, interesting attempt Dr. Linscomb made with *shock* treatment. The treatment *of choice*."

"I'm thinking of it."

"And then didn't you threaten Linscomb?"

"Yes, I threatened him."

Back in his office he thought, When is Dr. Steiner going to call? It might be soon or it might not. Was there anything he ought to be doing before that call came?

Jimmy. The eyes of that quieted kid seemed before him in the room. That famished face had a certain expression: the flame of resurrection. When the kid had begun to sweat and I was holding him, that surprise that said, I'm alive, and that trust that said, I'm safe. At least once before it's too late, go and see Jimmy.

Miss Davis waved from down the corridor and hurried toward him. "Gee," she said, straightening her cap, "I didn't expect to see you here."

"I've been put out of bounds with Ethel, but I haven't been told I can't see Jimmy."

"Then of course you must see him. He's doing so well. He's been eating fine—hungry, you know? And, Doctor, he asked for you."

Asked for me. The kid asked for me. He said, "By name?"

"Do you think he doesn't know your name?"

"No, tell me—" he was excited, he couldn't help it— "how did he ask for me?"

She seemed trying to recall and at last said, "Well, it was something like, 'I wonder where he is.' Then I kept after him and he said, 'Where's this Dr. Marks?' but on his own. He said it—I'm not kidding."

"Something stayed inside of that psychosis."

She said, "But aren't they always there really?"

He pressed her arm: "That's quite a statement you've made there, young woman."

Jimmy was under a light cover. That head with its reborn look. Dr. Marks said, "Hello."

A smile. "Hello."

"Hello, who?"

"Hello, Doctor. Once—"

"Yes?"

But the kid said nothing more. Dr. Marks said, "How are you? You feel strong?" Jimmy looked up at him inquiringly. "Sit up. I want to see if you're strong."

Jimmy wasn't satisfied with sitting up. He got out and stood beside his bed in his bare feet. "You got any slippers here?" Jimmy glanced around the room. There was a robe hanging from a hook behind the door, and slippers on a shelf of the stand. Probably he's been going to the toilet.

"You been going to the toilet?"

"Yes." More loudly, "Yes."

"Good. You want to go now?"

"Somebody said—"

"Jimmy!"

Silence.

"I don't want any of that crazy talk. You want to go to the toilet?"

"He says yes."

"You say yes."

"Yes."

"Who am I?"

"My . . . friend."

"Sure I'm your friend, but what's my name?"

After a brief hesitation: "Doctor Marks."

He got the slippers and gave them to Jimmy. "Can you put those on?"

Jimmy put them on, and Dr. Marks handed him his robe. Like a normal person, Jimmy slipped his arms into the sleeves. "So you know how to wear a robe. Do you know where the bathroom is?"

The kid went toward the door, Dr. Marks following, and went straight to the men's lavatory. "You're getting sharp there, son."

As they were coming back, Dr. Marks stopped him and adjusted his bathrobe, tying the straps better and fixing the collar. He had an idea. "You don't look so bad. Come with me." He led the kid over to the elevator bank. (I'm hungry. Probably the kid's hungry too.) He rang.

When the slow-moving elevator stopped, he asked the operator, "Is there a commissary, a canteen, in the basement here?"

"Yes, Doctor." The tone, one of complete deference. "You want to go down, Doctor?"

"Yes, we'll go down."

As the car descended, he thought about that deference. Deference to him as a doctor. Deferring to him as the supreme figure in this hospital world. Nurses, attendants, workers, all bowing to the doctor. Well, what in hell had the doctors done that they were so supreme? What had they done for Jimmy with his fever-trembling? What had they done for Ethel with her gallery of murderers? What had they done for Mrs. Blumstein? A hospital of Uncle Johns, going flat-footed past the doors. Don't look. Don't listen. Silence is golden.

Two nurses got on the elevator. These gave him a somewhat funny intent look. Respectful but intent.

When they reached the basement, the operator pointed to the right and said, "You'll find the commissary down there, Doctor—where the music's coming from." The music was coming from a juke box in a room with some tables and a long counter. Over the counter a sign read: FOR PATIENTS, EMPLOYEES, AND GUESTS OF NEW STATE HOSPITAL.

"All right, Jimmy, step up here." Jimmy climbed onto the stool next to him, pulling awkwardly at his robe. He got himself settled and put both fists on the edge of the counter. "All right, what'll you have?" Dr. Marks asked. He was stunned by the answer:

"A malted."

"What kind?"

With no hesitation: "Chocolate."

The kid had slipped back into a pattern of normality that was self-contained and untroubled. You could probably give him a book and he would read it. You could probably give him a bicycle and he would ride it.

Dr. Marks ordered, "Two chocolate malteds," and the clerk said, "Right, Doc," and there was that funny look again. Like the two nurses. A kind of double take as if they were seeing something they were not used to seeing. And now various people around the room, at the tables, at the counter, had that same look.

He got it. (Look, God damn you.)

A doctor is with a patient. A doctor brings a patient to the commissary. A doctor makes a patient his friend.

The juke box had stopped. In the quiet that followed, Jimmy drank his chocolate malted. He began slowly, but after a few swallows, he took the glass in both hands and tilted it up so that a trickle of overflowing liquid rolled down his chin. He gulped and when he was finished, he put the glass down and stared at his reflection in a cracked mirror behind the counter. He quickly lifted the glass of malted and drank a final drop and put it down again. And again he looked in the mirror.

"How was it, kid? Good?"

"Yeah."

"Want another?"

"They said he did."

"Let's have it at a table." He drew the boy to his feet and led him deliberately to a table where the two nurses were sitting. "Hello," he said to them.

"Hello, Doctor," one of them said, surprised.

"May we sit with you? This's a young friend of mine, James Cady."

They glanced at one another, baffled.

"This is my friend Jimmy's birthday."

"Oh, congratulations."

"It's the first day of his second life."

Another flurry of glances. "Are you a doctor?"

"Dr. Marks. I guess what troubles you is that I have a patient for a friend—isn't that it?"

"Was he your friend before?"

"Before what?"

"Before."

"No, he wasn't. Only now." Jimmy sat with his hands in his lap. His robe fell open over his hollow chest, which rose and subsided with his even breathing. "Ma didn't like them—" he said.

"What? Where are you, Jimmy?"

The kid's eyes cleared.

"You know where you are," Dr. Marks said.

"At the fountain."

"All right. Remember it." Turning: "I wonder if I could get you girls something."

"Oh, no, nothing, thanks. We just had something."

"Sure you won't have something more?"

"No, thanks."

He had been speaking through the noise of a record. As it whirred into silence, "More music?" he asked.

"No. We have to go. Please excuse us," and deferentially they made their way among the tables to the door.

Dr. Marks beckoned to a free waitress. "Kindly bring us two chocolate malteds," he said.

An hour later he was writing, "RBC"—red blood cells —"4,500,000," when a nurse knocked on the door.

"Dr. Marks?"

"Yes?" He put down his pen.

"Dr. Steiner would like to see you in his office right away."

All right, it had come.

When he entered the large, open foyer of the Administration Building, an attendant was just unlocking the door going inside. Dr. Marks followed him through, skirting the receptionist's cage that hung like a globe, the goal of police cars with emergency cases and quiet warder of the gate to public visitors. He passed the well-furnished offices of the "elder" staff members, and at the end of the west wing, reached the Superintendent's office. The secretary said, "Dr. Marks? Go right in, please." He went in and his eyes adjusted themselves to sunlight, to a row of windows.

Then he saw that head and its whorl of hair. . . .

An isolated upper-lake boat landing at Lake George. He had been walking with a friend, Ted Rutledge, to Ted's summer place—when was it, three years ago? Along the way, he and Ted had passed a wall of spruce when a medium-sized hawk flew out and with predatory silence, head-on and unexpectedly (probably both for the hawk and for them), had glided straight toward them. It gave them a fierce, unwavering glance, and flew on into some trees on the other side of the road.

The eyes, still undeviating: "I'm sorry to have had to interrupt you in your duties," now Dr. Marks heard the muted sound of traffic from the arterial avenue bordering the hospital, "but really, Doctor, I'm almost at a loss . . . You'll recall, when you were last in to see me—"

He recalled it very well. He recalled the end of that interview when he had had to tell Dr. Steiner in detail how he had made a diagnosis of renal colic, how he had searched for and found blood traces. He recalled the whole talk very well.

"I believe I mentioned my satisfaction, I must have indicated how genuinely pleased I was—we all were—that a man of your caliber had come in here. Of course, I had not told you in so many words the plans we had for you, how we hoped soon to move you ahead." A long pause. "You could go far in the hospital here—I've heard of your excellent committee work with the County Medical Society. You have a great potential. But I simply don't under-

stand what has just happened." His voice, though he said
he did not understand, also said he did. "I hope I'm stating
this fairly—it has come to my attention that you threatened one of the doctors here."

"You mean he told you that."

"From what he told me—"

"I did grab his shirt."

"Dr. Marks, I think you must know that nothing like
this, nothing in the least like this, can possibly be allowed
in a mental institution. Treatment depends on the most
careful control of the patients, and that means unvarying
self-control on the part of the staff so that every employee
here—every nurse and attendant—feels that supportive
control. When there's any violation of that at the top or at
the bottom, our whole work is endangered."

A set speech, probably prepared beforehand. There was
only one answer to that. "I'm aware of that. I'm aware
that I made a serious mistake and I'm sorry."

But that was not to be the end of it. The way the Superintendent continued indicated that it was only the beginning. "Dr. Marks, serious as any implication of violence
may be in this institution and as seriously as I may have to
look at this matter of your conduct toward Dr. Linscomb,
I am much more concerned with something else."

He waited.

"There are certain arrangements in a hospital. An institution operates with certain commonsense assumptions.
You were brought in here as a doctor in residence, in psychiatry. In psychiatry you were here for training, and only
for training. Is that right?"

"Yes, it is."

"Had you had any previous experience in psychiatry?"

"No, sir."

"Yet, with this complete lack of experience, you took it
on yourself to go to the Medical Ward and to treat two
cases of acute catatonic excitement—diagnosed as in exhaust status—cases in danger of death—you did do that,
didn't you?"

"Yes, I did. I asked permission, though."

"Regardless—"

"Dr. Steiner, the way this came about—"

Interrupting: "I'm not interested in how this came
about. I'm interested in the fact that with six weeks' train-

ing in psychiatry, you felt qualified to treat two patients who were presumably dying."

"I didn't go there—to Medical—to treat anybody. I'd been to the Morgue to watch a post, and the post happened to be a man who had died from acute catatonic excitement. After I'd watched the post and found no infection, you can imagine that I wanted to see such patients before death. I went over to Medical and took a look at Jimmy Cady, and—"

"Once again, Dr. Marks, I'm not interested in how you came to undertake treatment, but in the astonishing fact that you felt you could treat a patient of this kind after only six weeks in the hospital. If either of these two patients had died from your interference, I'd have had to dismiss you immediately."

"But isn't the whole point that they didn't die? They were in exhaust status and they didn't die."

"Dr. Linscomb was telling me about that. I'm going to have to speak in Staff about the unconsidered way patients are being sent to Medical without carefully checking to see whether they're really a medical case—"

"You don't think Jimmy and Ethel were medical cases?"

"If they recovered, they were clearly not in exhaust status."

"But, Doctor, if you just took a look at Ethel, you could see she was. Even Jimmy—"

"Impossible."

"Please take a look at them. Several staff doctors, I know, will verify that they were in exhaust status—"

With anger: "What are you doing, building up a legal case?"

"What would be the use of my claiming something that isn't so? If it isn't so, it can be proved it isn't so. But suppose it is so. This hospital could make an unprecedented name for itself in psychiatry. It could save hundreds of patients from dying. For this, isn't it worth coming and looking at the patient?"

There was a subtle change in Dr. Steiner's voice: "Dr. Marks, are you undergoing analysis?"

"I am."

"Were you using analysis on these patients?"

"I *was* using the understanding of mental processes analysis makes available."

The eyes glided close: "I know that obscene understanding you're referring to, that sick theory about boys wanting to fuck their mothers—I heard you were saying such things, and others—"

"Dr. Steiner, why does psychoanalysis disturb you so?"

Dr. Steiner now forgot the fine control that he said should exist from top to bottom of the hospital staff. He pounded on his desk and yelled, "I forbid you to use psychoanalysis again in this hospital."

"You can certainly forbid me to treat. But if a person has a mental illness, you can't prevent me from having a mental understanding of that illness."

"I believe you're telling me that you will not obey my order."

"I'm not saying that."

"I believe I know what you're saying."

Here it comes, Dr. Marks thought. Here's where I get fired—here's where my hospital career ends. But evidently Dr. Steiner had not decided to carry it to that point—some restraint seemed operative—for he went on in a changed voice: "We need your medical services here, Dr. Marks. We're short of doctors who have your experience in pathology. But I have to make a number of things transparently clear if you're to continue being useful to us. First, there's a hospital order that male doctors may not go into the lavatories alone with female patients. Is it correct that on the evening of August seventh, you accompanied Mrs. Simpson to the women's showers and were alone with her there while she stripped and bathed herself?"

Am I accused of sexuality? Is a gynecologist accused of sexuality when he makes his examination? Is this hospital really insane? "What are you trying to say?"

"I'm asking you, Dr. Marks, why you did not have a nurse bathe the patient or accompany you into the lavatory as the hospital orders require?"

"I'm afraid I *am* new here, Doctor. I didn't know that the integrity of the staff could not be relied on."

In fury: "You don't care about hospital rules of any kind."

"It's not my habit to disobey rules, but—"

" 'Not your habit.' I have another notation here. One of the rules is that you do your work." Consulting notes:

"On August fifth you absented yourself from Reception for the whole day, and spent that day with a patient, James Cady, in the Medical Ward, making yourself completely inaccessible."

"Dr. Steiner, I work hard here and in the overall performance of my duties, nothing has been slighted."

"I fail to see how you can say that, Dr. Marks, when you admit to being absent from your regular duties for a full day."

"But during that day I was saving—"

The control from top to bottom broke again and Dr. Steiner again pounded the desk. "You will submit yourself to the rules of this hospital or get out. There'll be no further treatment of patients by you in any way, shape, or form until your period of training is finished. Furthermore, you will not leave Reception without proper authorization except to make rounds. Your work will be physicals, blood tests, and the required reports, the work you were hired to do. Is that clear?"

Silence.

"All right, Doctor, you may go."

8/12/43

MEMO TO:
DR. JOHN N. MARKS
   Pursuant to our talk of today, you will specifically not visit James Cady or Ethel Simpson, but will confine yourself to your prescribed duties.
                    DR. FREDERICK STEINER

He arrived early at Dr. Naumann's, and as if under analytic scrutiny, he asked himself why he had come early. It was not usual for him. Some need?

He felt alone. Did he need sympathy? Understanding? His nerves were singing uncomfortably. Steiner. He expected what he got from him. You don't expect better at the hieratic, let's-have-more-shock-treatment level. But Linscomb, head of the infirmary. He felt his eyes redden again.

He was unable to remain sitting in the chair in the waiting room and began pacing, his steps muffled by the heavy rug. The eyes in Freud's photograph followed him, the man who had listened to the Wolf Man and little Hans. Quiet. Quiet.

Eyes so quiet in the patch-light photo—surely this man had never grabbed a colleague's shirt. But he had not been passive. He had had to defend his beliefs by fighting.

But how had he fought?

Letters, writing, polemics with dissidents. Persuasion. The great, severe eyes looked down.

He did get sympathy from Rossman and Pirosh.

Naumann opened the door.

"You assumed the role of God?" Dr. Naumann said. He wanted details on the shifting of the transference to God. His excitement about it was evident.

When Dr. Marks had brought the story up to the point where Ethel was in contact, Dr. Naumann said, "This case is even more important than Jimmy's was, in some respects. I can't too strongly urge you to record these two cases in detail—make full notes while you have the cases fresh in your memory. Put down everything, including verbatim dialog. Put down every last thing you remember so that the full sense of the treatment can be conveyed."

Dr. Marks felt an inclination to stay in this pleasant area of his story, to extend it. "Did I understand Ethel correctly?" he asked.

Dr. Naumann said as if thinking aloud: "Everything in psychosis as in dream is overdetermined. Yes, many of your interpretations as you tell them to me seem right and perceptive. Some things you couldn't miss. The penis envy. The Oedipal material." Thinking: "This ravenous need of the patient's to be powerful. 'I command everything. I raise the dead.' I have the feeling that in real life the patient actually felt powerless. And angry at being so powerless."

I sensed it too, Dr. Marks thought. Though I never expressed it to myself.

"When does one feel powerless?" Dr. Naumann asked.

"When nobody cares for you?"

"Yes. Let me put it differently—at what age are you most powerless?"

"In infancy, of course."

"Yes. And then 'I live on water,' what would that mean?"

"Not enough love—?"

How he blocked on milk, on the breast! Dr. Naumann remained silent.

"Food. I told her I'd give her food."

It was like the catechism of a dream. With the censor blocking the meaning. Well, it would have to come in its own time. "How was Ethel today?"

The heavyset body adjusted itself on the couch. Dr. Marks continued the story of Ethel. . . .

Dr. Naumann said, "When Miss Alston told you Ethel had been taken to insulin—I'd appreciate it if you'd try to put yourself back there at that moment. When you were phoning to the insulin ward, and when you were on your way there—try to reconstruct that. What was uppermost in your mind, were you hating Dr. Linscomb or were you thinking about Ethel?"

"Both."

"You're sure?"

Silence.

"In that dream you reported," Dr. Naumann continued, "the dream about the tree growing out of the puddle, the patient appeared to you as your child. So, what were you?"

"Her—his father."

"What kind of father?"

"A good father, I believe we said."

"We began to get an idea how important it is to you to be that good father. Now, if you were a good father, what was Dr. Linscomb?"

With a reluctance he did not understand, Dr. Marks said, "A bad father."

"And you wanted him to be a bad father," the voice said.

"But he *is* a bad father."

"If he had given Ethel the glucose?"

He would have been a good father.

The voice continued: "Sitting beside Ethel, were you thinking about the best possible way to get Dr. Linscomb's cooperation? For Ethel's sake? Were you thinking, I'll go to see him privately at home so as not to antagonize him by confronting him on the ward?"

Quickly: "But if he saw Ethel, he might have more feeling for her."

"Were you thinking, I'll let him enjoy his triumph over me—let him humiliate me—so that he'll spare Ethel?"

Silence. Heavy breathing.

"Was your main interest the patient regardless of yourself? Did you try to exhaust every possible means of persuasion on Dr. Linscomb?"

"What you mean, I take it, is that I had some unconscious need to make Dr. Linscomb be vicious," Dr. Marks said.

Silence.

"If that's true, I ought to get up now and leave you. I ought to give up any hope of properly being a psychiatrist."

"What's in your mind now?"

"Nothing. Linscomb *is* a bastard."

Silence.

Dr. Marks too was silent, but at last said: "Linscomb—there was a man who came to the flat on Bushwick Avenue sometimes, selling needles. He had a suitcase that opened out into a tray, and he had needles, thread, scissors, such things. He looked something like Linscomb. But no glasses. One day he was selling Mother a needle and she wanted to see whether a certain thread would go through it, so this peddler gave the needle to me and said, 'Sonny, see if you can thread this needle for your mother.' I tried hard to do it but I couldn't and finally my mother took the needle and right away, the first time, the thread went through. I was embarrassed. I thought that the peddler must have a terrible opinion of me."

"He came often, this peddler?"

"No, only a few times. I'm surprised I've remembered this."

"Is there anything else you remember?"

"About him?"

"About anything."

He was silent almost a full minute, then he said, "Something I'm sorry I've remembered."

Dr. Naumann waited.

I'll tell him. He felt coldly unwilling to, but he felt too, in a curious way, that he would seek to gain Dr. Naumann's approval by telling this memory. "Gus, this boy that I've told you about. I remember that one day I was standing in front of our house there, I was still forbidden to go away from it, and Gus was there. I remember he was leaning against the window of the shoemaker's shop on the ground floor—it's a funeral parlor now—"

"It is a funeral parlor now?"

"Yes."

"Please continue."

"Gus saw some dried horse manure in the gutter and told me to kneel down and eat it. Of course I refused. He said, 'You're scared. You don't dare to.' I didn't answer him. He said, 'You can't do anything. You can't leave the block. Sissy.' 'All right,' I said. 'I'll do it.' I kneeled down. Then something happened the way it does in a nightmare. My father came out of the downstairs door of the house just as my face was going down toward the manure. I jumped up and said I was just going to pretend to eat it. I begged him and pleaded with him to believe I was just going to pretend. Without answering, he took me into the house and whaled me. Gave me one of my worst beatings. But of course that wasn't what mattered. What mattered was that I believed Father could never have a good opinion of me again in my life."

He wasn't approved by Father. All the things that happened in his childhood must have kept constantly saying to his Unconscious, I don't approve of you. You can't go across the street. You can't know things. You can't take care of yourself.

The needle man. Here again was the test for approval. Thread the needle. You can't. You can't put the projecting thread into the waiting hole, you can't do the man's job (disguised as the woman's). And the needle man reminds him of Dr. Linscomb. The two are one.

"Dr. Marks, you tried to explain what you had done with Jimmy to Dr. Linscomb, didn't you?"

"You can say that again."

"And what was his reaction?"

"He wouldn't listen."

"Why?"

With anger: "He had his mind made up whatever I had to say was meaningless."

"Worth nothing."

After a silence, Dr. Marks said, "I see what you mean. I was no good, in his opinion. That's the way I thought my father felt toward me too."

"What do you do when your father feels that way?"

"You mean I ought not to give in to it, I ought to keep trying to change his opinion? But it's hopeless."

Worse than that: You know Father is pleased when he

sees you eating shit, it means he was right all along: "Is it possible you can seem to be trying to persuade Father of your worth at the very moment you're giving in to him?"

Dr. Marks said, "That has psychological truth for me. I admit it. But it has none for the hospital. Neither I nor anybody else could have changed Linscomb. That I know. And I didn't tell you about Steiner." He told Dr. Naumann about Dr. Steiner. He told him in extensive, angry detail.

Dr. Naumann thought, He did the same thing with Dr. Steiner that he did with Dr. Linscomb. That terrible trap of the Unconscious, that it secretly provokes the opposite of what consciousness wants. Now Dr. Marks was forbidden to treat patients and was confined to his building.

"The hour is up," he said. "I could wish we had more time, and I urge you not to underestimate the insight you got here today. Also, this word about your situation at the hospital: I'm sure that Dr. Steiner and Dr. Linscomb have some uncomfortable awareness of what you accomplished with Jimmy and Ethel. But they have much to contend with when it comes to accepting it. To them you're what they say you are, an untrained resident, a beginner who jumps in and treats the most serious cases in the whole hospital, challenges their experience, challenges what they think of—and have an interest in thinking of—as absolute truth. That deserves consideration. More important, you could consider that in dealing with areas of irrationality, you must bring the most wholesome motivations to bear."

Dr. Marks, as he often had before, recognized his analyst's concern for him. "I will consider it," he said.

When he came home, Margaret met him in the foyer as if she had been waiting for him. She seemed not to notice his mood, but said, "Darling, something happened. A man committed suicide in the neighborhood this afternoon and Nancy happened to see them take away the body. We were out walking. Well—" She gave him a look. "The children, I mean all around here, have been discussing it."

"Discussing it?"

"Well, going over it. I want to prepare you."

"Yes?" What did that mean? "Where's Nancy now?"

"She's in the kitchen—I'm just giving her her supper. Her young friend is visiting her—Murray. You know Murray."

Yes, he knew Murray. He went to the kitchen and found Nancy seated at her own small table with Murray opposite her. "Oh, Daddy!" Rapturous—the rapture apparently waiting only for him to burst forth.

"Yes?"

"Daddy! There was a soocide here this afternoon."

Murray's interest was intense.

"Yes?"

"Yes. A man jumped out of a seventh-story window and jumped right down on the cee-ment. Oh—all his brains spilled out. He broke his back! He broke both his arms! He broke both his legs! And—" she seemed reaching for the ultimate detail—"he broke his dingus!"

Murray's hands were tight on the edge of the table, his knuckles white with excitement. "But not me!" he cried.

Dr. Marks went to the living room, Margaret following him. What had been coming out in his analysis recently—it wasn't just the male, the father, who castrated. It was the woman. His grandmother with her whip, lashing his father across the Siberian plain. Striking at his manhood —his prick—at what she didn't have. And all these women, including Nancy, striking in fantasy at your appendage.

Margaret's eyes met his, and immediately they began to laugh, trying not to let the sound reach the kitchen. "My God," Margaret said, "we shouldn't. That man died." And yet she added, " 'But not me.' "

" 'But not me,' " he said, choking.

Not me. Not me who was castrated. Dear God, dear father in heaven, it was not me.

I'm safe, I have the love of my wife, I need not die.

I'm safe, safe. Not me.

9

The following morning was the weekly staff meeting. He had to go and could not help wondering what the attitude to him would be. Authority had spoken. And after Authority spoke, the word always went around. "You will not treat patients." "You will confine yourself to your prescribed duties." But do I have to take a completely unhopeful view? Dr. Rossman was sympathetic. Pirosh. Couldn't there be others here who would have some interest, some sympathy? The whole meaning of Staff was presumably showing an interest in a patient. Wouldn't the word be around as to Ethel's present condition? Wouldn't there be some reaction to that? Wouldn't there be interest in Jimmy?

On his way down the long final corridor leading to the staff room, he met Dr. Edwards who was walking with another doctor unknown to him. There seemed to be a momentary hesitation before Dr. Edwards said, "Good morning," and added, "I'd like you to meet Dr. Massing, just been transferred over from Building Five."

Dr. Massing had a large, hearty look. He said, "I was just telling Dr. Edwards what a change I see as compared with the last time I was in a state hospital."

"When was that?"

"In the early thirties. What a difference since then! Unbelievable!" They were passing a woman whose hands were enclosed in large canvas mitts. She was rotating one of the mitts in front of her face. "In those days it was just custodial care. But now——" Where is my hand? Where am I? "——now they're doing something for the patients. The whole spirit is different. They're active toward the patient."

Active. Without commenting, Dr. Marks continued to the staff room at the end of the corridor.

As they came in, morning sun in a bank of windows

136

that had wire in them threw webbed lines down on four long rows of chairs. Some thirty doctors had taken places in the first two rows. The back rows were filled with student nurses who rustled in their striped skirts.

As Dr. Marks took a seat, several doctors nodded or spoke, but as the meeting was getting organized, there wasn't much chance for personal talk. At the long table in front, Dr. Cortiner and a woman stenographer were sitting and Dr. Cortiner was saying, "Dr. Broughton's case. Is Dr. Broughton here?"

"Not here yet."

"We'll wait," Dr. Cortiner said, frowning. He had a voice like a broadcaster's. His gaze kept going toward the sides of the room and he rubbed his hand over his chin.

"Erna. Erna Greenly. You know her?"

"A nice girl."

"She was assaultive the other day."

"Really assaultive? You know this girl, Wellman?"

"—has trouble eating."

"I understand she's up from the South, came up—"

"A country girl! Comes from the country there."

"Low IQ?"

Dr. Cortiner folded his hands heavily on the table. "I believe we'd better get started. Dr. Hughes, would you kindly read the anamnesis?"

Dr. Hughes took the patient's chair in front, at the end of the table. Dr. Cortiner handed him the chart. Whenever there was a chart read, Dr. Marks felt embarrassingly ignorant. The terms other doctors used so easily—"hebephrenic," "degenerative anlage," "ego-hypertrophy," and so on—he still had to look up. Taking a case history, he put things down only in plain language. ("The patient stuck out her tongue.") Dr. Hughes was just now reading "—with what was adjudged conspicuously inappropriate affect." Very likely every chart I write, Dr. Marks thought, shows my ignorance.

The group of doctors listened attentively to the chart being read. He listened too, trying to understand, but had to admit to himself he found it difficult.

When the reading was finished, Dr. Cortiner nodded to a nurse at the door. "Have the patient come in."

A girl in her twenties entered and took the chair Dr. Hughes had just left. She was short, and her head did not come up much above the back of the chair. She wore a dress with a lacy collar. She folded the collar over her throat, held it, let it go, laid her strong forearms on the arms of the chair, and gazed out over the doctors. Her bearing did not have the arrogance or tension of many of the patients. Her eyes were large, black, and round, and glistened, and seemed sad to him. Her carefully combed hair was cut in a neat line over the nape of her neck.

Dr. Cortiner turned his head to the side and said with apparent casualness: "Now, Erna, this is a gathering of doctors from the hospital here who are interested in what may be troubling you, and we thought that if you would like to talk to us, answer some questions and tell us about yourself, we might be able to help you."

"Yes, Doctor." Erna's voice was clear and had a quaver of sweetness. It projected well. The double row of doctors seemed pleased that this patient was going to talk loud enough to be heard.

Dr. Cortiner continued: "Erna, would you tell us how long you've been at the hospital?"

Without hesitation: "Since May twenty-third. Before that, I was committed March second to Bellevue and was there I guess ten days."

"And in between, you were home."

"I was home."

"At your mother's."

"Yes."

"Why were you first committed? Could you tell us about that?" His voice had become more authoritative as he began to establish the question-and-answer rhythm.

"Yes. I got up one morning and wanted to be proud like."

"And what do you mean by that?"

"I don't know." Melodious: "It's just how I felt."

"Was there something specific you were going to be proud about? Something special?"

"I wanted to go out and tell the people."

"Tell them what?"

"The message."

"You mean something religious?"

Smiling shyly: "Oh, no."

"So what happened?"

"I don't know." She said, "I would tell you if I knew."
Dr. Marks noticed that her lips had an unusual shape, the

upper lip coming out in a sharp line from her nose, and the lower lip seeming to rise to meet it.

"Then what happened this last time, after you were home again?" Dr. Cortiner asked.

"Well, I wanted to wash my feet and there was no hot water and Mom forbid me to use cold water." Gazing around: "It was my time."

"Well, why were you so set on washing your feet?"

Surprised: "If it's your time, you got to wash your feet."

"I see. Was that all?"

"Oh, I got over that. But then later that same day I begun to laugh."

Examining chart: "And then they took you to the hospital?"

"They did." Asking to be believed: "But it don't mean nothing, really, me laughing. It don't take but the least thing to make me laugh, to make me happy." She said it as if explaining some simple thing to a friend. She said it as if anybody should understand it, this thing about happiness, and yet at the very moment she talked about it, Dr. Marks glimpsed terror.

"What about people in glass houses?" Dr. Cortiner asked.

"What, please?"

" 'People in glass houses shouldn't throw stones.' What does that mean?"

This was a routine question to test the intelligence of the patient.

"It mean if you got faults yourself, you shouldn't go around talking against somebody else got that—them faults."

One of the doctors called out, "A rolling stone."

"Yes, what does it mean when you say, 'A rolling stone gathers no moss?' "

"Why, that mean a person goes here, goes there, don't settle down to nothing. Don't like to get ahead."

"Yes." Casually: "Now I'd like to ask—you live with your mother when you're home. How do you get along with her?"

"Oh, very well. She done everything for me, raised me. My mother loves me." Her gaze was steady.

"But," glancing at the chart, "it does seem you have trouble with her."

"Oh, yes, kind of a way. It's hard for her to realize I'm grown up and got my own life to live now."

"You did fight, it seems."

No response. The hands again clasped.

"Did your mother call you names?"

"Depends on what you mean by names."

"Did she call you any names?"

Low: "Hardly any."

"Well, what did she call you?"

"I don't know," she said, very troubled.

"Well, can't you tell us at least one?"

" 'Heifer.' "

Taken aback: "What's that mean?"

"You know, calf, little cow."

Dr. Edwards called out, "It means a cow that has not had a calf."

Dr. Cortiner to Erna: "That's a strange thing for your mother to call you."

"That about all the mean she call me any time. She call me sweet things too."

Consulting chart: "You didn't like to go out?"

"I liked to go out sometimes, once a week maybe. Once or twice. But I liked to be by myself, too."

"Why's that?"

"I just liked to."

Glancing aside: "What do you do when you're by yourself, Erna?"

"Sew. Radio. Seems I just like to be by myself." Dr. Marks had the impression that perhaps she didn't sew or do anything. Perhaps she just said this to please Dr. Cortiner. He had the odd feeling of being in touch with her mind.

"Don't you like people?" Dr. Cortiner said.

No answer.

"Suppose you're alone and reading, do the characters seem to be alive?"

"How?"

"Come out of the book? You ever make them do things themselves?"

Embarrassed: "I can't read."

Dr. Cortiner rubbed his chin, contemplating this phenomenon, his questioning balked. He said, "Do you day-dream?"

She seemed to revolve this through her mind and an-swered, "The silverware." Murmuring: "The fork is Mama, the knife is Papa, the spoons is the little ones. There's Brother. There's Grandma and Grandpa and un-cles—"

This would be how to find out something, from the knives and forks.

"Your father, we haven't spoken about him," Dr. Corti-ner went on. "Can you tell us something about him?"

"He didn't help us none. He went away and left Mama the work. She work; my brother and me just scrabbled up."

"So what did you feel about your father?"

Angrily: "No feeling, one way or the other."

"You seem upset as you talk. A little angry."

Ethel, enraged at being abandoned.

"Maybe I am." Her lips tightened. "I did think one time, Be nice to have a papa who love you. But I forget about that now. I got no father now."

"How did you get along with your brother?"

"All right." Sunk in thought.

"Do you have friends?"

Low: "Hard to have friends, hard to depend on any-body. I had one friend—"

"Yes?"

"A girl I met in the restaurant, I was working there. I do everything for her. When she don't work, help her and even give her money to buy stockings. Then—"

"Then?"

Low-voiced: "She just cut me."

"Cut you?"

"Even say mean things about me."

"Like what?"

Choked: "That I wore my welcome out."

"But some people are good, aren't they?" Routine ques-tion.

Into her dress collar, faintly: "Mighty few."

"Do you think you have any enemies? Would you say you have any?"

"No. No, I wouldn't say that."

"Nobody who did anything against you?"

"One."

"Yes?" The head on the side, listening.

"Landlady downstairs." Puzzled: "When I come back from the hospital, why'd she have to keep coming up so much? Coming up all the time? She knew I was cured—I heard the doctor tell her I was cured by the shock treatments. What'd she have to come snooping around for?"

"Well, why do you think?"

Seeming to flinch: "About the water. You know how rust come out the faucet sometimes? Well, the water run like rose color all the time. Why should it run rose color? It never done that before. Why just then when I come back from the hospital?"

"You think the landlady made it do that?"

Shaken: "Why'd she keep coming up all the time?"

"Erna," Dr. Cortiner said, referring again to the chart, "what is this business about you not wanting to eat here at the hospital?"

"I'm overweight, about ten pounds overweight. If I eat every meal, I gain weight. I keep gaining. So, few days ago, I just didn't want to eat."

She was clearly not overweight.

"I understand you had a fight with a nurse outside the dining room."

"It weren't a fight." The pointed lips quivered. "I grabbed her arm, pulled it around like this. I didn't hurt her. You go into the dining room, it's a temptation to eat. She wanta make me go. After, I found out it's the rule you got to go in the dining room because there's not enough nurses to watch you out in the hall. If I'd understood, I'd have gone." She had slumped down in the chair into a peculiar position, with her legs out in front of her. It was as if she was trying to slide from view. "I'm sorry 'bout that. Some people do things and forget about them. But like me, I keep thinking about them."

"You keep thinking about that?"

She nodded.

"Other things?"

"Yes."

"Like what?"

Clearly: "Sins."

Dr. Cortiner turned his head more directly toward her. "Sins," he repeated. "What sins?"

"Well, like eating is a sin. The sin of gluttony. Times I eat too much, I think about that." A strange sin, Dr. Marks thought.

"Other sins?"

She brooded.

"Sex?" Dr. Cortiner said.

"Few times. I think about that too."

"When did that first happen?"

As she answered this question, there was the same unchanged, clear yet hushed, melodious tone to her voice as when she spoke about eating. A man "come from that part the country, there where I come from," and there was some "promise like" to marry her, but "after that" he went away. What he did to her did not seem to have stayed much in her mind. Something then about "another one" who held her and "argued her." It was hard to know whether her few "sins" of this kind had been from any strong active need or from compliance.

"Tell me, Erna, do you feel depressed sometimes? Low?" A stock question.

"Yes, I do."

"Do you ever feel like killing yourself?"

Shocked: "I do think about it." Breathing deep: "I get to the point where I think how to do it. But I'm— It's awful." Strangling: "I do want to do it. How'd you know I have those thoughts?"

"What do you mean?"

"Somebody told you?" An accusation.

"No, it just came into my mind to ask you. I only asked."

"Oh." Not too relieved.

"What troubles you especially?"

"One thing. I think about it and think about it. I can't help myself."

"What?"

"Terrible." She raised the collar of her dress and put her hands over her face in evident despair. Her body slumped further. Now her hands, one after the other, began to tear distractedly at her mouth.

"If you don't want to tell us, if it troubles you too much—"

"I'd rather not tell. But if you insist." Her own fear and desperation insisted. "It really happened, I know it did.

Because my mother she remember that boy come." A lucent hint of fantasy. "I was five, it was an upstairs room —" Now her voice died out.

Dr. Cortiner asked, "How old was he?"

"About fifteen."

"And what happened?"

Her body, still extended and braced with its strong legs, twisted, and she said, "He came over me." She tore again at her lips with her hands.

Dr. Cortiner asked, "Did he actually, did he—"

"Oh, no. It wasn't that way."

Now all the doctors were looking at her hands and she stilled them and covered her mouth.

The hunger. The sin of gluttony and the desperate fasting. The symbolic fight with the nurse in the hall. Hunger, hunger! The lace collar caught in her hands. When she took away her hands, her cheeks were flushed and wet with tears.

"Thank you," Dr. Cortiner said without expression. He signaled a nurse standing near the door and as she came forward, he said to Erna: "The doctors and I appreciate your cooperating with us today. That will be all."

As the door closed on her, Dr. Parker said, "Intelligent. That answer to the rolling-stone proverb. I believe that's the best answer we ever had here on that."

"Excellent. Wonderful powers of abstraction."

"Although I don't know if I approve of that proverb," Dr. Spencer said. "I don't know if staying in one place is so good." Laughter.

Dr. Cortiner said, "Dr. Spencer, what do you say?"

"I'd diagnose her as paranoid. No question. That rose-colored water and her friend, the one who said things about her."

Dr. Marks thought, What are they doing? What attempt is being made to understand this girl? As Erna had concluded her interview, he had felt such anguish, such a passion about her. He would have put his arms around her.

How she had looked, walking toward the door! Her body had seemed to become shorter. She seemed stunned —confused—and at the door she gave one last glance back.

Dr. Edwards: "I'd say the patient was manic-depressive. She had a suicidal depression, and you'll note the clear affect."

"You could say euphoric," one of the doctors said.

"But that's not necessarily manic," Dr. Wellman objected. "And we ought to take into consideration the cultural level."

"Poor whites?"

"They can fool you with a reactive elation. That's all I mean."

"One way to find out would be to give her an intelligence test."

"Yes, we could test the patient's intelligence and I'm sure that would be helpful," Dr. Cortiner said, "but we have a good deal to go on as it is, and I think we should be trying to make a diagnosis." Dr. Cortiner glanced along the two rows of doctors and located Dr. Broughton who had come in late. "Dr. Broughton, perhaps you'd like to comment."

"I must admit I was impressed by the showing she made."

"You think she was trying to make a showing?"

"Oh, yes, definitely. She was much better than I ordinarily see her. That's what makes it so hard to judge. Either they're a lot better here, or at their worst."

"From your overall knowledge of the case, how would you diagnose?"

"Psychopatic personality."

Dr. Cortiner seemed not pleased at this offering.

A woman doctor: "There's every indication of a character disturbance."

Dr. Cortiner said, "We can't keep her on that. Dr. Lantz, what do you say?"

"Well, I'd point out the marked dissociation. The patient clearly had difficulty relating to anybody—mother, father, friends. I even see a trace of hysteria." A jar lid used as an ashtray dropped on the floor with a loud clatter. "We must get to a diagnosis," Dr. Cortiner said, turning his head from side to side.

Dr. Marks noticed Dr. Wellman glance over toward him. "Possibly Dr. Marks would offer a suggestion," Dr. Wellman said.

The skirts of the student nurses could be heard rustling.

"I'm not as qualified as others to diagnose. I'd say simple schizophrenia." Would he have the courage to go on with what he wanted to say now? "But is it so important to spend all our time on diagnosis?"

"I suppose you know a diagnosis is required by law." Dr. Cortiner did not say this impatiently.

"A number of things are required by law, but need we keep to the letter of the law always? I'm thinking of meaningless chart entries. I'm thinking of a number of things familiar—more familiar to others here than to me." Silence allowed him to continue. "Isn't it important that we should feel compassion for this girl? And think what a chance there is here—this isn't a catatonic out of communication—out of ordinary communication—this girl can talk to you. And she's in terror. No matter how she tries to conceal it—no matter if she made a good showing as Dr. Broughton said, she's still in terror. Suicide, hate, there are signs all over. So shouldn't we be doing everything in our power to find out whom or what specifically she's afraid of? Try to understand her?"

Dr. Wellman said, "What Dr. Marks seems to want is deep questioning of the patient. Questioning Erna deeply would break down her defenses and then we would have a full-blown psychosis to deal with."

"You may have anyway." Wasn't anybody going to support him? Wasn't anybody interested in Erna? He said, "The way she pulled on her lips seems to ask us to go further in trying to understand her. Her trouble with food." He glanced quickly around. "Can't we try to help her?"

Silence.

Dr. Cortiner: "That's all you have to say?"

"That's all."

"I'm glad to have had your comment. I'm glad to have had the comment of the other doctors, and my opinion is that it is a simple process schizophrenia and we will so diagnose it. What treatment shall we give the patient?"

"In view of the depressive features underlying the elation," Dr. Wellman said, "I recommend electric shock."

Dr. Cortiner: "Electric shock is indicated, but because of the particular circumstances of this case, with its obvious need of special handling, I'm going to suggest that this girl be sent to the insulin ward. I think the nurses are better there."

Sixty sweating comas. *I'm dying, I know I'm dead.*

"All right, that's all, gentlemen."

10

Erna sat on a bench in the dayroom of the insulin ward, her legs extended in front of her as they had been at the staff conference. She sat this way for a long time, then she raised her hands and put them over her ears.

On Ward H in Building Eight, a woman patient was talking with one of the attendants. In a bitter whisper she said, "Martin Luther threw an inkpot at the devil, and everybody thinks he's wonderful. But I see the devil and they don't believe me. I do see him."

"Yes?"

"Yes." Brooding: "And other people see him too. I know. Their eyes follow him."

In Ward C in the same building, Myrtalene Hall flapped her robe over her pear-shaped belly, in the last stage of pregnancy. She moaned happily. Mmmmmmm, mmmmmmm. She had it inside, she had it. Wires made fiery spurts and contacts and protected it. From her camisole couch—"I announce to one and all that my gift is about to be forthcoming. Listen, all."

A nurse going by in the corridor looked in and thought, That one's going to pop any moment. Jesus, what that kid will have for a mother! She stopped.

"Myrtalene."

Myrtalene glared at her.

"How do you feel?"

The singing was fading now and the wires were not humming. She put her hands down at her sides, frightened. Then the humming began again and she said, "I announce to one and all—" her voice rising, proud "—I announce to one and all—" With great happiness she ran toward the door. "I have it. I have it," she cried.

147

The rectangle of the sixth-floor men's dayroom, with its rows of benches, was like a lecture hall or a classroom. But the students sat mute and motionless. One man climbed on a rear bench, talking silently. His eyes protruded and now and then his body trembled and when it did, his moving tongue stopped and he seemed to be listening to the voices.

An attendant ordered him off the bench. "You'll fall. You mustn't climb on the benches, you know that."

When the man had falteringly got down off the bench, he remained in front of it in an upward-straining position, his tongue flicking.

Jimmy went over to him and said, "Who was it?" and went back to the wall. The room gave him a sensation of dream, of having dreamed it. Something threatening existed among the steam pipes in the corner and he had an impulse to stand still. He stood still for some time, but, tiring, took a seat next to the man who continued trembling, flicking his tongue, and straining forward and up.

The attendant came over and made the old man sit down and said to Jimmy, "How are you?"

Jimmy rubbed his hands over his denim pants. His lips puckered. "Nobody comes to see me," he said.

Notation on James Cady's chart: "Aug. 12th. Since transfer back to Ward L, continues in partial contact and improving."

Johnny sprawled on the sofa while Dr. Marks sat in his usual armchair, smoking. He held the cigarette holder in his teeth. Johnny started humming. Thousands of suffering patients (children) in the hospital, and this kid sprawls and hums—Satchmo Armstrong himself. Why is he so damn normal? Who gave him an ego-resistance of a hundred? Who fixed him up so he never had to worry about the noises of the primal scene or the security of his genital organs?

(I have to listen to him hum—I can't see Jimmy.)

"Dad."

"Yes?"

"That's a wild daughter you've got."

"Why?"

"What she said at dinner."

At dinner she had been allowed to sit with the family

again and had made the most of it. Female to the bone, she had given her father a number of deliberately melting glances, and he had finally succumbed and leaned over and kissed her. He said, "You're the most beautiful girl in the world."

Smug glintings of those perfect eyes.

He said, "I don't know what I did to deserve you."

More glintings.

"Break it up, break it up," Bob said.

"You do love me, don't you, Daddy?"

"The whole world knows I love you."

With a straight face, delighted: "God told everybody, didn't he? Because you have to work and you wouldn't have time to tell everybody."

At the shouts of joy this produced, Nancy was even more delighted. She stood up on her chair and waved her arms.

Dr. Marks now tapped his cigarette on the ashtray edge and said, "That remark she made—'God told everybody.' That's what the insane say. There's a big likeness between insanity and childhood—you ought to hear them at the hospital."

Johnny gave him a wise look. "But what you said was insane too," he said.

"How's that?"

" 'The whole world knows I love you.' "

"Well, that's just an expression."

Johnny was laughing. "Okay."

So it was true. What he had said was insane too. But everybody used these large expressions. What the hell was sane and insane in this world anyway?

Margaret came in and Dr. Marks said, "Where did Bob disappear to?"

"He went to a movie."

"Who told him he could go to a movie?" leaning forward aggressively.

"He has an allowance. Since when can't he go to a movie?"

"When I was his age, I asked my parents if I could go to a movie. And then they said, 'No.' "

"Are you your parents?" she said.

He checked an angry answer.

What was this constantly growing irritation he felt until the very happiness of his family bothered him? Margaret was much happier since he hadn't been going nights to the hospital—and now even that annoyed him.

Back to physicals. Fifty a week. Eyes, ears, nose, mouth, throat, chest—heart and lungs—abdomen, any masses or palpable organs, extremities and reflexes, urine —spinal tap—blood from the arm, blood from finger. Today he had discovered an RBC of 2,000,000 and his first thought had been starvation (a Jimmy or Ethel). How persistently his mind went to them!

And writing up the mental on the charts. He had mentioned the legal idiocy of chart entries at Staff—the law says you have to have some kind of progress note for every patient every six weeks. He himself wrote up notes for a hundred seventy-five patients he didn't know— couldn't know—and he had heard of doctors in some hospitals who had nine hundred to write up. "Patient assaultive during past two weeks." "Condition unchanged." "Patient continues on Ward 21—condition unchanged." How many tens of thousands of "Condition unchanged" got written into the charts!

The law!

And from a thousand rooms, the cry of fear and confusion. Desolation, despair. "I can't stand it. I can't stand it. I'm going to give up. Why don't they just kill me and get it over with?" Constant yelling. A woman had caught him in a dayroom today and shuddered against him, that utter haggard caving in of the face, that storm of giving way. Screaming like a child in tantrum: "I won't stand it. I'll kill somebody. I don't care what I do. I don't care. I don't care."

"Condition unchanged."

The phone rang. It was Dr. Rossman. He said, "Something I wanted to tell you and I hate to call you on the phone at the hospital—"

"What is it?"

"Erna Greenly who was presented at Staff last week—"

"I know. What about her?" Dr. Marks said.

"She was put in restraint today. Really violent. Terrible."

Two days later, on August sixteenth, it was his turn to make rounds and stay in the hospital overnight, a routine duty that fell to him every nine days. He knew that Jimmy had been transferred back to his ward, and he had been looking forward to rounds as a legitimate excuse to see the kid. Hurry the rounds a little and maybe he could stretch it into a visit.

He finished work in his office, writing down the final red blood cell count for the day (4,500,000), and he recognized how he was rushing. He closed the last folder. All he had to do now was make time from ward to ward. No extended talks with the nurses. No talks, period.

When he came out of the sixth-floor corridor into the low-benched dayroom of Ward L, the late summer sun was still shining. The men on the benches looked uniformly depressed and quiet. Then he saw Jimmy, with his back to him, standing at one of the windows. There seemed a suggestion of interest in something in the kid—not the complete passivity of the rest of the room.

He came to his side and said, "Hello."

Jimmy turned sharply.

"It's me. You knew I'd come, didn't you?"

Jimmy's eyes filled with tears.

"You knew I'd come, didn't you?"

No answer.

"Didn't you?"

"Zzzzzzzzz."

"That's crazy stuff. You can forget that. Listen."

Silence.

"I can only come to see you now about once a week, once in nine days. But I'll see you. You understand?"

One of the men on the benches stood up and muttered. Then, stepping forward, he said clearly to nobody, "Son of a bitching bastard. Get out of here." Jimmy was watching.

"Who's that?" Dr. Marks asked.

"Who?"

"Over there. That man you're looking at, who is he?"

"I don't know. Joe—"

"Joe's your brother. He has nothing to do with that man over there."

Jimmy shook his head. His hair waved to and fro.

"Joe's in the army. What makes you think of him when you see that man over there?"

Jimmy flattened his hand along his pants leg. "Fighting."

"Who's Joe fighting?"

Silence. The man so phantasmally disturbed sank down again on the bench.

"Who was he fighting?"

"No."

Dr. Marks took Jimmy's face in his hands. "Look at me. Who was he fighting?"

"The . . . the . . . Eddie."

"Not Eddie. Not Eddie. Who was he fighting?"

"Me," Jimmy said.

Softly, "Yes, you. You. He wants Mama to love him, not you. He wants Papa to love him, not you. Yes, he's fighting you. And you think he can get the best of you, don't you?"

"No."

"Everybody can get the best of you. Everybody's better than you, aren't they?"

Jimmy trembled.

"They're not. You're the best. I know." When Jimmy had quieted: "You feel better now, don't you? Let's have your hand." He took Jimmy's hand and felt the palm. Wet. "Take it easy. I love you and protect you, you know that. Who am I?" he asked.

"Doctor—"

"Yes?"

"Some doctor."

"What doctor?"

"Dr. Marks."

"And who are you?"

A look of confusion. "Me? My name?"

"Yes, what's your name?"

"Why—"

"Are you getting scared about something?"

"I'm, I'm—"

"What're you scared about?" Intuitively guessing: "Did something come into your mind?"

"No."

"Yes, it did. What did you think of just now?"

"They said a girl."

" 'They'?"

"Am I a girl?" His eyes questioned Dr. Marks with desperation. Every Goddamned thing Dr. Naumann said was true. The Unconscious doesn't know what sex it is any more than it knows what age it is. "Son, you're not a girl. You're my son. A man likes to have a son."

"Son."

"Yes, son."

"I'm your son," the kid said.

"You certainly are, and I love you. So who are you?"

Low: "You mean my name always?"

"Yes. Your name always."

"James Cady."

"Right." He said it with emphasis on the "t." "You just got confused for a minute, didn't you?"

"Yes."

As the room darkened, the men became shadows. Jimmy looked toward them. Dr. Marks touched his arm. "Where are you?"

As if awakening: "Where? In the hospital."

"That's not good enough. Whereabouts in the hospital?"

"A—a room."

"You don't think I don't know it's a room, do you?"

Jimmy smiled, embarrassed. The embarrassment was good.

"What room? Where?"

Unsmiling: "I don't know."

"When they brought you here, did they tell you anything?"

Jimmy shook his head.

"They told you something, all right. What did they tell you?"

"Moving me," with a propitiatory nod.

"Yes, that they were moving you. And where were they moving you to?"

Trying hard: "Here."

"Where's 'here'?" Again Jimmy was puzzled. "Jimmy, were you ever here before?"

A quick glance at the room. "No."

"Yes, you were here before. This is the ward where you used to be. This is one of the wards for crazy people—insane. This is Ward L. Come here." He took Jimmy to the door and showed him "Ward L" inscribed on it. "You see it now? Ward L."

"Ward L."

"I want you to know it. I want you to know where you are. You're getting better, though."

Jimmy nodded and gave a faint "zzzzz" sound. "Papa—" At the start of Dr. Marks's frown, he quickly corrected himself. "Not Papa."

"That's right. Who am I?"

"Dr. Marks."

"Right. Keep it in mind." Quietly: "Did you dress yourself this morning?"

"Yes. Yes, I did."

"Take care of yourself all right?"

"I—I do."

Dr. Marks gently buttoned a button at the top of the boy's blue shirt. "Keep on doing it, Jimmy."

"Yes."

"I'll see you in a little over a week. You'll be all right until I come. You understand?"

The man who had got up before got up again. "Jesus, Mary, and Josephine," he cried loudly.

"Good-by, son," Dr. Marks said. "Take care and I'll be seeing you soon."

Dr. Marks, after he left the kid, involved himself in certain delays. He questioned sedation orders he usually okayed. He had an argument with a nurse, about nothing. He walked more slowly. But at last he reached the women's insulin ward.

His first impression was the one he always had at this time of day. Now the patients were calm, they touched one another, they spoke; with the deliberately languid slope of an arm or the steady lift and fall of a breast, they said that they were hardly different from people outside in the street. Look at us, their eyes pleaded, don't look at the cloth straps on the beds or at the gleaming rows of "molasses" mugs.

There were exceptions. At a glance he saw several who couldn't "come up." One was arching her thighs. Near him a dark-eyed woman lay face down with one white breast pulled out of her nightgown, repeating endlessly, "Esperanza, esperanza, esperanza."

"Where's Ethel?" he asked.

Ethel was on a cot on the far side of the room. She was lying completely still, not in restraint: no restraint was needed. Catatonia. He passed his hand in front of her eyes and there was no flicker. "Ethel," he said.

Silence. Very low breathing.

He said to the nurse, "Is she like this all the time?"

"Yes. Yes, it's real stupor, Doctor."

"Is she rigid?"

He lifted Ethel's arm a few inches above the bed. It remained there. He thought of something that had happened once with Nancy. He had left home on an emergency call and had forgotten to kiss her good-night. When he came home later, Margaret told him Nancy had cried herself to sleep. He went to her room and found her lying in a tangled nest of her covers, her head toward him. He lightly kissed her and whispered, "I'm sorry."

What good does it do to be sorry?

He gently replaced Ethel's arm on her breast.

Two hours later, in the early night, he had finished rounds, but was not yet ready to go to bed. When he did go, it would be in a small bedroom in the Administration Building where, as he slept, he would be on call. Now he went to his office and turned on the small desk lamp.

He had something important to consider. What was left to him here at the hospital? What was the use of going on? What would he be going on for?

To see Ethel on rounds once in nine days? He had promised to see Jimmy and that was important. But even Jimmy could manage now.

No, something told him, Jimmy needs you.

Why am I so alone here? That was the aching question. Why isn't there anybody here with any power who has any interest in anything but shock treatment or the Emperor's Clothes of one-minute psychotherapy? Why do they want to keep away from the patient, not look?

No "deep questioning." Wellman had said it. Deep questioning was dangerous. But it wasn't dangerous to give insulin shock that produced an Ethel and an Erna. And might kill them.

Why isn't there somebody in power here who's willing to "intelligently observe," as Freud put it? (". . . a single intelligent observation of the psychic life of a neurotic, a single analysis of a dream, must force upon the physician the unshakable conviction that the most complicated and the most accurate operations of thought, to which the name of psychic occurrences can surely not be refused, may take place without arousing consciousness.") And it was not the minds of neurotics that these doctors had before them to observe. It was the far more exposed minds of psychotics. Minds with windows.

What was he to do now?

He felt as he had felt when he had been stood in the corner by his father and told to remain there until he apologized. He had remained there, it was true, and had fallen asleep standing up after hours of refusal, his will unbroken. He could do that now. He could refuse to accept what Steiner and company believed here. He could refuse to acknowledge their will. But what good would that do—a program of denial? He might as well resign.

He realized he had been smoking. He killed the cigarette and tapped his cigarette holder on the edge of the tray, which rang with a glassy knell.

Dreaming (asleep in the small bedroom on the third floor of the Administration Building), he was holding in his hand a filing card that was not only a filing card but a telegram on which words were printed one below the other. The last printed word was DELUGE. Below that, in a neat handwriting like printing, was the word EATS. As he woke up, he had his hand sprawled out and realized he was reaching for the telephone, which was ringing.

"Dr. Marks?"

"Yes?"

"This is Miss Brown, Ward C in Building Eight. One of the patients, Myrtalene Hall, is having a baby. Can you come right away?"

Yawning. "What's the hurry?"

"Hurry! She's so disturbed we never knew it was happening. You'll just about have time to get here."

"All right, I'll be right over."

Myrtalene—where did anybody get a name like that? Some crazy mother. And now another gob of the same flesh was coming into the world.

He hurriedly dressed and, rather than wait for the slow night elevator, ran downstairs and let himself out. High up above him, above black porches like superimposed cages, he could glimpse Dr. Steiner's penthouse.

Wide spaces between the buildings. He continued running.

When he reached Building Eight, he jabbed the elevator bell hard until an elevator rumbled down and took him to Ward C. The nurse there, Miss Brown, took him to Myrtalene, a stout woman in her middle thirties who was proudly grasping the top bars of a small metal bed. He asked the nurse to hold a light while he made his examination. He found an area of the baby's head about the size of a half dollar already visible, black-haired and pressing out. The patient had a look of great satisfaction. She arched her legs and orgiastically moved her thighs. When her pains came, she caught her breath. "Take her to the delivery room," he said.

Two attendants transferred the woman carefully to a wheel table and trundled her down the corridor. He followed to the bare operative anteroom, washed himself at the large sink, and got into the sterile gown, mask, cap, and gloves. The gloves fit well for once.

That disk of head beginning to show. A new life. Would it be born wholesome or sick? He thought, Why not wholesome? A one-legged woman gives birth to a two-legged child. A birth is a cleansing. Why not wholesome?

But what kind of life would it have with that mother?

The delivery room waited with its glare. Another nurse had joined Miss Brown and both nurses were masked and ready, and he walked forward, conscious that he was going to be bothered by the heat of the mask, under the hot lights in the hot night.

Myrtalene lay with her eyes dilated, her hands gripping the edge of the padded table. He said to her firmly, "Bear down." She seemed not to hear. "Bear to the pain," he repeated.

"Thank you, one and all. Thank you, bastards." The voice was hard and self-satisfied.

"I'm your doctor. I'm here to help you give birth to your child." Something might get through to her. "Bear down, please."

"Announcements, all. This is the—" She closed her eyes and shook with pain under the blazing lights. When the pain relaxed, she opened her eyes and said, "Happy holiday."

The baby's head slowly emerged until it was completely out. He released the tiny shoulders, then he became aware that Myrtalene had raised herself and was staring downward. "Lie back," he called to her.

"What are you taking off me? Put it back!"

He grasped the baby under the armpits. Myrtalene screamed. "Hold her!" he ordered the nurses as he gave a steady pull. Despairingly: "Mama, you took it and now you got it, oh, you got it, you got it, you got it!"

"What have I got?" He had the now-yelling child in his hands and noted that it was a baby girl, the usual birth-beet color, but clean and well-formed. "What have I got?" he repeated, busy tying the umbilical cord.

"Taking it away from me." Gasping: "Bastard!" She reached her hand down. "Keep her hand back. Taking what away from you, Myrtalene?"

Whines. Screams. He cut the umbilical cord. "All right now, Myrtalene. Just a minute. Wait. Just a minute now." He wrapped a bellyband over the baby's stomach, and tied it, and went with the baby toward Myrtalene.

"Doctor, what are you doing?" Miss Brown's eyes, deprived of expression by the white swath over her mouth, seemed only wider than usual. "That's not allowed."

"What's not allowed?" he said.

"You hand it to me, Mama? I got it? I got it?" A flame of joy lit Myrtalene's face as he put the child into her arms. Her arms closed on it and she fitted one hand over the baby's small naked buttocks while he stood poised above her. As he watched, into her eyes came the lucidity of patients who, after a long flow of strained rhetoric, lapse tiredly and with relief into their own natural voices. He had seen it happen on rounds. They ask for a cigarette, or mention a physical hurt, or make some other normal remark. Myrtalene held the child for one moment with that natural look, with her hand curved over the buttocks. Then the insane excitement returned and she cried, "Announcements, all."

The nurses were violently shadowed from above. Their heads bent forward, their foreheads glistened.

'*I have it, I have it.*' And the '*it*' being forcibly taken from her. '*There's no meaning in what they say.*' '*Bizarre speech.*'

"Myrtalene."

"Yes? Yes, Mama?"

"The nurse has to have your baby now. I have to give it to her so she can take care of it." He withdrew the baby from her and handed it to Miss Brown.

Confusion was rising in Myrtalene's eyes. Frightened: "It's gone. It's gone!"

"But you understand, daughter, you'll get it back."

Bewildered: "But, Mama, you took it."

"You'll get it back."

"No. No, I won't." Loudly: "I won't, I won't."

Dr. Marks grasped her shoulders. Firmly: "You'll get what you want." Miss Brown was going away with the baby. "You'll get it."

"Yes, I'll get it, I have the divine order." Lifting her head and staring around proudly, she called, "Announcements, all."

"Yes?"

"This is the day—" But she was unable to go on. She said, "No, it's the wrong day," and broke into violent sobs.

11

Dr. Marks turned his head on the couch. It was one of the few times he had looked at Dr. Naumann during a session. And there was that small bald head above the not too well-pressed coat, multiply conscious, listening. Perhaps for one moment that head was caught off guard, was seen as it was throughout the hour. Then Dr. Marks was aware of a wordless reproof. I'm not to be looked at. All right, he thought, resuming his normal position, and he said, "My intention is desperate, I agree. But think: here is this baby born and it has no mother. The mother is alive, but of no use to it. I know I have no right to believe I can get her out of psychosis, but if I could, the baby could have a mother. I began to get some insight there into what's troubling her—"

"This is not a Jimmy."

"I know. I know I had the right to treat Jimmy because it was life or death—that or nothing. I know also that part of why I was able to help Jimmy was that he was screaming to be saved from death. I had his terror going for me, you could say, and that may be crucial. But to help a mother—"

"The hospital has ordered you not to treat."

"Do I have to respect such an order? There may be some way around it. What's the use of my being there if I can't do anything?"

After a moment: "You'll do something later. Now you're there to fulfill your requirements for a residency, to become a psychiatrist."

"I feel so useless."

Dr. Naumann was silent. He seemed to be thinking. At last he said, "You must understand that I sympathize with you. I too came up against the hospital hierarchy in my early days though I never provoked it as you have done. And I found ways around them, and the torment of the insane will somewhere be accessible to you, too. Meantime you are learning. You've learned from this Myrtalene yesterday. You will have other undoubted opportunities to learn at the hospital. I know how you must be feeling—"

"A baby without a mother—"

"I know. Now I wish that you would be silent for a moment or two." It was Dr. Naumann's technique occasionally to insist on silence before the actual work of the session. To put a gap between the pressure of the outer world and its concerns, and the analytic process. It was like the moment of ~~silence~~ in a theatre as the house lights dimmed, lulling and conditioning an audience.

And Dr. Naumann noticed something, in this short interval of silence. As Dr. Marks lay outstretched on the couch, he seemed to be holding something in his right hand. "What do you have in your hand?"

"A penny. Your previous analysand evidently dropped it from his pocket." He showed the penny.

"Yes. So—" Dr. Marks seemed quieter. "What's in your mind now?"

"I was thinking about rain. It looked like rain as I was coming here, and I heard a sound of the wind outside as if perhaps it was going to begin to rain. The windows are open in my car—well, it doesn't matter."

"Please put everything immediate from your mind." Dr. Naumann waited, but there was no response from Dr. Marks. It was a defense. Dr. Marks knew that he should comply with the analytic requirement, but he continued silent. Dr. Naumann wondered whether to help break this block, and decided not to.

At last Dr. Marks said, "The dream I had before I went to deliver Myrtalene—"

"Yes."

"I think of this word, 'deluge.' "

"Take your time. Think about it."

Something suggested itself to Dr. Marks. "I seem to see a man carrying a child. Up some sort of mountain path. ~~He's~~ climbing rocks that look like the lines that were on the telegram. Like steps. Water's following him and he's saving the child. I see a woman half lying in the water. It's as if I were remembering something— Yes! In one of my aunts' houses in Brooklyn, there was a picture like that and I think it was even called 'The Deluge.' Something else—last night just before I went over to the Administration Building to bed, I was thinking that the floor of my office looked like a pool, like water." Water. The water he had seemed to see as a child, past the brewery dome, to the north from Meserole Street. He mentioned it, and went on: "But I don't know why I thought of that—yes, because I was thinking of myself as a child, I was a child being carried by his father."

"You mean in that picture."

"Yes."

"Being rescued from a flood. Would you please associate to 'flood' or 'deluge.' "

"Drowning, the flood in the Bible that was to punish wicked people. Death." *Castration,* Dr. Naumann thought. "Unconsciousness. I was never—I never fainted in my life that I can remember. Never lost consciousness. I always fought anything like that—anesthesia—"

"You've told me that. But it may be meaningful that just with this dream, your thoughts go to that episode of breaking your arm, that time you fought the anesthesia. Please tell me that whole story over again." He had found it useful to make the analysand go over the same material again. Often something new could be discovered. With a shift in the defenses, new facts or feelings were uncovered, and with these there was a possibility of new associations. Sometimes the gains were important.

"Well, I broke my arm, and when I got to the hospital—"

"How did you break your arm?"

There seemed a slight breath of embarrassment. "Well, it was this kid, this girl—she pushed me off a bench in school."

A girl broke his arm. Again castration, but now Dr. Naumann thought, A girl did it. Did that represent to him the castrative female, his grandmother with the whip? "Yes."

"I can't remember the name of the girl or who she was or anything about her. Can't remember her at all. I just seem to remember we were having some sort of hassle on the bench, and she gave me this big push and I fell off."

"Yes."

"Well, then when I got to the hospital—"

Dr. Marks's haste in saying this was suspect to Dr. Naumann. You get to know this kind of haste—a hurrying on that leaves things out for conscious or unconscious reasons. "Tell me—who took you to the hospital?"

Dr. Marks again betrayed embarrassment. "My father," he said. "He carried me."

Why hadn't he told this before? The soul's defenses—always operative. Dr. Naumann: "Let me understand—wasn't this during the day when he was working?"

"Oh, they telephoned the place where he had his wagon —it wasn't far away—and he was there. He came running. He just came running to the school as fast as he could, and carried me to the hospital."

"In his arms?"

"Yes."

That was an expression of fatherly love. Why had Dr. Marks been so reluctant to mention it? An almost conscious embarrassment.

But there was another interesting thing: the father in reality had been carrying the child not away from but toward the flood, the anesthesia. "And when he reached the hospital, was he with you when the nurse said surgery meant they would cut your arm off?"

"Yes, he was with me."

"He didn't correct the nurse?"

With fury: "No, you know he never explained anything. He just took me on up there."

"And what happened when you got there?"

"I've told you about that. I made a terrible scene. I wasn't letting them give me something to put me to sleep and then they'd cut off my arm or something. Finally they had to do it without giving me anything and it hurt like hell. My father held my shoulder while the doctor pulled my arm."

"Please go back to the moment when they were trying to give you the anesthetic. Would you tell me about that, please—"

The ether cone. Did they get as far as actually putting that damn cone over my face or do I imagine it? He felt himself screaming and fighting. No! "No, no, no! I don't want it. I don't want it!" His father tried to hold him down. The doctor, a nurse— "I won't! I don't want it!" He told Dr. Naumann everything. The palms of his hands were wet, and the penny he still was holding in his hand was also wet, and he put it on a small table beside the couch and wiped the palms of his hands off on his pants.

"And so they didn't give you the anesthesia."

"No, they didn't."

Now his breathing quieted. After a few moments, Dr. Naumann said, "I notice you put down that penny you were holding. You held it rather a long time."

Silence.

"What are you thinking?"

After a noticeable silence: "You know—I've told you —that I had to be taken to school. I didn't tell you that even when I was seven or eight or more, my father each morning would give me a penny to pay one of the shoemaker's sons downstairs to take me to school."

Silence.

"That's why Gus called me a sissy."

And you think about this after you reexperience the threat of anesthesia, and you stop holding the penny. The penny that makes you a girl. "I wonder why you never told me before about your father carrying you to the hospital and being there when your arm was set."

"Well, that's just details, isn't it?" As soon as he had said this, Dr. Marks realized it was transparently a defense. As he started to tell Dr. Naumann that, Dr. Naumann cut him short: "That's a defense too, philosophizing about it. Taking the treatment away from the point under discussion. I asked, Why were you unwilling or unable before to tell me all the details about your broken arm?"

"I don't know. I don't know that I had really forgotten."

"Each time you rushed your story to the hospital and avoided saying anything about what came before."

Silence.

"Your father carrying you. Running to the school because he was so concerned for you and carrying you to the hospital. Why did this bother you?"

Reluctantly: "I didn't want to acknowledge he was—he felt that way about me."

"To put it plainly—loved you."

"Loved me."

"Why do you suppose you were so disturbed about the anesthesia?"

"I told you. I thought my arm was going to be cut off."

"Was that a realistic fear? Your father may not have explained or reassured you, but the doctor did, didn't he? Didn't he tell you he was just going to set your arm?"

Hotly: "I didn't believe him."

"Most children don't make that kind of scene. Not to the point of struggling the way you did, and I've been thinking that you were struggling with a broken arm that pained you every time you moved. You endured that pain and you endured the pain of having your arm set without an anesthetic. This was far beyond the normal reaction to such a situation."

"So it was."

"You say that sullenly," Dr. Naumann said. "You're not trying to understand what went on."

"What went on?"

"May I ask you another question: Why do you think you had such sympathy for Jimmy?"

"I was like him. And he was my child—"

Silence.

'Papa, don't cut off my balls.' Dr. Marks said aloud: " *'Papa, don't cut off my balls.'* He was afraid of castration. Just as I was when they wanted to give me the anesthesia."

"Cutting off your arm 'or something.' "

Silence.

"Did Jimmy trust anybody?" Dr. Naumann asked.

"No."

All these similarities to me, Dr. Marks thought. It was true.

"There is another likeness," Dr. Naumann said.

Dr. Marks waited.

"His fear and your fear. May we examine it?" When Dr. Marks said nothing, Dr. Naumann went on: "When does anyone have the most reason to fear?"

"When what is feared is powerful, dreadful?"

"That just puts the question off. When is it powerful or dreadful?"

"I don't know. I don't know what you mean." (But beware of Naumann's riddles.)

"Jimmy had some other significant productions that you told me: *'I have Frances in me.' 'She's a man now.'* What do all these productions mean?"

"That he wanted to be a girl."

"Yes. No temptation by Mama, and Papa would love him. So when do you fear something most?"

Silence.

"When do you fear something most?"

"When you want it."

"You treated Jimmy. You treated him well. Why have you struggled so not to tell me your father carried you to the hospital, why do you suppose you haven't wanted to admit it?"

Angrily: "I hated him."

" 'Papa, don't cut off my balls.' Why did Jimmy have so much fear?"

"I always fought anything that made me passive—"

"We know that. We know the cause of that. But will you kindly tell me: Why did Jimmy have so much fear?"

Silence.

"Why did he have so much fear of castration?"

As if exhausted, Dr. Marks said, "Because he wanted it."

"And you?"

A silence of breathing. A murmur.

"What makes it so hard to admit you have that likeness to Jimmy? What gave such force to your struggle against anesthesia even when they told you it was just to set your arm? Why must you assert your own will always, if you have the least chance? Why did you put the penny down?" After a pause: "That's all," Dr. Naumann said. "The hour is over. You will remember about the wanting."

The next day, he found out in midafternoon that Myrtalene's baby had been transferred to the nursery on the Medical Ward. He telephoned Medical and got Miss Davis.

"This is Dr. Marks."

Warmly: "Hello, Dr. Marks."

"I guess you know I'm in solitary over here."

"I know. Well!"

"Look, you have a baby there."

"Oh, I guess you mean the one you delivered. A real little doll. Yes."

"How is she?"

"Wonderful, just wonderful."

"Normal?" he asked.

"Healthy as they come."

"I'd like to come over and see her. That's just between you and me, of course."

"Could you come now? I'll slip you in. What about the elevator?"

"I'll wear dark glasses."

She laughed. "Yes. Yes, you better."

When he hung up, that last sentence lingered in his mind.

Myrtalene's baby was sleeping in her white wicker basket, under the canopy of a blanket. "Isn't she a love?" Miss Davis said, standing back.

What incredibly small hands! he thought. That human hands could be so small! The head was larger proportionately and more acceptable. And the mouth. A baby seems all mouth. A baby tells all its secrets with its mouth, a mouth always working, opening, sucking or making sucking motions, a mouth that seems always speaking, silently or otherwise. Even in sleep it has a dream or sigh of motion and seems about to open.

If it could have Myrtalene's breast. He felt resentful of Naumann. I promised Myrtalene she would have "it" back. It really seemed as if she could—that moment when her rhetoric and madness dropped away.

That thing of the child's need of the mother . . .

One night lately when Margaret was out, Dr. Jones had come to give Nancy one of these children's routine protective injections (Dr. Marks always had another doctor do these things for his children). After Dr. Jones had given it, he said, "All right, good-night, Nancy."

Nancy managed to say good-night, but with such a reproachful look that Dr. Jones smiled.

After he left, Dr. Marks asked her, "Where did he give it to you?" He knew, but it would help her to tell him.

"In my hinie." Her face was still reproachful.

"Feeling better now?"

"Yes." He had a game he played with her and he thought it would be good to play it now. The idea was this little turtle named Mixmaster told his mother he was going to hide on her. Dr. Marks took the role of the little turtle and Nancy was the mother.

"I'll find you," Nancy said.

"I'll change into a ball of string."

Happily: "I'll change into a girl who finds the ball of string and flies a kite with it."

"Then I'll change into a big basket."

"I'll change into the big basket's handles," Nancy said.

"Then I'll change into some grass."

"I'll change into some rain and rain on you—rain kisses and things."

"All right," Dr. Marks said, "I'll change into nothing."

She was momentarily baffled by this so Dr. Marks whispered to her, "I'll change into next to nothing."

"I'll change into next to nothing."

Another whisper: "And be next to you."

"And be next to you."

"Then I'll change into a river," Dr. Marks said.

Now Nancy foresaw the ending of the game and on her face came a grave look of pitying condescension toward Mixmaster, the little turtle. "Then I'll change into some rocks in the river and tickle you."

"Then I'll change into a little turtle and I'll have a shell so you can't tickle me."

"Then you better not try to hide at all because that's what you are now, a little turtle."

The little turtle with all his changing hadn't been able to escape his mother's love.

His mother's love. And here this baby lay, separated from her mother's love. And the barrier between her and her mother was unreal. An imagination of the mother's mind. If Myrtalene nursed this baby, might it not bring her more moments of lucidity? "When is her next feeding?" he asked.

"Four o'clock."

"I'm wondering." He described to Miss Davis the moment when Myrtalene had held her baby. "If I could bring her baby to her now and let her nurse—"

"Nurse!"

"Yes, why not?" Miss Davis, he thought, of all the people in the hospital, would understand what he was after.

"No, that wouldn't be possible." She started to say something—

"But what's more natural than letting her nurse her baby?" he said. "It might be a way to bring her back to reality."

"You haven't had a maternity case in the hospital before," she said.

"No, I haven't."

Unhappily: "It's something about their milk. Something in their milk always makes the babies sick, always gives them diarrhea or colic. No, nobody in the hospital would let one of them nurse her baby."

One of them. As if they were outside the human pale.

"Then the responsibility," she said. "Dr. Marks, it's just a baby, no strength of its own. One move and she could hurt it. You just can't take that chance."

"But suppose that way you could give the child a mother."

"I know what you mean, and I'd say do it if it could possibly be done. But it can't. It just can't."

He said: "What'll become of this baby?"

"She'll be put out somewhere in a foster home. Until maybe Myrtalene gets better."

Until maybe Myrtalene gets better.

Back in Reception, he talked to the nurse on the ward near his office, a Miss Robechek.

"What's this thing," he said, "that a psychotic woman can't nurse her baby if she has one here in the hospital?"

"There's something in the milk."

Something in the milk.

"Sometimes the babies act like they're poisoned," she said. "I know it's hard for you to take my word for that, but believe me it happens. I've seen it. We don't even have the less disturbed mothers nurse their babies."

The following week, on rounds again, he found that Jimmy knew what day of the month it was and what day of the week it was, he knew he was a patient in a mental hospital, and he even knew what ward he was on. As soon as Dr. Marks asked him, he gave his name and faltered only when asked about his baby sister, Frances. "You know you have a sister, don't you?"

Silence.

"How old is she?"

"That was another one."

"Another what?"

"Frances."

"You know your sister's name, but don't know it's your sister. Is that right?"

Confused: "My sister?"

"Yes, your sister."

"Eddie—"

"Frances is your sister, you know that."

Silence.

The problem of sister. I was meant to be a girl. I should have been a girl. "Jimmy."

"Yeah?"

"You know Papa and Mama have Frances, and they don't want any other girl but her. You can be a boy. They love you and want you to be a boy."

"I'm the strongest."

"You're my boy."

Jimmy relaxed now.

"I only want you to be a boy," Dr. Marks said. "Boys can do things girls can't do, of course." After a moment: "How about that sister?"

"Yes."

"How old is she?"

"She's about five years old."

"She's not five, Jimmy. You know better than that."

Angrily: "How long've I been in this place?"

Mocking: "Not that long. Of course it's hard to know how long you've been here, isn't it?"

"Yes."

"How old is she?"

"One."

"Thank you, son. That's right. Do you have a comb here?"

Jimmy produced a pocket comb and Dr. Marks combed his hair for him. "You need a haircut. I'm going to leave an order in the book for you to get a haircut."

This thing about Frances, the baby sister, he had it straightened out now, but who knew what would go on in the kid's mind in the nine days between rounds? Maybe Frances would get lost again. Maybe other things would get unsettled. The kid looks good, but I ought to be working with him. Dr. Marks felt a surge of anger against the restrictions on him.

"You're getting better, kid."

"Yes," smiling.

"I'm sticking with you. I've got to go now, but I'll see you again."

"He says yes."

"You say yes."

Embarrassed. "Yes."

"All right, good-by for now. Take care."

Jimmy smiled.

Three attendants held a new male patient while Dr. Marks did a spinal tap. "Where are those blackout strips?" the patient cried as soon as he was released.

"What blackout strips?" Dr. Marks said.

The patient, a man of about thirty, had what almost amounted to a speech defect. Something that muffled his words. "Those—those bastards. They sail in there." "There" sounded like "thur."

"Who do you think 'they' are? Where are 'they'?"

Now the patient crouched back and trembled. His eyes opened wide. "In the room. In the room," he cried.

"Who?"

"R. W." He began pulling at his penis.

"Stop that," Dr. Marks said.

Some indistinct words.

"It's a good prick. You can be proud of it, you know."

The patient stopped tearing at himself. "R. W.," he said.

"What?"

Staring: "No," the patient said, "no."

If I could only talk with him, listen to him for hours, what might I not find out? Dr. Marks thought. How could any doctor not want to listen—it was so interesting. It was the finest of all labyrinths, where the Minotaur of the soul was hidden.

"Blackout strips." He felt haunted by this man even after he left him.

In the dining room. Dr. Marks overheard:

". . . one very sick one on the men's disturbed ward now."

"What's the matter? Why don't they send him to Medical?"

"Steiner's been kicking if you send anybody to Medical who isn't just about dying. This one's approaching exhaust status, but Lane says he's going to wait a day more."

At dinner Dr. Marks was heavily abstracted. "What gives with you?" Margaret said.

"Excuse me," he said. "What did you say?"

The wall clock in the men's disturbed ward said ten o'clock (P.M.). Joe Huber, the attendant on duty, had a writing pad on his knee, preparing to write a letter. On ei-

ther side of him out into the dark stretched rows of
enamel beds on which men of all ages lay sleeping. A few
refused to sleep. A mutter: "Keep that damn—" Another
voice: "Thursday. Who is this fluke or freak of nature?"
The voice called, "Joe," but Joe did not turn his head.
"Joe, let's do it. Let's sue them for every cent they got and
try to find this character. It's your life against his. Hey,
Joe?" Then a long silence. "Dear Charlie," Joe wrote, "it's
too quiet here after the insulin ward. I sure wish I was
back there. On night duty you do nothing. Eight hours of
nothing. I would rather be down there with you guys."

On the insulin ward there was something doing. You
came in and tied the patients in in the morning. You
cleaned the stairs and corridor and side rooms. And when
the doctors came in, you kidded with them. "Here's a
vein, Doc. Right here— Uh oh, you looked away that
time. You took your eye off. I got to report that to the
supervisor." And the doctors kidded back.

Not that there weren't bad moments. Patients you
played cards with and got to like died. That Benny, that
kid, we never brought him out. He thought about other
things: at lunch there were often just three of them who
had to take care of over forty patients and maybe you
couldn't coax some guy to eat. And there'd be no doctor
there to tube-feed him. Or some guy would fool you. Then
in late afternoon or in the evening, he'd fall over in shock.
You could be talking with him and right then he'd drop.

He sat smoking, the heat of the lamp drawing the
smoke up. "Hey, Joe, he's got the secrets," the voice
called. "We got to find him. You want to become famous,
don't you, Joe?" On and on. You just stopped noticing, or
you noticed only the breathing. That's how to know things
are all right, the breathing, how each one breathed. Each
one had a way.

He heard a car below on the grounds. It approached the
building. The night was cloudy and dark and with the hu-
midity, sounds carried far. He heard the motor stop. He
finished his cigarette and walked down toward the end of
the long room where the dark seemed to hang heavy
under the corrugated white ceiling. Passing the beds, he
sniffed to detect a soiling, not that he was anxious to go
through that again. Twice already tonight. He stared out
into the night, through the large windows, and saw a car
parked below.

He returned up the uneasily resting aisles and settled in his chair, but a few minutes later he heard somebody opening the stairs door. Who could that be at this time of night?

Now the same somebody was unlocking the ward door, and a large, heavy-set man entered. He wore dark glasses, but took them off as he came forward.

"Hello," Joe said.

"Hello. You alone on duty here?" The man spoke with authority.

"Lingman is on the side rooms."

"Uh huh." Taking out a pack of cigarettes: "Cigarette?"

"Thanks."

"I'm Dr. Marks."

"Dr. Marks. The one cured somebody over in Medical? And got in trouble?"

By this attendant I cured somebody, Dr. Marks thought. By the staff, I didn't cure anybody. "What's your name?" he asked.

"Joe Huber."

"You surprised at seeing a doctor here?"

"Some."

"I understand you have a case here with fever and excitement."

"Yeah, Tommy Kupfer. He's got a fever all right. He ought to be in Medical. That's just my opinion."

"The kid I cured in Medical had fever and excitement. How old is Tommy?"

"About twenty-two."

"You like him?"

Joe glanced down the room. "I like him."

Dr. Marks let smoke out along the stem of his cigarette holder. He said, "You ever listen to these nuts?"

"Sure, I listen to them all the time."

Of course, Dr. Marks thought. He has to. Nurses can protect themselves behind attendants, doctors can hide behind nurses, but the attendant has to be there all the time. "What about what they say?"

"How do you mean?"

"You think what they say means anything?"

"Yeah, it means something. But you gotta know what it means."

Somewhat taken aback, Dr. Marks said, "How's that?"

"Well, like Jonesy. He'll lay there in the corner and say,

'Keep away. I got a bad body. Very bad.' Then he'll shake
—like tremble. Well, one day he was laying there and I
tried to get him up and he was shaking and he said, 'Don't
take my body. Your body's all right yet—honest. I got a
bad body.' So I figure what he's afraid of is that like
somebody wants to get into his body and if he can convince them he's got a bad body, he'll be safe."

"Suppose we were to tell him we could keep these people out of him—off him." After a pause: "Of course, it
isn't real, what he's afraid of. What do you think he's
really afraid of?"

"There's a guy keeps coming on about some man with
secrets who's going to kill everybody."

"Yes. Who's he really afraid of?"

"Atom secrets," a voice said, rising spectrally. "Joe,
you want to become famous? We got to find him. It's him
or you, Joe. I give you the warning through the newspapers. Don't say I didn't."

"That goes on every night."

"And he's afraid," Dr. Marks said.

"Sometimes he talks like he don't care one way or the
other. 'Hey, Joe, he's got the secrets. He's got all them
controls. Let's take off on him.' But other times he shits
his pants. He hangs onto the bottom rail of the nearest
bed and shits."

"He ever hard to handle?"

"Sure."

"Tell me, you ever hit a patient?" Dr. Marks asked.

"I come close to it. But I tell myself, they don't know
what they're doing. And I light a cigarette. That helps.
No, I never hit one. *I* didn't."

"I know it happens. I wasn't asking you about that. I
just wanted to know how you feel about them."

"I feel all right."

"You afraid of them at all?"

"Oh, no, I'm not afraid."

Serious: "You mean you're really not afraid?"

"Oh, you got to be careful. I don't say you don't. You
got to watch. But you get a kinda sense. Like the only
time I been hurt by a patient. I had this kinda sixth sense
and turned and seen this chair coming at me. I pulled back
so it just caught me a little in the lip, but it give me a cut
there, and this guy, his name was Henry, right away he
said, 'Oh it's you, Joe,' and he began to cry. I told him I

had to go to Medical to see about it, and all the time I was gone, he was crying."

"That's the only time you were hurt."

"Yeah. Something like that hardly ever happens."

"Does it get on your nerves when they keep talking? Like this atom secrets stuff?"

"Sometimes. If it gets too much, I don't listen."

"How do you mean?"

"Ah, shut my ears. You know."

"Joe," the voice called, "you want to be famous?"

"You got any kids?"

"Two. Boy and girl."

"I have three. Two boys and a girl."

"Makes a nice family."

Dr. Marks said, "Tell me, doctors ever come here and talk with the patients?"

"Well, yes. They come in sometimes and talk."

"How much?"

"Not much. Oh, they come and see if a patient's improving sometimes. I tell them or a nurse tells them the patient's improving. They want to see that, see how the patient is. Maybe he should be put on a better ward. Even discharged—that they like."

"Otherwise?"

"Not much. A kind of check now and then."

"A kind of check?"

"Yes, you know. Just go through."

"A doctor ever stay with a patient and talk with him for an hour?"

"Never."

"Two hours, three hours?"

Joe was smiling.

"Four hours. Twelve hours. Sixteen hours?"

"Who'd do that?"

"I did it with Jimmy Cady. I had to, so I did. You ever feel like a patient was your child? Or say, a relative? It ever come into your mind it might be a relative?"

Mildly: "I guess maybe I have thought that."

"I believe I can help this Tommy Kupfer."

"I like him," Joe said.

"I'm not supposed to be here. I guess you know that. I walked up the stairs, didn't take the elevator. Nobody knows I'm here. Where's the night nurse?"

"She's in her office on the floor below. She has the two floors."

"Does she come up here?"

"Nah, she won't be up."

"The doctor?"

"That's Dr. Lane. He comes up around midnight. He won't be up before then, maybe not then."

"It's safe till midnight?"

"It's safe."

"Suppose I could save Tommy Kupfer's life. Work with him, treat, talk and listen a long time—hours—bring his fever down like I did Jimmy and Ethel. You know what'll happen if the fever doesn't come down?"

"I know."

"I'd like to try."

"Why don't you go ahead, Doc?"

Both of them were looking the length of the room. Dr. Marks said, "Good. You know anything about him?"

"He's a schizo, you know. I think he went to high school. He ain't dumb. He wasn't so bad there for a while, but two weeks ago he blew up. He had a fifteen-round boxing match with somebody he called Peppy—" Pappy? Dr. Marks thought "—and that laid him out. Hughie, one of the boys on day duty, told me about it. They were all laughing like hell about him, even a couple of patients were laughing."

"What family's he got?"

"Father and sister. They was all living together. Then he was in the Army—you hear him talking, you know he's been in the Army. He got discharged as a 'psycho,' then he was living home again and he got a job. But then he had a row with his father and cracked up again."

"You know this much about most of the patients here?"

"Oh, you get to know them."

Dr. Marks put out his cigarette. "There's this Lingman outside, on the side rooms. He likely to look in here?"

"Pretty likely." Smiling, "But he won't see anything if you can get him a bottle of whiskey—"

"I can bring it. I'll bring one for you too."

"Nah, you don't have to bribe me."

Dr. Marks pressed his arm and said, "Let's see this kid."

They walked down the middle aisle and came to a bed that revealed only a gross shape. The boy's arms were folded over his breast, inside the straitjacket. His face was in shadow. Was he asleep? No, there was a steady trembling of the whole body that shook the bed. Joe took a flashlight from his belt and snapped it on. The light picked out an open-eyed, hollow, elongated face. The boy's jaw moved to the side repeatedly in a tic or stereotypy. The small frame of light gleamed on his forehead, which seemed dry.

Silence.

"Here I go." Very low, shuddering: "Down." Tommy's arms pressed hard at their bands.

"Down where?" Dr. Marks said.

"You bastard. Clear out! I had that one in the Midway kennels, pushed her right over. You got no gun." Still trembling: "I got the stick, you hear? I'm climbing. *I see her down there*. She's floating. Here I go! I have her centered. Here I go! Here I go!" Tommy screamed the same volumeless ghost scream as Jimmy, and his shoulders pitched wildly as Dr. Marks held him.

12

Three months later, on the couch: "I dreamed I was in a house like the one Robert has, and I went through a door there and somewhere in a nearby passage I had to get through a very narrow place. I had my coat on, and first I felt I ought to take it off, but I didn't. I pushed around a narrow corner and then I had to get through a still narrower space where I'd have to slide downward and sideways. Margaret was visible beyond this space, and I asked her if I could get through. She wouldn't say and I woke up before I actually tried.

"That's the dream. About the coat—the night before last I came home from the hospital at two o'clock, and I had a kind of momentary collapse. I sat down on a chair in the bedroom, and Margaret knew something was the matter and got up and helped me take off my coat, and she was going to help me undress, but then I felt better and was able to undress myself. Then she wanted me to have some hard-boiled eggs——"

Hard-boiled eggs, that went back to his courtship. He had met Margaret at his brother's when he was just beginning to practice medicine. It was near the start of the Depression—those Depression thirties. Robert had called him professionally. He had hiccoughed for a day and a half. So he had called John for his rather ridiculous malady, and John, the young doctor, had arrived with his small black bag. And Margaret, a school friend of Robert's wife, Lisa, had been there. A sedative cured the hiccoughs, and John had his eye on Margaret, and he suggested that the four of them go for a drive around Prospect Park. It was a warm fall evening and that was how it began; the curving park roads, the softness of the dying trees and the dying light, and this lithe and pleasant young woman.

With a glint of easy mockery in her eyes.

He had made a date with her. They had had some kind of argument about whether Syracuse would beat Columbia in football, so they made a date to go to the football game, and she bet a necktie against a pair of stockings—

Naumann (at the second session): "A necktie."

"Well, she lost. She had to give me the necktie, so she sent it in the mail. Then I didn't see her for a few weeks."

"Did you like the necktie?"

"I don't remember. That was a long time ago. Well, I had an Auburn roadster, that was what I drove her in that first night, but ordinarily part of the time I had this colored chauffeur, Roy. He was a young colored boy, he was from the neighborhood, and he just sort of— He had a chauffeur's cap and he wanted to drive this sporty Auburn for the doc, so I said, 'Fine, Roy, you can have the job.' And sometimes he drove me and sometimes he didn't. He got eight dollars a week. That was the Depression; that was back when I got twenty-five cents a call. So about three weeks after this football date Roy was driving me, and didn't I see Margaret in the street! In front of her house! This was a sports car, so to ride in the back I had to ride in the rumble seat, so there I was, some class, with my chauffeur with his chauffeur's cap, and I told Roy to pull in to the curb. I was sure showing off, only getting out I tripped off the mudguard where that— I came tumbling down flat on my face, but Margaret behaved with considerable dignity. She wanted to laugh, but she didn't. She didn't even snicker. After that, we began to go out together regularly."

He had liked her father a lot. An extremely kind, considerate, unaggressive man.

He began going there for dinner three or four or five nights a week. He had some dubious thoughts about her Victorian-type mother—so insecure behind her controls—but she could cook. She was hospitable in her way. So he got to be the regular caller, played chess with the old man until he went to bed, then necked with Margaret in the living room till five or five thirty in the morning (always wanting to go further, but the old man might come downstairs and anyway you were proper in those days). Each morning he stumbled back to his office-apartment and caved in till nine o'clock when his office hours started.

But the thing about the hard-boiled eggs. Whenever he

was hungry, Margaret rushed him some. "She wasn't a cook, God knows, but she fed me."

Naumann noted his seeming to make fun of his courtship.

They had been engaged two years, and that had been a rather long time for the state of feeling between them. But it had been the Depression. He had had to get his practice established. Or perhaps it was a streak of final caginess, the last protest of the male.

When he was away sometimes, he wrote her and this was the ultimate tribute, for he hated writing. He found later that she had kept all his letters.

Their marriage night made up somewhat for the long wait. Again there was no sleep that night, but the hours were well occupied. Margaret was quick, ready, and had no inhibitions about showing her pleasure. That first night, the neighbors might easily have thought she was getting murdered. (They started their marriage at his place on Ocean Avenue because he had to be in his office the following morning at nine o'clock, come what may.)

But the hard-boiled eggs. "I don't know why Margaret still has that thing about them because she sure got to be a good cook. Maybe it's love. But I think she thinks hard-boiled eggs are especially good for me."

Silence.

"But to go back to the night before last. She gave me the business then about how I'm overworking, and I'm going to kill myself and so on. She's been having a pretty rough time lately. She even said, 'You don't play poker anymore,' like that's the end. I know I'm overworking, but I can't help it. Lugano last week—I see him dying, don't I have to do something about it? And can I help it if I have to do it after my regular hospital work? It's that insanity of the hospital. To save a life, you have to do it at night, moonlighting."

"I'm not distracted by your light tone," Dr. Naumann said. "Let us return to your dream about the coat and the narrow space and Margaret. You don't often dream about your wife—"

"That's usual, isn't it?"

"It makes it more meaningful when you do. You've given me some associations to your coat. Do you have any more?"

"Well, you take off your coat to have a fight. But I

didn't have any thought about fighting in the dream. This narrow space and Margaret, that might suggest intercourse, but so why would I want it? I'd just had it. I don't think it was intercourse, I think it was birth. It was 'sliding downward.' At least three of my patients at the hospital showed they had thoughts of being reborn, to be more acceptable to their parents. God knows I want to be more acceptable to my parents—at any rate, that's what comes out here."

Silence.

"I was reborn in one way."

Silence.

"And that had to do with Margaret. She gave me a father who accepted me, her own father."

Dr. Naumann recognized the truth of this. Dr. Marks had told him a great deal about Henry Alexander, Margaret's father. Henry Alexander was a top official in the Board of Education when Dr. Marks first knew him—he later retired. He had been an orphan and was largely self-taught, he had had to fight for an education, and so when he established himself as a civic leader in Brooklyn, it had been with a special interest in the school system. Some of the current improvements in Brooklyn schools were due to him. He was also on the board of the Borough Federation of Charities. He was widely and popularly honored, but he was curiously aloof and had few close friends. This may be why he developed so deep an attachment to Dr. Marks as a son-in-law. He told Margaret her husband was "a genius" and would "do something someday." This feeling he had for his son-in-law was in marked contrast with the feeling Dr. Marks got from his own parents.

"She gave me a father who accepted me, her own father." So he was reborn.

"I have another idea why I dreamed this dream," Dr. Marks went on. "I knew that collapse I had where Margaret had to take off my coat made her think about Henry's dying."

Her father died three years ago. On the day of his death Henry had walked a long time at the World's Fair, and that night he came over to Dr. Marks's apartment—he lived near them—and Margaret noticed that he was pale. He had had a coronary previously, so the pallor wasn't good, but he played a game of chess with Dr. Marks and then insisted on walking home alone. He walked the few blocks to the lobby of his house and fell dead.

When Dr. Marks was called and came and pronounced his father-in-law dead, he wept. Dr. Naumann knew—Dr. Marks had told him—that this was the only time in his adult life that he had wept publicly.

"Go on," Dr. Naumann said.

"I sometimes think I feel a tremor in my own heart, but it evidently isn't anything except plain fatigue. I had a checkup at the hospital last week, and my heart is all right —I didn't tell you about this checkup, I know. What I ought to do is take it easier for a while, but I can't."

"I can't" means "I won't," Dr. Naumann thought.

"My father wants me to let up—he wants me stop entirely. Go back to being a 'real doctor.' Just last week he said to me, 'They're probably better off the way they were, before you did anything.' And now I'm going to sell my office equipment. You can imagine the screams there are going to be: 'You're giving this up for this crazy business?' The X-ray machine and the fluoroscope that moves vertically to horizontally by electric motor that I 'saved and saved' to buy, the diathermy machine, the examining table, the sterilizer, the waiting-room furniture—everything."

"Why are you selling all your equipment?"

"I need the money. But mainly I don't want any temptation to go back to my medical practice."

So you are tempted still to please your father. "These patients at the hospital who want to be reborn, why do they think they're not acceptable to their parents?"

"They're worthless—"

"Why worthless?"

Why am I worthless, why was I so scorned as a child? Dr. Marks thought. And even now? I'm stubborn. I want my own way. Flickering over that thought was a further thought: "These patients at the hospital, so many of them believe everything would be all right if they could be reborn a different sex. They'll do anything, undergo any suffering, hope for any miracle—they all believe in miracles—if they can just please Mama or Papa."

"Whom mainly, Mama or Papa?"

"They, Mama. I, Papa."

"Are you sure?"

"Of course I'm sure." But as soon as he had said this, he began to wonder.

"The hour is up," Dr. Naumann said. He stood and quietly waited as Dr. Marks went out.

*   *   *

That night, Margaret and he were having a pre-Thanksgiving party at the apartment. Dr. Arthur Chandler, a former colleague at The Vansittart Clinic, came early. He asked Dr. Marks, "How's your edible daughter, Nancy?"

" 'Edible—' Oh, you remember that story."

Nancy was very fond of ice cream. One day Bob asked her, "Do you like ice cream more than Johnny?" "Yes," she said. "Do you like it more than me?" She still said "Yes," so he asked her, "Do you like it more than Daddy?" and at this crucial question, she hesitated, but finally said truthfully, "Yes."

"Obviously still at the edible level," Dr. Marks had said. He said now to Dr. Chandler, "She's been developing very nicely. She even seems to understand something about my work, when I talk about it."

Dr. Chandler entered the living room and sprawled his heavy length out on the sofa. "Bill Widener's been telling me about some secret work you're doing at the hospital, treating acute catatonics."

"I told him, but I told him I hope nobody at the hospital knows, not that I'm absolutely sure they don't."

"It will go no further with me. But tell me about it."

Dr. Marks described what he had been doing, telling first about Jimmy and Ethel. "Those were real acute catatonics, in exhaust status. I mean it was obvious and uncontrovertible. The ones I've done since had to be ones that hadn't yet clearly gone into exhaust status or they would have had to be sent to Medical. But on all of mine, the excitement and fever had begun and the terror was there, all over the place. By me they were all acute catatonics, though Staff would argue the diagnosis possibly. If they had seen them before I treated them. After I got them out, obviously by Staff there had been no acute excitement."

"How many have you treated?"

"Sixteen."

"How many have recovered?"

"All of them who haven't had more shock—they're all out of psychosis or on their way out. Fourteen."

"But that's a lot in three months."

"They come out pretty fast, some of them. None of them takes very long. That's the thing, they have to get better or die. It's a very special thing, apparently."

"Special. You think less than acute excitement would be different?"

"Very possibly. These are screaming for help—wide open. As soon as you relieve the fear, the recovery is rapid."

"So you just do that one thing," Dr. Chandler said. "You haven't worked with any other type of case?"

"No. If I was taking that risk, it had to be for patients who might die."

"I can see what you mean." Dr. Chandler seemed to brood. "You said you aren't absolutely sure it isn't known at the hospital, what you're doing?"

"Suppose it is known. Suppose somehow it has gotten to Steiner—that could happen. It's conceivable. In that case, the bastard hasn't wanted to make an issue of it, hasn't wanted to face up to it. He'd have to say all these recoveries are meaningless, and that's hard to do. So officially nothing is known."

"Still, you're living dangerously there."

Dr. Marks shrugged.

"Do you think—"

They were interrupted as Margaret brought in the Mandels and the Rutledges who had arrived together. Ted Rutledge was one of the patients from his medical practice who had become a friend. His wife, Linda, was a bow-lipped, rather innocent person. Ruth Mandel was a cousin, a real A-1 ego, and her husband, Harvey, was an awkward man with a deep-troughed face, a good, kind man. That was what got the Ruth Mandels of this world.

"Nancy wants her good-night kiss," Margaret whispered to him. "Maybe you could go now." He excused himself to the others and went to Nancy's room.

She was sitting up in bed, looking rather sober. Reproof. "It's a little cool," he said. "You take care of yourself. Button up that pajama top."

Since she didn't move or answer, he sat down beside her and buttoned the buttons himself with his blunt fingers. He thought of how he buttoned up Jimmy Cady's shirt.

"Daddy."

"Yes?"

"You gowaway all the time."

"I have sick people to take care of. I *have* to take care of them."

"But you gowaway every day."

"Not every day. I'm here today."

No happy reaction to that.

"I have to take care of those sick people," he said.

"Why?"

"They might die."

"But you won't let them, will you?"

"I won't let them," he said.

"Can anybody die?" She was casual, but the question wasn't casual, for her or him. When you talked to a child about death, you had to be very careful. He had had an example of it (of not being careful) just lately, from Jimmy.

In the depth of the psychosis, Jimmy had kept saying "trap" and "anzel—angel—" When he had been a child, it seemed he too had asked about dying, and his father's sister had told him "angels come for you and take you up to heaven." To make it real good, she added, "They might come any time for anybody. They might even come and take *you* up to heaven." That same night he woke screaming with a nightmare. When his mother came in, she found him looking over the side of the bed. He thought there were traps there "to catch the angels" and save him. He had to be saved. Somebody or something had to save him. Jimmy: Angels are coming for me because I'm guilty of incestuous desire for my mother and I deserve to die. *'I'm a puzzle.' 'It's awful.'*

His own child kneeled before him, exposed and waiting, only apparently casual. He had to be careful with this life. Margaret had to be careful with it. "You gowaway all the time," as if guardedly saying, "Why do you go away? Don't you love me? Perhaps I don't deserve to be loved." And now death suggests itself to this child.

"Dying usually happens after you've lived a long time. When you're old. It's like resting."

"Are they old, at the hospital?"

"No. So that's why I'm trying not to let them die. I'm taking care of them."

"But could they die, Daddy?"

"They might."

Cautiously: "Could I die?"

"I won't let you. I love you too much. Now you'd better

get under the covers." Obediently she got under them and he kissed her and said good-night. But going back to the living room, he asked himself, Did I handle it right? Well, perhaps it was all beyond conscious precaution. Perhaps there was nothing—nothing important anyway—that didn't communicate itself unconsciously, for better or worse.

He met Harvey, who was standing at the small desk just outside the living-room door, reading a postcard. "Q to KB5—what's that?" Harvey asked.

"My next move in a tight chess game I'm playing with your cousin-in-law Steve Marks of Denver."

Harvey nodded, smiling. His eyes were gentle. His nose was bent and injured, but attractive. (The thought occurred to Dr. Marks that the nose disfigurement might be a result of forceps. Birth.) Bill Widener (Dr. William Widener) and his wife, Alice, came in and greeted everybody. Bill was a rose-colored MD of thirty-two who was taking some of the same courses with Dr. Marks at The Psychoanalytic Institute. A nice guy and very sharp, as Freudian in his way as Naumann, and a good foil to Arthur Chandler. Dr. Marks said, "So you told Arthur what I've been doing at the hospital."

"Yes, but I warned him to keep it quiet."

"I trust Arthur."

Linda Rutledge asked, "What have you been doing? Please tell us."

"All right, I've already told Arthur some of it." Once he had determined to tell them, it was like a catharsis and it all poured out. Jimmy and Ethel, murder-in-law and God. Climbing to the men's disturbed ward at night, removing his dark glasses, and walking down the aisle of beds. To Tommy Kupfer, to Sullivan, to a succession of cases like echoes of one another. "In all, I've done sixteen of these cases," he said.

"Remarkable," Harvey said.

"Have you noticed any change as you go on?" Ted asked from the sofa beside Dr. Chandler. "Do you do it better?"

There was Lugano last week. This man took his hand and held it as the words rushed out. "Dee, dee, unnerstan'. Dee. I take her in a church . . ." The strong pressure of the hand, repeated and repeated. "No. Please. Dee. Where the blude come." Fountainous Italian scattered itself among fragments of English, and the hand pressed and pressed.

"He was out of psychosis in half an hour. My hand was a mess. I felt as if we'd been in a dream together and woke up together."

"Out of psychosis? That's rather a statement," Dr. Chandler said.

"By me he was out of psychosis. He never went back in as far as I could tell."

"He really had catatonic excitement, you believe?"

"His temperature was over a hundred and four before I started. I took it. We took it."

" 'We?' " Linda asked.

"The attendant and I."

"But what's really the matter with them all?" Ruth wanted to know. With her tone, he felt on guard.

"Fear."

"You said that."

"I mean that." He put a cigarette into his cigarette holder.

"But what did this Italian fear? Did you understand what he said enough to know?"

"Evidently. I caught on that like Jimmy he feared castration, but it was something technically called *vagina dentata* he feared. I could spell out the productions. It's no use, it's something you wouldn't understand *or* believe. But we must have communicated and I must have been able to explain things to him and reassure him because he recovered."

"John," Dr. Chandler said, "you have this enthusiasm, which is good, but how can you be so sure about this interpretation thing. Aren't there a great many possible meanings for any single production, just as there are for any single element of a dream?"

"That's a fair question. But they tell you the same thing over and over. If you lose it one moment, you find it again the next. They keep on telling you."

"They seem to tell *you*, all right."

"That deserves a break." Getting to his feet: "Margaret, how about drinks?" Margaret began to serve drinks. She was wearing a red dress. He had on his coat. He felt like taking it off and remembered his dream of the night before. A coat was unimportant, but Freud says the dream memory recalls "subordinate and disregarded things."

Those around him began joking. Harvey was telling Arthur about a dream of his, and Linda was laughing. In the distance a plane throbbed and receded. "John, what do you say it (Harvey's dream) means?"

Laughing: "Ask Bill."

"When you gonna play some tennis?"

"Come on, he can't play tennis. No handle to his racket."

Margaret returned with the drinks, and gradually the general talk quieted, and Dr. Widener said, "John, going back to this thing, you say these patients of yours are dying of fear, just fear?"

"You ought to see them—"

"What accounts for the intensity of the fear?" Dr. Chandler asked. "I mean, why do you think some patients go into catatonic excitement and not others?"

"Possibly some had to take more. Maybe some are more archaic in the Unconscious than others."

"More 'archaic'! I don't buy that. What makes you think that—Jung?"

"No, Freud. Maybe I'm wrong, but in *Totem and Tabu*, he suggests the Unconscious of savages is different from ours—at least it's less controlled and needs more barriers. So tabus set up an automatic punisher, even an executioner—in the savage's mind. Jimmy and other patients at the hospital have had a mild psychosis compared with what Freud describes in *Totem and Tabu*." He told about the Pakeha Maori warrior who ate from a chief's table without knowing it and when he found out what he had done (he had violated a strong tabu), this perfectly healthy young man died in a matter of hours, just collapsed and died. "That's an instantaneous psychosis. Fear killed him."

Dr. Chandler picked up from an end table near the sofa a small tan ceramic donkey out of whose back a plant was growing. The plant had two half-dead leaves and Dr. Chandler inspected these leaves. Margaret, Dr. Marks thought, always getting these plants and not giving them enough water. Sometimes, in irritation, he'd get a glass of water and water the plants himself.

"All right, it's fear that kills them," Dr. Chandler said, setting down the donkey. "And what saves them is what you do psychoanalytically, right?"

"I'd say so."

"Bill, what do you think of all this?"

"This term 'psychoanalytically.' " Turning to Dr. Marks: "It's not *analysis,* what you do."

"You mean there's no free association."

"No free association, and without that—"

Dr. Marks said, "I wonder if the patients' productions aren't some kind of free association. I've talked with Margaret about it. They wander along any way they want, jump from one thing to another. But actually—this is the point—you don't need free association, you don't need it at all. The whole Unconscious is right out in the open there anyway. All resistances are gone, or almost gone. It's all there to see."

"It sounds easy," Dr. Chandler said.

Dr. Marks shifted in his chair and said, "In a way it *is* easy. Freud said understanding the Unconscious hadn't turned out to be as hard as he expected. That's in the Dora case. He said nobody can keep a secret. No, the thing that stops you from understanding is your own resistances."

"Your own resistances are important."

"I couldn't agree more." (How long I waited to get the first clue to Jimmy!)

"All right, that's association," Dr. Widener said, straightening up, "and I don't give it to you. Now what about transference?"

"I'm sorry—transference—" Ted said. "What's that mean?"

"It means you transfer to a present person feelings you had long ago, as a child. Hate or love, confidence or fear. Feelings you have toward a parent or sibling, toward somebody meaningful in your life." He breathed some smoke over these feelings so barely and clinically evoked.

Dr. Widener: "Psychotics certainly can't transfer in that sense."

"I know," Dr. Marks said, "that's why I create the transference myself—"

"But transference has to develop spontaneously—"

"In neurosis—"

"And then it has to be interpreted out of existence," Dr. Widener said, finishing what he was saying.

"I interpret it into existence."

Dr. Chandler began to laugh. When he laughed, his mouth rounded like a baby's. In this baby mouth, his tongue lifted like a gigantic palate and made his laughing both sardonic and innocent. "Well, it seems you do everything just the opposite," he said.

"The condition is just the opposite, isn't it? In neurosis, the Unconscious is repressed. In psychosis, it's exposed with almost no repression. The job in neurosis is to get rid of repression. In psychosis, the job is to restore it. You could put it another way. In neurosis, the patient is out of touch with his Unconscious and in touch with reality. In psychosis—full-blown psychosis—he's out of touch with reality and in touch with his Unconscious."

"Damn, you've got something. He's got something, Bill."

"I withdraw from this discussion. I'm just listening now," Dr. Widener said. "Just put me down for one big reservation."

"This business of interpretation—" Dr. Chandler started.

"I know. I've heard the same thing from Naumann," Dr. Marks said. "You can't interpret or you'll upset the repressions. But the psychotic hardly has any repressions."

"Why do you interpret?"

Dr. Marks raised his arms slightly in a gesture that meant self-reassurance. "Try to suppose you're Jimmy and I tell you I'm your father. You don't believe me, you have no reason to. But now you say, 'Don't cut off my tongue,' and I say, 'I know you're afraid I'm going to cut off your prick, son, but I'm not going to do it.' Then you see that I know your secrets, and you begin to believe I'm your father."

Dr. Chandler flicked his fingers. "But there are always things you don't know. You didn't know what this angel trap business meant until Jimmy told you."

"I admit there are always things you don't know. But Jimmy was afraid of the angels because he was afraid he'd die. Be castrated. If I don't understand the angels, I understand heads and tongues being cut off." He smiled: "Or if I'm too dumb, Jimmy knows it and tells me in plain English."

"You win."

Ruth said, "What's this?" She was staring down at a small green turtle in a round glass bowl. The turtle had its head drawn back into a single wrinkle like a green and red muffler.

"That's Mixmaster," Dr. Marks said. "Nancy and I have

a game about a little turtle so we had to get her one. It's a pet."

"She probably loves it."

"Very much."

"Ugh," Ruth said. "Do you get the child everything she wants?"

Dr. Chandler grasped his arm and drew him down on the sofa beside him. "I want to talk with you."

"Yes?"

"I've been thinking about you, since what you said tonight—about all this." Margaret came and sat with them. Dr. Chandler: "Yes, you listen to this too, Margaret." To Dr. Marks: "How long do you intend to keep on treating these patients this way?"

"As long as they're sick."

"That's endless. Do you see any chance of a change in the staff attitude?"

"None at all. Oh, Dr. Rossman started a personal analysis and I think he'd like to do something. But probably he'll just leave the hospital. A few others are having analysis. I don't know which ones. It's considered damaging to have it known. So you could say a few of them are making a start, but change the general situation there? No."

"Then you're in a serious spot, you know it? You looking forward to taking the Boards in psychiatry?"

"Yes, I am now."

"You run a danger at New State that you may never get to take Boards. I have a suggestion. New State isn't the only place you can work. You could possibly do your work at The Psychiatric Research Center and not run up against the official block you've got there at New State. It's freer at the Center. It's a big endowed place. Plenty of funds for training and research and not as rigid, I believe. I think it might be a good idea for you to look into it. Of course I wouldn't go there and say I'm going to cure acute catatonics—"

"No no," Dr. Marks said quickly.

"I'm not even sure they'd have any exhaust-status cases. They have only a relatively few patients, selected on the basis of interest for research."

Myrtalene. Florence. "Well, you know I was telling you before that all I've really done so far are these cases that all follow the same pattern, the same screaming for help,

'I'm dying.' All approaching exhaust status, all with fever. What I'd like to do is something different, a more usual case, say the cases I keep seeing by the hundreds on rounds. I wouldn't mind full-blown insanity, but not acute."

"I see what you mean. You might very well get a chance at that there. I'm not guaranteeing it."

"I know you can't guarantee anything," Dr. Marks said.

"But it might be a solution for you. Go in on a residency and you'll still be using your time toward the Boards."

Dr. Marks glanced at his wife. "You might have something," he said.

"Meantime, let up a little. You could get yourself into real trouble there at New State."

Let up a little. Margaret was much too responsive to that. That would mean he'd have more time at home. Less strain. But that would mean letting patients die. Try watching these patients and (if you were like him) see if you could consign them to death.

As Dr. Widener was leaving, he said to Dr. Marks, "No hard feelings."

"I'm on your side, Bill. You just don't know it yet."

When the door had closed behind the last guest, Dr. Marks looked at the time. Almost one. Earlier in the day, Joe Huber had told him that there was a patient on the ward showing increasing excitement, an older man—Fischer. He had a momentary impulse to go to the hospital now, but he knew it was impossible. Leave Margaret after the party? Still he had that terrible pull.

Margaret was walking back from the door, toward the bedroom. Okay. He noticed that very nice curve of her red skirt as she leaned to put out a lamp.

13

The next morning as he sat at breakfast, he studied a chess game he was playing by mail with Dr. Howard Pierce of Washington. This was the friend who had believed the orphan girl walking with an attendant on Fifth Avenue had a mother. Dr. Pierce was a good player, and his latest move, just arrived by postcard, Kt to KR4, was giving Dr. Marks some trouble.

"Less noise, you kids."

I can play chess, he thought. Does that have anything to do with thinking ahead of patients?

He had three games going now by mail: Steve, Howard, and a game with a former colleague now in Chicago. He was losing two games out of three, which was not usual.

Well, he was tired. It would have done him good to sleep later this morning.

Fischer, he dreaded starting with him tonight.

He went to the living room to the piano. It was a Saturday, the kids were home and would come if he started playing. Good. He needed them, needed that much relaxation. But watch the time. He had arranged to see Lugano before he started his day's blood counts. He'd worked out a thing with the attendant on the ward where Lugano was now (Lugano'd been taken off Joe's ward) to let him in if he got there before nine.

He opened his book of melodic notations and began pounding away. "Walk into Jerusalem just like John." Lugano, still gripping his hand like mad. Depending on him. And holding his gains. He heard running feet and the kids burst in. "Come on, get with it," he said and they quickly found their places and began to sing.

When they had sung four or five songs, he said, glancing at his watch, "Well, that's it, guys."

"No—more, more," Nancy cried.

"Sorry," he said, getting up. "I have to go." Margaret who had come in said, "Where?"

"To the hospital. I told you I had to go in early today."

"This early? Saturday?"

How a woman's face could change, he thought. Anger. Just that fractional thinning of the lips, just that fractional narrowing of the eyes, and the same face became a different face. "If you have something to say about it, come out in the hall," he said.

They went into the hall and the kids remained standing awkwardly around the piano.

"All right," he said.

With those narrowed eyes: "How long did you spend with the kids?"

"Fifteen minutes." He said it calmly and deliberately.

"Fifteen minutes," she said in a fury. "And you say it like that! And Nancy wanted you to stay." The edges of the lips, that's where it showed. That convulsive change.

He said, "The last two nights I've been home. I was here all last evening."

"Oh!" Catching her breath: "No, no you weren't here last night," she said. "No, I think you're mistaken about that. You were at the hospital."

A fair crack, he had to admit. "So."

Now she said, as if it had been saved and was ready to throw at him: "I guess I could expect it. You never considered us when you played tennis or poker, when you wanted to go off with Harvey or Ted for a weekend fishing. Now I shouldn't expect anything different."

He felt the justice of what she said. What he had done in the past with his male independence made what he did now harder to take. She had been good. She had understood his needs at the hospital even if they were at a certain remove from her, but he knew the strain had been building—it was taking him away from her, it was exposing him to overwork and exhaustion, threats of dying (like her father).

"The kids know I love them. You see anything unhealthy about them? I gave them some time—"

"Give them an hour, John."

He started to put on his topcoat. "I have to be at Lugano's ward before nine to get in."

"Arthur told you, if you keep on like this—"

He continued buttoning his coat.

Threateningly: "If you go—"

"Yes?"

Now he saw that she would cry: it would be one of the few times she did. Disregarding it, he went out the door and left.

He did not come home until two o'clock in the morning. Fischer had had a discordant face, loosely held together like a puzzle. That looseness of the jaw. Tomorrow night he might pull that face together.

Reaching home, he found Margaret deeply asleep. Now that he was gone many nights, she no longer stayed partially awake for him. She slept for herself. Seeing the soft curve of her body, seeing her in the defenselessness of deep sleep, he regretted what had happened that morning. Perhaps he could have been more diplomatic. He had not been able to. It was an incapacity he found it hard to cope with. "Never give in to an adult?"

She had been helping him recently. He took notes during treatment, scribbling in a notebook. It was the only way to get the exact productions, and Naumann insisted that he get them. "How can I treat if I'm doing that?" he said. "You can treat," Naumann said. And it was true he could. The patient seemed not to mind his taking notes. He had been amazed when, in the middle of a long "word salad," one of his patients said, "Write that down." What part of the mind had spoken out of the psychosis and said, in a completely normal voice, "Write that down"?

This Fischer tonight. He had taken pages of Fischer. He emptied the wads of notes out on the dresser. Tomorrow Margaret would type them for him.

As he got into bed, her soft breathing touched his shoulder. Some part of her now knew that he was here, he thought. He was too tired to sleep. A reddish light shimmered behind his eyelids. In that unreal light, he saw Fischer again, and recalled something that had happened. As the man's terror got less, he had kept examining his right forefinger as if to reassure himself that it was there.

Finger, tongue, head—the castrative link.

"Darling?" he said.

"Mmmmmmm?" He liked the easy way she woke, at the least word. "Would you want to write something for me?" he said. "I'm too dead tired to write it myself."

She immediately got out of bed, bending as she rose so

that her nightgown flattened, from her shoulders down, as if a hand had run over it. She shook her head and her eyes opened fully and she said, "Look out, I'm putting on the light." Then she got her notebook and sat beside him.

He said indistinctly: "This—put it down—Fischer, schizoid jaw, kept examining his finger as if he wasn't sure it was there. And Jimmy worried about his tongue. They're all afraid they've lost something important. Would male patients possibly be reassured, when they're coming out of psychosis, if they were told to hold their penis? I saw one patient who did do that though he was tearing at his penis, actually." He thought, I couldn't have written that down myself. It would have been too much for me. And these thoughts that come in the twilight state get away. Get away as completely as a dream.

"Anything else?" she asked, raising her head, waiting. The low collar of her nightgown touched the spheres of her breasts.

"Just put down, *The Problem of Acceptance of Unpleasant Ideas,* Ferenczi."

"Anything else?"

"I love you," he said—"get back into bed."

Jimmy was going home. It seemed to put a period to part of Dr. Marks's life. And it seemed to determine his life to come. Every nine days he had been able to see Jimmy on rounds, and steadily in spite of all alternations, as steadily and inconspicuously as growth, Jimmy had improved. The zzzzzzz had stopped as if some psychic gasoline had been used up. Now the kid had reached the point of making sense most of the time, and talking clearly.

He seemed pleased with his progress. Occasionally he would be boastful, but different from the way he had been in the acute excitement. The boastfulness now had an overtone of conscious humor. Taking the role of doctor, he would ask, "What's your name? Where were you born?" Or he'd say, "All right, son, I'm going to protect you," his intonation indicating that this was a joke.

This pleasant phase came to an end when he learned he was going home, that he would have to go out again into the real world. Then he seemed depressed, almost as if sanity was not too welcome.

One thing could not be disputed. He had begun to dream.

As Dr. Marks arrived for a session with Dr. Naumann in late November, he was filled with the fact of this dreaming by Jimmy. During psychosis, Dr. Marks still believed there was no dream in the ordinary sense, a dream you have during sleep and remember when you wake up, because the psychotic was dreaming all the time. His whole life was the psychosis of a dream. And so something had radically changed for Jimmy when he could report that he had had a dream.

Dr. Marks had been making rounds and had met him as usual in the dayroom. But this, he knew, would be their last time together in the hospital.

The kid looked swell. Physically. Psychically there was that somewhat depressed look. "Hello," Dr. Marks said, grasping Jimmy's arm. "Say, how are you really feeling?"

"I don't know." Honest: "Last night I got afraid again. I don't mean bad—"

"I know. Nervous."

"I woke up in the night. A dream frightened me."

Be casual. "What was it?" Encourage him to speak. Not easy yet to speak about dreams, those messages of the Unconscious.

"I dreamed about a bet."

"Yes?"

"I was in the street, in front of the house where I live. Two men came along and I said, 'There's a grocery store two blocks down.' "

"Why'd you say that?"

"I don't know."

That's true. You don't know why you do things in dreams. "Go on."

"Well, so one of the men said, 'There ain't no grocery store there.' He was big, a big guy. So I go and bet him. I bet him a buck there was a grocery store there. So we started walking and right when we started, I knew I made a mistake. The grocery store's three blocks down, not two. But I knew I couldn't get out of the bet then, and then I woke up."

"Anything more about this dream?"

"The big guy, he was fat. Like— I don't know, it was funny how he was fat."

"Anything else?" (The hardest parts to remember mean the most.)

"Well, how I felt. I was so sure about where the store

was. I wanted him to bet. I even said, 'All you got to do is walk a couple of blocks and you make a buck.' That was to make him bet. I was sure. Yeah, but he was sure too. And it was him that was right."

"You're troubled about going home, aren't you?"

"Kind of."

"Who wouldn't be?"

Dr. Marks thought, He feels bad, depressed, but having this dream was a triumph. Because dreaming had been put back where it belonged. It had been taken away from waking, it had been ripped off "things." A tongue had become only a tongue that you talked with. An airplane was an airplane—it was not your male prowess or a zzzz-ing motor with which you drowned out something that threatened you. And voices were real voices. Jimmy's eyes now were focused on nothing but what was actually in front of him.

"What do you suppose your dream meant?"

"Well, I was there in the street so I guess I was thinking about being home."

"Looks like you wanted to be home."

"But I was scared."

"What were you scared about?" Dr. Marks asked him.

"The bet."

"A lousy buck." Jimmy was staring at him with some of the old confusion in his eyes. "A buck isn't much to get yourself into a sweat about, is it?" Dr. Marks said.

"No."

"This grocery store. What's that mean?"

"It's a store near our house."

"You've lived in this same house a long time?"

"Where we live now? Yeah."

"Since you were a kid?"

"Yeah."

"So what about this grocery store? What's it mean in your dream? Whatever happened there?"

Jimmy shook his head. "Nothing."

"Why the grocery store? Think about that."

Jimmy frowned. He said nothing.

"What about that bet?"

The eyes brightening: "I went to the store once. I didn't have enough money."

Here it comes. "Yes?"

"The man said something mean."

"The clerk?"

"The man at the store. He said, 'Go back and get the money.'"

Was that mean? It could be mean to a kid. A kid who needed enough money. "How much money did you need?"

Jimmy looked down. "I don't know."

"Something like that happened to you, you felt bad, and you can't remember?" Silence. "You probably do remember."

A very troubled look. "I'm not sure."

"If you know, what reason do you have, do you suppose, for not telling me?"

A confused silence.

"Perhaps it's embarrassing." Sharply: "All right, if you don't want to tell me."

"No, I'll tell you. It was a dollar."

"What you bet in your dream."

"Yes."

"And who was the fat man in your dream that you bet the dollar with, the fat man who knew he was going to get your dollar?"

Jimmy stared at him.

"Who was the fat man?"

Jimmy: "He was my mother when she was having a baby."

Only a postschizophrenic would know it, Dr. Marks thought. He had observed this phenomenon before, of what they knew. He said, "What do you buy at a grocery store?"

"Well—things to eat."

"Yes, stuff to eat. Food. And what's that?"

Jimmy shook his head.

"What is food? You know what food is."

"No."

"It's love. And you know it's love. Jimmy, listen to me. You know what that dream meant. It meant you didn't have what it took to pay for love, for your mother's love. That's what you've been afraid of all your life. Not enough of what it took to pay for love. Unworthy. Unworthy of being loved. So you had to work yourself up into something terrific—you listening to me? Into a genius, a billionaire, anything to be good enough to be loved."

It seemed to him now that Jimmy was feeling better. It does so much for you, to be understood. But there was

more that had to be done for him before he went home.
"You're pretty slow catching onto these things," he said,
putting a note of annoyance into his voice.

"No."

"Yes, you are. How many times do I have to tell you
these things?"

"I know what you told me."

"You know it with your head, that's all, but do you feel
it?" He hit the kid's chest. "Do you feel worth being
loved?"

Silence.

"Do you? Tell me."

The kid still silent.

"That was your mother you were trying to pay for loving you. Your mother. You think I'd let you worry about
buying my love? When did I ever ask you for anything?"
He held the kid's face up. "When did I? When did you
ever have to come with any lousy buck to me?"

The kid's eyes were threatening to get wet.

"You think I stayed with you till I almost dropped because I was getting paid for it? No, I wasn't getting paid. I
did it because I loved you and I knew you were worth-
while. I knew you deserved everything I could do for
you." To Dr. Marks's surprise, his own eyes were getting
wet, and it was true. Everything he had said was true.

"That's all. That's all I want to say to you. But I want
you to remember what I just said no matter what happens.
You going to remember?"

"Yes. Yeah."

When he told Dr. Naumann about it, Dr. Naumann
said, "You know there is a strange thing about all this."

"What?"

"In the first treatment, when you first treated Jimmy,
you were the father. Last night you were the mother."

"Well yes, but the kid himself got me into that, with
this dream."

"You completely forgot the father."

Yes, he had.

"You became the mother in place of the mother."

"You could say so," Dr. Marks admitted.

"The mother had wanted a girl, not a boy. The mother
had been castrative as well as the father. Who knows the
compelling power of this mother? It seems you sensed it."

(It was not the first time he sensed it, Dr. Naumann thought.)

"I did what I had to do. I follow these hunches. Anyway, mother, father, what does it matter as long as I keep him well?"

"It matters that you know what you do. But that's not all. You're not expecting to see Jimmy again."

"No, I'm not."

"And yet you know that instead of ending the transference, you deliberately continued it?"

Deliberately. Hell, he hadn't even been thinking of transference. He'd just been doing what, at the moment, clearly had to be done. "That kid is going back into a tough situation. He had a right to be depressed. Who's really going to keep him going there?"

"If he's well, he won't need anybody—not you anyway."

"Remember he hasn't been well too long, and I haven't been able to see him regularly. And if you'd seen him today— You have to go by a certain warning you get."

"I understand your impulse, but I can't agree it's wise not to end the transference."

Transference, transference. "I can't believe it will hurt the kid to know I still love him."

A long silence. Then Dr. Naumann said, "What's in your mind now—"

After dinner, Bob usually helped Margaret clear the table and do the dishes. Nancy tonight wanted to help too. "I thought you were supposed to be in bed," Bob said.

"I can stay up. I can stay up sometimes." She took a dish from the table and walked toward the kitchen with it.

"Ma, for God's sake take that dish away from Nancy."

"Thank you, Nancy," Margaret said.

Nancy said to Bob: "See, I can take it." When she came back into the dining room, Dr. Marks led her over to look at Mixmaster. The small turtle rested somnolently on a flat stone. "He's gone to bed, hasn't he?" Nancy said.

"Yeah, he's sleeping."

She said, "We have a turkey. You know we have a turkey? Tomorrow for dinner we're going to eat it."

"Yes?"

"Yes, it's Thanksgiv-giving."

"How do you know about Thanksgiving?"

"Well, it's—" She was puzzled. She went away and ran back with a piece of paper. "I drew a turkey. See?"

It was a vague outline that might be considered to be a bird. Two thick lines stuck out from it. "What are these?" he asked, pointing to the lines.

"Feathers. Two feathers. That means it's the mother."

"How many feathers does the father have?"

"One."

"Why did you make this a mama turkey?"

"I just wanted to." With a touch of disdain.

"But why?"

"Because—I wanted to."

Bill Widener at The Psychoanalytic Institute might be interested in this. He picked up Nancy's picture and folded it and put it in his pocket.

"Do you like my picture?" she said.

"Yes, I like it," he said. "I'd like to show it to somebody."

Also in his pocket were two letters that Joe Huber had given him, that Gus Fischer wrote. Fischer had written a series of these letters before he went into acute excitement. Accompanying one of them had been a piece of tissue paper containing some mucous.

The letter read:

TO Yourself in hell, compared to what you should be in—from DAMNATION, from Cain. ik ik cain cain cain ik ik;

my very beloved

Please know in advance that Cain, who writes this, is 100% hypocritical a complete liar and welsher: I will tell you what I do for happiness, and advise you to do it. I don't do a small fraction of the things I advise you to do but I advise you to do it in any case. Wear a solid statue of my self, of a rich metal, around your neck: also a cross around your neck, always forever, of diamonds. Eat little: remember that I am a complete hypocrite: eat nothing whatsoever ever, and remember that I am a hypocrite: act as you would have others act to you always: work maximum, the best you can do, for the poor, poor in soul and materials, day and night. Give blood, hair, your waste, nails, anything else you can think of free, to the poor as often as possible, directly, personally. Accept nothing, give everything. Go to heaven now: send the poor there: send them there from everywhere, always. Eat only, continually, wooden crosses: bed with the poor of the same sex and opposite sex, and such of course: remember that I am a 100% hypocrite: tell contents of this letter personally aloud to the poorest poor— of the world—continually; you must not be the hypo- crite that I am: if you eat medicine, or bathe, overdo it always, unlike myself who underdoes it: contact the poor personally throughout the world—the poorest— and bring them to heaven: make them do all these things; act like you were mentally sick: stay alive; you will grow happier faster if you do all these things.

I give you all my love, strength, authority, goodness, virtue, power, brilliance, money, food and wisdom, irrevocably forever, to do the above.

I love you.

CAIN CAIN IKCAIN CAINIKIKIKCAIN CAIN CAIN

Imagine the suffering of the person who would write such a letter. Dr. Marks was on his way to class and planned to show this to Bill Widener.

Fischer who was afraid of his father and of his son.

In class he brought up in discussion the problem of the symptomatic meaning of the patient's difficulties with eat- ing. Or not eating. He did not bring out Fischer's letter and did not mention Florence or Erna, or any other pa- tient from the hospital. The instructor had several times expressed his annoyance at discussing "psychotic material" in a class devoted to neurosis. Specifically he was annoyed with Dr. Marks. Dr. Marks had once asked him if Freud had not said that the dream is a psychosis, that the dream is "the royal road to the Unconscious," and that the psy- chosis is a "permanent dream." But he made no headway that way. And so he made the approach now of asking if other students had not had the experience of finding eating difficulties in their patients. There was general agreement that they had. One of the students said, "This business of not eating. I have a male patient right now who refuses to eat—blocks on eating—and the unconscious reason ap- pears to be that he wants his belly to be empty, so that he won't have a child."

After class, he asked Bill Widener if he'd like to have a cup of coffee. They walked together down the street, and something about it reminded him of Lugano, the Italian who had been afraid of the *vagina dentata*. The street seemed to have the form of a hollow tube, with jagged edges, conceivably teeth. Amused, he mentioned the thought.

"John, not many people see streets as vaginas, let alone a *vagina dentata*," Dr. Widener said with an odd look.

"I guess not. But you deal enough with these things. Don't you occasionally see things symbolically?"

"I can't say to that extent."

"Don't you ever see a building in a certain shape and think of it as a penis?"

"Yes."

Why not the vagina? Dr. Marks thought. Can't I be interested in cunt too? In anything? What was wrong with seeing things symbolically—even illusionally? He told Dr. Widener about how he had come into Ethel's room that night and her bed had seemed like a coffin over a grave. At twilight or at night, didn't you often see things as something else? And what was psychosis but a constant twilight or darkness?

He thought of Nancy's drawing—highly relevant. Dr. Widener was saying, "What you're saying is close to not being in reality."

They entered a restaurant on Lexington and ordered coffee, and Dr. Marks said, "I have had one experience that maybe fits what you're saying," and he told about the time he had touched the privet hedge when the world had become unreal.

Dr. Widener had been listening to him silently as if to a patient. "You know, John, I've been thinking about you. After the party, I was talking with my analyst—you know him, Dr. Beechhurst, he's on the Educational Committee —and he's completely against treatment of psychotics. When an analyst takes a case, he observes the case for a week or ten days to make sure there's no evident danger of psychosis, and if later—and it does happen—the patient should show signs of going into psychosis, he terminates the case right away."

Echoes of Staff.

"But the main reason I mention this," Dr. Widener went on, "is there's danger to you, treating psychotics."

"What danger?"

"Well, this—this weakening of reality that you describe."

"But mine was just momentary—"

"Just the same. When you get inside the psychosis the way you do—when you join the psychotic, for if I understand you, that's what you do—when you join him for considerable lengths of time in his psychosis, there must be danger in that."

"But I still don't see—what danger?"

"The danger that that derangement, that distortion, whatever it is—that you'll become lost in it."

"I am lost at certain moments, but I always come back."

"You have so far."

"So far. Well, if I really understand you, Bill, what you want to come right out and say is that there's nothing to be done for a psychotic."

"Well, I wouldn't go that far. Analysts have always been interested in psychosis. Even Freud."

"Interested." With a roll of his shoulders, Dr. Marks said, "But most analysts aren't too interested, right?"

"Well, not on the scale that you are."

"And so one must be very careful, is that it? Measure out the hours very cautiously? How many hours a week with these schizophrenics would be safe, do you think?"

Dr. Widener was silent. (What was he to say? To answer the question would trap him into an absurdity.)

"I appreciate your concern for me," Dr. Marks said, "but these are dying patients—"

"I understand that, but I don't think you should plead a special case from them. I'm talking about psychotics in general, who can even be homicidal."

"That's much exaggerated, that they're homicidal."

"There's no limit to what they need and demand."

"That much is true. And a child is demanding and exhausting, but we have children and we love them."

"The psychotic isn't a child. The psychotic is a regressed, archaic, and dangerous adult—"

"Who has been a child." Insinuatingly: "Who could be your child."

He had come out with Widener wanting to show him Nancy's picture, wanting to share with him that humor and symbolism of hers, and wanting to show him Fischer's letter too, discuss its ties with Jimmy (that thing of Jimmy's self-despising and at the same time needing to be the greatest), the ties with all his patients. Well, he couldn't, obviously he couldn't. He might cut in a little on his next analytic session and show them to Naumann, but he couldn't show them to Bill. And it was too bad.

At the hospital, a new development. Huber told him that Fischer had been transferred to another ward, a better one. Had it been deliberate? Did they know (he couldn't help wondering) and were they taking Fischer away from him? Well, Fischer had been practically out of psychosis (I pulled his face together, all right) and they had a right to move him. He could now join the many other patients seen on rounds or by minor connivances with attendants.

Huber: "There's another guy looks like he might be getting pretty bad. You want to take a look?"

"Not tonight. I've got to get some rest before I start a new one."

When he came home, the kids were in bed, but Margaret was still up. She said, "You're home early."

"They transferred Fischer, sent him to a better ward. There's another one starting, but I was too tired—"

"I'm glad you came home, dear. Would you like something to eat? Some hard-boiled eggs?"

"Nothing, thanks."

"How was class?"

"Neurotic," he said, making a bad pun. He explained it to her and told her about his talk with Bill. He said, "You were worried too after that thing with the privet hedge, but you saw I was right. It was temporary. I've been all right since and I've been working even harder, been closer to this whole thing."

"Yes, but there *is* something." That voice of hers. Even if he knew she was going to say what he might not like, he liked its quality. She said, "You're getting too much in touch with the Unconscious—"

He laughed. "This from you," he said.

"You can laugh, but you told me when Fischer said he was afraid of a crime wave on the waterfront, that meant he was afraid of being castrated—"

"The penis is the waterfront, isn't it?"

"Just the same, you're getting too close to it—something's happening to you from this working with psychot-

ics. You say things that aren't entirely real. You exaggerate. You say things in a certain way. You said to Bob the
other day, 'You're going to have six kids, all boys.' I guess
that's to make him feel manly, but that's something you
tell patients, not Bob."

"You don't think I was serious when I said that to
Bob."

"Well, I don't know. You even know my own thoughts
sometimes in an unbelievable way."

He took her hand. "With you it's different," he said. "I
have a right to know your thoughts."

"No, you don't."

He said, "I've been putting off something I have to tell
you."

He saw her apprehension.

"I've been looking into the setup at The Psychiatric Research Center. It seems to be everything Arthur said it
was, but there's a hitch."

"What?" she said.

"They don't pay residents there."

Now he saw fright leap to her eyes. He said, "I'm going
to have to borrow from Robert."

"How much?"

"Ten thousand, perhaps."

He saw the great effort with which she controlled herself.

"I'll pay it off later," he said.

"How will you pay it off? How are you ever going to
get paid for this work with psychotics? Nobody even
wants you to do it."

Glancing at her: "I have to do it." It isn't in the realm
of argument.

Parental feeling.

Atonement.

Hope.

Even paranoiac pride.

But he had to do it.

The second letter from Fischer in his pocket—

DEAR FAMILY:

I am feeling better. How are you? I wish that you
were here very much indeed. Please take me home
immediately; I am entirely well in every way: this is

known to every body. There is a fellow named Cain living here, messing things up completely. I am completely well, and in the best possible condition in spite of him, however. He is the world's worst; i am completely well, and so is every other male and female patient here including all those mentally and physically sick, in spite of Cain's efforts at deception.

I give you all my love, strength, power, and authority, my brilliance, decency, goodness, and virtue.

Please get me out of here at once.

Yours affectionately CAIN CAIN CAIN CAINCAINCAIN-IKIKIKCAIN

Robert had a large house in the Bay Ridge section of Brooklyn. As Dr. Marks drove up to it and stopped his car, he thought, How often I've told Naumann about this house, which seems to intrude constantly into my dreams! The outward sign of Robert's success. Robert had followed Pa in his unvarying business sense. Pa had built an enormous delivery service after he gave up his selzer route, and he had partly helped Robert establish his chemical plant. Now Robert had more money than Pa.

Do I mind? Not consciously. But that push to get to the head of the medical profession? The Medical Examiner asking him, "Look at this case, look at that case." And Emmanuel Libman recommending him for acceptance and qualification for taking the examinations for The American Board of Internal Medicine. And now he was driving in a new direction. Who knew these things?

Strange what had happened to a couple of kids who played on Bushwick Avenue. If you looked at Robert now. Once he had the privilege of being with him when he was getting into full dress (this kid brother I played with in the streets): he put a silk handkerchief carefully around his neck and then put on a dress shirt, tie, and cummerbund, and just before putting on his coat, he slid the protecting handkerchief out from under his shirt collar. The trouble was, he had seemed to be doing a familiar and accustomed thing.

Uncle John, that's what it was. I became a doctor. Robert became a dresser.

"You say it will take you the better part of two years more," Robert said.

"That's what I figure."

"You have Dr. Naumann to pay. Altogether, a hundred fifty a week?"

"A hundred thirty."

"You sure that's enough?"

"I believe we can manage on that. Margaret will see that we manage."

"But she's not happy," Robert said.

"She's resigned," Dr. Marks said.

"This is a very difficult thing for her, a difficult thing you're doing."

"I know. It's like going back to the days when I was starting practice, but worse—now we have children. And the children are the one thing she's really edgy about."

"I know how she is. Nothing must touch the children. But it will work out." His brother spoke with sympathy. He said, "No use hoping Pa and Ma will understand this, and even I can't understand it completely. But after what you've done, you have to go on."

"That's about it."

"Let's have Lisa in."

That was Robert. You don't make a big thing of it. You get it settled and leave it alone.

Dr. Marks had made an appointment to see Dr. Steiner. When he entered the office, Dr. Steiner seemed alarmed just at his presence.

"Could we discuss something?" Dr. Marks said.

The alarm noticeably increased. "Yes, I'm at your disposal."

"One of my associates—former associates—at The Vansittart Clinic spoke to me about The Psychiatric Research Center the other day. He mentioned its being a focus for research, with many programs for physical and psychic testing, and I began to think about my possibly going there." As Dr. Marks said this, he felt the alarm subsiding. He said: "As a matter of fact, I was wondering if I might not make application for transferring my residency there in the near future."

Readjusting fast: "Why yes, yes, the Center's a very fine place, of course. I can completely understand how it might appeal to you—to your particular interests. Yes."

"Good."

With increasing enthusiasm: "I even wish some of us might have thought of that possibility for you before. It certainly does appear to be a solution."

Solution to what? Dr. Marks thought. But the main thing was that no obstacle was being raised to his going there. "I'll assume then that I may have a recommendation when I make my application to the Center?"

"You certainly may. I could write it for you right now—"

"No hurry."

"Whenever you want it, just let me know. I can have it for you the same day."

Can't wait to sign the terminal slip, Dr. Marks thought.

"Of course," Dr. Steiner was saying, "we will be very sorry to lose your excellent services in pathology."

Getting the touch of sarcasm, Dr. Marks said, "And I'll be sorry to lose those with whom I've worked here."

He had the satisfaction of seeing Dr. Steiner frown.

The head of The Psychiatric Research Center, Carroll Carey, M.D., gave him an appointment for the following Monday. After lunch on Monday, he drove to Manhattan and uptown to the tall Center building, one of the long white teeth in the city's skyline. Dr. Carey's office, on the top floor, was at least twice as large as Dr. Steiner's and was lined with medical books. The Head made a curious impression on Dr. Marks. He seemed the forceful, even hard executive type, but about his eyes was an overlay of sympathy. It would be pleasant to trust that sympathy, but Dr. Marks had had experience with power, with the push for hieratic success, and he told himself to be cautious.

Best not mention anything about psychoanalysis. Dr. Steiner's letter spoke about his "outstanding work and devotion to duty" and Dr. Marks let it go at that. Dr. Carey said that in view of the warmth of Dr. Steiner's recommendation and with his superior medical background, he would certainly be most welcome at the Center. Dr. Marks gave as his main reason for wanting to change that he hoped to have more time to "learn" here.

"Yes, that's so, we are not as hard-pressed here. You should find your residency here an ideal opportunity for advancing your knowledge of psychiatry. Everything you need for study is concentrated here in one building. We even have time for pure science, and allow for that along with our more practical programs." Dr. Carey became more positive as he talked. His voice was a carrying one, used to public speaking. He questioned Dr. Marks about when he could come and seemed somewhat disappointed when he said not immediately, that he would have to set his time.

Dr. Marks had discussed with Dr. Naumann the termination of his residency at New State Hospital, and they had agreed that he should stay long enough to do the important follow-up work on the remaining patients he had treated, those who were not being given shock and whom he could still manage to see. "Give it at least three months," Dr. Naumann advised him. "It's just possible that now that it's known you're leaving the hospital, there will be less chance of your being interfered with. But under no circumstances must you begin a new case."

"I don't guarantee what I'll do."

"Patients will be dying there after you're gone—"

"At least I won't see it."

"If you stop taking new cases, you'll have a better chance to terminate properly with the ones you have," Dr. Naumann said. "Being responsible with the patients you have is part of your decision to make this change to The Psychiatric Research Center. The decision is right. You must accept the terms it imposes."

Dr. Marks stirred restlessly.

"I don't often give you an order, do I?" Dr. Naumann said.

"I don't know that you ever have."

"I give you this order: no new cases."

Grudgingly: "All right."

"I count on you to follow it."

"I'll follow it."

And he began to get more rest, even an occasional game of tennis. He had one session of poker, paid for with irrational guilt feelings. It was perhaps the night tension, the same night tension as when he bent over the bodies of Kupfer, Lugano, and Fischer. Through the fan of cards, he saw those wildly pleading eyes.

14

The spring blew in with rain. At the hospital, crocus and jonquil shoots appeared in the lawns. Windows went up, and hands and arms signaled to imaginary saviors. A few hieroglyphic notes—save me, save me—mingled with the scraps of paper that floated down and were lost around the hospital trees. On Women's Ward K, a young patient wearing a wide red belt like a sash sat at the nurse's desk, writing.

THINGS TO BE FEARED IN INSANITY

1) Destructive habits.
2) Being in a state of infancy.
3) Loss of muscular control.
4) Voices as the interfering agent which keeps a person from facing the facts about himself to himself.
5) Cruelty to oneself and to those who love you.
6) Dreaming when talking or working, or doing any other thing not in reality.
7) Overemphasis.
8) One thing especially to be feared is rotting away.

As the patient wrote the last item, a nurse walked quickly up to the desk and said, "Sally, what are you doing here? You know you mustn't come near this desk. What have you got there? What is it?" She picked up the torn envelope on which the patient had been writing and glanced at it, and her expression changed. It said that the patient had become human for her. "If you want to write . . . I mean. Ask me for some paper."

Lowering her head, the young woman said, "Yes."

Under a single-column caption on a back page of one of the metropolitan papers:

"The Women's Guild of Friends of the Mentally Ill had

as their guest yesterday Dr. Howard Steiner, Superintendent of New State Hospital. Dr. Steiner described the various forms of shock therapy and the hospital's constant improvement in shock-treatment techniques. The women of the Guild donated four radios for the wards and two hundred books for the hospital library."

Dr. Marks had brought all his patients to a point where they were either discharged or well prepared for discharge. Only two remained in the hospital, and he had the feeling that his leaving might even be psychologically good for them. They would then insist on discharge.

He thought, Ought I to see Mrs. Blumstein before I leave? In a week he was going to the Center. Mrs. Blumstein was now on one of the worst of the back wards, he had seen her there twice, and he wasn't anxious to go through that punishment again. But he could phone and find out how she was. He got the nurse on the ward. "I'm Dr. Marks," he said. "Would you kindly tell me how Mrs. Blumstein is now?"

"No improvement, Doctor."

"Does she still just sit on the floor against the wall?"

"I'm afraid she does."

He could see her in that unspeakable reeking ward—

"Doctor—"

"Yes?"

"Did you know her daughter Rose is now in the hospital?"

"No, I didn't. Where is she?"

"She just came in. She's on Ward H."

He thought, Starting where Mrs. Blumstein started.

He went up to Ward H. The same oval in the door where the "ell" had been cleaned off, the same soft blind eye. He knocked on the door, feeling as though he were repeating a scene *déjà vu*.

The nurse said, "I didn't know you were coming up or I'd have told you—Rose has gone for shock."

"Shock."

He asked for Rose's chart. A whimpering voice from a nearby bed kept saying, "I never saw," perseveratively. "I never saw I never saw I never saw—"

He read through the chart quickly. The main facts were that she had lived at home after her mother's breakdown and had cooked and cared for her father and one brother. That would be a chance for her symbolically to take the place of her mother and do herself some fine psychic damage.

"I never saw I never saw I never saw" (the voice rising) "such filth."

He gave the chart back to the nurse and went to the shock-treatment floor. It was late; a long row of women by now would be lying with their legs tied to the bottoms of the beds, their thighs curved up and their shoulders caved in, like drunks.

When he reached the shock-room line, he called out, "Rose Blumstein?" A nurse beckoned to him. "Rose? Here, Doctor." She took him to a frightened-looking young woman with fair, soft-textured skin—definitely Mrs. Blumstein's daughter. She was wearing a neat beige skirt and blouse, her own, apparently, from home.

"Rose," he said, "do you know who I am?" An unreal question.

She shook her head quickly.

"Do you know what I am?"

Again the shaken head.

"A doctor."

"Yes," she said eagerly, wanting to agree.

"What's your name?"

"Yes," just as eagerly.

He took her hands and said, "Rose." Her hands stirred convulsively and with one loosened finger she touched one of his fingers. She pressed it searchingly.

"You can love me if you want to."

"Ma."

She sprang against him and her arms went around him. He held her and noticed her lips beginning to hunt for a nonexistent breast. Without thinking, he bent his finger and thrust the projecting knuckle into her mouth. She sucked and after she had nursed in this awkward way for a moment, she disengaged herself.

Her eyes still seemed eager and vacant.

He said, "What's your name?"

"Rose."

"Where are you?"

"I don't want to be here. Please, I don't want to be here. I don't want to be here."

"Where are you?"

"That—that. That street."

"Where are you?"

Frightened. "I don't like that river. Or that—that. That smell."

"What smell?"

She listened as if trying to understand.

"What smell?"

Arrogantly: "He's especially powerful. He has seven trucks and does it easily. Easily. The—the—the little ones run all over."

I can't do an interpretation here in the corridor, he thought. "Slow up," he said. "Just answer slowly. What's 'seven'?"

She began to tremble.

He put out his finger and she took it. "What's 'seven'?"

"No. No, the trucks were never—no. I didn't. I never did."

"Who drives the trucks?"

She tried to speak, her large, hinged, perfect eyes watching him.

"Who drives the trucks?"

"That way, over there."

"Who drives the trucks?"

Her eyes—

"You can tell me. Tell me. Who drives the trucks?"

"No."

"Who?"

Trembling.

"Who?"

"Brother."

He withdrew his finger from her hand and released himself. He went into the treatment room, stepping behind a small screen that partly blocked the door. Dr. Wellman was holding the electrodes above a woman's head and glanced across them at him. "Yes?" he said. He lowered the prongs.

"I wonder if there's any possibility you could release one of your patients from shock this morning so that her case could be reappraised?"

"Which one do you mean?"

"Rose Blumstein."

"You know I'm not authorized to do it even if I wanted to."

Dr. Marks stepped outside and Rose was brought in

next and shocked. As she was brought out and wheeled away, to be tied in a bed in the adjacent ward, he stood and watched the rest of the line fearfully going in, one by one. It was tempting to wait till Wellman was finished and would go and wash his hands in a small bowl in the ante-room—it would be tempting then to confront him and ask him if he didn't think he ought to read some of the literature on shock, read how they made experiments on stunning cattle at the Chicago stockyards in nineteen thirty and found it caused tissue damage throughout the body—spoiled the meat. Read how total hospitalization time showed no significant difference between shocked and non-shocked patients. The symptomatic gain (where shock fit a psychic pattern of relieving guilt or giving the illusion of rebirth or where it simply temporarily dulled down the symptoms) was offset by the patients' terror, by varying brain damage, and by a total lack of any real curative value. It was lucky if the patient had a minimum of shock and the damage was minor and he wasn't noticeably affected. Wellman could find out all this if he wanted to. Pirosh would tell him, Dr. Marks thought. But it was hopeless. He himself had mentioned deaths from shock once to Wellman, and Wellman had said, "But the percentage of death is much lower than with many minor operations we do all the time. Nothing to compare with the help shock gives." No, Wellman, Parker, Spencer—they were so hysteric about the mere possibility of seeing the Unconscious that they were blind to any evidence against a treatment (marvelous for them) that offered or imposed the gifts of silence, death, and obedient resurrection.

Rose would be stirring now. Just stirring. Her foot might pull against the knotted towel with the fretful tug of an animal. Her breathing would be deep and strained, and murmurous with saliva. She would be coming back to life.

Dr. Marks was walking across the hospital lawn with Dr. Rossman. Dr. Rossman was saying, "I agree it's useless to try to talk to them, but I have said: Why does the hospital count go up if shock cures? They have an answer. They can be cured if they're really not schizophrenic. Those who come back have a 'schizophrenic core.' "

"You don't give up hope?" Dr. Marks said.

"No, I don't."

"Good. Are you going to stay here at New State?"

"I'd like to."

In a sense Rossman was right. This was where the patients were, in their thousands. But would conditions here ever change? Would Rossman or a few others he knew about—would their small company leaven this institution?

After he left Rossman, he did something he had had in mind doing for some time. He got Jimmy Cady's chart out of file and read it. He skimmed to the day when he had first seen Jimmy in the Medical Ward. From that point on he read carefully. "Intravenous amytol given . . ." "Temperature at 4 P.M. 105.7." "Patient talking continuously with confused flight of ideas, hypermanic and fearful." (He was fearful, all right.) "Encephalogram shows abnormal electrocortical activity of a diffuse nature." "Sedation . . . Temperature . . . Sedation shows little effect." Then, without explanation: "Temperature normal, marked decrease in excitement. Patient in partial contact." Now (in a new handwriting) it was noted that the patient had returned to Ward L, and after that, "Patient eating normally." "Patient improving." From here on there were fewer entries. "Patient increasingly in contact." "Patient able to dress and shows interest in other patients." "Patient cheerful." The intermittent entries continued until the final notation of Jimmy's discharge from the hospital.

Nowhere was there any mention of himself.

Part 2

15

A week later, he drove up to The Psychiatric Research
Center for his first day there as a resident. He had just
moved to Manhattan. That had not been a simple matter,
and the problems were not yet over, but they were moved.

He slowed into the doctors' parking lot—certainly
swell-looking cars here. So mine isn't a Cadillac. At least
it's a nice, tasteful maroon.

The Center building was better designed than any New
State Hospital building, windows in shining vertical bands
on functionally plain stone walls. The front door was wide
open. No guards and no questioning and no keys. It was a
relief not to have that prison routine going in.

He stopped at a small desk near the door and said to
the receptionist, a woman who actually was pleasant, "I
have a ten-o'clock appointment with Dr. Carey."

"Please go up," she said, indicating the elevators.

As he waited at the elevator, he could see doctors and
nurses coming into the lobby from the street. They walked
rapidly and funneled out to side corridors and stairs, and
he couldn't help thinking, Alert, something special about
them. Now a doctor was standing beside him, knifelike
creases in his trousers. The elevator door opened and the
operator said, "Good morning, Dr. Gates," and bowed.
Dr. Gates—that must be Newbold Gates, a psychoanalyst
often spoken of at the Institute. He a staff member here?

The elevator rose noiselessly, small, antiseptically clean,
not one of those creaking boxes at New State smelling of
paraldehyde. At the thirtieth floor, he was let off into a
crown of silence. By comparison with New State, this
whole place seemed notable for its quiet.

In the foyer of Dr. Carey's office, his secretary, Miss

Blake, said, "Dr. Carey's down with Dr. Freer and asked if you'd wait a few minutes. Won't you have a seat?"

Windows were open. As he waited, on an incoming draft of air he believed he could smell the sea. The sense of it coming up on both sides of the city. Viewed from up here, the city's buildings stretched out like corrugations, a haunting structure resting in an amniotic pool.

What would the Center be like? New possibilities, surely, from what Arthur had said, from what he had heard elsewhere. He had learned that at least four members of the staff were members of The Psychoanalytic Institute.

"Good morning, Dr. Marks," Dr. Carey said.

"Good morning."

"You're here early on your first morning. Come in." Dr. Carey opened his office door, indicating to Dr. Marks that he should precede him. The office windows were open. Walls and ceiling reflected and rereflected the bright sunlight.

"What a great day!" Dr. Marks said.

"I noticed it too, leaving home this morning. A day for spring fever," and as Dr. Carey said this, he smiled and Dr. Marks felt disarmed. This must be a man you could like. And a force in psychiatry—a force on the side of the mentally ill. Dr. Carey went on, "I just wanted to see you briefly before you go down to see Dr. Stieglitz." Dr. Henry Stieglitz, chief of the service on the female side. "I take it you're ready to go to work?"

"Quite ready."

"You're replacing Dr. Belos who's finishing his residency. You'll see him today and talk with him a little, that is, if he feels like talking. There's no need to, otherwise, for you'll have no trouble getting started with your duties here."

"I'm very pleased now to be here."

"But I suppose you were right, taking your time about coming over. It shows a good attitude toward New State and your work there."

Dr. Marks had a moment of alarm. But of course Dr. Carey couldn't know the real meaning of what he was saying.

"I believe you'll find this a fine place to work," Dr.

Carey said. "You'll see your opportunities concretely from day to day. This is one of the great centers of psychiatric research. For example, we have some extraordinary physical research under way. Dr. Johanson, head of the laboratories, could tell you about it, and you should get acquainted with him—he's a good man, well trained and highly talented. Go and talk with him. You're a pathologist—you can talk his language."

"I will."

"He's shocking monkeys to see the effect on the brain. Do you read foreign languages?"

"Just German."

"Our library downstairs has an important collection of German works. Use it."

Dr. Marks thought of Dr. Naumann's recommendations that he read. But this, perhaps, was not the reading Dr. Carey meant.

"On the seventh floor are the children's wards, and you'll find them most interesting. We have excellent personnel there—"

Miss Blake's typewriter drummed in the background.

"Speaking of children, I understand you have three children of your own," Dr. Carey said.

"Two boys and a girl. Nancy is still small and she has a fixed idea I'm going to work now in a Bicycle Center and she's to get a bicycle."

"You're in trouble there." Dr. Carey smiled, and again Dr. Marks was aware of a disarming sympathy. "Well, you'll want to get down to see Dr. Stieglitz and I mustn't hold you. I'm happy to have seen you and to have you here."

The ninth-floor corridor seemed to have been recently painted, and glistened. At Room 914 he knocked and a voice called, "Come in." He entered a pleasant office, the walls of which had an eggshell sheen, and the man who got up to greet him was handsome, with a black beard cut straight across.

"Dr. Stieglitz?"

"Dr. Marks? Dr. Carey just gave me a ring that you were on your way down."

Dr. Stieglitz's voice reminded Dr. Marks of Dr. Naumann's (let's not get a transference going here).

"I do need you," Dr. Stieglitz said. "I'm told you have a fine background in internal medicine."

"I'm qualified as an internist, but I'm not formally experienced in psychiatry——"

"That's why you've come here. I may say the whole range of psychiatry is here at its best, and nothing is excluded. The various work and reeducative therapies, the physical therapies. I imagine Dr. Carey has spoken to you about the laboratories——"

"Yes, he did."

"You'll learn diagnostic work, you'll learn how to join the care of body and mind." There was a moment's pause. "Did Dr. Carey mention to you that I'm a psychoanalyst?"

"No, he didn't!" Dr. Stieglitz seemed to be watching his reaction.

"Yes, and the Center, you'll find, makes the basic contributions of Freud an important part of its approach."

Dr. Marks said, "I'm glad to know that. I'm under analysis myself."

"You are!" Dr. Marks noted the surprise. A kind of readjustment seemed to be taking place in Dr. Stieglitz. "Well, that's most interesting. But with your background——"

"That's it. I found many instances where medical practice wasn't getting me anywhere. So I began trying to find out about the mind——"

"May I ask who your analyst is?"

"Dr. Erich Naumann."

"Naumann. You've certainly gone to the top."

"He's wonderful," Dr. Marks said.

"I don't know him well personally. He's very dedicated, very absorbed in his work."

"Yes, he is."

Could I speak to this doctor about my work with Jimmy and the others? Dr. Marks thought. Why not? A man who knows of Naumann, who admires him. But a last caution held him back. Instead he said, "You haven't said anything specifically about a psychotherapy program."

Without commenting on this, but as if picking up a thought, Dr. Stieglitz said, "I'm certainly pleased at the overall qualifications you bring to this work. Perhaps I'll do some of the work I've wanted to do through you."

"Do you work directly with any of the patients?" Dr. Marks asked. As soon as he had asked this question, he felt it had been a mistake. He explained himself: "I'd be so much interested in watching you treat, if that would be possible."

"My analytic work is mostly in private practice, with neurotics," Dr. Stieglitz told him. "Here I'm handicapped with administrative work. With other duties. I do guide the younger men in psychotherapy, and I'll try to help you. You'll have eight patients." He gave Dr. Marks the list of his patients. "None of them requires too much attention, but as soon as a case comes in that looks interesting, I can perhaps assign it to you and give you personal guidance with it."

"I have only eight cases?" Curious: "Do all the residents have as few cases as this?"

"We don't believe in this hospital in having too many beds. For our purposes I sometimes think we may even have too many as it is."

Eight cases.

"Take your time today. Familiarize yourself with the place. Try to see your patients if you can. One of them, you'll find, is a state senator's daughter, Mrs. Bell—she's made remarkable progress, not that she was a very serious case. As I say, look around and tomorrow morning drop by and see me again."

Miss Blake had no typing at the moment and, the door between her office and the Head's being open (it usually was), she heard Dr. Carey speaking on the phone. He was speaking with Dr. Stieglitz.

"So you like him." A silence. "I had a good impression of him too." A longer silence, then, "I'm surprised at that. Who's he getting it from?" After a moment, "Naumann. Well—"

They were talking about Dr. Marks, she knew. "Well, I just hadn't expected it. I wonder a little that he said nothing to me about it . . . But isn't he supposed to be an internist? I . . . Well, so long as you're happy."

This Dr. Marks, Miss Blake thought. Anybody would like him, but then again he looked rough, like some common person, maybe a laborer— He didn't look like a doctor, actually. But then you can't tell from the outside, she told herself.

The library faced east and was shadowy. As Dr. Marks came in, he noticed a bust of Freud—as always, serene and thoughtful—between the two center windows.

A young man waiting near the door said, "You're Dr. Marks?"

"Yes, you're Dr. Belos?"

"Right. Let's go outside where we can talk."

In the hall outside, Dr. Belos said, "You have your office key?"

"No, am I supposed to?"

"I turned mine in to the housekeeper. She'll be expecting you in for yours."

"Will I have your office?"

"Not automatically. No telling what Mrs. Seebright will want to do. She may assign you to mine or she may not. The way it works, several residents use the same office. She'll tell you."

Several in one office.

"Aren't you a little old to be coming in as a resident?" Dr. Belos said.

Dr. Marks: "I'm interested in psychotics and this seemed to me the best way to find out more about them—"

"You're interested in psychotics?"

"Yes—aren't you?"

"Oh, yes, of course. But you'll have to hunt around for them here—I didn't have any. The real psychotics they ship off to the state hospitals unless their families have a lot of pull."

"But I thought this was where you studied psychotics."

Dr. Belos acted as if it wasn't worth his while to argue. He said, "Did Stieglitz give you the list of patients?"

"Yes, he did."

"Well then, good luck. You'll find Mrs. Seebright in Room Two Ten. I might mention: two cases you'll have show signs of being psychotic, but they'll almost surely be transferred to Creedmoor." Having said this, Dr. Belos bowed and said, "Good-by."

Dr. Marks felt confused. Surely Dr. Belos must be mistaken. A psychiatric research center would be meaningless if what he said was true. Perhaps he hadn't been prepared to take advantage of the opportunities here, or wasn't adept in finding them.

That must be it. After all, Arthur Chandler had said this was a place where he could work, and Dr. Naumann had agreed. This was the leading research center in the East. What did Belos mean, no psychotics?

He remembered too that Dr. Stieglitz had specifically promised to find him something "interesting," a case he could "guide" him with.

No, Dr. Belos must be mistaken. Dr. Marks began to disregard what he had heard.

He went to the housekeeper's room and she got him his keys and told him his office would be Room 319. He chatted with her. "How old is this building?"

"It's not old at all. Only a few years. But—" with a flicker of exasperation "—it's terrible how quickly it gets beat up. They scratch."

That was what mental illness represented to this woman. "They scratch." But he knew what she meant. He had seen it at New State—grooved lines of desperation on walls and doors, angry, magic communications.

He held his strangely old-style hospital passkey as he walked away. Large and emphatic like a phallic symbol. He wondered if a time might not come when an ordinary small key would be all that would be needed, and the common jail atmosphere associated with this key could be dispensed with—perhaps even the key itself.

To the elevator operator he said, "I'm a new resident— can you tell me where to go for lunch?"

"The sixth floor, Doctor." At the sixth floor: "Straight back and to the left."

It was a large room, but not as large as at New State. Dr. Carey presided at a table in back. Dr. Marks seemed to detect interest in the Head's glance as he came in.

"Were you meeting someone, Doctor?" the waitress said.

"No, I'm a new resident—"

"Oh, then you'll want the residents' table. This way, please."

He came to a long table. He said, "May I join you?"

"Please do," a young man said. "I'm Dr. Emory."

"I'm Dr. Marks—John Marks."

"This is Dr. Sands and this is Dr. Hoagland." Several doctors nodded to him and he felt how definitely they were young and he was not.

"This is your first day here?"

"Yes, and I'm afraid I have a lot to learn."

"What school you from?" Dr. Emory asked.

"Washington University, nineteen twenty-seven."

"Say, I went to Washington University too."

"What's doing there now?" Dr. Marks said. "Now" meant this doctor was just out.

"Oh, mainly they're rebuilding the hospital—"

Voices around him:

"She put chewing gum in the lock and Mrs. Seebright—"

"Where'd she get it?"

"His newest is he thinks there's a Socrates movement in France, something to do with literature."

One of the doctors took a piece of paper from his pocket and passed it around. It came to Dr. Marks. In a highly eccentric handwriting in which the verticals were all heavily widened, a letter evidently written by a patient:

Macy's
Gentlemen of the
      MAIL ORDER DEPARTMENT
Please send me the following items C. O. D. special delivery, at your earliest convenience:

1. 2 boxes of food
2. One statue of GOD (12 inches high approx.)
3. One Madonna
4. One incense burner (large)
5. 1 piece of rope

                 ESTELLE BROWN

Dr. Marks said, "This handwriting—"

"Oh, lots of them write like that. Part of their system."

How much I don't know! Dr. Marks thought. He felt the table talk pour over him, and it reminded him of the first days of his medical residency. There had been just such a residents' table then, and young voices, young eyes. The same eyes.

"A complete paranoid system—"

"And then Kobelev—"

After lunch, he studied his list of patients as if in it he might find a focus, a source of stability. They were all women. Linda Bates, Seven south. Hilda Sorensen, Four south. The thing to do was go to the floor of each patient and get the chart.

Linda Bates—he started with her. He got the chart by himself, from its usual place in the nurse's office. A brown binder. The mental, presumably taken by Dr. Belos, was long, certainly long by New State standards. He read it through and went to look for the nurse who must be somewhere around.

This was the first restricted floor he had been on. The "women's side," he had been told, was nine floors on the south side of the building, and he could hardly believe what he saw on this floor. He thought of New State, which he was sure was typical of most hospitals, maybe even a little above standard: plain walls, plain windows, no furniture that wasn't screwed down or too heavy to pick up. Walls damaged, gouged—not just scratched. Inveterated ugliness. But this! The ward beds had bedcovers that matched the window drapes. There were partitioned alcoves. A radio played to two women who sat in light wicker chairs. Even the odor of the room was pleasantly feminine.

He found the nurse in a private room with a patient. He waited until she came out. "I'm Dr. Marks, the resident replacing Dr. Belos."

"Oh, yes. I'm Miss Morrison."

"Can you tell me where Linda Bates is?"

"Oh, she's at RT, Recreational Therapy."

Recreational Therapy. "When will she be done, when will she be back on the ward?"

"Not till after supper now. Most of the patients on this ward are kept busy during the day."

Looking around: "It's quite attractive here."

"It is, isn't it? Just the drapes, maybe—" Her expression disapproved of the drapes.

He said, "Tell me, patients on a ward like this can't be in very bad shape."

"No—most of them could go home right now. A lot of them are voluntary commitments."

He was thinking of what Dr. Belos had said. "But aren't there any bad cases?" he asked.

"Oh, they are worse on the shock wards—these aren't shock here. The few really bad cases you'll find on the tenth floor."

The tenth floor. "Thank you."

Hilda Sorensen, Four south, was also in one of the therapy groups—art therapy. The next patient was a retarded woman who worked in the kitchen and had been working there a long time. He did not see her.

He interrupted his search for patients and went to the tenth floor. "Go all through the place," he had been told.

Here was a row of cells with small, shatterproof windows in the doors and, inside, nothing but a light mattress on the floor. He looked through window after window. Nobody inside. Why are these cells locked up? Finally surprised, in one cell he found a woman lying on a mattress. She was in a straitjacket, and in addition, she had been rolled in a blanket so that only her face showed, an edematous, numb, drugged-looking face. Heavy sedation. The lips slightly parted, the eyes frozen almost closed, but not seeming asleep.

The door of course was locked, and did not open to his key.

After a last look at the woman's seemingly nonsleeping stupor, he walked on. At least there were *some* difficult cases here.

It was on the shock ward that he caught up with the first of his own patients, Reba Schwartz—Mrs. Reba Schwartz. She lay outstretched in bed at three thirty in the afternoon, her black hair wound tight against her forehead and her hands restlessly moving. She said calmly, "How are you, Doctor?"

He thought, That's turning tables on me, all right. "I'm your new doctor, Dr. Marks."

"Very good. You'll please put in an order at once for me to go home."

No matter what the disasters of the mind, this one mental concept they had—they asked or pleaded or gave God's order that they should go home. "Do you think you'd be better off there?"

"Doctor, I've had forty shock treatments," she said. "I think it's forty. I think it's enough. It's ruined me."

"What do you mean, it's ruined you?"

"I've lost my memory."

"How's that? What do you mean by that?"

"I know my husband and my children came to see me, but I can't remember it. No, I can't see into that great hole here." She touched her head. "Think, Doctor. It's like they hadn't been here."

"But you remember that they were here."

"I remember I tried to say their names—that comes back—" She looked as if she wanted to cry. A patient on another bed raised up on an elbow.

He'd had a senile patient in medical practice who tried to remember his son's name and couldn't. He would call his son, "Moe," and then, "No, no, Ruth," using a girl's name. It was an organic loss of memory. That's what this woman had—she knew she should remember, but she couldn't.

She pressed her hand over her black hair.

"Well, Reba—"

"Thank you, Doctor."

"Thank me for what?"

"For wanting me well."

"Yes, I want you to be a 'well Reba.'" The nurse on the ward here had told him that Mrs. Schwartz was to be transferred "very soon" to Creedmoor. She wasn't improving—if anything, the opposite. "We only keep patients sixty days. After that, if they aren't going home, they have to be transferred to the state hospitals." Creedmoor. Amnestic. Untreated or rather shock-treated. He thought of Creedmoor and he thought of this woman and he wondered how long it would be before she too would be in the back wards.

Early for his hour with Dr. Naumann, he waited to be called in. He avoided looking toward the door behind which God listened—that god, that godhead so remote that his colleagues (Dr. Stieglitz, for example) didn't really know him, knew only his constantly extending track of books and articles. This article, in *The International Journal of Psychoanalysis* this month, on "Closed Rooms" —I have to read it. I wonder if the so-and-so has me in it (my parents' bedroom?). How does it feel as a patient to find clinical material about yourself in print? Troubling, but such material has to be used. Naumann makes postsession notes in that little scrawl of his in German, translating what I or others say into his own language, then he puts that dialog in his articles, then some translator translates it back into English. Well, maybe the old man checks over to see if the dialog is like the patients'—he's capable of that.

I ought to be writing my own article, on the cases at New State. I ought to get onto that before I mix those cases up with any new cases.

That started him thinking about the possibilities of a new case. He hadn't seen anything yet that looked like what he had in mind, not even the tenth-floor woman stuporous on her mattress. He didn't want a drugged, physically caused stillness. He wanted a psychotic who wasn't screamingly accessible as all his cases had been so far.

He thought, Will I be able to do anything for them if they're not dying, screaming, *in extremis?*

That was what he had discussed with Margaret when he had called her earlier in the day. Putting the call through had not been as simple as he expected. He had called from his office where he had found a telephone.

"Yes?" the switchboard operator said.

"May I have an outside line, please?"

"This isn't Dr. Belos, is it?" she asked.

"No, it's the new resident taking his place—Dr. Marks."

"We like to keep the outside calls to a minimum, Doctor."

He said, annoyed, "I'm calling my home."

"Yes, Doctor."

She put through his call and he had a talk with Margaret: prospects wonderful, but the strange thing was that as yet he had no cases like he had had in mind. The setup here was different really from what he had counted on. No cases kept over sixty days, or hardly any. Apparently it wasn't going to be so simple to get a real sick case, and he had thought the place would be filled with them.

"Well, what kind of cases do you have?"

He detailed them to her: two shock-treatment amnestics, a group of what he judged were borderline neurotics (including Mrs. Bell, the state senator's daughter), and one moron who had a permanent job in the kitchen.

"Cheer up, you'll surely find something soon," she said.

"I hope so. You know, even if I do get a tough case, what if they take it away from me in sixty days?"

"You mean it would take you longer than that?"

"What do I know about a really bad case?"

Now, sitting in Dr. Naumann's waiting room, he recalled the utter silence of his office after he finished talking with Margaret. It had struck him as an intensification of the whole quiet of the Center, and he began to miss the sounds of New State. He missed the nearby dayroom from which the women came and sibilated their "Please."

"Dr. Marks?" There stood God in the doorway, thin, splendid, dressed like an unsuccessful small businessman.

Dr. Marks went to the couch perhaps more than usually aware of the special sanction of the analytic hour, and the special privilege. Here insecurity at least had available a rough comfort, and immaturity at least could yearn toward a foster father.

How different from psychotics! They had no hour, no place, and nobody with them except as they lived continually with dreams and voices, dreaded shapes that they must stare and stare at—watch.

The Voice (dispassionate): "What are you thinking?"

As if awakened: "Why, I was thinking of the analytic hour—I was thinking that it's something psychotics don't have."

Too logical, and he knew Dr. Naumann wouldn't approve of this opening. Here you have to associate.

But what is association? In the waiting room his mind had been busy unpacking itself in a series of thoughts. But not exactly association. Not association as it is understood in the analytic hour. If he repeated only what had been going through his mind up to now, he might get from Naumann, "Your associations seem to be defensive today," or, "Your associations are not very productive, it seems."

One thing was allowed:

"I think perhaps I had better tell you what happened at the Center today."

Naumann was silent, which meant consent. He would permit a short interval of reality, and then he would turn the reality to account for his own purposes. They would soon be back to work.

His account of his day ended with the thought he had had in the waiting room, that he had not found yet a case of the kind he had in mind.

"Tell me, are patients at the Center first entries—first commitment to a mental institution?"

"A good many, yes. But they tell me they admit them according to what they have in mind—you know, the research projects. So I understand they do bring in some cases from the state hospitals, like if they want to do research with hebephrenics, they bring in hebephrenics." But where were the hebephrenics, the bad cases? Long-term schizophrenics?

They must be there. He hadn't been everywhere. He just hadn't seen them.

Silence. Then, "What are you thinking?"

This was the real signal to get to work. "I'm thinking of this Center—it's classy. When I was there in the lobby this morning, and saw all these people coming in and out, like this Newbold Gates—" It flashed into his mind: "A real Uncle John type. Yes, I guess it came into my mind for a moment, that he was an Uncle John type."

Silence.

"My Uncle John would have fitted right in at the Center—no accent, you know. He was my mother's side of the family, my grandmother's brother, he had a real Harvard accent, and he was married to a woman whose family came over with that Jewish immigration in eighteen forty-seven or forty-eight and they were all pretty cultured."

Continued silence.

"He was the big wheel in our family all right—nobody disputed it. I used to think later it wasn't fair because he had an older brother, Joe, who was really a nice guy, and bright, but compete with this production, this striped morning pants, wing collar and cravat, this 'I'm it' who delivered all the kids—all four of us?" Thinking: "And then there was that operation he did on me."

A slight motion in the chair at the head of the couch. Listening.

"But the first time he operated wasn't on me—it was on my brother, Robert. Shall I tell you? . . . He came to the house with another person, his anesthetist or somebody, to take Robert's tonsils out. Something about it started to scare me. I didn't know what it was all about, but when they took Bob into the kitchen to do this to him, whatever it was, I ran into the bedroom and stayed there. But then while I'm in there they bring Bob all dripping blood and smelling ether, looking like he's dead, and shove him into bed in our bedroom—we shared a bedroom—and then I really shit my pants. The ether smell. The smell of that stuff."

Was this the start of his fear of ether? Perhaps this session would open it up. You never know when it will come. "What is it like, this smell of ether?"

Slowly: "Well, sweat—urine."

The danger of a drop in the emotional level of the productions. Keep silent.

"That smell you get from your crotch sometimes—if you need a bath. If you've—I remember when I was about four I woke up one night and I felt a flow of urine. At first it had been pleasant, but as soon as I was awake, I got terribly afraid. My father would beat me. He did use to lay into me for bed-wetting. Something else—much worse than this about the bed-wetting. I had this terrible curiosity— I'd seen my sisters undressed a few times, but I wondered what women were like, then one day—" now he was closing and unclosing his right hand "—one hot day in the summer my grandmother was in her room asleep, she was lying there sleeping, and she was naked, just had a sheet over her. I tiptoed in and lifted the edge of the sheet at the bottom of the bed and peered up there between her legs to see what was there. I saw some hair and I smelled that crotch smell. I got awfully scared."

That grandmother, that was the matriarch he feared and hated. "Was it not an act of defiance, toward your grand-mother?"

"I don't know why I did it. I was excited. Then I was scared."

Crotch, ether, incest. As he stood fighting anesthesia that time, Dr. Naumann thought, in Surgery—with his broken arm—he smelled incest, and there before him was Uncle John with his knife and instruments of punishment. "Associate, please, to the ether cone, that time your arm was broken."

Now marked signs of disturbance. Dr. Marks twisted and stifled a yawn—not a real yawn. He squinted. He began: "Well, it means something over your face. You struggle to breathe . . . Oh, that first tonsilectomy Uncle John did on Bob. I remember something else about it. He apparently blocked Bob's breathing, maybe with blood or something. Anyway he had his mouth down to Bob's mouth or nostrils and was breathing air into him. I heard about this afterward, my mother looked into the kitchen or something and saw it."

This sounded like a defense. "The ether cone."

Dr. Marks began scratching with one finger at his thigh, and the movement seemed tortured and compulsive. "Any smothering. I've always been frightened. If I even thought of the breath stopping. My sisters had temper tantrums as kids and the little so-and-sos'd hold their breath until they got blue in the face. I'd get terrified. I wanted to breathe for them, make them breathe. Stop that choking."

Silence.

Angrily, made to go on: "I'd watch Babe when she was

a baby and she'd roll or something in the crib and I'd think, Maybe she'll get caught and smothered in the bed-clothes."

A death wish. And now it seemed to Dr. Naumann that Dr. Marks's skin had a film of moisture, some bestial hint of other odors. He occasionally seemed to have an awareness, though minimal, of such delicate changes in his patients that gave him a sense of revelations to come. "Yes?"

"I saw her at the breast, one time—"

At the breast (keep still).

"I remember, even if I wasn't so old when I saw it. Yes, Ma had Babe up against her breast, and she reached out to push aside a curtain that was blowing and squeezed Babe up into her breast and Babe choked, began to smother. My mother loosened her right away and Babe began to suck again. But at that moment I distinctly remembered a time when I myself had been nursing—it wasn't so long before that—and had felt that smothering —being pressed into Ma's breast, and yes— Anything that stops the breath, the windpipe!" And now Dr. Marks was touching his mouth.

Orality at last. In the usual burst, Dr. Marks had reached for the source of this pandemonium about ether and the ether cone: the s-mothering breast. The crotch, Uncle John blowing air into Bob and saving him from the strangling clot of blood, then the breast. That hint of revelation had indeed been fulfilled, and perhaps it would be as well to terminate here, Dr. Naumann thought.

"All right, that's enough for this time."

Let him remember that suggestion of the hostile breast.

16

Margaret looked at him sitting with his arms stuck well out sideways as if to give himself room. Stubborn. "Why don't you eat two eggs?" she said.

"Because I only want one. Feed your children two eggs. My mother spent years feeding me two and three eggs and special cream. All I want is one egg."

Stubborn. It had made a problem with the apartment (or was I the problem? she thought). First she had resisted coming to Manhattan. Brooklyn was her home and she had unexplained anxieties about leaving it, but of course John was right that Manhattan would be nearer everything, work (the Center), Naumann, the Institute. "I can get home easier. I won't be tempted to sleep over at the Center." It was true. She couldn't argue. And he promised to find a rent-controlled apartment within their means. Robert would send a truck and help them move. It was feasible.

That part was all right. She gave in on that. But then he found a large, cheap apartment on the seventeenth floor of an old apartment house in the East Seventies. He was determined to have it. She still didn't know how she got him out of it. The seventeenth floor and there would have to be windows open, and with children—with Nancy? Children did fall. And she had a right to worry about them. Just knowing she felt that way, how could he insist on taking such a place? Did he have *no* consideration?

Well, she got him out of that and they kept looking and at last saw this one on East 64th Street, on the second floor, big too, but not that big, and they began thinking how their furniture would do in it.

This was the one they took. But the kids. All their friends were in Brooklyn. Nancy was leaving Murray! ("But he can come over here to see you! You'll see him." Boohoohoohoohoo.) Bob and Johnny had walked around the new apartment sullen as cats. Johnny said, "Where do we put the globe?" He proved there was no place to put the globe.

She had to admit she was tired from the moving. But not John. A change of pace for him was a rest. He was already recovered from his long months of work at New State Hospital.

They were having breakfast in the dining room that connected across a hallway with the kitchen. Across another hall behind her was the open entrance to the living room. Already John was planning to put folding doors in to close off the living room the way he had been able to close it off in Brooklyn. Settling in to home. Already he had personally unpacked the pack-plant donkey and watered it and put it where it belonged, and had put his large armchair in approximately the same place it had occupied in the living room in Brooklyn.

He finished his egg and got up, intent, undeviating, probably the way he looked standing over patients.

Stubborn.

Later before leaving, he said to her, "I'm not making excuses for New State, but maybe there's this to be said: When a doctor goes to his first dissection, he smells guts and disinfectant everywhere and loses his appetite—you'll see him buy ten-cent lunches at the cafeteria. Sometimes he faints. Maybe the first experience of the Unconscious is the same—guts, blood, mucus—stuff that should stay inside out of sight."

This thought was steadily with him, the disturbing quality of the Unconscious. You never seemed to get used to it, the way you did with physical guts and blood.

But in spite of that, you *had* to do something. And it was the sense that they (the staff) hadn't the slightest intention of doing anything that had made his last day at New State so awful.

In one of the corridors that day he had passed a woman standing facing the wall, one hand to her mouth, the other to her ear. "Hello, hello. Put—put through the call immediately. Please!" Wheedling: "Listen, please." Whispering: "I must have help right away. Right away. You ever hear of Bessie De Vois, the voice? She's after me. Help me before—before— Help!"

In the dayroom at the end of the corridor, he came to a

young woman whom he knew. Margie. Quickly she walked to him and said, "I want something to drink . . . What shall we drink? Do you have something? When shall we have something to drink—at tea?"

"What do you want to drink?" he asked.

"Pomegranate juice and snow from heaven."

She hurried away. She came to another patient and announced, "I'm going to heaven."

"Says you."

"I am."

"How'll you get there?"

Proudly: "I have a private ladder. Through the air."

She hurried back to Dr. Marks. "My mother's in heaven," she said. She walked quickly away again.

Another patient said, "Stew four times a week, but there's no meat in it. Chocolate pudding four times a week, but there's no sugar in it. They put the bread through wires."

Margie approached him again and said, as she glided by, "What's the word about the crops?"

Unchanging, always the same, nobody listening, nobody interested, and these hurt souls called out endlessly in their Aesopian language for understanding and help.

Would they ever be heard?

When he reached the Center, he went directly to Dr. Stieglitz's office. His secretary in a side room said, "I'll get him on the phone for you. He wants to see you." The calling system began ringing and Dr. Marks realized that it was ringing throughout the building. Two long and a short. "Here's Dr. Stieglitz," the secretary said.

"Dr. Marks?"

"Yes."

"I wonder if you'd like to come down to Six south. I'm looking at a new case there."

"Of course, Doctor."

In Ward Six south, as attractive a ward as those he'd seen the day before, on one of the beds with its beige cover stripped down, lay a young woman in a straitjacket thrashing her head from side to side so rapidly it was hard to see her. Her hair flew all over her face. "This is Nora Paul," Dr. Stieglitz said, and continued as if she couldn't hear him, "She was brought to us because she took an overdose of sleeping pills and she believes she's ugly. She believes she's so ugly nobody could love her or want anything to do with her." Sharply: "Nora?"

"The engines make deep impressions, don't they?"

"What?" Dr. Marks said to her. But she did not answer, only continued ceaselessly writhing. When her head stopped at last like a halted motion-picture film, her hair fell back and revealed her as not only not ugly, but beautiful. And with the most appealing kind of beauty, for him: a look of sadness.

"Her father could afford the finest private hospital for her, but he wants her here. Her husband too—he's some big brass in the Army. He's overseas." Dr. Stieglitz gave a nurse directions to have Mrs. Paul transferred to a private room on the floor. "And, Dr. Marks," he said, "you stay with her, please. Give her sedation and then come to my office."

"Yes, Doctor."

Dr. Stieglitz left.

In spite of the straitjacket, Nora now tried to get out of the bed. Dr. Marks put his hands on her shoulders, holding her: "Easy. Easy."

"Phil orders—" She made a sudden attempt to bite his hand, but he evaded her.

Two uniformed male attendants wheeled up a stretcher table and lifted and slid Nora onto it, and the table headed for a single room like an extension of the ward—the same beige bedcover and window drapes. "This is it," one of the attendants said. "Would you help us, Doc?"

That meant help them put her in restraint. Always a messy job, always something repellent about it. Patients always fought it, and it always seemed an indignity to any human being, no matter how sick. But it had to be done. He helped lift the girl to the bed and caught a breath of her closeness. Then as much in one motion as the attendants could manage, they were tying her legs, fastening the coarse worn canvas straps to her fine, silk-sheathed ankles. Quickly and expertly they ran the straps down over the end of the bed and made them fast. So they had her roped to that extent. Now they fastened the canvas sheet to one side of the bed and tossed its gray panel across her body, and immediately she raised her legs. Automatic, that resistance to the sheet. "Put your legs down," one of the attendants said and as the legs did not go down, he pushed on them. Still they did not go down. "Sit on them," the other attendant muttered, and whether the patient heard this, or whether it was coincidental, her legs went down and they fastened the canvas in place.

The sedative. Dr. Marks thought, Should I give it? She had screamed several times, had shouted, "Mother." That deluge of sheer panic motion. He put his hand on her forehead. It was not too dry, but it was hot. If he had been shown this case, if Joe, for example, had tipped him off that there was the male equivalent of a case like this and he had come and examined it, he would have taken it. One straight-on glance such as this girl had given him, its appeal singing and bleeding with terror, would have been enough.

He simply knew he would be back, and if coming back was to mean anything, he could not give a sedative.

Let's hope Stieglitz doesn't ask if I gave it.

When he entered Dr. Stieglitz's office, Dr. Stieglitz smiled and said, "I've been looking forward to the chance of having a private word with you. I wanted to tell you—I called New State Hospital yesterday—I was talking with Dr. Parker there and you know what he said to me?"

"No, what?"

"He said you had the patients in the hallway calling you Papa." With amusement: "I'm sure Dr. Parker has no idea what transference means or that there might be sense to it. However . . . Did I understand right that he said you had treated two and possibly more patients there?"

Well, this was it. There was no use trying to avoid it any longer. "I did treat a certain type of patient at New State Hospital." He told in detail what he had done with acute catatonic cases in exhaust status. Dr. Stieglitz listened. Dr. Marks felt encouraged by his listening and finally said, "What do you think of it, of these results?"

"Astonishing. I'm not sure I understand it all entirely, but there's no doubt you must have some natural flair. I'm thinking about this Nora Paul case—what's your opinion of a case like that?"

"It already occurred to me that this is a good deal like the ones I was doing at New State."

"It is?"

"Very much."

"You're under analysis with Naumann." As Dr. Stieglitz

said this, he touched his carefully trimmed beard. "I suppose you know Freud knew Naumann's work and spoke highly of it."

Dr. Marks decided to make no comment.

"You're an older man. I have confidence in you. Would you like to take this Nora Paul case?"

"I'll take it."

"Mr. and Mrs. Bridenbaugh, Nora's parents, have an appointment to come in at ten thirty. Suppose you see them and get as much as you can about her from them— be as thorough as you possibly can."

"I will, Doctor."

"About your other duties today. Take it easy with them. There's nothing that can't go except—I did speak to Dr. Bently to say you'd make yourself available to him to help with insulin. You'd better speak to him."

Taken aback: "I hadn't been doing any shock at New State."

"You haven't had any experience with insulin?" Dr. Stieglitz said with surprise.

"Well, yes, but I stopped giving it. I didn't believe in it."

"Oh, well, that's understandable, but you shouldn't object to what we're doing here. This is a thorough investigation of every aspect of shock therapy to find out whether it should be used or not. Proposals have been made that different methods of giving shock—different combinations and so on—affect the results. We want to go into all that and see whether we can settle the matter."

"I see."

"You don't object to being part of that?"

Put that way, it was difficult to say no. "All right," he said, "I'll see Dr. Bently."

When he was finished talking with Dr. Stieglitz, the Bridenbaughs had arrived, and Dr. Stieglitz suggested he go to his office and wait for them. At his office, he asked the switchboard operator for the nurse on the ward on Six south.

"Miss Jones," a voice answered.

"This is Dr. Marks who's on the Nora Paul case. How has Mrs. Paul been since she's been put in restraint?"

"She's making a lot of noise. Maybe you can hear her."

He heard a distant screaming. "Doesn't it let up?" he asked.

"Yes, it lets up."

"I know it isn't pleasant to have that disturbance there, but I have a reason for keeping her off sedation until I can come down. If it gets too bad, will you call me? My extension—" he looked at the number disc on his phone—"is two forty-seven."

"Yes, Doctor."

That blond hair—he could see it. Lashing from side to side. And the eyes with their panic sadness. Breaking the image, there was a knock on the door.

"Come in."

The man who came in, carrying a fedora and a camel's-hair topcoat, impressed Dr. Marks as self-possessed, his wife perhaps less so. She was blond like Nora and had a somewhat similar disarray. He seated the Bridenbaughs in comfortable chairs facing him, and let them collect themselves.

"Dr. Marks," Mr. Bridenbaugh said, "Dr. Stieglitz says you're an experienced therapist."

"I have had some experience, and some success, with mental cases."

"Cases like our daughter?"

"I've had very little time to examine your daughter, but from what I can tell—yes."

"Doctor," Mrs. Bridenbaugh said, "is there hope for our girl?"

"What does Dr. Stieglitz say?" Dr. Marks asked.

"He said there was hope."

"I take it he bases that on the fact that many first breakdowns like your daughter recover. This *is* a first breakdown, isn't it?"

"It is. There was never any sign of trouble before this."

"That would be hard to say as definitely as that."

"Yes, I believe it would," Mr. Bridenbaugh agreed. "And I think you're right—"

"She was a little depressed sometimes," Mrs. Bridenbaugh said.

"It's just that it didn't seem serious. Really there was nothing so serious that we would have expected this."

Dr. Marks: "Would you tell me about the breakdown, please?"

Mrs. Bridenbaugh said, "She had seemed all right, just once in a while she seemed quiet—a little moody—didn't go out much. Then you know about the sleeping pills. She left a note before she took them—you know about that, I guess—saying she felt worthless. That's what I can't understand." Catching her breath. "Why, we've always . . . She did so well in her studies. And athletics—she had such a fine build. I always said she would have made a wonderful boy."

Mr. Bridenbaugh said, "My wife wanted a son."

"I suppose you didn't," his wife said.

Quietly Dr. Marks asked, "How old is your daughter?"

"She's twenty-one."

"Other children? Does she have brothers or sisters?"

"We have two other daughters."

"Their names and ages, please?"

"Rita's twenty-seven. Betty's twenty-five."

So Nora was the youngest. The disappointment of a third girl.

"Can you tell me any circumstances about Nora's birth?" Dr. Marks now had out a pencil and was beginning to write with the same rapid scribble he used taking down the productions of patients. Everything had left his mind except the pursuit of traces of pathology.

Two days later, at the beginning of his session with Dr. Naumann, he told him that Nora was out of psychosis. The day before, he had said he was sure she was coming out. Now he said she was out.

"Completely out?" Dr. Naumann said.

"She's out of restraint—out of the straitjacket. She's back in reality. If you saw her, you'd agree. I don't mean that I'm not going to go on seeing her and working with her, trying to build her insight. But I've told you—it's easier to build up insight in these patients than in neurotics. They remember psychosis as if they'd had a dream. She'll get better. I know. I know from my experience at New State."

"What do they think of this at the Center?"

"There's quite a lot of excitement, of course. Dr. Stieglitz has talked with her. He knows she's out of it, but he expects some kind of relapse. I don't. Or if there is, it won't last. She *is* depressed, but not as unrealistically as she was before. It's more—" he tried to think what it was "—it's more as if she was embarrassed at having had to take this way out of her troubles. And sad at coming back into reality again and finding it much the same." After a pause: "But there's one difference."

"Yes?"

"She feels that there's somebody around now who values her and understands her."

Silence.

"She's a fine girl. Really fine." A fine intelligence and a fine delicate something about her lips and eyes, even in her sadness. Her psychosis was as if she had been "crowded" in some unexpected way, taken by surprise. The sadness had leaped on her. He told Dr. Naumann something of what he had felt about her, the rush of intuitions that so often—perhaps always—accompanied these quick cases. A sense of knowing by a series of explosions and a sense that the patient knew with you, and just as quickly. "I felt that if I could have seen her before it happened, perhaps it wouldn't have had to happen at all. But of course that's probably just subjective thinking. They have to go through this experience to get back to themselves."

The Bridenbaughs were overwhelmed with a most evident and even awkward joy. In their gratitude, they even went so far as to try to give a present to Dr. Stieglitz's wife.

Nora had talked with her parents. Somehow Dr. Marks had shivered when he undertook that interview, but it had gone all right. But she had not wanted to see them long.

"What are you thinking?" Dr. Naumann said.

He said, "I was thinking about Nora. About her parents. They—well, let me put it this way. They seemed to share her embarrassment about the whole thing. Maybe that's a good sign. Maybe that will help them get together."

Dr. Naumann now remained silent. As the silence went on, Dr. Marks knew that he must start the work of the session. He thought of a dream he had had the night before that had troubled him more than its content seemed to justify. Strange dream in a way. "I dreamed I was angry with Robert—my brother. I told him he was putting too many machines in his plant and not to do it, and I felt it very strongly."

Silence.

"I'm never angry with Robert. I felt upset when I woke up and carried over that angry feeling from the dream—

felt that funny anger. Of course, right away it went away."

Robert was somebody else. Or merged with somebody else. "Have you ever been angry with Robert?"

"Oh, as kids we'd fuss. Yeah, we'd have fights. But that's long over and even then we stuck together. Anybody touched Robert had me to reckon with—had to fight the both of us."

Stuck together. Dr. Naumann said, "Is there anything that happened yesterday that might have led to this dream?"

"Well, I went to see Dr. Bently late in the afternoon. I'd telephoned him the day before and I guessed I couldn't put off seeing him, so I went to his office. And there on a table near the door were several bottles of glucose. That killed me. Dr. Bently killed me too. He's one of these professor types. You know, makes you feel small just by the way he talks to you. A real Uncle John. He deigned to tell me about his experimental program—yes, that anger I felt with Robert was just like how I felt about that whiff of electric shock and insulin, and the reason I passed it on to Robert is I do have a feeling he's overexpanding a little at the plant and ought to slow up. Too many machines (shock machines?). I've spoken to him about it. Possibly there was a little irritation when I told him. I suppose one thing is that—"

"Yes?" Dr. Naumann said.

"Well, it's a little embarrassing—petty, I guess. I was afraid he might think I'd rather he invested the money in me, but of course there's no real issue about that. What he gives me is a small matter. He'd urge me to take more if I needed it."

Silence.

"I associated Robert, I guess, to this Dr. Bently, and Bently to Uncle John. Well, there is one reason for that, for associating the three of them. All three of them are swell dressers. I'm aware Robert and I are fighting it out to be Uncle John, Robert as a dresser, me as a doctor. Unconsciously, of course. There's no real sibling rivalry between us, that I know of. I'm fond of Robert. Really am. But I suppose there can be some rivalry you're not aware of."

There can also be unconscious homosexual fondness. That expression, "we stuck together." Clues had occasionally appeared before. If there is fondness, you resist it.

"I mentioned going after Uncle John's role, being a doctor. You know it wasn't just that—and this is strange. He had a peculiar affection for me when I was a boy. He used to take me out in the automobile, the Stevens Duryea he had at the time. Then he bought a Franklin that was air-cooled, and then a Kissel car—all Kissel cars are out of existence now. He'd take me along in his car and I'd wait there while he went in to see a patient. I'd make believe it was me going in to make the call. In later years he'd invite me up to his house—for breakfast he'd invite me up—when I was already in medical school, and he'd quiz me about things that were happening in medicine. He had a technique that I got on to. First he would try to impress me with how much he knew by asking me some obscure point in obstetrical anatomy that I couldn't answer, then he'd ask me, 'What is this about red blood cells, this work with red blood cells, what is this about the blood cells?' Even if he was one of the attendings in the Brooklyn Jewish Hospital, and also at Long Island College Hospital, the finest hospital in Brooklyn, his medical background was limited compared with what I was getting—what was considered scientific then—and so he'd quiz me that way, not letting on that he didn't know, and I'd tell him things. And about that time there was a change in him. It was a real change that I could notice. He began to dislike me. He began to try to run me down in the family, said I wouldn't make a doctor and would be a drawback to the profession and so on, and that got me terrified. Because he was like Father. You couldn't do anything about Father. It just wasn't in the cards."

Here the associations had come back to a familiar pattern as they so often did—from a new angle. Uncle John. His father was identified with Uncle John in a number of ways, and here in a new way. Father wants me to fail. Uncle John wants me to fail. Father says I can do nothing for the mentally ill. Uncle John (though he is dead now) also says I can do nothing.

But, Dr. Naumann thought, there is something else. Dr. Marks knows that he really knows more than Uncle John. He knows he's right and Father-Dr. John is wrong. We've worked it through, and there should be much less unconscious need now to give in to Father. But these patterns persist. Insights lose freshness and have to be reinstated.

"What are you thinking now?"

"Nora. In the psychosis she said, 'I can't shoot down any of those toy soldiers,' and she told me afterward that her mother did give her a set of toy soldiers to play with. Imagine how they told her all the time she was worthless. Not in so many words like my father did. But, 'You ought to be a boy who can play with toy soldiers, shoot them down.' A kid like that and they go to work on her. She did almost succeed in killing herself."

"Shooting the toy down?"

"I suppose killing herself was equivalent to shooting. She did what they said she couldn't do. The way I do what Uncle John says I can't do."

"But you also do what he wants you to do, and what Father wants you to do."

Dr. Marks answered now with urgency, "No, I don't. Yes, I do—or I have. You mean she has some of that in her?" I'm always the patient, he thought. Always. And what I learn about myself here I carry as therapeutic tools to the patient. And I make that offering of myself. "Her thinking she's worthless," he said. "And they got her to believe it, right in the middle of that blob of brain of hers, they made her believe it. I just said I don't believe it about myself, but then why did I have to knock them dead by curing a case in two days at the Center? Why did I have to show off I was so great?" He frowned. "No, it doesn't feel like that." He glanced upward nervously. "Nora was just something I had to do—a girl like that. I had to help her."

Silence.

"Didn't I? Didn't I have to do it?"

The evening meal that night was centered around a large baked ham garnished with apple like some baronial boar.

"I suppose I have to carve this damn ham, work all day and work all night. Bob, aren't you old enough to carve?"

"Weak wrists," Bob muttered. He made no motion to get up and take the knife from his father. Dr. Marks cut the ham with surgical precision, laying out slices like organ sections, and finally he spread his elbows as the presiding male and began to eat. "Well, this was quite a day at the hospital." Talking as he ate: "I cured another patient, I mean I cured my first one at the Center." Nancy shook her hair back and forth admiringly, like Nora's tossing hair. Also blond.

Margaret said to the children, "Your father really did quite a thing there." To her husband: "I guess they don't usually get them out of psychosis in two days, do they?"

"You can damn well say they don't." He described the case, his enthusiasm boiling up like a happy fever. Nancy said, "What's 'worthless'?"

"Well, like you're worth a lot to me. I guess I would pay twenty-five million dollars for you. Maybe more. But Nora thought she was worthless. I mean, worth maybe five cents."

"Five cents is a lot."

"She thought she was worth nothing. That's what being worthless means." He held up a tiny sliver of ham. "Not worth even that much."

To try out the new word, Nancy held up a crumb of bread. "Worthless," she said.

"Yes, that's about it." He addressed the table in general. "Nora reminded me of several patients at New State. Well, I guess she reminded me of all my patients there. She wasn't screaming around as much, but she sure was crazy. You know, she thought she had to kill herself. She thought she had to do that to make somebody happy. But also maybe she thought somebody else wanted to kill her."

"Who?" Bob said.

"Who knows?" But he was beginning to have an idea.

Margaret thought, He's really on a tear tonight.

"Of course, Naumann sure got me over this pint-sized pride. An interesting thing," Dr. Marks said to Margaret.

"What?"

"I'll tell you about it later."

Later, alone with Margaret in the living room, he told her about his session. "I still seem to be fighting to be worth something," he said. She sat near him on the sofa, her attractive legs folded under her. "He got me around to seeing that."

"But you said that's an old insight."

"It is. You go back and back. And then you go on." He rubbed his jaw, tactilely aware of what he minimized in the mirror, the rough, coarse lines of his skin. He frowned. "I was too high about Nora. What does it mean? A quick score, yes. But that isn't what I came to the Center for." Now the insight was beginning to work for him.

"But isn't it good that they let you do it, were happy you did it?"

"Yes, that part's good. But I was just repeating New State. But that isn't my main business at the Center, that isn't how I'll get to learn anything new there." He fitted a cigarette to his long cigarette holder and began to think of the Tenth Floor, the small, porthole-like windows of the cells there. He eliminated from his mind the woman on the floor there and replaced her with other silent forms. Truly withdrawn patients. Patients unencountered as yet, patients with symbolic (not real) blankets wrapped around them, patients who lived hidden away in the nuclear cell of the psyche. "It's something else I'm after now."

Later that evening, Dr. Marks's brother Robert appeared, quietly as always. He hadn't been able to come during the moving. Now he went through the entire apartment and approved of it. "You'll be comfortable here. It's a nice place." He looked in on Nancy sleeping.

How could I have had that dream about him? Dr. Marks thought. But in the shape of Robert's nose and in a certain curved line at the side of his lips he saw his father, and in spite of himself he saw on Robert's face for that moment the shadow of his father's censoriousness.

It didn't matter. Affection was what mattered. You needed a brother. It wasn't just that it made you a little stronger to stand against the world, and in Jewish families that meant a lot, but the thing was: a brother had had the same life experience you had. Nobody could be closer in that one sense. The same blood, tissue, memory, love. The same suffering. Same from the cradle up. Often it seemed to him that he could see inside Robert's head. Head? The whole damn organism. When he's tired or angry, I know why. I walk with him between those machines in his factory. He looks out of my eyes at patients.

That identification in love. You grow to have it with a wife. You're given it with a brother (or sister, let's not forget Dora and Babe). That identification of love. Isn't it what you have with patients?

"Margaret," he said. "Can't you break out a nice hard-boiled egg for Robert?" He watched her pout. That was what you called bringing the family close.

17

When Dr. Marks arrived at the Center at nine o'clock Monday morning, he decided to take a chance on seeing Dr. Bently, and started up to his office.

This Dr. Bently. After the session with Naumann on Friday, Naumann had stopped him a moment as he was leaving. "Is that a Dr. Josiah Bently whom you saw yesterday?" Dr. Marks said it was. "Well, he's an analyst, a member of the Society. I thought you might wish to know." Immediately Dr. Marks had wondered how he could have had such hostile feelings toward an analyst. It alarmed him. I really have got to watch that transference thing. But—the thought came to him now as he was walking upstairs to the second floor, up the wide low steps of the stair shaft (which above the second floor was protected with a wire door)—why does an analyst have a position supervising shock-research programs? He found no answer in the institutional-looking brick-walled stair shaft, and came out on the second floor.

Dr. Bently's office was at the end of one of the corridors where it widened into an alcove for his secretary's desk. Somehow it made Dr. Bently rate a little under Dr. Stieglitz that he didn't have a private office for his secretary, but had her in the hall. She seemed like a watchdog for his closed door and said, "He's in, but he's on the phone. I think he'll soon be through and then you can go in."

So he would wait (as he had waited as a child for Uncle John to make his visits).

"Good morning, Dr. Marks." Shaking hands: "You know since speaking with you Friday I've heard about the Nora Paul case. I almost feel we ought not to be putting you on insulin service, taking your time that way, but then it's only for a month, and I suppose the other residents will feel better if you take your expected turn at it. And it won't mean too much time anyway, an hour and a half—eighteen patients." He went into a detailed discussion of some of the cases which he said were "interesting. You'll want to read the charts on them. They help us in evaluating the results." Dr. Bently had a moustache whose gray was at variance with his darker hair. He went on, "I wanted to mention, you're probably familiar with Lauretta Bender's research program at New York University and Bellevue, with children?"

"No, I'm afraid I'm not."

"Well, I'll give you her material to read, then. It's quite important. I know this kind of research is difficult to face, but we're committed to finding out what can or can't be done with shock." What did that mean? "We have two children we're giving insulin to, and during your service we're going to add another boy. I want you to meet him. He's here, he's up in the children's ward now, and we'll see him and then—" he looked at his wristwatch "—it'll be a good time for me to take you down to the insulin ward."

Children, Dr. Marks thought. Older adolescents, probably.

And now he had an involuntary shudder. It was quick and sharp and definite, as if some charge of horror had run along his spine. That wasn't like him, that kind of reaction. Embarrassed, he wondered if Dr. Bently might have noticed it. What gives with me? You're a doctor and you have to take things as they come. He had had suffering children in his private practice and he had been able to care for them—in fact he'd done very well with them.

"Have you been on the children's wards?" Dr. Bently was saying.

"I haven't seen them yet." They were now leaving the office and going along the corridor.

"They're beautifully organized: playrooms, gym, a classroom—regular schoolroom accredited by the city school system."

A schoolroom. But how could psychotic kids be going to school? This didn't sound like they were very sick.

Dr. Bently continued talking as they came nearer and nearer to this children's ward. Rather desperately Dr. Marks said, "From a Freudian viewpoint, isn't it hard to accept this insulin and electric shock approach to mental illness?"

"Well, the work has to be done, and you know Freud began with physiologic—neurologic—interests. There was that near-miss of his with cocaine, and he published a whole series, well, several, papers on neurologic subjects and always considered the possibility of an organic basis —a chemical-organic basis—for emotional disturbances."

Dr. Marks knew that Freud had carried over into his early period certain misunderstandings that he got in his medical school days that led him to make some guarded statements about the organicity of psychosis, but to quote that . . .

He heard children's voices, subdued, but with the flooding freedom of childhood—the soaring sound that seems all eagerness and laughter. And he had a presentiment. As they were passing an open door, glancing sideways, he saw what was evidently a gymnasium. At one end a heavy net hung between the ceiling and a wall, and a woman instructor was talking with a boy who seemed to be climbing the net. This was a boy of about twelve. But that sound he was hearing ahead, that must be still younger. "George will be in the playroom now," Dr. Bently said, and further down the corridor, he opened a glass-paned door. "Go in, please, Doctor."

A dozen boys and girls, most of them on the floor surrounded by toy ambulances, trucks, and blocks. None of them was as old as the kid in the gym. Dr. Bently grasped Dr. Marks's arm and guided him to a horse made of a barrel. A horse's head, rather small for the large barrel, had been nailed on one end and a tail on the other and stirrups were fastened to the sides. "This is Tar. We call him that because he's made of a tar barrel," Dr. Bently said, putting his hand on the horse. A boy, obviously not more than eight, was sitting astride the barrel. "Do you like him, George?"

This was the boy! There must be some mistake. Dr. Marks looked around the room for an older boy, but there was no older boy, and Dr. Bently was introducing him to this small boy perched on Tar. "This is George Golding. George, this is Dr. Marks. He's going to be your friend. Will you shake hands with him?"

George put out his hand (touch precedes speech). His hand moved actively and in a friendly way, and small as it was, it took hold of Dr. Marks's firmly. George gave a single kick of his legs against the sides of Tar, and smiled.

This is what I have to give insulin to.

"Let me up on Tar," another boy was calling. He tried to climb up in front of George and George pushed him down, but when the boy climbed up in back, George let him stay and both boys cried, "Giddyap, giddyap."

Dr. Marks and Dr. Bently left the room. The child roar softened.

"About George's history," Dr. Bently was saying. "He's an only child, eight years old. His mother brought him in because he's something of a problem child. In school, he insisted on sitting in the first seat of the aisle. He wouldn't sit behind any kids in school. When the teacher once put him in the back of the class, he fainted. He has eczema—"

"Was he doing badly in school?"

"No, he did fairly well. No, the main problem was the eczema—at least that was what was bothering his mother. After a few psychotherapy sessions, she came in and said, 'What's the use bringing him here all the time? He still scratches his eczema.' Then we found out she had some old-time family doctor and he had told her to put heavy mittens on his hands and tie his hands to the bed at night and she was doing that. Of course we told her to stop that at once."

Who's crazy? Dr. Marks thought, the mother or the child? How can an eight-year-old kid be crazy anyway unless there's brain damage? At eight he's in the latency period so maybe he's neurotic or has some neurotic problems, but psychotic? Structurally impossible—you have to develop at least to puberty to regress.

And in the latency period you don't have any heavy pressure or suffering. That comes in puberty when you have to face life.

Or am I wrong? But this kid doesn't look a bit psychotic to me.

"I told her not to tie his hands," Dr. Bently said, "but I suggested he'd be a good patient for insulin. That would quiet him down and make him amenable—balance his emotions. The eczema, of course, is psychosomatic. So his mother agreed and we're going to keep him here at the Center while he's on insulin. He'll begin tomorrow. Of course, the real purpose of this is for the insulin research."

"But he isn't psychotic!"

With that superior, Uncle John tone: "You're only

going by the surface. Underneath there's a schizophrenic involvement. You'll have a chance to talk with the mother and it'll be part of your job to talk with the boy and keep the chart up. Read the chart and talk with Dr. Smith who's been doing the psychotherapy. You'll see what we mean about the involvement." Psychotherapy!

"How old are the two other children who are on insulin?" Dr. Marks asked in a low voice.

"They're about the same age. Tina Howard and Tommy Da Costa. You'll see—they're probably out of insulin by now, or we can bring them out."

An hour later he had gone to his office. He sat there in the full morning light—his office, though small, faced on the Hudson—but he was not aware of light or morning or spring. What could be done about this? He could not go to Dr. Stieglitz or Dr. Carey—an inexperienced resident talk down the program of an experienced analyst? Neither could he back out of it now, for he had been assigned for a month.

He had an impulse to call up Margaret. No, somebody might overhear the call at the switchboard.

He was boxed in. He felt numb and felt a droning in his head. He had met the other two kids on the insulin ward, just being brought out—a sweet little girl with long, gawky legs, and a perfectly pleasant boy. Neither of them was any crazier than George was: it was obvious. Dr. Bently talked about them in their hearing (that universal insensitivity), and said a few words to them. Around them, men and women—adults—were being wakened out of coma. Not to keep the kids in a room by themselves. Tina whispered that she wanted to go back and "play."

And tomorrow they would bring George down there.

No, there must be some way out of this. He just couldn't do it.

Like a faint tremor, a part of his mind communicated to him, Take it easy now. You're just starting here. Don't fall again for that Father-Uncle John thing. You don't actually give the insulin. The nurses give the insulin injections, at five in the morning, and the doctor comes in at nine and gives the glucose (so a most serious part of the program was left to the nurses, and the doctor, of course, didn't have to come in so early). And so, whether you took the insulin service or not, the nurses would go right on with their daily injections. And if you took the service, you could console yourself with the rationalization that you could possibly arrange the results on the charts so that it wouldn't look so good this month for the concept of shocking children.

You better calm down out of this. You have to see Nora. At least Nora hasn't been put on shock. You were able to stop that.

Ahead of him was a day's work to do.

The next morning he was up at five and over to the Center at six. He had not been particularly conscious yesterday of what the insulin ward looked like, just that it seemed stripped compared with the regular wards. And that cloud of sweat that dimmed it into the usual phantasmagoric purgatory. As he approached it now, walking through the early-morning emptiness of the corridor, he listened. Like something predetermined, he heard a scream of terror, clear even down the distance of the hall and through the closed ward door.

When he knocked (the door was latched inside), a nurse, a Miss Fitzhugh, let him in. "Good morning, Dr. Marks. Aren't you awfully early?"

Her tone was friendly and it pleased him that she remembered his name. "I want to see George. Is he still awake?"

"Well—yes, they're awake."

He saw three beds together at the end of the room and walked down through an aisle of gray-blanketed adults to the three children. They were still conscious. Their faces moist and red, they looked frightened. He patted Tina's damp hair and kneeled down by George's bed, taking his hand in a firm grip. "I'm Dr. Marks. You remember me." The hand clenching his gave a spasmodic twitch. A man nearby raised up with the standard precoma "I'm dying." George said, "Am I gonna die?" his voice thick and hoarse.

"Didn't the nurse explain it to you?"

Dilated eyes stared at him.

"It will just make you sleep a while, and then you'll wake up and be all right." Tina had closed her eyes. "That little girl in the next bed," he said to George, "Tina—she had insulin before and she's still all right."

"Stay," the small breath said.

He promised to stay and the boy seemed to relax. The hot minutes of the insulin went by and its power everywhere began seeping down through the brain. Several of the men and one of the women moaned and screamed. They twisted. The nurses and attendants held them, keeping them from falling out of bed, tying them in or readjusting their canvas bonds. Now the time of drowning, the time of those hoarse cries between terror and sleep. Let him be unaware of it. On one of the beds a man had begun to protrude his tongue, over which he seemed to have lost control, and foam formed on his lips.

Let George not see it. Let him go under now.

But now Dr. Marks began to notice a slight twitching. The boy's arm jumped slightly. Alerted, he noticed an uneven motion run through the muscles of the boy's neck and upper chest, a jerk of fibrillary twitching. It was certainly fibrillary twitching. He had seen it too many times with diabetics to mistake it. This kid must be sensitive to insulin. He watched carefully, waiting, delaying, to be sure. But the twitching of different muscle groups continued and he went to Miss Fitzhugh.

"How much insulin did George have?"

"Forty-five units, Doctor. Why, is something the matter?"

"Did he have any testing for sensitivity?"

"Not that I know of." She appeared anxious. Another nurse came up.

"Couldn't he have been started with a smaller amount?"

"But that's what Dr. Bently ordered, Doctor, and the other children started with that."

"He's sensitive to insulin. I'm going to bring him out immediately."

"Yes, Doctor."

He got a syringe of glucose and at the pressure of the slow-moving plunger, George's stuporously pale body warmed into its natural color and he opened his eyes. He blinked.

"You see?" Dr. Marks said. "You just slept a little while."

George rubbed the spot where the injection had been given. He stared around at the comatose bodies near him, some in the thrashing convulsions of shock, some lying still like the girl and boy in the next beds. "They gonna wake up now?" he said.

"No, they have to sleep longer than you. But they'll wake up later. Meantime you can get dressed. Miss Fitzhugh, where are George's clothes?"

"I'll bring them, Doctor."

When she brought them, he said to George, "You can dress yourself, son." To Miss Fitzhugh: "I'll take him back to the children's ward when he's ready."

Lucky he had been there, for who knew what might have happened? The kid could die. And now he was puzzled. A research hospital, up on the latest in technical procedures, and not testing for sensitivity. And not ordering a doctor in attendance the first day. If he hadn't come in on his own—

He put his hand on George's shoulder, comforting him as he slipped into his clothes.

"I'm glad I woke up," George said.

At eleven, he went to Dr. Bently's office and was able to go in without waiting. Dr. Bently said, "Well, so you're finished. No trouble?"

"Yes, there's been trouble." As he started to explain, Dr. Bently interrupted, saying, "You felt it necessary to come in at six?"

"It seemed to me if it was George's first day, a doctor ought to be there." Later in the story, Dr. Bently interrupted again: "You brought him out before coma?"

"Of course."

"But it's very important that we have all three children on the same schedule."

Puzzled: "But can't we begin again tomorrow with perhaps fifteen units? Then we can build it up and find his tolerance."

"No, we have to have all three children on the same basis if we're to work this program out as we've planned it."

"But there was fibrillary twitching."

The Uncle John tone (already present) now became marked. It was not annoyance. It was simply as if Dr. Marks were a novice who could not understand. "You're exaggerating this whole thing, Doctor. There's commonly movement like this. You're probably overconcerned about

George. If you'd watched the other children, I'm sure you'd have seen an equivalent movement with them too. Children in general can be expected to be a little more sensitive to insulin than adults. No, George is to have the same strength as the other children. I'll leave word about it with Miss Fitzhugh. You'll continue him like the others."

Dr. Marks made one final effort. "Would you possibly come there tomorrow and see George?" That meant, of course, that he was asking Dr. Bently to get up in time to be at the hospital at six in the morning. Still in the tone of patience-with-the-novice: "Doctor, we'll keep to the regular schedule as planned. You'll see that George will be all right."

The next morning Dr. Marks came to the insulin ward at five thirty. Miss Fitzhugh let him in as before and mentioned that she had specific orders from Dr. Bently about George's insulin. He made no comment. What could he be expected to say? He went over to George and sat beside him and George asked, "You'll take care of me?"

"I'll take care of you."

The fibrillary twitching repeated itself and at six thirty Dr. Marks got a syringe.

"You're going to bring him out?" Miss Fitzhugh said.

"I have to. But I won't be able to take him back to the children's ward today."

"I know, or they'll report to Dr. Bently."

The look between them said, We understand each other. He said, "The others here I don't suppose will say anything."

"I think not."

He was thinking, New State all over again. Well, what the hell could he do? Out of the side of his eye he saw the heated rows of faces, the tied bodies, sweat, foam—he heard hoarse hints of dyspnea that shook him with their likeness to terror and that perhaps were in fact the panting of unconscious fear. Two men were convulsing.

He plunged the syringe point in and George awakened. "Hello."

"Hello," Dr. Marks said. George was in the end bed. Dr. Marks brought a chair and sat between him and the rest of the ward, shutting off part of his vision. The hoarse breathing could not be shut off and unfortunately two or three beds directly opposite could not be shielded. "Do you feel like going back to sleep?"

"No," George said.

"Well, I'm afraid you're going to have to rest here then. I can't take you back right away this morning to the playroom. But I'll stay right here with you."

A look of fright. "Right here?"

"Of course." Softly: "You like stories, don't you?"

Low: "Yes."

"What stories do you like?"

"I dunno."

Eight? Too old for fairy stories? No, he ought to be just right for them. "Do you know the story of Hansel and Gretel?"

"Yeah." Quick: "Tell that one."

I'm stuck with it. He started: The mother wanted the children taken out into the woods and left there. "The stepmother," George broke in. "The stepmother," Dr. Marks corrected himself. How the kids noticed that! It wasn't your own mother that wanted to do the bad thing, leave you out there to starve. Your own mother loves you. And Father does too, but he gives in to the stepmother. This seemed like the schizophrenic pattern, domineering mothers and weak fathers. How these fairy tales talked to the Unconscious! He went on telling the story; twice the kids were taken to the woods, and the second time they came to the witch's house, made of cake and candy. George's face began to show a remarkable change when Dr. Marks told about the witch's house. It was delighted, ecstatic. "I'd like to go to that witch's house to live," George said.

"But the witch tried to eat Hansel afterward," Dr. Marks said, surprised.

George was not interested in what happened afterward. He dreamed only of the "little house" that he could eat and inside which he would be cared for with so much love. The witch fed you there. She gave you "pancakes and sugar." And "milk and apples and nuts."

"But then she would try to eat you."

George said, "I'd just like to live there."

"Why?"

"It's nice there."

"Why?"

"That witch is nice."

But it was George's face more than anything that told Dr. Marks he was dealing with a state of mind that was not open to ordinary logic. The child had separated out an element of the fairy tale, and was not interested in anything else.

"Do you think about that house?" Dr. Marks said.

A quick look, as if startled. "Yes."

"When do you think about it?"

"When the bird flies around."

"I don't understand, son."

"I see the bird." Then silence. George was staring up in the air, toward the ceiling.

"Do you see the bird now?"

Smiling: "Naw, not now."

"When do you see it?"

"Oh, in the street. Like—it flies up in the sky."

"Why does the bird make you think of the house?"

A confused look. No answer.

I'm not letter-perfect on that story, Dr. Marks thought. Maybe there's something in the story about a bird. "Is there a bird in the story?"

"Yeah, the bird that takes them to the house."

So there you were, with the hidden answer. For a minute he thought the kid was talking crazy. They don't talk crazy, but you can find out from kids something about the early processes of thought and language. Splitting and projection and all those mechanisms. Symbols.

He remembered Nancy and her drawing of the turkey.

This kid, he was a perfect doll! A dark line of eyelashes and a small dimple near his mouth. The eyelashes were prettier than some girls'. Thinking of girls, Dr. Marks looked at the small girl in the next bed, still in coma, her very small body running out of the covers into a dead-white face. In the rumpled bed it was hard to be sure he even saw her body. Her face was like something on a dissecting table, waxen and still; then her lips formed a speck of foam. By watching the space where her chest must be in the bedclothes, he detected her breathing.

How hot it was here! He himself was sweating.

"You didn't finish the story."

Dr. Marks smiled. "But you don't want to hear the rest of it, about the bad witch."

The boy smiled, but whether he was amused or whether

he just wanted to answer Dr. Marks's smile, Dr. Marks did not know. George's small face was normally flushed from the warm room. "I'll listen," he said.

"Gretel had to feed her brother," Dr. Marks began, and he told the rest of the story.

Dr. Marks talked with Dr. Smith who had done the psychotherapy with George. To his surprise, Dr. Smith was a resident like himself, not too long at the Center. "But, Dr. Smith, have you had experience with psychotherapy?"

"No, I never did it before, but I'm doing a little now."

"Well, does somebody show you how to do it?"

"No, I just do it and then talk with Dr. Bently." Dr. Smith seemed embarrassed. "The fact of the matter is I'm not very good at it. I don't know exactly what psychotherapy is."

"Haven't you watched them doing it here?"

"No, I don't think there is anybody to watch."

"Do you do psychotherapy with other patients?"

"A few."

"Are you in analysis?" Dr. Marks asked.

"Oh, no," Dr. Smith said, as if analysis was the last thing he would be in.

"Tell me about George."

He told Dr. Marks a few things. "His father, I'm afraid, has been rather rough with him. And then he has some story about his father taking him to some bridge, and he was afraid his father was going to fall off." This man must have some sensitivity, Dr. Marks thought. Dr. Smith took a key chain out of his pocket and wrapped it around his long, flexing fingers. "I mention this because he seemed very much disturbed about it. He cries when he talks about it."

'If I sit behind somebody, I'll push them.'

'I don't hurt anybody else. I scratch and tear myself' (eczema).

"Are you going to lunch?" Dr. Marks asked.

"I'm sorry, I have an appointment during my lunch hour."

Would it be useful to try to give Dr. Smith some insights about George? But why wasn't Dr. Stieglitz doing that? And how did Dr. Stieglitz expect Dr. Smith to do "psychotherapy" anyway? With nothing to go on but his own evident sensitivity, but was that enough?

The whole thing was hard to believe.

After lunch, he went to see Nora. "How do you find it?" he said.

"All right. Yes—all right."

"Nothing wrong?"

"They want me to eat more than I want, but—no, it's all right."

"You look as if you could stand to eat a little."

"I know. Well, hospital food. Even in the best hospital." She lowered her eyes, and her long lashes brushed her cheeks. He thought, She hasn't yet smiled. So many were like that, at this stage of recovery. Discouraged maybe, looking for something different that might be better, inside themselves or outside. "What's the people?" he said.

"Oh, nothing. No, really nothing."

"I've given orders that your parents are not to see you for a week. That doesn't bother you, does it?"

Now for the first time a faint smile. "No."

"What about your husband? Could we get him back from where he is?"

"Oh, no, Phil couldn't come back."

"Is there some reason why you weren't with him?" Dr. Marks asked.

"I guess it's my fault. He wanted me over there, but I wouldn't go."

"You may wish to later." When she was sure she wasn't ugly.

He indicated the empty ward outside. "Where are all these people?" he said.

"Well, they go to art and things."

"Do you want to go to art?"

Worriedly: "I won't be here that long, will I?"

"Until the staff discharges you. Until they're convinced you'll be all right outside. You know there is some reason to be worried about you."

"I know. But I won't—I would never——"

"Illuminations, cathartics, all from sperm oil," he heard a voice cry down past the end of the ward, from a private room.

"Is that a new patient?" he said.

"Yes, a very fat girl. I shouldn't say that."

"Why not? What's her name?"

"Minnie something." Nora listened. The girl's voice that had been loud for a moment dropped to a murmur that seemed happy. He said, "She sounds happy, doesn't she?" The same deception they all practiced.

Almost indignantly: "She's not."

"What do you suppose she meant, 'Illuminations, cathartics, all from sperm oil?' "

" 'Eliminations, cathartics.' "

"Yes—we'll have to make you a therapist." Another faint smile from Nora. He thought, By mentioning sperm and elimination (urine?), might Minnie be confusing her sex? It was impossible not to catch such meanings and the high condensation in "illuminations—eliminations" that also included the sperm oil for lamps. "Cathartics," that might mean defecation and giving birth. Did she want to give birth? How loaded these productions were! He said, "Can we talk about you?"

"Yes."

"You dream last night?"

"I did have a dream. I have a friend, a girl named Marianne. She's been married, but she's divorced. I dreamed I went into her bedroom and her husband was there and I felt like an intruder."

"What's an intruder?" he said.

"Oh, a person who encroaches on somebody else's property—I mean, trespasses. A dirty little brat—"

A child who goes into the parents' bedroom. "Keep on."

"Nothing head—"

"What's a 'nothing head?' "

"Oh, just something my mother used to call me. Then he—she gets angry. She's very egotistical. She's a megalomaniac really. She ought to die."

"Who ought to?"

It was as if she woke up. "I wasn't talking about myself."

"Who were you talking about?" he said.

"I don't know."

She had been talking about herself, and he hadn't missed the verbal slip confusing he and she. You're worthless so you have to be very valuable, but he had seldom seen the confusion come out so clearly and in a relatively sane state. For this girl was no longer psychotic, he was sure of it, and he knew how fine the line was, that fraction away. At New State, patients would talk along, protecting themselves and covering up, keeping away from any gross betrayal of their pathology. Such a patient would talk "straight" for an hour, then after that long period of control, say, "And that spoon being left that way, do you suppose it could be a message? If one understood?"

"I think you were talking about yourself."

"But how could I be?" she said.

"You're not consciously afraid of dying. But who knows what's going on underneath?"

"I thought someone wanted to poison me."

"The someone who considered you an intruder?" he said.

"I don't know who it was."

Interested: "When did you think that?"

"Those last two days."

Before she became crazy, he thought.

"Well—how were they going to poison you?"

"I'm not sure, but I felt— It was as if somebody near me was going to do it."

"How?" he persisted.

"I don't know."

"Would they put poison in your food?"

"No!" She seemed shocked.

"But then how could they?"

A baffled silence. As she continued to say nothing, he said, "Were you afraid?"

"I'm sorry I'm not clear about it." She pushed her hair back.

"Did you ever feel like you might be poisoned in the past any time?"

Thoughtfully: "I would sometimes be sick or nauseous and I'd think it might be something in my food. But that's different, isn't it?"

"When would that happen, can you remember?"

She looked at him as if inside she were asking herself the same question, and hoping to get it answered. "No," she said.

"Sperm whales are very useful," the voice outside called. "They make soap."

He thought, driving home that afternoon from Dr. Naumann's, Some sessions seemed to repeat previous sessions in spite of every conscious effort to break through and go forward. There seemed a fascination that held the mind to a fixed point. Like insanity. Turning and turning on one point. He had been thinking about patients at New State.

He had known one who had had a delusion that objects around her were extremely valuable, and she had had to observe them "intently." He had been told she had been that way as long as she had been there. She spent hours walking along the corridors and around the circumference of the dayroom, or in and out of the ward and around every bed. She would find a small bit of fur. "That's Canberra rabbit—very valuable. I once saw just a palate and a few teeth, just think! Look there, there's an amethyst." She would speak of object after object and all full of "wealth." "Nobody knows the effort, the effort," she would say. "There's a Malay mahogany." One day, and this was why he remembered her, she said, with that incredible relaxation of the strained voice into a natural one, "I was a fat little girl, and always hungry."

If it was hard for Naumann to move him out of his closed circuits sometimes, how much harder it must be to get the insane moving. Except in crisis. What could it really be? And why did he keep thinking of case after case, trying to think what it basically was? Were they doing for their single case what he did for all: were they trying to solve a problem? How often he thought of them as concerned with "their problem!" But they could no longer think about it helpfully or directly. It was all confused and confounded with symbols and indirections; it was a circuit where they ran the chance of being indefinitely lost.

'I was a fat little girl, and always hungry.'
He would have to look in on this Minnie.

That night at home, Nancy came to him importantly and said, "Somebody on the phone for you." She had taken to answering the phone, and would call whoever was wanted, and would feel quite grown up.

"Thank you. Did they say who it was?" he said.

"No. It sounded like a man."

He went to the phone and said, "Yes?"

"Hello," a soft voice said.

"Who's this?" But already he knew.

"Jimmy."

"Jimmy! Hey, I thought it was you—"

"Yeah."

"You could have called me before! How are you?"

"Good. I'm working."

"Wonderful to hear your voice! What are you working at?"

"Cashier in a chain store. It's fun. Two girl cashiers."

Dr. Marks whistled. "I'm coming over, man."

Silence.

Dr. Marks said, "How are things at home? How's Frances?"

"Great. She's walking, running all over—"

"Your brothers. You handling them?"

A laugh. "Joe's still away. He was back home last month. Looks like he's getting married."

"Well, you'll get married too when you want to," Dr. Marks said. "So everything's all right?"

"I wanted to ask you something."

"Yes?"

"Should I get a car?"

"What's the problem? Why not?"

"I don't know," Jimmy said almost inaudibly.

"You don't think you deserve one?"

"It's expensive."

"Your folks pushing you for money?"

"No."

"Well, would they mind?"

"I guess not."

"So get yourself a car. So maybe it's beat up, so what?"

The kid sounded pleased. "All right," he said.

"Never mind 'all right.' Just get it. Is that all?"

"Yeah."

"It means a lot to me to hear from you. I'm here any time, you know?"

"I know."

"Take care."

When the kid said good-by, he sounded happy.

He went back and told Margaret: "Jimmy called. Something?" He told Nancy and he told the boys.

Jimmy called me on his own.

Two days later he went through a bad episode on the insulin ward, fortunately after one of the attendants had taken the children back to the children's ward. One of the male patients did not respond to glucose intravenous, and turned blue. Dr. Marks started emergency measures with the composure of anger: "The blood pressure cuff." He pushed the feeding tube rapidly down the man's throat and got the glucose running to the stomach. He gave plasma. After a two-hour battle, the man came out of coma, but appeared to be in a state of permanent shock. Dr. Marks wondered what kind of damage his brain had suffered with the insulin going too far down into the medullary centers. If I hadn't acted fast enough, if my tendency wasn't to bring them all out a little on the fast side, would this man be dead now? Nurses and attendants themselves were pale and shocked. One of the attendants sat on a bed, head down, his hospital uniform gray with sweat. To look at him, you might think he was a patient.

Let's not have this again, Dr. Marks thought. He wondered if, in the excitement, all the patients had been properly fed. If not, you could expect convulsions later in the day. He checked on the feeding.

He went down to the children's ward to see his three children before he continued with his regular duties. The little girl was drawing a picture of a little girl, giving her a green-crayon smile that had the horror of a crocodile.

"See?" She showed it to him. "She's happy."

After lunch, he remembered what Dr. Carey had told him on his first day at the Center: Go and see Dr. Johanson. At New State he had always intended to see what this brain damage from shock was that Dr. Pirosh was always talking about. Maybe he would find out now from Johanson. Perhaps what he would find out would tell him what had happened to the brain of Nick (the patient on the insulin ward) when that deadly stillness had descended on him.

Dr. Karl Bjorkman Johanson was not a difficult man to get to see. Dr. Marks just walked into the Pathology Department lab and found him seated near a large camera microscope. He was wearing a lab jacket like a worn wraparound. Dr. Marks explained to him about Nick, and Dr. Johanson said, "So you want to see the brain damage."

"I've heard you have slides of shocked monkeys."

"Monkeys?" Dr. Johanson smiled, not a pleasant smile. "No need to look at monkeys. They can argue about monkeys. I can show you the human brain. Fifty brains of shocked patients."

"Fifty!"

"Yes, and you're wondering where I could get fifty? None of course is a death from sickness. They could argue that sickness caused the brain damage. No, these are all deaths from shock itself or from suicide. A slit throat or slit wrists can't hurt the brain." Again the not pleasant smile. "But take a look." He put a strip of glass under the microscope. "Here's loss of ganglion cells typical of whole areas of the brain. You mentioned this patient who almost died of insulin shock. This is insulin shock. Do you see where the cells are replaced by lines of scar tissue? You see the lines? Petechial hemorrhage. If any of it hits the cardiac or respiratory center in the medulla, the patient dies."

Dr. Marks studied the lines of scar tissue carefully. He looked at slides of Metrazol and electric shock. The Metrazol was less scarred and electric shock the least. But all showed the revealing lines.

"Monkeys are the same," Dr. Johanson said. "The same destruction of the ganglion cells. You want to see?"

"No, this is enough."

"Enough. Are you sure you're really convinced?"

"I can't imagine why I shouldn't be."

Dr. Johanson pulled his wraparound tighter. "I can imagine. Dr. Bently, who's in charge of what is called 'research,' research presumably into the psychological effects of shock, hasn't once been up here. Perhaps he thinks it would belittle his work to see what the physical effect of shock is. He says what I report about it is 'silly' and he sees no connection between what he does—his series of experimental shocks—and what he calls 'the brains upstairs.' But a few of these brains, I may say, were previously downstairs."

Dr. Marks said, "I can't see that this doesn't really mean hostility to the patient—"

"Of course it does. And how about this? In the middle of the last century some doctors treated mental illness by castration. Masturbating causes insanity, ergo stop masturbation. I have just a single simple-minded reaction to all this. The flesh is innocent. The cells have done no wrong. Why must they be assaulted, mutilated? What is it in these professors of the soul, these psychiatrists, that makes them so angry with body tissue?" The panels of Dr. Johanson's wraparound seemed to float in and out like a rib cage as he breathed. "I don't often say what I think, but let me ask you: If the brain tissue is quiescent—in, say, non-dreaming sleep—then surely it's guiltless, isn't it? Or consider it as an instrument, a mere potential. Would you smash a violin, a Stradivarius, because it was imperfectly played by a child who didn't know music? Is the brain, the cellular structure in itself, guilty and punishable? Is it at fault for the way it responds to human cruelties? I object to shock because it's nonspecific, there's no scientific methodology there and there cannot be."

"Can't you say this to somebody in authority—"

"To whom?" Dr. Johanson asked.

"Dr. Carey told me to come and see you."

"I'm part of his program. I'm a talking point. I'm a carefully separate department: neuropathological research." He picked up a folder and balanced it on his hand. "As the head of a separate department, I give my reports and I'm appreciated."

Dr. Marks: "But they're shocking three eight-year-old children on the insulin ward."

"I've heard about it. There seems to be a schizoid gap at the Center, as everywhere. I don't think that you or I will close it, or not soon."

Staff. The blank wall of the weekly staff sessions at New State. Again Dr. Johanson was speaking: "Isn't it a very simple thing to notice that strokes produce convulsions and that those same strokes produce damage? And that shock produces artificial convulsions and damage to tissues, to bones, to life? Why must it be so hard to see this?"

Why?

What about the freedom at the Center, the welcoming of Freud, all the analysts there? Dr. Marks felt confused. He felt a darkening. Surely it was a mistake, surely there was a sane, carefully planned total program here that honest men could agree on and want to forward. Otherwise—

After dinner that night, he closed the newly installed doors of his living room, establishing a pseudoprivacy that satisfied him. All day at the Center he had little sense of privacy. He lit a cigarette. Bently—Bently had called him after the insulin-ward episode and acted in his smooth way as if it had been some kind of mishandling that the thing had happened at all. Mishandling—everything on the insulin ward was done exactly as Bently wanted (except George).

Smoking calmed him and he began to feel better. The hell with Bently. Even Naumann would tell him, You have to let go. He blew smoke over the pack-plant donkey. He liked this apartment. He liked the enormous (it seemed to him) hallway that started between the dining room and kitchen, and continued past his own and Margaret's bedroom to Nancy's room and the boys' room—the boys' room was across the hall from Nancy's. The layout was good. There was a large foyer where he had put the piano so you might say they had a music room.

Johnny was finishing his school term in Brooklyn, subwaying there, and the day after they moved, he had lured a friend, Dave, home from school with him. Of course right away Dave called up his mother and said, "I'm over at Johnny's," so his mother thought he was just up the block. To hear the kids tell it, you'd think that this great story was the complete justification of their moving here from Brooklyn.

Now they went over the story every night and even Nancy knew it by heart so she could tell anybody who was willing to listen. So family legends are created. Who knew what similar legends are tied into the nets of association of psychotics, being told over and over, gradually shortened to catchwords or slogans? Like Minnie at the Center and her "sperm" whale. Then he'd been talking with another patient—

The living-room door opened and Margaret came in. She said, "You don't know what it does for me to have you home here." She came over and sat beside him and said, "Nancy today was talking about marriage. She say anything to you about it?"

"No. What about it?"

"Well, she wants to marry Murray. I said she was rather young for it, but she said there was a law, 'if the parents let you.' Where she gets this." As he said nothing: "I started to explain that your husband has to earn a living—"

"Why don't you just tell her she's married to me until she grows up."

"John!"

He went over and felt the plant in the donkey's back. "This plant needs water."

"Well, you water it so much I get out of the habit."

Bob came to the door, opening it a crack. "Am I interrupting anything?"

"It depends on how you look at it," Dr. Marks said. "What can we do for you?"

"Can I go out?"

"Do you know your sister wants to get married?"

"I heard. She tell you you should let Murray live here so they can be married?"

"Say, what goes on around here? Can't I hold my women? Is the Oedipus complex breaking down or something?"

"I want to take a girl to the movies," Bob said.

"That's different. You're past your latency period. You got your homework done?"

"Yeah."

"So go."

The head disappeared.

Life, you add up a few billion small things. Somewhere he had read it took a hundred and forty thousand stitches to make a man's shirt (he was going back to Minnie in his thoughts, he had his eye on Minnie). So how can you undo insanity that comes from a billion assaults made during a thousand or ten thousand days? He breathed out some smoke and said, "I've been thinking about this insulin research program."

"Yes?"

"When they do research at the Center, they go back and start doing what they used to do: They make a production of insulin or electric shock. It isn't routine anymore. All those nurses and attendants get interested because it's research, and act like Mama who's cooperating with the doctor who's going to save her sick child. I saw one nurse lean down and kiss a patient. And that thing that happened today, it wasn't, Some guy is gonna die. It was, Nick is gonna die. That kind of feeling is all gone in the state hospitals, but this doing research brings it back. So they measure the insulin, but can you measure units of love?"

She said, "When are you going to start working on your article?"

"You and Naumann. All right, I'll start now. Where are my notes?"

She came back with the notebook paper filled with his rapid scribbling, and her transcripts. As he read, he could see Jimmy, that panting, hollow face with its *hochgrädigster-Angst,* and Ethel with her arrogance. He read some of the notes on later cases: " 'We'll break it down, beat it down. He's so full he should drown. We'll make him brown in some goddamn style. . . . ' " That was one who liked to rhyme. Rhyming can distort what you're really saying and turn it into nonsense. " 'Don't you get it, damn you? Forces of oil, horses of oil. . . .' "

How they talked to you sometimes through the non-sense! One of them said, "It's going to be a new world, I'm creating a whole new world and there isn't going to be any language—just understanding."

"Well, how am I going to write this?" he said.

Margaret brought a pad of paper and a pencil and put them into his hands. "So write," she said.

With a sly look: "Maybe you'll write it for me."

"I'll typewrite it after you write it."

He wrote, "The Treatment of Acute Catatonic Excitement." He crossed out "The Treatment of" and substituted "Resolving." He had the article title. Well, what was so hard about writing?

Two days later he passed the window of a candy store and saw some small houses—they looked something like dolls' houses—made out of candy. George. The witch's house. He went in and bought one, then, going out, he remembered he'd have to have houses for the other two kids too, Tina and Tommy. And the insulin—that was a problem. He could give them candy only after they'd had insulin, and he'd have to keep it hidden until all three of them were out of coma. Such Goddamn problems! He went back into the store and bought two more houses. What's a house? he thought. A mother? A womb?

George was transported with his house. He immediately began to eat it. A little piece of eave broke off and he said, "Can I give this to Tar?" (the horse in the play-room).

Tina watched the two boys eat, but no matter how Dr. Marks urged her, she wouldn't touch her house. "It's too pretty," she said. He curled one lock of her hair over his finger—mustn't let her see any mockery. It *was* too pretty to eat. And she was too pretty to eat, too, to be ground up in the teeth of Bently's Goddamned research program. If Bently just came and looked at these kids, he might get sick to the stomach and stop the whole damned thing, but mainly if Dr. Carey would look, if only he could see the gentle curve of this face trembling with its pleasure—

George had finished his house, unbelievably. Well, that would sure wipe out any last trace of insulin.

Dr. Marks thought, In a couple of weeks I'll be off this insulin duty. Then what? This thought had been increasingly troubling him like a drumbeat behind music, moving in on him at odd moments compulsively. But really what was there to worry about? He'd talk to the new doctor. The nurses were with him, they knew the whole thing. He'd lay down the law to whatever new resident they put on the insulin program, and it would be all right. Fibrillary twitching, for God's sake.

The work on the article went slowly. He looked up again the literature Naumann had referred him to when he was treating Jimmy—Kozowski, Redalié, Claude and Cuel, Binswanger and Berger. Particularly Scheidegger and Fischer's material on post-mortems. He took notes and began dictating his article to Margaret. He decided to limit his clinical presentation to his first three cases. You couldn't put in everything. At least now he was started. He probably lacked the fine technical wordings the real pros used, but let that go—the thing was to convey what was really taking place (if there was any possibility of that) between himself and the patients.

Naumann urged him to read some more of the literature, not material specifically on acute catatonic excitement, but some of the extant articles on treatment of psychosis.

"But I've read Freud. Who wants to read the rest of that junk." Since he wasn't a reader and resisted reading, long periods would go by when he wouldn't read anything. Then, reversing himself, he might stay up all one night reading.

"You've read Abraham and Ferenczi."

"I've read you," Dr. Marks said.

"Let me urge you at least to read two articles—"

Two days later Dr. Marks had trouble getting to any of his regular patients: It was the usual rush of art therapy, OT, physical therapy. "I thought I had an appointment to see Miss Bates," he told Miss Morrison.

"I'm sorry, Doctor, she seems to be staying late in art therapy."

They even had Minnie off somewhere. (God knows what they were doing with her.) Free for a while, he took the elevator down to the library and got out—for room reading—Ruth Mack Brunswick's article on the analysis of a delusion of jealousy.

In the calm afternoon light—shades of the Academy of Medicine Library—he began to read this long article. Dr. Brunswick was a German-speaking American analyst in Vienna in 1927 (imagine being there with Freud at that time) and she was pretty bright. Could write anyway. He read along. This girl Dr. Brunswick was analyzing had been diagnosed by her as psychotic, as paranoid. But it wasn't psychotic the way he understood it. The girl, a working-class girl, could come to Dr. Brunswick's office and lie on the couch and follow the orthodox analytic procedure. Was this a psychotic that you could treat like a neurotic?

Not only could the patient free-associate, she could dream. He remembered with Jimmy what an advance it was when Jimmy was first able to dream (in the normal sense).

Well, read this anyway and see what Naumann had in mind. Maybe there was fear, then he'd know where he was. There ought to be the all-out fear Jimmy had, that you could only get an idea of from your own nightmares.

No fear.

Dr. Brunswick at any rate was not getting the fear. The girl "dissimulated" (what doctors at New State had called "being evasive" maybe), and the fear showed through only in hints or hysteric gaps in the ordinarily sound defenses. But knowing it was there, Dr. Marks wondered at not finding any emphasis on it in Dr. Brunswick's article.

The case. This girl had an older sister with whom she had had some homosexual play when she was very young. Later the sister became a sexual delinquent, went with boys, and abandoned the patient. The patient hated her and wished her dead. Years afterward the patient seemingly was on better terms with her sister again, but there was reason to believe her hate continued, and this was important because the sister died, and now the patient felt "that dreadful sadness," and wanted to die too. But this wish to die was strictly a phony, Dr. Marks thought. For example, she had a dream of being carried in a coffin, but reported a pleasant undulant sensation as she was carried by the pallbearers toward the grave. Far from dead, she was identifying with the sister in her sexual pleasures. And for that and for her death wishes, she felt she herself should be killed. This is where the fear came in. That fear that you yourself have of dying, that talionic, basic fear, that fear that shook you to the depths—that's what this girl really had. Like Jimmy. Jimmy wanting to kill and trembling with fear. Ethel yelling, "Bitch. Murder-in-law. I'm outwitting her." But in the borderline state this Viennese girl was in (neurotic mainly), you couldn't see it. She was calm enough as she associated and told her dreams.

His interest picked up again at one point. Dr. Brunswick of course was the girl's sister in the analytic sessions. And one day Dr. Brunswick broke free of the orthodox analytic technique and coerced the girl, suggesting and even insisting on the transference. Forcing it. (What I do.) The girl had missed a treatment session because she had gone somewhere to do some sewing. Dr. Brunswick said: "How could you do such a thing? How could you fail to come? You must be very angry with me." She told the patient it was insulting to put her sewing work ahead of her analytic "work with me." Perhaps you hate me, she said. "Perhaps I'm your sister." That was as much as Dr. Brunswick did. She didn't act out or carry it any further. It was limited to that one *'Perhaps I'm your sister.'* But this much had a remarkable effect—note. The patient admitted that the day before while she was sewing, her thread broke. She heard a mocking laugh, her sister's (I can get boys and you can't—boys can have me and you can't). She believed her sister was actually there, and in terror she put out her hand to feel her, and her sister wasn't there. When she got rid of her illusionary sister in this way, she thought: "If only she was dead."

So Jimmy had been killing his hated brothers and making his baby sister disappear in a frightful omnipotence. I can kill, dissipate, annihilate, and if I have such power, what might not be done to me? I deserve it. I'm guilty (for my hate and for those secret things I did or thought of doing).

But all this catechism of fear seemed unknown to Dr. Brunswick. She went no further. She apparently left it to the girl herself to take care of her haunting terrors and desires. Or she considered that the techniques of ordinary analysis would handle them.

Psychosis? Treatment of psychosis? He didn't see much

here that would lead anybody to treat the Jimmys and Ethels of this world.

No, he was going to stop reading. It might mix him up. Freud said his "splendid isolation" of the early years had not been without its advantages—he didn't have to read "the medical literature," and "following the unforgotten advice of my master, Charcot, I looked at the same things again and again until they, themselves, began to talk to me."

When he lay down on the couch at five o'clock, his eyes felt tired. It always tired him to read. He was glad of the green coolness of Dr. Naumann's office, like a pool he could rest in. "I was reading today. Ruth Mack Brunswick, one of the articles you told me about. I'm sorry—there's not so much there that has to do with what I've been doing. A little, yes. Not much."

Silence.

"Her case wasn't psychotic, that's all. And there's a technical point I want to ask you about. I've been thinking about it and that article makes me wonder. Can a psychotic sleep in the sense that a normal person does?"

"I think we said something about that, or bearing on that," Dr. Naumann said. "Didn't you tell me once that there is no complete waking and no complete sleeping?"

When I was watching Jimmy. "Yes, I said that. But that's not what I mean. All that proves is that something isn't completely one thing or the other. But still you sleep —that is, a normal person does. What I want to know is if psychotics really sleep."

"I would almost say, no." Dr. Naumann walked again through the aisles of a Berlin hospital where he was treating a psychotic patient. The patient was never without a wakefulness that was like a continuous cautious listening. In the deepest silence, there was this sense of waking awareness.

"Then what about this girl in this Brunswick paper? She has dreams. That she's being carried in a coffin, and she dreams about having intercourse with somebody who wears a bow, so she associates to it. The bow is like one her sister wore."

"I believe there's this difference. There are dreams, but the dreams of a person just going into psychosis foreshadow the type of delusion and hallucination they're going to have. And when the person is coming out, the dream content repeats the delusions."

"But an actual psychotic doesn't dream," Dr. Marks said emphatically as if to make a point to himself.

Dr. Naumann moved his hand along the arm of his chair. Dr. Marks heard it. "How shall I answer? Once, in the late fall, I saw an apple tree with a single white blossom. Did that make it springtime? I should not like to make any categorical remarks about what can exist in this world and what cannot."

"Okay," Dr. Marks said. "But when I was at New State, I never heard about any of these deep psychotics dreaming. The whole psychosis is sleeping and dreaming. I never knew any that dreamed, in the usual sense, that could tell me about it, anyway. But here at the Center, it's dreams dreams dreams, and I can't believe they're psychotic patients. Borderline maybe. And this Brunswick woman's case, that's borderline too. It's not a Jimmy or an Ethel. That's what I'm getting at."

"It may be."

Angrily: "No maybe about it."

"You like to be clear-cut. But you will find when you have more kinds of cases that nothing is as definite as you think. One case may go quickly into deep psychosis and the psychosis is the sleep and the dream, as you say. Another case may go in slowly, with elaborate defenses, and for a long time repression may continue, and normal dreams."

"Well, that may account for this Brunswick girl dreaming. But this case doesn't teach me anything. Some good clinical writing. But you can't get the answers from an ambulatory case."

"You have a strong feeling about that."

"I do."

Dr. Naumann said, "Whom have you always wanted the answers from, from whom you did not get them?"

"From Father. You think there's a connection?"

Silence. Now Dr. Marks said, "I'll give you one thing. I had the funny feeling she was a man."

"Who?"

"This Mack Brunswick woman. Maybe her name did it. Or just the way she wrote."

With a shade of sarcasm: "Or possibly the way you read?"

"No, she writes like a man," Dr. Marks said. "Very little of herself as a woman gets into it." Naumann of course would sense this as a defense.

Calmly Dr. Naumann said, "Still she was in it. I had a patient once who believed that he had eaten me and that I was he and he was I. He would even say, 'Let me ask myself a question,' when he meant, 'Let me ask you a question.' All through that, he was still himself. There is no way to get completely away from oneself."

Dr. Marks shifted on the couch and felt tight and oppressed.

"What are you thinking?" Dr. Naumann said.

"There's so much I don't know. I realize it. I'm trying to learn from myself. And I said I want to learn from my cases. But even there I can't make headway. The right way would be to get a really new type of case. Like this Minnie. She's different, she has her defenses up all right. I've told you about her—she's the one who talked about 'sperm oil' and is so fat." Fat. It came to him: The fatness (she ate ravenously) could be pseudocyesis. "You know this fatness of hers may be a false pregnancy? Why didn't I think of that? I thought of it at the time of that Brown cadaver when I saw that woman with the lipoma of the mesentery. But what threw me off with Minnie—she never says anything that gives her away. Why is it they never mention such a thing directly? Never refer to it in so many words?"

Silence.

"Why don't they say it?" Dr. Marks asked.

"Would they say it in a dream?"

Of course he was right. She was saying it with "sperm oil"—just what Naumann had been trying to tell him.

The hour was ticking away. Not that Naumann had anything as obvious as a ticking clock anywhere in the room. But you were aware of the steady escape of the minutes, particularly in a session like this of unconscious stalling. Not so unconscious at that.

Naumann was silent. That silence said, I can wait it out, but perhaps you will still wish to work.

Did I dream last night? Dr. Marks thought. Any flickering memory of dream had vanished. He wondered what was the matter with him. Ever since this insulin thing, he had not been able to settle down to "work," in that state of necessary looseness and drift. He asked himself, What's in my mind? "I can't seem to think of anything to say."

"Mention some object in the room."

"The desk light." The soft light out of sight.

"Please associate to it."

"It's out of sight, like you. It's a kind of green, has a green shade. This whole room is restful and green, like it was under the sea. In a motion picture once, this wreck was being lifted up after it had been undersea a long time —and everything was covered with like coral and weeds. It was hard to recognize things. The masts and spars seemed to be trees, for example. So maybe that's how it is with things in the Unconscious when they lie there a long time—they get hard to recognize too. It's like the world used to be when I was a kid, with people all around me speaking Italian or another language I only half understood."

"Yiddish."

"Yiddish. Even when they didn't talk Yiddish, they might just as well have. They didn't tell me anything. You know—didn't explain anything. I figured only grown-ups knew things, and it made me sore and I wanted to grow up fast. I guess I was grown up when I was six or seven. I refused to smile. And I'd go around balking my mother. Sometimes—"

"Yes?"

"I'd stop talking to her."

"Yes?"

"Then I was grown-up the way I'd take care of my younger brother and sisters. I'd—"

"What was this about not talking to your mother?"

"Well, I didn't."

"For how long?"

"A day, several days sometimes."

"When did this start?"

Sullen: "When I was eight maybe. I'm not sure."

"What would make you do that?"

"Oh, never anything serious. Just something got it going, and then she was as stubborn as I was." Dr. Marks felt the heat of some solemn ugliness, some stubbornness carried to a hateful extreme.

"You mean she wouldn't talk to you?"

"That's right."

These memories, Dr. Naumann thought, that suddenly came to the analysand, offerings made after days or weeks of resistance.

"But I was the one who would stop talking first," Dr. Marks went on. "I always started it."

"How would you start it?"

"Once I dropped a plate and she hollered at me. My father was there and I thought he was going to beat me—I thought with her hollering like that he'd surely beat me—"

"Did she get him to beat you like that?" Dr. Naumann asked.

"Well, I have to be fair to her. She'd never deliberately try to get my father to beat me. But I was afraid that was what was going to happen, and that made me mad and even when my father didn't beat me, I didn't talk to my mother for three days." Angrily: "I couldn't stand that hollering. Like a woman."

"Did you ever refuse to talk to your father?"

"You didn't try anything like that with him. You didn't tangle with him."

"Well, didn't he interfere when you wouldn't talk to your mother?"

"He didn't care."

His mother hollering at him. Like a woman. "Would you associate to 'hollering'?"

Dr. Marks hesitated before he spoke. "Well, anybody who hollers or fusses. A man lays down the law and that's it. Beats you. I hate any fuss or argument. Like—"

"Yes?"

"No."

"What were you going to say?" Dr. Naumann asked.

"Well, it bothered me before when you fussed about how I was doing in my analysis."

There was a pleased breath from Naumann. "I didn't fuss, but you felt that I did and that's the same thing. Then what did you do?"

"Why—what do you mean?"

"What did you do?" he said.

"I don't understand."

Firmly: "What did you do to me?"

"I stopped talking."

"You stopped working analytically."

There it was. Right back to himself. "But this has been

going on for some time, that I haven't been able to work."

"Did you say you sometimes didn't talk to your mother for several days?"

Dr. Marks felt that this was too good. Angered: "Yes, I did."

"It might be most helpful to ask, What threatened you that you had to defend yourself that way, at that very early age? You were threatened, you know."

"I was sore, I was mad."

"And you wouldn't speak. That's quite a defense, isn't it? And now you're looking for a patient who doesn't speak, who's withdrawn."

He was. A patient who was himself.

Was I afraid of my mother? Was I afraid?

Of what?

"I'd like to know myself what I was afraid of," he said.

"Yes. However, not today," Dr. Naumann murmured. "Unfortunately your resistances today have left us no time." But as his small figure came into sight and as he walked with Dr. Marks to the door, he touched him on the shoulder. It was a sign of satisfaction.

18

The day Nora was discharged seemed to be a good day to ask for a new patient, and Dr. Marks spoke to Dr. Stieglitz about it—he said he had heard Minnie yelling while he was on Nora's case, and had become interested.

"You know, don't you, that that's Dr. Sands's case."

"Possibly Dr. Sands wouldn't mind if I took it."

Dr. Stieglitz stroked his black beard. "I don't know. Dr. Sands may feel that he has an investment of time and effort in that case, and we don't usually transfer patients that way."

"Is Dr. Sands doing psychotherapy with Minnie?"

Dr. Stieglitz said, with a trace of annoyance, "No, she isn't at a stage where psychotherapy can be undertaken."

"Then if I took over now, I wouldn't be interrupting any continuity of treatment."

"Well, of course, there's other treatment than psychotherapy, but the important thing is that she's not accessible, not at a stage where you can do any good, and I don't like to see you use valuable time on a case that's about to be transferred out. Now I do have a case that's likely to interest you, in fact I've already spoken to the girl's—the woman's—husband about you. He's a brother-in-law of a top radio-communications official and he was frankly rather excited when I told him about you, that you had been having success with this type of case. It's a first breakdown, rather florid—some things about it will remind you of Nora. I may say it could be very important to let some of the key people in radio communications see what psychiatry can do."

"What's this patient's name?" Dr. Marks asked.

"Jeannette Stone."

"May I see her before you assign her to me?"

"Of course."

On the way up, Dr. Stieglitz said he had told Mr. Stone

not only about Nora but about Dr. Marks's success with Mrs. Bell, the state senator's daughter, who had just been discharged. (Great success—the woman had had no need for treatment.)

That afternoon, out of a cynical curiosity about her background, Dr. Marks asked for Minnie's chart. She was married to a postal clerk.

"Did you hear," the nurse said when he returned the chart, "that Minnie is being transferred to Creedmoor?"

"No, I didn't hear," he said.

"Yes, the order just came through a half hour ago."

The next morning, he found a message in his office asking him to phone Dr. Stieglitz. "How are your children coming in the insulin project?" Dr. Stieglitz said with marked cordiality (Dr. Marks had taken the Jeannette Stone case). "I'd been meaning to ask you about them. Would you care to bring me their charts after lunch?"

Dr. Marks had been expecting such a request, and had kept the charts up to date, including George's. Each day he put notations on George's chart as if he were actually receiving insulin, and unfortunately it was something of a problem. Because George was the only one of the three who wasn't showing any serious damage. On Tina's and Tommy's charts, his notations were easily and nonfictitiously such as not to encourage shocking children. Tina was thoroughly frightened and would hardly talk to anybody. She was beginning to stare at her hands and dream for an hour or two at a time, as if duplicating the insulin coma, and it was hard to draw her out. This was about as close to psychosis as he had ever seen a young child.

And now on the children's ward, a special side effect of the research program: the other kids were taunting George, Tommy, and Tina because they "had to have insulin."

"Dr. Stieglitz, don't you want to consider taking Tina off? It obviously isn't having a good effect."

"I might speak to Dr. Bently about it, but he believes strongly in following all the research programs through."

"Well, who originates them?"

"Dr. Carey has charge of the overall conception. But of course he's influenced by the reports of programs at other centers of research, and wants either to confirm these or start new lines of investigation."

"With eight-year-old children," Dr. Marks couldn't keep himself from saying.

"But you're evidently not in touch with what's going on in this field," Dr. Stieglitz said. "At Stony Brook they're shocking infants from six months to a year and a half—"

"Six-month babies? But how can babies be insane?"

"They can. Distortions of the fundamental life pattern can be detected early."

Dr. Marks found himself not listening anymore. Perhaps he was becoming hysterically deaf?

The initial stages with Jeannette were difficult. She drew around herself a cloud of her own creating, suffused with repressed anger that shaded off into disdain and then gathered blackly into a thunderhead so fulminating that he expected to be hit by some kind of psychic lightning. She walked around the room flicking her hair out behind her with her uplifted hand, screaming, "Pits of waters! Jacks and jackals! Who hears me?"

And then she would let her hair fall, and spit.

At one o'clock in the morning he went home, completely worn out. "I know I'll get this one," he said to Margaret. "But you have to have something approximating their own strength to do it. That's what's terrifying, how strong they are. No, they aren't strong. Their sickness is strong. But their ego is weak." Under the lightnings and the fires of sickness, such patients were functional nothings, they were helpless, childlike fractions of themselves.

Margaret said, "You'll get through. You said you used to give your patients a transfusion."

"Well, my blood is just draining away." He made a slurping sound. You get back into bed and we'll see if I'm drained away.

But later he was still unsleeping.

'Pits of waters! Some special jackals now. Where is the particular bastard who unhinges those damned upper currents?'

He had to sleep. The voices of insanity had to slide off, had to let him go.

He had worked with Jeannette all day, trying to find out what the "upper currents" were that seemed to prey on her mind, troubling her eyes with a far and frightened look. It was something to do with electricity, but only in the sense of a strange power, or now and then there were hints that it was "spying." The "upper currents" came in through the wall at about the level of her shoulders. They came in all around her room, but she seemed to locate them on the second shelf in a small wall cabinet over her washbasin. She would open the door of this cabinet and touch the shelf, and she would move a container of talcum powder infinitesimally to one side and back and jerk her hand away as if the "electricity" had burned or warned her.

Toward four o'clock in the afternoon, he noticed her come to the closed cabinet door and, putting her hand on it, lean forward and seem to kiss her hand or press her lips to it. And then, backing away, she turned her head slowly from side to side as if searching, her lips sucking. He found it hard to trust his eyes. Her face was becoming a baby's face, unlined, smooth, wrinkling its lips—

"I guess she was looking for the nipple," he said to Dr. Naumann.

"It would seem so."

"You'll remember my telling you about Rose Blumstein, how she tried to nurse off my chest—"

"I do remember."

"And I gave her my knuckle to suck. Maybe that's what I should have done with Jeannette." The treatment room as usual suggested a hypnogogic quiet, and Dr. Marks was surprised at his wakefulness, that, exhausted as he was, he could not relax. "Milk. That's what the 'upper currents' are, currents of milk. Just at the level of her lips. But if she needs milk, why is she always saying, 'Pits of water'?"

Silence.

"Amniotic fluid?" A rush of thoughts. Was it she giving birth or was it she going back to the womb, searching for rebirth? So many of them wanted that.

He said what he was thinking, but said, "Maybe 'pits of water' means no milk. Why is she afraid of that shelf? Why is the shelf electricity? Something that can hurt her? And all that fear and that babyishness, and all that arrogance gone. And there was Nora thinking she was poisoned."

Silence.

He began talking about other productions of Jeannette's and Nora's, and Dr. Naumann said, "May we perhaps take an interest in you, in your oral resistance to your mother that still remains unsolved?"

Oral resistance. That was pretty good. Dr. Marks said, "I was sore at her."

No reaction to that.

"I guess it might have been her having all those kids in a row. I was sixteen months old when Robert was born. When I was three years old, Dora was born, and when I was five years old, Babe was born. As the oldest, I had the responsibility. I told you how I took care of them, my brother and the girls. But did I get any privileges? Oh, no. When the time for going to bed was advanced to nine thirty, it was advanced for all the kids, not just me. No privileges for me. No."

Dr. Naumann thought, He's carefully keeping away from the orality.

Dr. Marks said, "Maybe there's another reason for my getting sore. Pa and Ma never told me anything so maybe I wanted to shut up and show them. Keep my own mouth shut." Now he thought of how his parents' secretiveness had trained him in reading minds. Jeannette believed her thoughts could be read. There were "devices" in anything round (like that talcum-powder container) and they knew what she was thinking. Her cloudy torrent of language occasionally slowed and became clearer, to let some sort of communication break through. Not that she talked sane. No, but she would say, "He gave me a bialy. That's round. I guess that's from Bialystok. I know he put a device in it, the bastard, and he can hear my every plan. But I can outplan him. I have those special powers. Genesis. I know where to work."

He said to Dr. Naumann, "I'm thinking about Jeannette. Her worry about being spied on. She has a lot of productions about that, and that has to do with the 'upper currents' too. Then she'll say 'genesis,' and I think it means 'genius' or maybe 'God.' Or maybe being born. There's so much doubletalk. Nothing clear until she started hunting for the breast, and that was sure plain enough. That was like Jimmy saying, 'Don't cut off my balls, Papa.'"

"But Jimmy was frightened."

"And you mean Jeannette isn't? Yes, she *is* frightened: all those wires and enemies."

Dr. Naumann crossed his legs. Dr. Marks knew the sound, the cloth sound and the slight creak of wood. "Enemies, fear. We were going to try to find out what you were afraid of, that you wouldn't talk to your mother. That anger with its inseparable companion—"

"I don't remember any fear."

"If you remembered, we would perhaps not need the analysis."

That will hold me. That was Father with the strap. You listened to that. Now he felt a moment of panic and rushed to defend himself. "I don't think of anything, except that I shut Ma up. That was a benefit. I didn't have to hear all that yapping: 'Eat your egg.' 'See that you take your books to school.' 'See that you come home right after school.' "

Silence.

"Yapping. Like a dog. *Kelev.*" He snickered. "I still remember how my father hated that and almost took the strap to me. My mother didn't have any equivalent of the strap, not that I can think of. And I think she loved me in her nutty way."

Silence.

"I'm blocking."

A sigh that might be interpreted as sympathy. "This could help—can you remember any dream you had at that time, that may have stayed in your mind?"

"I'm in Prospect Park and some car—I can see it—runs out of gas. Then another car drives up and stops and puts a gasoline nozzle in the back tank of the car and fills it up, and the car can go again—it's happy."

"What kind of tone did this dream have?"

"It was a good dream," Dr. Marks said. The dream had come back as if he had dreamed it the night before. Strange that such a restitution of a commonplace dream should occur precisely at this moment. And he had an immediate association to it, to the nozzle. "This nozzle," he said. "Uncle John was always prescribing a big enema —anything to hurt, the bastard. I can still remember Ma shoving a damn enema nozzle up into me and filling me with warm soapy water."

Silence.

I'm supposed to say what's in my mind. "I suppose it was a penis."

"But the car was happy," Dr. Naumann said, without expression.

Dr. Marks felt taken aback.

"You did say it was happy?"

"Yes, it was funny that I felt that. Of course this isn't the first time I've presented dreams that suggest homosexuality."

"What did Freud say about the ultimate basic goal of homosexuality?"

After a moment's delay: "To be united with the mother's breast."

"Then what is the nozzle?"

Just what Jeannette was hunting. He made the admission by his silence.

"Perhaps you will tell me, what do you use when you nurse?"

"My mouth."

"Wasn't that what you were afraid of using?"

"Afraid of homosexuality?"

There was now the closest to an explosion of disgusted breath that Dr. Marks had ever heard from the head of the couch. But in a calm tone, Dr. Naumann said, "Were we not pursuing another area of fear? But again the hour is over, I regret to say, and we must wait till a further session. But I wish to say, this session was not unrewarding. It is ringing with *vielleicht*."

The new resident assigned to the insulin ward was Dr. Emory. At home, Dr. Marks said to Margaret, "I know things have been rough for you lately, with me working late on Jeannette and going every morning on the rescue detail with George, but now it'll be better. I'm off insulin day after tomorrow. The only problem is this new resident. I have to see him, I have to get to him. I've had the impression he's an intelligent young doctor. I hope so."

At the table at lunch the next day, he asked Dr. Emory —Stewart—if he would be kind enough to talk with him privately some time during the afternoon. They agreed to meet in Dr. Marks's so-called office, hoping no other resident would want to use it while they were there.

The day was pleasant, bracing, carafes of burning sea

air being poured over the panels of the windows. It was like his first day at the Center, the same splendor and fire.

"Stewart, I have something difficult to tell you, but it couldn't be more serious." Dr. Emory's crew cut seemed to shine as he relaxed in the comfortable office chair opposite Dr. Marks. "You probably know I was well thought of as a doctor and internist before I came to psychiatry. I had many years of successful practice and my father still thinks I'm crazy to have closed my office and sold my equipment. But that's neither here nor there. I mention it because I want you to know that my medical knowledge is at least adequate, perhaps good."

"I'm sure it is."

"I've had many diabetics in my practice and I've had reason to know what fibrillary twitching is, as a sign of undue sensitivity to insulin. That's important because—" And carefully Dr. Marks told Dr. Emory the whole story of George.

"You can understand, then, that he must be brought out of coma by six thirty at the latest."

Dr. Emory seemed stunned. "You mean you've been going there at six thirty every morning?"

"Yes, earlier. I haven't wanted any chance of a traffic jam or car breakdown. I've wanted to be there. And that's what you'll have to do too. And of course you'll have to phony up the chart."

"But, John man, I can't do that. And you shouldn't have done it. You're breaking regulations—going against orders. If a doctor goes against orders and something happens—"

"Something will happen if you *don't* go against orders." Stupefied: "I can't possibly do it."

"But why not? You're intelligent. The damned experiment is fouled up anyway. What will it prove if George gets the balance of the series? The point is he won't *get* the rest of the series. He won't live. He won't live to get it."

Nervously Dr. Emory said, "You talked this over with Dr. Bently?"

"Never mind Dr. Bently. He hasn't seen George's meningeal stiffening. He stiffens up, his head, you know? Like strychnine poisoning. Because it's getting to the central nervous system. Different sets of muscles start twitching.

You'd recognize it. Do one thing. Promise you'll go there tomorrow morning and look at George."

Nervous and disconcerted: "I don't want to get mixed up in a thing like this."

"You already are mixed up in it." Desperately: "Come down now and let me introduce you to George."

"Dr. Bently already introduced me to the children," Dr. Emory said.

"Then didn't you see what a great kid he is? He's got humor. He has more stuff than any kid I know, except my own." Angrily: "Why, you could give your life for a kid like that."

Dr. Emory was now sitting straight in the chair. His lips were thin and stubborn. "I have to assume this hospital knows what it's doing," he said. "I'm sorry. I can't believe Dr. Bently would ask to have something done that was mistaken like that, that could threaten the life of a child." As an afterthought: "You know, of course, that I won't say anything about what you've been doing."

Dr. Marks: "Are you familiar yourself with fibrillary twitching?"

"I've seen it."

"You understand what it means? What it's signaling?"

"I do—"

"Then you must do this. Go there and look at it. Just go and look at it and see how serious it is and see if then you won't agree with me. Watch the different sets of muscles. Even the nurses know. They won't say anything if you bring the kid out. Bently hasn't seen this, you understand. He wouldn't. You go and see it."

"I just can't believe—"

"Go. You have to go."

Dr. Emory, looking miserable, sat and shook his head.

In the dining room at lunch the next day, as Dr. Marks came in:

"How did it happen?"

"What?"

"Henry just said—"

"Did you hear—?"

"They say Emory is almost out of his mind."

Emory. "What's happened?" Dr. Marks said.

"George Golding, an eight-year-old kid on insulin— Say, weren't you just on insulin?"

"What about George Golding?"

"Dead, never came out of his coma this morning. You knew the kid?"

"Emory and several other doctors worked on him for two hours—couldn't save him."

"Excuse me," Dr. Marks said. He hurried to the elevator senselessly, as if in spite of all reason something might still be done.

He took the elevator to the insulin ward. All the steam of its morning heat was gone, and all the cots but one were empty. George had not been removed, he lay on his cot, covered with a light sheet. Sunlight came in warmly, outlining his small body. When Dr. Marks drew back the sheet, he saw that all the blood had left the skin, but what seemed the remnant of a smile was still on George's face.

Miss Fitzhugh was glancing at him and he went over to her. She choked and when he put his hand on her arm, she began to cry. Through her tears she said, "He was so sweet. Didn't you tell Dr. Emory?"

"Of course I told Dr. Emory."

"Oh, God. No wonder he was in such a state." She said, "Something ought to be done. He was just a child. And these other children—"

Without a word he left her.

"I well understand your rage," Dr. Naumann said, "but you must consider. Assume you did create a scandal. I'm not saying it wouldn't be tempting, but what would it accomplish? The Center would have the medical profession behind it: If the parents charged that Dr. Bently gave insulin without testing for sensitivity, he'd answer or the Center would answer that the law of malpractice here doesn't apply. Malpractice is what the average physician in the community would not do if he was prudent. But in research nobody knows what you do. The very nature of research is to investigate the unknown, so the court would consider that to be a bonafide defense and would support the Center."

"But I could shake them up—"

"Later perhaps, when you have standing. Now you're a resident, a person without standing. Even that you have brought patients out of psychosis does not weigh with a Dr. Carey or a theoretical judge, you may be sure of that.

But there is one thing you can do," Dr. Naumann said.
"Go to Dr. Bently—have him take the little girl Tina and
the other boy—have him take them off insulin. He will do
it."

"You think so?"

"Yes. You will find that that much is possible."

"I wish I could be as detached as you are. I can't. I'm
burning."

"Burning—"

"I can't work. I couldn't do a thing with Jeannette
today. I don't know if I'll be able to treat her tomorrow."

"You will treat her tomorrow. You will make the
human adjustment that has to be made to grief and injus-
tice, even to death. Someday you may not have to make
the compromises you make now."

Jeannette, flicking her hair behind her head with her
hand and striding up and down.

Lying on the couch, he let one last vibrating heat go
over him, over his tired eyes. *The bird flies around* and
George smiling at him. George had gone to the witch's
house all right and had eaten candy (glucose), not knowing, not admitting the witch was there.

Wrong to think here on this couch silently. Thought
here was supposed to be aloud. But thought went with incalculable speed in its privacy, sometimes. And a thought
he was really blocking telling Naumann was that he felt as
if a child of his own had died. He had fought off seeing
George's parents because it would remind him that they
were the real parents, who had the real right to grief.

He did finally tell that dubious thought to Dr. Naumann. Dr. Naumann said, "I can understand that that
thought may not seem to you a good one in the ordinary
sense, but I would not censor it or condemn it. You *were*
the parent."

"What I feel mainly is anger. Total anger at hospitals.
They don't just kill George. They put him through all that
fear, down in the adult insulin ward. Like me when they
said Surgery meant they cut your arm off."

Dr. Naumann said, "The ether cone."

"The ether cone. The fear of that. We've been trying to
find fear lately in myself. I have a vague notion—" He
blocked.

Silence.

"I think I can go back now to Jeannette."

"You said, 'I have a vague notion,' " Dr. Naumann said quietly. "I believe it was something not connected with Jeannette."

"I can't think what it was." It had gone from his mind.

"Did you have a dream last night?"

"I have only the vaguest recollection of this dream."

Vagueness again, Dr. Naumann thought.

"I'm trying to remember it better. It seemed to have something to do with an automobile. I was driving over a mountainous road, and somebody said, 'You drive well,' and I felt happy." Embarrassed: " 'Happy,' that's the car in Prospect Park that fed from Mother's breast. I had to dream about it again after that reminder, I guess. And this was a good dream, too. But I seemed to have some anxiety too, about this dream or in this dream. I needed to be told I was driving well because I didn't think I was driving so well, actually."

"Go on."

"I have a general feeling of uneasiness just now. I wonder about my work with Nora and Jeannette, whether it's being accepted, whether I'm really doing as well as I seem to be doing. I seem to need to be told I'm doing well."

Silence.

"I also think about George and the long time I've tolerated people like Dr. Bently and Uncle John, and I think, Is that good?" He felt a slight tightening of a muscle at the base of his back.

"Why did you put the car in the mountains?" He could have put it on the plains or anywhere, even over water, Dr. Naumann thought. The mountains were his wish.

"I don't know why I did. I've driven in some mountain areas where I felt nervous, frankly. I remember one place that just had dirt bulldozed along the edge of the road in maybe a two-foot—one-foot—barrier between you and death." He became completely silent. Naumann also waited in silence. "Once—"

"Yes?"

He felt oddly strangled and unable to go on.

"Yes?"

"I saw a car being pulled up by a wrecking truck. It had gone over the side of the mountain and they had attached a rope to it and were pulling it up."

"Why does that disturb you so?"

"What is this state you enter into in analysis? This state

that makes the green room into a "pit of water" in which you drown, a wall-less sea filled with fear. "I don't know. I think it goes back to childhood when Father drove us off to the Catskills in his rattletrap car. When he first had a car. I can't explain it. I—"

"Yes?"

"I remember the vague thing I was going to tell you before. I hesitated because I never wanted to believe it myself. Ma said I almost died when I was born, from the placental cord choking me. She said I was a 'blue baby'—how's that? You arrive that way. But she also told Robert the same thing about himself. Maybe it was him, maybe it was me, maybe it was nobody."

"But you have this image, this thought in your mind."

"Yes, it's the rope." He felt satisfied to get that out.

Silence.

"So that's probably why I was so disturbed when Robert got that blood clot in his throat and Uncle John had to breathe into his mouth. Strangling. Death. I can't tolerate it. I have to breathe, live—I love life."

"Do you think you are exceptional in that?"

"No, but I've always felt it so much."

"And when your mother pressed you into her breast?" Dr. Naumann said.

Could that be a reminder of that strangling, of that placental thing, something he wasn't sure even really happened to him? "You know, later my mother had an abscess of the breast that Uncle John had to cut, all full of blood, pus, and poison, and my mother claimed it happened as a result of the way I nursed, and I suppose bacteria had nothing to do with it, lack of cleanliness, Uncle John's failure to advise her about cleanliness."

"You're just now telling me about this."

"Well, it's not too important."

"Your mother did not make you feel too happy nursing," Dr. Naumann said.

"Evidently."

"Then later you refused to use your mouth."

Those long silences, two days, three days, that stubbornness, Dr. Marks thought. He was refusing the tit. As simple as that. He was—

"What are you thinking?"

Silence.

"Please say what you were thinking."

"I was refusing the tit."

Dr. Naumann thought, The tit that smothered. Fear deeply and curiously connected with death. He was tempted to say something, but didn't. He remained silent. And the silence produced a benefit: "I guess I was afraid for myself when I was afraid for George."

Silence. The silence said, What led you to think that?

"This institutional idiocy. They won't talk, won't listen, won't come down and see George."

Dr. Naumann finally said, "So what were you afraid of?"

But he lay unspeaking, refusing to speak.

Perhaps, conceivably, he never would. He refused the tit, he refused to talk to his mother, but he defended her too. Resistances, his slowness to remember, to admit things, to understand—it was all explicable. For when he went back from penis to breast, he still had some support. Hard as the mountainous road had been for him, for that baby, for that child, he had had a saving love, the love he now poured out on his patients; somewhere his ungracious, awkward mother had given him that love and had saved him from death.

Little wonder his defenses were strong. That they were loyal to that love, that they refused to let him give evidence against it. The same passionate defenses were in operation in his patients—and in my own, years ago—who held to any least decimal of that haunting and saving hope, that they did indeed have a loving mother.

But it would be important for Dr. Marks to identify the threat of the breast if he was to make progress in understanding his patients.

Dr. Naumann said quietly, "Thank you for your cooperation today."

The next morning a phone call came that Dr. Marks should report at once to Dr. Carey. He felt nervous, going up. Had something got through about his one-man anti-research campaign? Was he about to be *persona non grata* again?

But the Head could not have been more sympathetic when Dr. Marks came in. He swept across the office and put his arm across Dr. Marks's shoulder. "This terrible thing about the little boy. I've been badly upset by it. Dr.

Emory, he's very much on my mind. You were on insulin before Dr. Emory, weren't you?"

"Yes."

"A terrible thing for him, that he should lose the boy his first morning on the ward. This is the kind of thing that makes or breaks a doctor—I've seen it. You're an older man, you've been through this, but Dr. Emory hasn't. He's young. I'm told that he's taking this very hard. He isn't in today. Terrible."

Dr. Marks said nothing. The sun burned in a point of light on the back of *Mirage of Health*.

"I understand Dr. Emory got help quickly and did everything that was humanly possible to save the boy. There's no blame—no least blame—for anything done or not done on his part. I think you, as an older doctor, as the doctor who was previously on the ward—you could do a great deal to comfort and reassure him, to get him over this crucial hour in his young life."

"I'm afraid my own feelings about George get in my way. I definitely wouldn't be the one to speak to him."

There was a worn look on Dr. Carey's face. "Then I'll have to do it. I'm not happy having to take responsibility for programs like this. One hopes to find out something helpful, something that will prepare the profession to cope with these awful areas of human suffering. Then this happens."

The sunlight now had left *Mirage of Health* and was shining on *Statistical Summary, Electroshock Therapy*.

Dr. Marks saw Dr. Bently at three o'clock. It wasn't necessary to say more than a few words. "I'll speak to Dr. Carey," Dr. Bently said. "I believe I can persuade him that with only two cases remaining, the program has lost its usefulness." He added, "In any case, the little girl isn't reacting well."

Orders went down that evening to take Tina and Tommy off insulin.

DEAR STEVE:

I don't think I'm going to be able to send you the next move in our game for some while yet. I've gone through one of the worst things I've ever gone through in my life. I wrote you about George. I thought surely the new resident would go along with what obviously had to be done, but he balked, the fool. He was young. He couldn't stand up to the Establishment, and yesterday George died in coma.

This is one of the decisive moments of my life. Once before, when I was a kid, I saw a baby die of circumcision and the result was I was nonreligious from then on. You know what I mean. I mean in the conventional sense. And now George. I can't get over it. I know now I'll never be a psychiatrist in the usual sense. I'll go my own way and do what I have to do.

I can't write you a long letter. I'm trying to get hold of myself. All of us send our love to you and yours.

As always,

JOHN

As he wrote the letter, Dr. Marks was thinking of his session that afternoon with Naumann in which they had discussed the Head's wanting to comfort Dr. Emory. Naumann had seen that Dr. Carey himself was after comfort. The Establishment itself can waver. Then its automatism goes on.

19

Spring was coming strong and green in the trees along the near bank of the Hudson. The river's hurrying surface flowed under a cascade of willows.

Dr. Marks drove downtown from the Center, exhausted but enjoying the warm weather. He had not rested yet after bringing Jeannette out of psychosis—he had slept a few hours and then rushed back to see her again. The stunning thing: she had become modest and shy. Her glance seemed to say, What could have happened to me in that terrible dream? What did I do? How could I have let myself become lost in that maze?

It had needed hours of reassurance before she could begin to remember the time of "dreaming." "But think," he said to her, "how much you learned then and how much you can teach me now." She shook her head, switching her hair. "But I'm not a good teacher," she said.

But he would get her to talk. Soon.

He had tried, in the last days before resolving her psychosis, to get Dr. Carey to come down and watch the treatment. Dr. Carey had said that he was getting full reports on it from Dr. Stieglitz and was satisfied with that.

Well, now she was out. Nothing more to see except a girl regaining control of her own mind and (though this would probably be difficult) revealing what had sent her into psychosis.

He drove on home, had a comfortable dinner with his family (Margaret had set out a casserole of tender lasagna, one of her better dishes), and went up to East Eighty-second Street to The Psychoanalytic Institute. He was taking a seminar course there with Dr. Bertram D. Lewin on the problems of identification. Identification had been problems for him, all right, both in his training analysis and in treatment.

The classroom was full, with its usual dozen or so men

and three women, and Dr. Lewin was already there. By an odd coincidence, he lived in the same building with Dr. Marks. He had an unreconstructed Texas accent, glanced over his glasses like any classic schoolteacher, and dripped cigarette ashes continually on himself and on anything near him. He was one of the more brilliant psychoanalysts in New York.

"Gentlemen and ladies," he said, bringing the group to order, "we are going to consider tonight identification by oral introjection, and I assume all of you have reread *Totem and Tabu*. Let me ask you a question, to begin. What do you suppose are the implications of the minute of silence on Armistice Day? Dr. Mercer? Dr. Marks?"

None could think what the implications might be, and Lewin said, "Well, it seems *we're* celebrating our minute of silence too. No suggestions? Then let *me* suggest: Collectively on Armistice Day we're aware of having killed, so we are as silent as the dead. We're making an identification with the dead. In a talionic moment, we stand mute like the dead ones."

Dr. Marks thought of his silence with his mother. He made her be still, he made her dead. But he also was silent himself and so he too was dead as if *she* had said, Be still, be dead. And in fact Dr. Naumann had found a great deal of death behind that silence.

"For the moment we have accepted the dead into us. I've spoken about the palpitant ecstasy of the saints who are in God and who feel that God is in them—"

Easier to kill a woman than a man. You don't tackle the old man, that's too deadly, but the old lady's a little softer and you can express your hostility to her.

"Freud mentions the delicate attentions given to the head of a slain enemy by the savages on the island of Timor. They sing to it and ask its forgiveness. And the See-Dayaks of Sarawak put morsels of the best food into their dead enemies' mouths and plead with them to become one of them. In mourning the dead, you too want the dead to become one with you, not just one of your group, but in your violent, immediate grief you want the dead person there inside you, incorporated and not really taken away from you."

Dr. Marks thought of the patient who was convinced he had eaten Dr. Naumann.

"I could say," Dr. Lewin continued, "that then you go

through a period of distressing egoism where the superego merges with the ego and the normal boundaries are lost. But from that period of grief and suffering, usually you emerge with new sympathy for the world around you." He discussed the cannibalism of primitive races as identification: they ate parts of the body of the dead person so that by eating they could take on the qualities of that person. "I mentioned religious ecstasy. Many of the saints reported it to be an inexpressible state, a state whose content cannot be described. I ask what is the chronologic state before words and thoughts? Before the person can put anything into words?"

Dr. Mercer said, "Infancy."

"Yes, babyhood. And the baby's bliss is to be united with the mother's breast, to incorporate the mother."

That's getting close, Dr. Marks thought.

"You know Karl Abraham's thesis, that there are two significant periods for the baby: the nursing period before teeth, and the biting period. He makes a great point of this, the cannibalism of the child—"

You were a vicious feeder. That's what Ma said.

"—but he overdid it. He had this obsession with stages —good in a way—but it obscured the main thing, that the baby ate, was eaten, and went to sleep happy."

"How do you mean, 'was eaten'?" one of the women doctors interrupted.

"That's how it must seem to the baby. He's pressed into the breast, the breast enfolds him, and he's eaten, and then he falls asleep. Being eaten, you know, is not necessarily an unhappy experience. An uncle or aunt of a child will say, 'You're so sweet I could eat you,' and I've had children tell me about the happy sensations of a cookie being eaten."

Good God, George and the witch's house. But this thing of being pressed into the breast: That's all wrong. That's too easy, anyway there's another kind of breast, and he made a note to go up after class and perhaps talk with Dr. Lewin or perhaps they would go home together.

Dr. Lewin continued elaborating his thesis about identification through the beneficent breast and finally, in a wave of cigarette ashes, dismissed the class.

When the other doctors had left, Dr. Marks said, "Are you going home?"

"Yes. You?"

"I wanted to mention something, about this breast thing. You know the breast can be threatening too, smothering—"

"Yes, that's right," Dr. Lewin said, "but it still doesn't contradict what I've said. For some there may be a threat, but not for all, not for most. One of the things I've been discovering in my practice is that suicide may not necessarily be felt unconsciously as death, but may seem to be an eternal content-less peace like the fantasy of sleep at the breast. It's very hard to separate threat from attraction. Come, let's have coffee together and talk about this."

When they were settled in a nearby restaurant booth with cups of coffee, Dr. Lewin said, "You were telling me about the Jeannette Stone case. How has that been going?"

"Oh, she's out of psychosis. And now she's just the opposite of the way she was when she was crazy. She's shy and even affectionate—"

"That's interesting, and not so surprising." Ashes fell on the tablecloth. "But tell me what you do."

"I'm not sure I know. I don't seem to have time to understand while I'm doing it. I just do it. It feels right when I do it right. It feels wrong when I don't. But what I do wrong luckily doesn't seem to hurt the patient."

"You find that." After a long drag on his cigarette, Dr. Lewin said, "But you mean you can't say specifically what you do?"

"I'm trying to write a paper and maybe there I can clarify it a little. Part of it seems to be acting out a role in the psychosis, being the parent and changing from an imagined (or real) destructive parent into a good, loving parent. 'Reparative' is the word Dr. Naumann likes."

"He's a formidable person, that Naumann."

"He is."

Dr. Lewin drank some coffee. "You know, going back to what we were saying, I'd like to tell the group next week what you've told me about the threatening breast. Not that I haven't known about it, but it's a rather concealed thing in an analyst's ordinary practice, like mine. I do know this, that I often find that happy dreams have a latent content of death wishes or thoughts about one's own death. Just as I said about suicide."

My dream about driving in the mountains. Mountains —could they be breasts?

More and more orality. It was coming to focus.

It felt good that here he had somebody to talk to, somebody on his side. There was such a pressure from the other side. It was almost like paranoia, the way they distorted your thinking. The top-echelon doctors at New State saying there was no brain damage ("they" said it). Like Uncle John said you could cure appendicitis with an ice bag. But I had studied anatomy and I knew the appendix was six inches inside the abdomen. You couldn't freeze the back of your hand if you put an ice bag on the front of it. But Uncle John said it. It must be so. So I never went up to see Pirosh's sections. I had to wait until I saw Johanson's sections.

Well, that was back in the past. Now I have Naumann and it seems I have Bertram D. Lewin, and maybe there will be others.

Dr. Lewin drank his coffee and said, smiling, "Well, both of us must get some rest, get to a happy reunion with the maternal breast."

"From what we've discussed, that's an optimistic remark."

"No, it isn't. There is such a thing as normal happiness, normal sleep, and even normal nursing. That's why we say 'good-night.' "

The next morning he practically assaulted Margaret. Afterward, pleased and detumescent and holding her against him, he said, "I always said you had a nice front."

"Front, did you say?" As he snickered, she whispered, "Let's do it again."

"Physically impossible."

"Nothing's impossible for you, honey. You're swell."

"Well, not just at this moment." He made motions of getting up.

"Wait. I want to tell you about Nancy."

"So what about Nancy?"

"Well, it's something funny about the long hall down to her room. Bob noticed it. Whenever she goes alone down that hall, she runs. Runs like something is after her."

"I'll speak to her. This isn't a plot to keep me from the Center? There's a new case—"

She screamed, "John! . . . You were supposed to take a day off when you finished Jeannette."

"Jeannette isn't finished. What will make her stay well is for me to work just as hard with her now as I did in the psychosis—"

"How are you going to play poker?"

"I've forgotten what poker is."

"Nancy must think so too. She said to me yesterday, 'Poker isn't a game,' so I asked her, 'Why isn't it a game?' and she said, 'Because nobody plays it,' so I said, 'Why doesn't anybody play it?' and she said, 'Because it isn't a game.'"

"Circular reasoning," he said. "That kid's a mess. I'm going to go and talk to her."

He put on a light robe and went to Nancy's room. As he expected, she was awake.

He tried to define the quality of her face. It followed his own rugged contour, and had that craggy look that said, When I want something, I want it and I'm going to have it. But it also had a shyer look, the mouth ready to round into something between a sigh and a smile. She'll be a tough contender in the years ahead. Dozens of boys will suffer.

He said, "Come with me."

Surprised, she took his hand and they walked together down the length of the hall to the space between the dining room and the kitchen. Then he turned her around, patted her behind, and said, "Now go back to your room."

She started slowly enough, then broke into a wild run. He followed her and said, "What's this running? Why do you run down the hall?"

"I have to."

"Why do you have to?"

"I just have to."

Totem and Tabu, I have to. Something says "run" (that I listen to) and I have to do it. But he had watched her running and had taken note where she ran fast, which was past his and Margaret's bedroom door.

"Do you close your eyes when you're running?"

She was surprised. "How could I see?"

"I didn't ask you how you could see. I asked you if you closed your eyes."

"I don't close my eyes *much*."

"So you close them *some*. How about your ears?"

Laughing: "I can't close them!" Afterthought: "But if I run, I can't hear."

What can't you hear? he thought. This Freud, does he always have to be right? He tickled her and she fell on her bed and he went on tickling her and the bed began to jounce and creak. (What nice sounds—my bed can creak too.) He let her catch her breath, and said. "You know I'm afraid I love you too much to let you marry Murray."

She gave him a sideways look. "Well, if you don't want me to."

"We could see if he makes ten thousand dollars a year."

Giggling: "All right." And she let out a little sigh and seemed happy.

Staff. He had been to a number of Monday Staffs and now, with Jeannette doing well, he decided he had time to go again.

Staff was held in the same auditorium used for state-wide psychiatric conferences, and it gave the ordinary staff meeting an overtone of some extraordinary gathering. The floor sloped to the stage in the half circle of an amphitheatre and on the west side rose two-story windows topped by Roman arches. Doctors sat in front, nurses behind as at New State, and promptly at two o'clock, a hush fell, and Dr. Carey entered with Dr. Stieglitz and Dr. Charles Vance (in charge of the male side) and went up on the stage and called the staff to order. There was a small lectern in the middle of the stage, and Dr. Carey leaned over this, his wide shoulders contracting like a bellows. "We have an unusually troubling and difficult case to offer you today. Dr. Smith will speak to you about it. I ask your most considerate attention." He went to the side to greet Dr. Smith, beckoning him up from the audience, and accompanied him back to the lectern.

Dr. Smith was the same one who had done psychotherapy with George. He seemed nervous now, but his mouth and jaw had a sensitive, good configuration. He said:

"Rita is a young woman who has just reached her majority and as you will soon see, is rather thin and unhappy-looking. Her mother is a laundress and her father is an electrician who is a chronic alcoholic and works only occasionally for a shop on the upper East Side. (Dr. Marks thought, They never have a wealthy patient in here, never have them made a public spectacle of.)

"Rita has been ill for four years and what happened initially is that she became increasingly nervous, suspicious, and would pull down the shades in her room, her bedroom —would generally stay in that room and simply withdraw. Said she was afraid of somebody, but would not say who it was. The precipitating event was that she heard about a caffeine test in which caffeine was concealed in milk without people knowing they were drinking it—to test whether sleeplessness from coffee was psychological or real—and she became sure her milk was poisoned. She refused milk. Then immediately after that she had her first deeply psychotic episode. She recovered, but she has had two recurrences. The present one is rather mild, but has some intriguing aspects. She's convinced that she knows when persons inimical to her have been in her room even if she hasn't seen them. She goes around the room making slight indications with her finger, that that article of furniture has been altered in such a way that the inimical person quite evidently did it.

" 'Altered,' you mean 'moved'? I asked her.

" 'No, changed.'

" 'In what way?'

"But she is unable to tell you. She does know she is the object of some widespread conspiracy. She fights it, and in this struggle, she consistently divests herself of things. She no longer has any personal possessions. The other day she even tore up her handbag and put it in the garbage, not telling anybody and not willing to answer questions about it if I asked her. But she will tell some things.

"She believes hostile rays enter her room through the window if any part of it is left unprotected, and then at times she has at her disposal a 'counterforce' that, quote, 'sends them back to the originating box and blows it up.' "

Jeannette and her "upper currents." Rays and currents —milk from the breast?

Dr. Marks was forced to think of this because everything about Rita seemed to go back to babyhood. "Divest" yourself of things—the very word meant undressing, and he had had another patient who destroyed her clothing until she was almost naked. Babies are naked. Babies have nothing but their mothers. Certainly in all this report about Rita there was no hint of any sexual attack or any thoughts of pregnancy or things that might be detected in the Oedipal period. When something sexual was mentioned during treatment, he was more and more coming to believe it was a screen memory. Dr. Lewin spoke about a patient who said, "For a baby, a nipple in the mouth seems as large as a penis does in the mouth of an adult." When the patient remembered fellatio, it might be a screen for the nipple.

"I asked Rita what was the matter that she took the handles off the faucets. She said that they would hurt her."

His own dream of the New State chimney crumbling. Dr. Naumann had said it was a "pleasurable fright, possibly." It was going to come down on him, crush him. Much later in the analysis, it had become clear that this might be his father's penis entering him. But now, at this moment, surrounded by rows of doctors and student nurses, with Dr. Smith's voice going sympathetically on, he remembered that one of his associations to that dream had been the Eiffel Tower and in the Eiffel Tower you go up to a restaurant, a place to eat. The breast, the breast! The chimney had been both penis and breast, and that he should not have known it until now! It was so simple when you saw it: You yourself have these defenses, all this operates in you the same as it does in patients. So many Oedipal memories and fantasies that must be evasions and then they drop away, leaving only the breast, that rosy globe of milk that can be sustaining but that can also threaten with some unnatural element of hostility, of poison and death.

Dr. Smith: "She was a premature baby and had a cyst on one lung and had to have part of the lung removed. This experience made her overdependent on her mother and vice versa. She acted as if she might die if she let her mother out of her sight."

The milk might be gone. But the milk was poison. What a trap to be in! What a bind for the yearning little mouth!

And now it came to him that the patients always gave the impression that they had a single problem. They never mentioned it, no, but how completely you felt it, how you felt and knew that if just one condition could be satisfied, they would be at rest, they would have that essential relief they needed: a bellyful of milk and a dreamless sleep (Lewin's bliss).

But they never got that one answer to the problem.

Rita was brought in. She was frightened, but as the questioning began, she seemed to regain her composure.

Dr. Marks noticed how thin she was, as if the slow fire of pathology was getting rid of her body as well as of her possessions.

"Do you know where you are?"

She did know. When asked why she didn't eat more, she said there were "bad intentions" in the food.

"What are these 'bad intentions'?"

"I know there are." And she rubbed the palm of her hand over her mouth.

"Do you think the cooks here would do anything to the food?"

"Oh, no, it's not the cooks."

"Who is it then?"

"I can't have anything with a seven in it." She offered this explanation diffidently.

"What's a seven?"

She made a jagged gesture that might be conceived of as drawing a seven in the air. "Three and four," she said. "You know what that is."

He had the sense of rehearing the same thing, that sense of paralogistic repetition.

He thought of all the patients, valuable human material, given to the Dr. Smiths of this and other institutions, men often of goodwill but no adequate training or preparation. Maybe it was part of the same philosophy by which the young beginner in medicine is given what is called the "scut work"—he does the urine and the feces examinations, the sputum and vomit. The dirty work. The psychotic is the "scut work" here. Oh, presumably research is being done with them, but the work goes to the residents. Even actual contact with the patients on the shock-treatment wards was left to residents.

Was is that fear of the Unconscious that he had talked with Margaret about?

Why wasn't Dr. Stieglitz doing some work himself? Or Dr. Vance? Or even Carey?

Rita now was led from the stage and the staff meeting was thrown open for discussion the way it always was. Now the routine about diagnosis, immeasurably frustrating after as rich a presentation of psychic clues as Dr. Smith had just finished making. Arguments of the most standard kind went on and on: "Seclusiveness—" "withdrawal—" "defenses." In spite of himself, he raised his hand.

Dr. Carey: "Yes, Dr. Marks?"

"The patient's seclusiveness has been mentioned, but shouldn't we be considerably more concerned—excited— by a specific thing like the patient's having torn up her bag? This has to be related to the paranoid fear of poisoning. The usual meaning of the bag is a vagina, but with so much regression, couldn't we consider an alternate possibility, that it's a mouth?"

Dispassionately but firmly: "I don't like to interrupt you, Dr. Marks, but here at Staff we must exclude this kind of discussion, interesting as it may be—"

"But the patient is literally self-starved and if—"

"I'm sorry. We've got to limit discussion strictly to diagnosis."

Dr. Marks heard a murmur around him and, embarrassed, sat down.

Two hours later Dr. Stieglitz gave him a ring on the intercom. "I wonder if you'd like to see me."

"Certainly."

When they were alone together, Dr. Stieglitz said, "I'm concerned about what happened at Staff this afternoon. What you said there was well intentioned, but inadvertently you may have done yourself some harm with the Head. Dr. Carey admits the importance of Freud and analysis, but doesn't use it here or recommend it to the staff. He'll offer the reasonable argument that analysis hasn't been demonstrated as a therapy for psychosis—"

Dr. Marks said, "Then what is this psychotherapy everybody is doing here?"

"It's a psychiatrically oriented therapy."

" 'How are you today?' 'Do you hear voices?' " Dr. Marks said.

"It's not what *you* do, obviously," Dr. Stieglitz said with a smile that indicated, We understand each other.

"And if I were to present a case in Staff, I wouldn't be allowed—or expected—to talk about its specifics?"

Softly Dr. Stieglitz said, "I don't think you will be asked to present a case, and in Staff discussion, if I were you, I wouldn't press my viewpoint too far."

After that there was an educated pause and Dr. Marks recognized that he was not supposed to carry the argument further.

In the next month he made a significant discovery. If he diagnosed a patient "schizophrenia," the patient was sent right down to one of the shock treatments of choice, whatever was being "researched" at the moment—insulin, electric, Metrazol, or combinations of the three. But if, after an elaborate work-up of a case, with an exhaustive case history and all the physical tests, he then made any other diagnosis than schizophrenia (for example, "mixed psychoneuroses"), he could keep the case from being shocked. When Bently or somebody wanted recruits for shock research and leaned over his shoulder sniffing for a new case, he would say, "But obviously you don't want this one. It's mixed psychoneuroses, and psychotherapy is indicated. Insulin is only for schizophrenics, isn't it?"

Then Bently would frown, but knew Dr. Stieglitz would back Dr. Marks up. (Often the cases were so mild, he was tempted to diagnose "neurosis" or "tendency to fantasize.")

Important to get that paper finished. "Resolving Acute Catatonic Excitement." The title would flash into his mind intermittently, like phrases patients used perseveratively. He would wake up from a dream, or wake up and be aware that a dream was dissolving, carrying some anxiety or happiness away with it. Often it would be a dream of driving. Not necessarily his own maroon car. It might be any car, Robert's Cadillac, or Dr. Carey's car that he'd seen one day pulling out from the Center. He had dreamed about it that night, some harrowing nightmare of backing up Dr. Carey's car in a narrow street in great fear of hitting parked cars on either side: Who wants to be in the Head's seat? But this continual driving. It had something to do with writing the paper, he was sure, some need to get into motion, to make progress.

RESOLVING ACUTE CATATONIC EXCITEMENT.

Margaret sat at her beat-up typewriter, played with by all the kids, even Nancy. She hunched over like a Goddamned hot-rod driver, as if they were going to career through the work of completing the article slam-bang in one go. In scribbly pencil he was revising the section on the Jimmy case, and she was busy retyping away. He had taken the night off from the hospital. Let the patients treat themselves for a change. Let God do it ("we bind the wounds"). Now as Margaret happily zinged along (winging caressing looks at him that said, "We're jumping, aren't we?"), he tried to figure out how he was going to end the Goddamned article. He had written up three cases and stayed with his decision that three were enough. Let the rest go. Let the productions of the others drift through his mind, edging out into his current cases like overlaps of dream. Three would do it. Better keep the article short. Have a better chance to publish it, and maybe have somebody read it.

He wondered what that would do, having a few persons read it. They sure as hell weren't going to start rescuing Jimmys at New State Hospital, or anywhere else as far as he knew.

Well, it would be off his conscience, at least, and from then on, it would be somebody else's responsibility, not his.

This writing block: Who knew what caused it? But one reason was that he didn't even have a private drawer in his so-called office at the Center, no place of his own to leave his notes and first drafts, the result being that if he wanted to write in the hospital, he had to carry all the material there and back again. And maybe lose it. The thought of losing any precious words he had actually written or that Margaret had typed made him go pale. But was this, or the continual drain and interference of patients, an excuse? Was this anything you'd want to tell Naumann? Probably, if you wanted the literal truth, it all came down to his being afraid of somebody laughing at him: John Marks of Bushwick Avenue writing "a paper."

He handed Margaret three more sheets and with this much ahead, thought again about the ending. "Woman," he said, "stop making like a submachine gun there for a minute. Get your pencil and paper." Obediently she gathered up her long pad and pencil, pushing back a strand of hair. "Okay," he told her, "take this." More important to get some more words down than to revise, and something had come to him. " 'In nightmare, the dream fails to succeed in preserving sleep, but on waking up, the psyche has at hand all the reinforcements of the conscious ego so that life can go on in a relatively normal way. In the excited catatonic, we deal with a continuous nightmare from which there is no waking up, inasmuch as the conscious ego, which would have to come to the rescue, consists of remnants or shadows of the normal ego and therefore must fail the sufferer.' "

He thought of Jimmy's *triebmassige Angst* as he first saw it. That was nightmare all right and never explored before. And how important to explore it! It also occurred to him how he had felt as if he was giving an ego transfusion. Get that in. "Having gained the least access to the patient, one pours through it the dynamic force of the therapeutic effort. Perhaps one may take the liberty of calling this an 'ego transfusion.' "

How about paying a tribute to Miss Davis? "That it requires more than the administration of sympathy to relieve this state was fortunately proved by the fact that the nurse in charge of these patients happened to be a tender person who constantly ministered to these sufferers with the utmost kindness."

Mention *Totem and Tabu* (Bert Lewin will like that). Margaret's pencil was racing. If he didn't look out, he'd finish it. He said, " 'Summary.' " Aside: "You always have to have a one-paragraph summary at the end of these articles. If you don't, you're not a grade-A, eighteen-carat professional. Okay." He dictated a "Summary" complete with complicated passive verbs and jargon all over the place, and ended with reference to the ego transfusion: " 'It is suggested that this method derives its efficacy from establishing a symbiotic relationship between the weak ego of the catatonic and the strong ego of the therapist.' "

He screamed, "Done."

"It sounds wonderful, darling."

"Don't butter me up. Just put it into English for me."

"Ha!" She went back to the typewriter. "I'm not changing a word."

"How soon can you get this draft typed?" he said.

Suspiciously: "Why?"

"Well, I just thought I'd go up and show it to Lewin."

She was ready to hate him, but thought, No, he's been worrying about this article for months—now by some miracle he has it done. Let him show it to Lewin. "Don't you want to lie down and rest while I type?"

"I wouldn't mind." He left the room—they were working in the big foyer where they'd just put a new Ping-Pong table next to the piano. An hour later she found him fast alseep in bed.

20

When he did show the article to Lewin, after class the next night, Lewin liked it. He said, "This ego-transfusion thing. You mustn't get too literal about that."

"Well, that's how it feels. It feels like you're pouring yourself into them by all the orifices: eyes, ears, nose, mouth, even the skin." That gasping look they have. Wanting to eat. "What does the mother do with the baby? Feeds it. I'm the foster-parent and it just happens 'foster' comes from an old English word that means 'feed.' "

"Mama Marks."

"Don't joke, man. They call me Mama."

"Have you told Dr. Naumann about this ego-transfusion?"

"Oh, he knows my thoughts about that, but I admit he hasn't read the article yet. I left him a copy today."

"I'll be interested to know how he likes it."

"You and me too."

At the beginning of the session, the next day, Dr. Naumann said, "I've read your article and on the whole it's good. I have several minor points to discuss with you. You could expand the German bibliography. I've made some notations for that. You should include papers to show the balanced opinion on whether there are or are not any autotoxic elements—even mention them in the article. If I were you, I would also not hesitate to draw on the German nonorganicists. Their descriptions have a rich fund of significant detail."

"I reread your own papers."

"No, it's the specific papers you need. Mine are in a different area. I would have mentioned these other papers, but I first wanted you to do your own work." He was silent, meditating. "You have a flair for expression, you successfully make the reader feel it in his heart, and I

313

wouldn't want to have anything I say make you change that."

"Dr. Lewin thinks maybe I go too far with the ego-transfusion thing."

"Leave it as it is. There is going to be widespread rejection of the article no matter what you do. Best to have it represent what you yourself experienced in treatment."

Dr. Marks said, "You think anybody will treat patients the way I did?"

"That's not what is at issue at this moment. The article is professional. It is honest. I believe it will be published."

"Your articles were published too."

There was a sigh now. "I would not like to say my articles were entirely without influence. Nothing any honest person does is entirely useless."

With that cheerful note, they went on to the session. Dr. Marks said, "As I think of my work lately, I keep thinking of this baby thing, that the patient is a baby. Wouldn't a baby have to be a little wary of the environment? Maybe it's almost physiological to be a little paranoid then, to be fearful of injury—something so small, so helpless."

Silence. That means I'm not working. "Well, that interests me," Dr. Marks said. "Maybe that's why psychosis generally starts with paranoia."

Continued silence.

"I had a dream last night that I can't understand at all. I seemed to be looking at Jeannette and she was choking. I wanted to pat her on the back, to help her, but I felt I mustn't do that. I mustn't have physical contact with her."

After waiting for him to associate, Dr. Naumann finally said, "What do you think physical contact might mean here?"

"Well, I hate to mention this, but there's something about her behind, when she used to raise her hands to her hair and dance around, it made me once think she'd be great to fuck the back way. That's the back part, perhaps. And fucking, that stands for feeding somebody, doesn't it? So maybe my Unconscious was wanting to feed her, maybe that's this ego transfusion Dr. Lewin was unsure about. Of course, my better self forbade me to do it. But what about this choking?"

He saw her choking so distinctly from the dream. All night he had been restless, he had the feeling of dreams coming and going like processions, shouts, something like a threat (that perennial gun), but nothing except Jeannette's face choking that he could see clearly. "I have one patient who had asthma just before she became paranoid and went crazy. All during the craziness, no asthma. Now she's coming out, and damn if she isn't having asthma again."

Asthma always got to him, he thought, slid the old appeal past his defenses, appealed to him so deeply because it was just the cry of his own fears, the cord at his throat—all that.

Should he speak about this obvious thing to Naumann?

"Asthma. That was me worrying about Babe holding her breath. That was me and the rope around my neck, that umbilical thing. Oh."

When he had been silent a while, Dr. Naumann said, "Oh, what?"

"Funny, I never noticed my mother's pregnancies." Now where did that come from? Umbilical? "I just didn't see them. As far as I could tell, she didn't gain an ounce, even though she must have been as big as a house. I didn't see it." *Umbilical*—Now he knew. Now it came back to him, the thing he had blocked along with the knowledge of those pregnancies: "The miscarriage. My mother had one miscarriage. I had no idea what happened until Bob said to me, 'Don't you know that Mother had a miscarriage?' and he showed me there in the bathtub the whole bloody mess, the placenta, the cord, and all that, and I almost fainted."

Silence.

Fainted. But I didn't. Never lose consciousness. "The umbilical cord. I guess that was overdetermined. That fear. I've been edging up to it lately, with ropes and ether cones and stuff. But mainly the breast, you'd say." But Naumann didn't say anything. I have to say it. "But couldn't my not seeing the pregnancies be just a simple thing of not wanting any more babies getting milk from her? Couldn't it be that simple?"

"Did you like her breast so much?"

"No, I guess I didn't. But how do I know? My patients sure go hollering back there for Mama's tits. And then they do nothing but scream around about how it hurts them. Not that they say it's Mama's breast, no, it's something or somebody *now* trying to hurt them, except almost always it's via the mouth. Poison. The 'upper currents.' Making the lips move, making magic signs and trembling. This is part of it: I can remember so well Nancy when she was a baby and couldn't talk, she'd just look at you with those big blue eyes, and I thought, What goes on in her mind? What does a baby think? Obviously they do think, but not in language, so Jeannette or any paranoid or psychotic has to find words for that baby thought that originally had no words. So it's 'caffein in the milk' that they read about in the paper. And they cover their mouths or they tear at their lips—" He was conscious that he was getting away from himself. But he was also getting into himself. And where was it better to get insights than right here? "The thing that's important about it is that I've been so dumb about the whole thing; myself, patients, everything. I didn't see the plain thing, that all the language part comes later and they have to use it the way they have it. I have to. I talk about ether cones and operations. Jimmy talks about getting his balls cut off. Jeannette talks about pits of water. Maybe she's just one letter away from the truth (tits of water). All of them trying like mad to tell secrets we can't hear." He felt he was having an insight such as he had never had before. He also had the strange feeling that he had gone through it as through a dream, that it would end in a dream dispersal and the disappearance of conscious memory. Well, did it matter? If any truth existed in it, it existed in him and it would come back to him. That phenomenon had happened again and again. He could relax and trust himself.

What was Naumann thinking? Silent at the head of the couch. Even if this must be of obvious interest to him, him with his Berlin patients and memories, there he sat, keeping the discipline, waiting.

"Do you think there's something to what I say?" Dr. Marks asked.

"There is much there."

"I've been working in the session, and I haven't been working. But this insight is more important to me than anything that's happened so far in my life, I think. It would be good of you if you'd comment on it." At least it would help fix it in my mind, if he'd say something?

"There is this parallel perhaps. In dream we use substitutes for the actual desire, the latent content: symbols, fragments, parts for the whole. Hints. You may have carried this a step further, that the adult, or the near adult, uses substitutes for infancy. In the psychotic dream."

As Dr. Naumann stopped speaking, Dr. Marks had the feeling that perhaps his insight, that he had felt was so new, was not that new, that it was just part of an existing body of knowledge.

At least the important thing was that *he* got it and that he had something that could from now on be steadily useful, suggestive, directive. It was like holding the steering wheel of his car. Or maybe it was like keeping an area of the windshield clean.

The thought of his car reminded him of the cases back at the Center. He was anxious to return to them. He had taken lately to sleeping over at the Center: the staff with its superior beneficence had adjusted to his needs and given him a night cot.

He had three cases under treatment at once.

But he thought too of the pleasure it would be to him to tell Margaret about his insight. And he was eager to do the final revisions of the article Naumann had suggested.

When things begin to move, they really move. You felt it sometimes, the sense of being saturated with unconscious power. It was as if whatever you touched worked.

But be careful. These things had to be consolidated. Gone back to and made specific. That's what counted, being specific. Then there were always surprises, the good surprises of reality.

He had the feeling that Dr. Naumann was looking at his wristwatch. There was that momentary hesitation, then, "We've done enough for today. Much, perhaps?" God is pleased. Could one shake His hand? No. The voice had spoken and He turned back into a cloud and disappeared.

As Fred Kleinerman crossed the Riverdale overpass over the Henry Hudson Parkway, he heard the cars roaring rhythmically. Like blood. Beat beat pulse pulse and touching your ears.

The car-beat, though it roared, was temperate in the twilight. The last daylight shone through vacant lots and trees as he swung to the left, along the feeder road bordering the parkway. He liked the sense of country. Each night he was glad to get home.

When he came into the apartment, Marta was doing

something in the living room, and turned. That pivoting
toward him, why was it so important and good? That
wave of black hair. He loved the pattern of her whole
body moving to him, the knees carried forward like a
child's.

Ruthie was running too and he hugged them both together.

Marta said, "Ginnie's coming over later."

That damped him. "Why?" Her cousin Ginnie, capable
of endless crises, a real chaosnik.

"It's something at the job. The boss is carrying too
many clients and ran away or something." Marta smiled.
The slightest thing could trigger that smile or she would
laugh.

He loved her vaulting laugh.

Ruthie loved it too and would laugh with her.

But then sometimes Marta would look at him differently
and he would be troubled by the thought that she *wasn't*
happy. Difficult to tell yourself that, for often he felt that
Marta was good for him because he tended to be too
sober, and that lightness of hers, that surge of laughter
like a breaking of some loving inner radiance that spread
out and included him, an intimacy that told him they
could defy any darkness together—he needed that. Then
why should he have the thought that she wasn't happy?
She might say such a thing as "Is my hair too heavy?" as
if some defect (nonexistent, anyway) was troubling her
when actually she was almost unbearably beautiful, or she
might say, "Why do you love me?" apparently playfully,
but was it entirely that? An overlong silence, sometimes,
and particularly a look that said, I'm not sure.

A girl named Ginnie Morris, an efficient but evidently
somewhat wild young secretary, came with her boss, James
Bergendahl, to the Center. She also came with several policemen, all considerably in awe of Bergendahl (even
though he was now well out of his mind), for he was one
of the top criminal lawyers in the city. Because of Bergendahl's important connections with the city government,
Dr. Vance, on the men's side, asked Dr. Stieglitz if Dr.
Marks might be assigned to the case and reluctantly, since
he thought of Dr. Marks as his own private protégé, Dr.
Stieglitz agreed.

He went alone to see Bergendahl. He found him in

moderate contact, but obviously psychotic. He could believe that when Bergendahl was well, he might be, as Ginnie said, "a nice guy," but now he was a mess. In his late thirties and never married, "James" could count the times he had had intercourse with women (if he had had any).

Before seeing his new patient, Dr. Marks had a talk with Ginnie. She told him James ("James is what he calls himself, not Jimmy") had always tended to overextend himself and recently was carrying about double the number of clients he should be handling, "then he took off in a panic. He just took an unscheduled vacation without making any office arrangements, and went up to Boston and the police there picked him up in the street, hallucinating. So now he's here."

Dr. Marks: "You say he's a good lawyer?"

"Wonderful. You can't imagine. He gets murderers off or gets them the lowest sentences of anybody you ever saw. Right now four clients at least are expecting the chair if James doesn't get straightened out pretty quick. And he's a nice guy."

All kinds of fantasies poured out of him. His father was two hundred years old. He thought somebody had licked his cock when he was ten and that had started him masturbating. He said, "Open your mouth."

Dr. Marks: "Why should I do that?"

"I never went to the toilet in the courthouse. The ones who say I did are definitely mistaken."

"Why shouldn't you go to the toilet in the courthouse?"

"Men get together in the cubicles."

Flooding indications of repressed (or unrepressed) homosexuality. He went to a boys' school and had himself sent home because he was "sick." He "hadn't" had anything to do with "smaller boys."

One incident seemed to have troubled him particularly. He was sixteen and was sleepless one night at home and went down to a basement playroom. His mother heard him and called, and he went to the bottom of the stairs and looked up. His mother was coming down with the light of the upper landing behind her. She had on an almost transparent nightgown, nothing more. She went back up after speaking with him, but the incident left him shaken. Dr. Marks thought: fantasy? Or did it happen? If it did, imagine what it did to him, how it helped force him not to want Mother or any woman.

He told these fantasies in between *non sequiturs* and full-blown insanities. He was evidently hearing voices. He called himself "King James" and said he was "Lord of the universe." We'll fix that, Dr. Marks thought. He said, "If you're Lord of the universe, please ask that chair to move to the other side of the room."

The chair remained motionless.

"I lost my connection just then," King James said.

James was given a private room, and Dr. Marks went there to treat him for the next several days. The third day when he came in, he thought James looked a little funny. His eyes were staring and he seemed flushed. He got between Dr. Marks and the door and showed him a jagged piece of metal and said, "I have to kill you."

Dr. Marks felt a beginning of sweat. James was a strong, heavily built man. But keeping his voice casual, he said, "Where did you get that?"

"Off the bed."

"It looks rather dangerous. I'm interested—tell me, why do you have to kill me?"

"They told me to."

"They probably don't like it that I'm attacking your insanity."

"I'm not insane." Angrily James came toward him.

Interpret. Disarm him with interpretations:

"If I attack your insanity, it's to make you well. It's because I care about your health. I can't let you go on being insane, but that's no reason to be angry with me. You say you're not insane. If you're not, don't listen to the voices. They tell you to kill me because you want to use me. 'Open wide—' you know what that means. Baby opens his mouth. He wants to suck my cock. He's hungry. What he really wants is Mother's tits. All you want is to be fed, to be loved." Dr. Marks walked a step forward and said quietly, "Give me that piece of metal."

James handed him the piece of metal. Dr. Marks said, "Thank you. You have to listen to me, not the voices." He felt relief, but somehow he had believed he would persuade James to yield to him.

Now James said, "I wasn't really going to hurt you."

"These voices must be very afraid of me."

"Yes."

"Who are they?"

"Maybe my sister."

"You never had a sister."

"I know."

"You know, then why did you say it?"

James said that in his late teens he had stayed in the house once for three months. He was afraid of the outside world, anything outside.

By the end of the session he was no longer King James. He was no longer writing the world's greatest book on criminal law practice. And the palm of his hand was cool.

Dr. Marks said nothing to anybody at the Center about this episode. That might be the end of his privacy with patients.

The "killing" session with James proved to be the turning point. That cool-palm thing was the tip-off. It was like Jimmy's temperature coming down to normal. In each case, there was a moment when you knew you had it made. This was the decisive moment with this case.

Four days later James was completely out of psychosis, and two weeks later he was discharged, but under strict orders about how long he was to rest and how often he was to come in for follow-up at the Outpatient Clinic. He agreed that when Dr. Marks let him return to his professional duties, he would carry only half his present number of cases. Ginnie and an associate at his office had covered for him by saying he was "sick." Two cases were court-assigned and these could be dropped on the plea of health. The problem would be to keep him from being persuaded to take on new clients, for his oral talents were prestigious.

Dr. Marks found the Outpatient Clinic indispensable. Jeannette had been discharged and had a schedule of treatment there, and he treated a number of other patients this way, insisting he be allowed all the follow-up work he wanted and believed necessary.

The office he used in the Clinic was hardly ideal. He wished he had his own office—all his patients so far could afford the fees that would maintain a private office on a cost basis. There was no couch here, no sense of complete privacy. About the only pleasant thing was a reproduction of a large painting on the wall—women in the dress of the last century standing near a tile-roofed house.

The first time he saw Jeannette there, she examined the house carefully, finally touching the round ends of the eave-terminated tiles.

"So you're still looking for the breast."

Eagerly she said, "I can remember all that roundness, how frightened I was—"

"You don't have to tell me. Once I tried to give you a glass of orange juice—not milk, God forbid—and you objected to the round rim of the glass."

She laughed, remembering.

"Don't laugh," he said. "This is serious. You know it's serious, don't you?"

"Oh, yes, I do."

"If you can remember so well, tell me something I've been wondering about. Why were you so frightened of the wall cabinet in your room?"

She said, "I thought a current came out of it and went across to a certain spot in the wall."

"What spot?"

"Well, I could show you."

"No," he said, "tell me. How high up was it on the wall?"

She indicated a height approximately on the level with her chin.

"What did it look like?" he asked.

She held out her hand with the thumb lightly against her extended index finger but leaving a small opening that looked surprisingly like a mouth.

"It looked like that? Like an opening?" As she nodded: "And the current went in there?"

"Yes, it went in there."

"Well, what was so frightening about that?"

"I don't know. It just was. I thought—"

"What?"

"I thought I ought to cover that spot, tape it over so the current couldn't come in."

He was excited. He was getting back into that state, that dream! How seldom you had any such chance. "Why did you think that?"

"Well, that current—"

"Was it the 'upper current'?"

"Yes, *you* remember."

"I remember. What I want is for *you* to remember."

"That current might hurt the wall," she said.

"The wall, the wall. What was the wall?"

Now she gave her pony tail a flick backward with her hand and walked around the room. That butt of hers, it was certainly attractive. "Why are you looking at me?" she said.

"What do you mean, looking at you?"

"You're looking at me in a certain way."

"I'll look at you any way I want to. You're an attractive piece of woman, you know. Is that bad?"

A flare of the psychotic arrogance: "Keep your eyes to yourself."

He said, "I wish you'd notice what you're doing. I asked you a question that disturbed you and quick you work up a fight with me. I asked you what the wall was, that the upper current might hurt. But you run from the question. Now come back to it and answer it."

The arrogance left her as if she had been struck. She said, "I don't know what the wall was." She trembled.

"Try to think."

"White. Sheets. Teeth—"

"Teeth," he said.

Frightened: "No, it couldn't have any teeth."

"Why couldn't it have teeth?"

"Well, it was like this." She raised her hand again with the toothless hole.

"You will think. Think carefully. Why couldn't it have teeth?"

"I don't know!"

Relentlessly: "What is it that doesn't have teeth?"

She put her face in her hands and her body quivered.

"You know what it is, don't you?"

"Me."

"Yes, it's you. You when?" he said.

"When I didn't have teeth."

He went over and put his arm around her. "You're brave," he said.

She pressed against him, but he gently separated himself from her. "Sit down," he said. "Let's be formal again like they say you have to be. You can tell me now what the upper currents were, can't you?"

"Milk."

"What milk? If that was your baby mouth?"

"Could it have been from a bottle?" she said.

"You're not sick now. You don't have to defend yourself now, or defend your mother." But he became quieter, he found himself smiling at her. "All those thousands of times you told me about the 'upper currents.' And all those other insane things. How patient I was! Because, baby, you were pretty boring, you know? I had to really love you to keep listening to all that nonsense you kept repeating."

"Yes, I guess that stuff was boring." Laughing: "It bored me too."

"And all the time you were telling me about how you were a baby, about how you were suffering and frightened."

"I was frightened, all right."

"Because those currents were going into that wall."

She shook her head in astonishment. "Yes."

"Tell me—that was the 'upper currents.' But you also talked sometimes about the 'lower currents.' What were they?"

"I don't know what they were." But she reddened.

"Where did they come from?"

"The windowsill, sometimes. Sometimes from the bedpost."

"And where did they go?"

"They went in the wall too."

"In that same spot, that same opening?"

"No, it was another one."

"Where was the other one?"

She measured to her hip, then her hand went a little lower.

"Thank you," he said. "That's all for today."

He told Dr. Naumann the gist of his treatment session with Jeannette. "I can't help thinking of what they're always saying at the hospital, 'The patient's out of contact.' That's what they say, 'Out of contact.' Well, what's so out of contact if the patient presents all that symbolism? If the patient is trying to tell you. There was Jeannette during psychosis fearing anything round. Well, what's round? The breast, obviously. She even went so far as to be afraid of coins, of money. Money is life and food. She was afraid of harmful 'currents,' currents feeding harmful milk into her mouth and harmful discharges into her vagina, which is more milk. Everywhere she was telling me, and I knew it unconsciously or half consciously all the time. All the time they're telling you, and it isn't the patient who's out of contact, it's the doctor." He straightened his body on the couch. "The terrible thing is that even when I know I'm in contact and know what I'm hearing, sometimes I don't believe it myself. I reject it."

Silence.

"The staff does too, at the hospital. Not one single staff doctor there stops and listens to a patient. And even Jeannette, she doesn't want me to listen. Look how she defended herself today, that shy one who's so good and cooperative now, how she tried to distract me." He blinked his eyes. "If she was still in psychosis, I'd have beaten her over the head with interpretations, but I can't now."

"Is there an exact moment when psychosis becomes neurosis? Would you want to define such a moment?" Dr. Naumann said.

"So I should go on fighting craziness."

"I notice you weren't exactly passive with Jeannette today, you let yourself get upset before you pulled yourself together—"

"But not the way I would with a psychotic."

"It's not the way you would with a neurotic, either."

"You know I had to react the way I did."

"I don't say you didn't." And after some moments of silence: "I notice the 'distract-him' game going on. Like Jeannette, no?"

No evading him, Dr. Marks thought. Then, Where am I in the sequence of these sessions? Orality. More and more I'm aware of the terrible possible attack on the mouth. More and more I seem to know what Jeannette experienced.

That nightmare was something she carried in her from the age of about one day.

A thought flickered through his mind: It might be well to see Jeannette's mother.

These mothers. He supposed now he expected in Mrs. Stone some life-coarsened woman who would account immediately for Jeannette's breakdown. The voice on the phone, when he had called her, was deceptive. It had a cadence of goodwill, even of humor.

Exact to the minute, a nurse brought her to his private room at the clinic.

"Hello, Mrs. Stone." A delicate oval of a face and, if anything, more beautiful than Jeannette's. You always expected the daughter to outdo, outclass the mother. Here the mother was a more vivid and striking version of Jeannette. It disturbed him. It wasn't natural, somehow, or right. It was a progression in the wrong direction as if the man (the father) had not done his part. Not that that was a biologically sound thought.

"This is where you interview my daughter?" Mrs. Stone said.

"Not interview, treat."

"I guess that was a defense. I'm sorry. May I say, I know you're generous to ask me to come here. A Pissarro?" she said, going to look at the tile-covered house.

He said, "I'm not generous. I want to learn some things I might not learn otherwise, possibly."

"I understand—then please ask me what you want."

"First may I ask: Has Jeannette said anything very specific to you about her psychotic episode, or her treatment?"

"She's mad about you, I know that."

"She doesn't tell you details?"

"A few, but I haven't made her feel she has to. I don't know if she even wants to. I don't know if I should. I'm not one of these mothers who need a dependent child. I've seen such mothers and they horrify me. They only seem to live inside their children's skulls."

"Can you remember back to when Jeannette was a baby, when she was born?"

"I think so. Certainly."

"How did you feel with her?"

"Happy. I was happy. I just felt happy nursing her—"

"You nursed her?"

"For over a year. It seemed one of the privileges of being a woman. It felt good, to have that little thing there attached to you—that's the time they're dependent, that's when you can enjoy their dependence if you want to enjoy it."

'*I thought a current came out of it and went across to a certain spot in the wall.*' That was what that ideal nursing had become in its translation into words, into dream image. And Jeannette had wanted to cover the hurt mouth in the wall.

There must be something else here.

"You don't want Jeannette dependent," he said. "But don't you think she wants you interested in the most important experiences of her life?"

Mrs. Stone frowned. "I think I am," she said.

After a moment: "What about your own life, are you happy?"

He seemed to detect a shifting behind the eyes. How delicate the spirit's movements were! "I thought you wanted to ask about Jeannette."

He said, "If this disturbs you—"

"No, it doesn't." Abruptly: "I'll answer this way—is anybody happy?"

"Are you very unhappy sometimes?"

Looking away: "Yes, I am."

"Could you tell me, do you think it incapacitates you in any way?"

"I don't know. I have times when I'm not sure I want to live."

"Does that go back—that feeling?"

"Yes. I'm all right now, most of the time."

"You've been honest with me. Let me ask this—do you ever feel Jeannette is angry with you?"

"Oh, yes. And I can't understand it. She was home a few days before we hospitalized her. And then—it was hard for me to believe—her arm would go back as if she wanted to strike me. Not that she ever would. I knew she never would. But to have her do that. And her expression."

That face, beautiful in its definition, changed. Shocked. Well, we all can lose confidence. "What do you think you had done?" he said.

"I don't know. I always loved her. I'd tried so much to do what was good for her."

That was what they all said. The primary thing happened outside of consciousness. That was what you had to keep remembering.

Well, so he hadn't learned anything particularly. Did he expect this woman would come to him without defenses? Exposed? You worked for weeks—months—to try to get through to some of them. Naumann worked for years.

Maybe one or two questions had probed the cracks.

But that something existed there, he had no doubt. Behind that beautiful face. You must always figure on the depth to which the surface is reactive. To which it adapts itself. Jeannette didn't get angry with this beautiful, intelligent woman for nothing.

She was saying, "Doctor, I may have seemed a little

cool with you. I came here distrustful and nervous, underneath. But I so much appreciate your having seen me. And I know Jeannette is benefiting from your care—is getting better."

"She is better."

There the flick of hostility showed, in the unconscious slip. My daughter isn't well, only "getting better."

But in his hope of really learning something, he was frustrated. He had to resign himself to learning only from the patient. From Jeannette. If not from Jeannette, from James. If not from James, from X:

"I turn flowers into shit for fifty billion years."

"Understanding like that—you love and every molecule feels good. You get clean. It's an internal bath."

Fred Kleinerman, in the middle of the night, heard a soft sound of weeping. It was somewhere in the room.

A form in the darkness, he had that nighttime awareness of movement, and Marta slipped down beside him in the bed. "Hold me." He held her the way she usually wanted him to, a kind of ritual: one of his arms went under her neck, sliding along the crevice of the pillow, and the other crossed over her breasts and responded gently to her breath.

"What is it?"

"I don't know. I was thinking about the women you'd had before me."

What could have made her think about that? "Why would you think about that?" he said. "They might as well not exist."

"There was one you loved."

He had made the mistake once of admitting he had loved somebody before her. "But that's over, long ago. It was like the crushes you get in school—you remember them, but you know what they were."

"I think maybe you still love her."

"I don't. But why are you thinking about it?"

"She sent you a postcard."

If that wasn't like a woman. Go all evening, lovingly, and in the middle of the night, bring something up: a card. "Where is it?"

"I tore it up."

"What did it say?"

"Nothing much. Nothing really. But I don't understand her writing you. Why should she write you at all?"

"I don't know. I'm not responsible for her impulses, whatever they are."

Again weeping.

"Marta, dearest, what is it? All this is unimportant. What's troubling you?"

"I can't tell you."

"No, please tell me." He pressed her against him, he kissed the side of her face.

"Something's the matter with me," she said.

"Darling."

"It *is*—"

"Then tell me."

A deep catch of breath: "It's—it's awful. I was vacuuming today and I got the idea the vacuum cleaner was going to suck in my thoughts."

He was disconcerted. "Well, that's not so terrible. All kinds of crazy ideas come into your mind sometimes. Especially if you're tired. You're working too hard. Ginnie should help you. She's over here all the time anyway. Or I'll get somebody."

"You don't understand," she said despairingly. "I turned the vacuum cleaner off."

Part 3

21

A year and three months later, in the early fall, Fred Kleinerman phoned Dr. Marks and said, "I'd like to see you.
It's about my wife."

"I can give you an appointment in my office. Where did
you hear about me?"

"My wife's cousin, Virginia Morris, knows you. Met
you when you were treating her boss, James—"

"I remember Ginnie. All right, come this evening at
seven. Can you make that?"

"I'll be there."

Dr. Marks hung up the phone and, being alone, was
aware in silence of the happiness of having said, "I can
give you an appointment in my office." He hadn't had the
office so long that he could yet be habituated to those simple words. Imagine, a ground-floor and with a private
entrance. And on Sixty-eighth Street not too far from
Fifth Avenue. His heart hiccoughed every time he passed
the gold-lettered nameplate: JOHN NORTON MARKS, M.D.
The first office he had had in Brooklyn, filled with his famous equipment, hadn't made him as excited as this one.

When he ordered the couch, he almost had to have
Robert come and watch it being delivered. A buff-colored
leather couch to go with the beige walls. He had to be different from Naumann with his green room. But he gave
Naumann one thing. Over the table in the foyer hung the
large photograph of Freud in his later years, his cheeks
shadowed, his figurines playing with mysteries beyond the
ends of his old hands. I have to have Naumann's Old Man
here in all his cancerous glory.

To the left of the foyer was a bathroom with a small,
high window (good thing, hard to climb out). The treatment room had a larger, normal-sized window, leaning out

of which he could glimpse the far-off edge of Central
Park. It was comfortable and, mainly, it was private. Here
any patient-initiated dramatics (or any therapeutic coun-
tercraziness) would arouse no shivers of gratified censure
in his "colleagues." Here he could be himself and the patient could be himself or herself. So true was this that one
patient just two weeks ago had given him a good kick in
the rear end. This was fine. He welcomed anything that
would help a patient get off dead center, get moving.

The office beat most doctors' offices he knew in furnish-
ings. One reason was that Margaret had given it her good
touch, selecting the vases and lamps, and she had had the
final decision on where to put almost everything, including
a rug she had allowed him to bring from the apartment—
"bring" literally—he had carried it rolled up on his shoulder.

"I want it clear the children are not to come here unless
invited," he said.

"Yes, Your Honor."

That was important because his office was an easy walk
from home (not its least advantage). As a guideline to the
kids, in a kind of inaugural ceremony on the first Sunday
the office was ready he had had them come there and
lined them up and explained to them that this was their
only visit for a while. "Any time from now on, if I have
to be reached, I can be reached by phone."

"Yessir," Bob said.

"You'll probably be pretty busy with your premed, anyway," Dr. Marks said. High school studies were now
called premed (family joke).

"Do crazy people come here?" Nancy wanted to know.

"I suppose you could say that. I'm not sure how crazy
they are. Don't you feel crazy sometimes?"

Nancy laughed. "I like crazy people."

"The landlord know what kind of business you're in?"
Johnny asked.

"I have this private entrance, don't I? A patient threw a
hairbrush out in the street Friday, I admit that. I spanked
her, of course. She won't do it again." (A follow-up patient from the Center.)

"Oh, John, don't tease them," Margaret said.

But the children stood in a circle, adoring him. He was
their hero, a father who "cured" the insane. And who had

to have an office to which you couldn't come, where he could be alone with his rites. He didn't even have a full-time secretary yet. (That would wait till his revenues were a little better.)

But he was finished with the Center, graduated with honors, and he had taken his Boards. He was a qualified psychiatrist. His analysis with Dr. Naumann (both training and control) would continue for several years yet, but he was ready now to have patients of his own.

And now a Fred Kleinerman was coming to see him, recommended by Ginnie Morris, who was James Bergendahl's secretary. That's how you got patients.

At five minutes to seven, a young man arrived. He was tall and had a certain lightness and directness about him. He wore a gray herringbone suit.

"Mr. Kleinerman?"

"Yes. Dr. Marks?"

"Please come in here. This is my office. Small but it gets some afternoon sun. Please sit down."

Mr. Kleinerman said, "Ginnie told me rather a good deal about you. Not just about Mr. Bergendahl. She says you've had a series of cases even though you're just beginning—"

"Yes, that's so."

"I'm desperate and I need your help. I guess the best is to tell you the whole story—"

"Please do. I have no further appointments."

"I mentioned on the phone—" the slightest hesitation, "it concerns my wife."

"Yes."

"How specific shall I be? There are rather intimate details."

"I think you'd better tell me everything, if you will."

Mr. Kleinerman began slowly: "My wife Marta is twenty-eight years old. We've been married six years and have a five-year-old daughter, Ruth. I was twenty-six when I married and I'd had some sexual experience, no involvement that meant anything. And Marta means everything to me. Simply no woman could mean as much—"

"Does she know you feel this way?"

"I believe she does—did. But she had this strange thing, she didn't think well of herself. I could tell."

"You speak of her in the past tense," Dr. Marks said.

"Well, since she's in the hospital now. And she's completely withdrawn, out of touch. Catatonic?"

"Please tell me what happened."

"Well, there were these things. Over a year ago I began to notice things. She'd say something real crazy now and then—oh, not often. I guess only twice it sounded really crazy and you can't believe anything like that, can't believe what it means. I thought she was tired. Anything." Pleadingly: "You understand?"

"Would you tell me about these crazy things you noticed?"

Fred told him about the vacuum cleaner "swallowing her thoughts—"

"That was pretty bad, wasn't it?" Dr. Marks said. Bert Lewin's triad. Eat, be eaten, sleep. But this was no play cannibalism. "What else?" he said.

"Another time she was nervous about the couch cover in the living room. She said it looked like knives."

"That isn't too bad."

"No, except that it was a plain blue cover. But you know, I had a funny feeling now and then that she wasn't telling me all the things that were in her mind. I'd catch her staring. I mean she'd have such a kind of a sad look. Once I asked her about it, but she pretended it was nothing—"

"Did you say anything to her parents?"

"No, somehow I didn't want to get them involved. I didn't think that would do any good. Her mother's not good with her."

"How do you mean?"

"It's hard to explain. If there's any real reason Marta doesn't think well of herself, it's her mother. She runs Marta down, somehow."

"Marta have any brothers or sisters?"

"No."

An image of Marta was forming in Dr. Marks's mind. You formed these images of people before you saw them. He thought of her as small, dark, dark-eyed. "How much does your wife weigh?"

"About a hundred."

"Small."

"Yes, but her height isn't too bad, five foot three. She's thin."

"What happened when she broke down?" Dr. Marks asked.

"Well, about the middle of August one weekend, the second weekend, we were eating in a restaurant and she noticed something about a glass of iced coffee I was having and suddenly didn't want me to drink it. She was convinced it would poison me—"

"Did you have cream in it?" Dr. Marks asked.

"Well, now that you mention it, yes." Mr. Kleinerman seemed surprised.

"Go on." The first time he had encountered the fear of poisoning projected on somebody else, Dr. Marks thought.

"The next day Marta seemed sick, so much so that I took her to a doctor. He came out and told me she was mentally ill and had to be hospitalized at once. She had told him I wanted to kill her and had asked him to call her father to come and save her. Then she came out and threw her arms around me and kissed me and whispered to me what she had told the doctor and she said, 'Why do I say those things?'"

Seeing Mr. Kleinerman's emotion, Dr. Marks said, "I know this must be painful to you."

"How *can* a person go insane? I just can't believe it. Even after the doctor told me, it was all I could do to take her to the hospital. I took her to a private place in Westchester—Findlay Hospital. When we got there, she read the voluntary commitment papers and asked questions about it—rather sensible questions—and then signed them. She kissed me, she kept kissing me, and the nurse took her hand and she still wouldn't leave me until I had promised her I'd be back to see her the next day."

The process of being "hospitalized"—always he had seen it only at or after pickup, Dr. Marks thought. Now he was seeing it as it was to a husband who had lived through it.

From what Kleinerman had told him, he sensed that Marta had fought a rearguard action. There had been 'things in her mind' she hadn't told him, and she probably recognized that what was real to her wasn't necessarily real to him. At any rate, she seemed to have kept the pathology inside her out of sight as long as she could. And her husband, cooperating out of love, had refused to believe what he saw as long as *he* could. That was what he was saying. The next day when he had gone to the hospital to visit her, she was like a person possessed: "I hate you. I love you. I lied, I lied—"

As she raved, the truth really dug into him.

Night had fallen in the office, now lit by the streetlights through the slats of the venetian blinds. Dr. Marks lit one of Margaret's lamps. He said, "Has she had any shock treatment?"

"Yes, but she got worse as soon as they gave her some shock—she became mute and then, the way they put it, she was negativistic, catatonic. They used those terms. It's just she wouldn't speak to anybody or do anything. So they're giving her more—heavier—shock and she's still mute and I don't think she's going to get better there."

"What do you want to do?"

"I've come to you. I want you to treat her."

"How am I going to treat her?" Dr. Marks said. "Her hospital's up in Westchester, too far for me to go there and treat her. Anyway I doubt they'd let me treat her there. What I do doesn't have any notable hospital acceptance yet."

"But isn't there some hospital nearby where I could transfer her and you could treat her?"

"We may come to that, but let's think a moment."

Fred waited.

Dr. Marks said, "Is her family helping with the present hospitalization?"

"Yes, I couldn't carry it by myself."

"Her father's concerned about her?"

"Very much so."

"Does he know you've come to me?"

"Ginnie's spoken to him about you. I know he'd be glad to have you treat Marta, I'm sure he would. He'd do anything."

"Could I speak with him?"

"If you're thinking about your fee—"

"Let's not worry about that now, although if I work with Marta the way I have to work with a patient, I have to be paid. What I'm thinking is, suppose we rented space in a hotel nearby—not too expensive a one—and got nurses and had Marta accessible to treatment. She's mute and quiet, so she probably wouldn't make any trouble at a hotel."

"If you think it could be done—" Fred said.

"Let's explore it."

"Will you need to see Marta before you take the case?"

"No, you've told me enough. I believe I have a clear idea of it. But I'd like to be honest with you."

"Yes?"

Dr. Marks laid his arms flat along the arms of his chair. "There is this to consider. I've had a great deal of success with a particular type of case. The cases I've handled have all been excited catatonics, cases where you might say the patient is yelling for help. You get that feeling. It comes to you from every fiber of the patient's body. The patient is in deadly fear, and I developed a certain talent for resolving that fear and excitement. Where I've had steady access to the patient I've had no failure and no relapse. But I haven't had a patient like Marta where there's no excitement, no overt fear. That doesn't mean there *is* no fear there—"

"I understand."

"But I haven't had this type of case. I don't know what I may be able to do with it. My impression is that this can be a very difficult kind of case, probably much prolonged. I've wanted such a case. I've wanted it to see if I could use my methods with it or if I could develop methods that could be effective with it. But I can't at this moment guarantee anything." After a moment, he said, "I can say I would bring to this type of case—to your wife—every last resource of my own energy and determination."

"Nothing is being done for her now. Nothing. I'd rather see you working with her than see nothing being done. That's why I came to you."

"Then that's clear."

"I'm sure her father will go with this."

"There may possibly be a long time with no outward signs of progress."

"It's all right if you're working."

"I may need courage too," Dr. Marks said. "Tell me a little about yourself. What do you do?"

"I'm an accountant." Fred leaned forward in the soft light of the lamp. He said, "I can tell you this. I sometimes think Marta's breakdown may be my own fault. I've been irritable, maybe just when she needed me. I'm not as sensitive as she is. Maybe I haven't understood her as I should—"

Dr. Marks said, "Isn't it worth considering that she might have broken down sooner except for you? Surface irritation doesn't bother anybody who knows she's loved. All my professional experience tells me you weren't the cause of this breakdown."

"Then what?"

"Isn't that what we have to find out?"

Four days later Fred drove Ginnie and a nurse to the Westchester hospital. He had arranged with the Director to have Marta released, but not without an argument. The Director had told him his wife's weight was down to ninety-four pounds, she was being tube-fed, "and she's in no condition to leave the hospital—we can't be responsible for what may happen to her, or to anybody else."

Fred had said that he understood that.

"Where are you taking her?"

"I'm putting her under the care of a private psychiatrist, Dr. John Norton Marks."

"I'm glad at least you're having professional guidance." More pleasantly: "If there's anything I can do to cooperate with her new doctor—"

Coached by Dr. Marks, Fred said, "You could give me your report on her. For Dr. Marks."

"Certainly."

The waiting room was high-ceilinged with windows whose frames and sills were enameled pure white. Everything about the room was clean and orderly. When Marta was brought in, her stockings wrinkled, her hair flat to her head on one side and looking as if it had been hastily combed, she seemed in marked contrast to her surroundings. Fred noted this contrast with annoyance. He signed some papers (only too aware that it was Marta who had signed them coming in), and he and Ginnie and the nurse gently helped Marta out to the car and put her in the back seat. She sat rigid as the car started and was rigid for a long time, then she raised her hand toward Fred and said, "I lied."

Ginnie smiled at her and said, "It doesn't matter, darling. We didn't believe you."

They drove on in silence.

Fred had engaged the hotel suite without saying what it was for. He arrived and took Marta directly up in the elevator, accompanied by Ginnie and the nurse, May Kinnell, who was not wearing a nurse's uniform. The employees took no notice of them coming in.

The quiet, upper-floor apartment had a living room, kitchen, bath, and bedroom. Two other nurses had been hired for around-the-clock care, and Ginnie would fill in occasionally for relief. Fred phoned Dr. Marks and told him they were there, and Dr. Marks said, "All right, I'll be right over. But I'm going to ask you now to leave your wife. This is a matter of professionalism. She should be completely by herself for a while. Later you'll be able to see her, but I don't even want Ginnie with her for a few days."

"All right," Fred said.

Dr. Marks introduced himself to the nurse, a capable-looking woman in her thirties, and found Marta sitting on a sofa. She was slight, as Fred had said, and had heavy dark hair. Her black eyes had a swollen look. He had an impression of a child who has been severely reprimanded and saddened. A beautiful child. As he studied her, she seemed inanimate. Not even too appealing.

"Hello," he said.

No answer. No answer of voice or body.

He touched her shoulder: "Listen. You can hear me. I'm outside, but you can hear me. I want you to know who I am. I'm Dr. John Marks, the doctor who's going to take care of you from now on until you get well. It's important for you to know a few simple things. This is a hotel apartment. This is not a hospital, there are no hospital doctors, no hospital guards, no shock treatment, only me and my aide here, Miss Kinnell."

Marta bent her head and her hair fell forward over her face.

"Marta."

Silence.

He lifted her face so that she was looking at him. "I was told," he said, "that when you were brought into this apartment, you did a crazy thing, you looked under the bed and under the bureau as if you were afraid. You don't have to be afraid now. I don't allow anybody in your apartment who could hurt you. I control everything around you now. Do you understand me?"

That long, deep gaze. You could sink into it, travel

down it into a consciousness he knew only too well by now: fear.

Softly: "Are you afraid?"

A change in that gaze that made him feel she was listening not to him, but to some other voice, some other presence, and in fact her eyes went to the side and stared.

An hour later he noticed that she seemed tired. It was hard to separate her unbroken passivity from actual tiredness, but already he was becoming sensitive to slight differences, a scale of unconscious signals. "Would you like to sleep?" Although there was no response, he asked Miss Kinnell to put her to bed.

He sat in the living room waiting. He felt just slightly unnerved. This was the case he had wanted, but it *was* unnerving. No reactive interplay at all so far, and so, nothing to work with. A sense in Marta of easy and illimitable resistance. Not even resistance. She made you not be there. The defense was to annihilate you.

And yet that deep gaze. He *had* had the glimpse of fear even though he could not say she was seeing him.

He would have to work now with every indication given him, he would have to become aware of slighter messages of the Unconscious than any he had yet worked with. Nonverbal communications. Movement, posture, breathing. Nothing should be too slight.

Miss Kinnell came out and said, "She's sleeping."

"She went right to sleep?"

"She seemed to."

He got up. "All right, you'll let her sleep. Phone me when she wakes up. And when she wakes up, I'd like you to wash her hair. Mr. Kleinerman brought plenty of clothing. Dress her in a clean dress. Something pretty. I'd like her to feel we value her. Much of the success of this case will depend on how you and the other nurses treat her. You've done psychiatric nursing, you know about this requirement, but this needs a special touch."

"Yes, Doctor," she said.

"This case is going to be difficult, you can depend on that. There's fear under that surface. Remember that that's what will *make* her difficult, if she is, not any personal feeling she has about you. I want to reduce the fear as much as I can—that's why I told her she'd have no more shock treatment. Patients fear shock. It's a fear superimposed on all the other fears they have, something deeply terrifying. If Marta doesn't have that, it may make a difference."

"I wouldn't want shock."

Good girl, he thought.

He gave her some further directions and left.

He went directly to the office and phoned Margaret. "How was it?" she said.

"Hard to tell. She's withdrawn, all right. She goes in and out of these catatonic rigidities. Her defenses must be formidable."

"That's what you wanted, isn't it?" Margaret said.

"It's one thing to want it, another to be right up against it."

"What's she like, I mean otherwise?"

"So often deep insanity gives people a look not like themselves. I get that feeling with her. I believe she must be beautiful—Fred says she is, or was—but it's hard to see it. Of course she needs her hair washed and needs caring for. But there's something that comes over these patients that seems to disarrange their features. A slackness. They're inanimate, without expression. It can be repellent. But then you see through it, you see terror, childishness. I don't mean I have with her—it's no more than a hint. Like a hurt child. But that's how I've seen it with other patients. And then your heart goes out to them." He was in his private office. The leather couch was glistening against the fine beige walls. The midday light was clear in the venetian blinds.

"I know how you must feel, but—"

"But what?" he said.

"What if you don't make it with this case?"

"You didn't say that before."

She hesitated. "Perhaps I shouldn't have now. But it's your first case. And to be that—"

"That's what I wanted," he said. "Exactly what I wanted. I asked for it."

"Yes, I guess you're right. At least she has you. That's something."

He felt better. That was an acknowledgment, and from where it counted. He said, "I don't know just what my schedule's going to be. I'll play it by ear."

"Come home when you can."

He hung up and sat looking at a picture of his children on his desk.

Four hours later Miss Kinnell called him: "Marta just woke up. And she seemed sane. She said, 'I feel so rested. Who are you?' I told her and gave her some chocolate milk."

"Did she say anything more?"

"She said, 'I can't forget last night or her.' I asked her who 'her' was, but she wouldn't say. She says a word or two most of the time, or nothing."

"But there was that moment when she woke up," he said.

"Strange. Just as if she was normal."

"Don't get your hopes up. Wash her hair and comb it and call me. That would be a good time for me to come. If she shows any signs of being interested in food, give her a poached egg. Or anything else she might like—the refrigerator's well stocked."

"Yes, Doctor."

When he came back, Marta was sitting limp in an armchair, her hair was combed out and drying. He said, "I'm glad to see your hair washed and combed. You have beautiful hair. I suppose somebody told you you *don't* have beautiful hair. That's a Goddamned lie, of course. I never saw more beautiful hair." He touched it. "I'm glad you have this lovely hair and I'll want you to keep it in good condition. I'll want to enjoy it when I'm with you. You understand I'll be with you a great deal of the time from now on." Silence. "That's a nice dress too. That belt goes well with your hair, and the dress sets off your hair well, too. I always thought I'd like to have my daughters wear yellow dresses. You're my daughter now of course. I wonder why you sit so limply there. Give me your hand."

No motion.

He took her hand. The palm was slightly moist. He felt her pulse. In spite of her being limp, her pulse was beating hard. "I think you're afraid, Marta. I wonder if you might not tell me why." He waited. "There's no need to be afraid of me, you know. All I'd ever do is attack anything that's hurting you. I'm here to protect you. I love you as my own child. I believe you're going to feel that love and understand it. You're probably hunting for some love right now and think you have to be limp like that—like a baby

—to find it. You don't have to crawl back there like a baby to get a little love. You can get all you want from me."

Miss Kinnell was watching. She told him later, "I never saw anybody work like that."

"That's just the beginning, I'm afraid."

"Do you think she hears you?"

"Some part of her does. I told her that."

"But how long will you keep doing that?"

"Indefinitely," he said.

The first week he spent eight to ten hours a day with Marta, one day eighteen hours. Her mutism continued unchanged. She said nothing to him, not a word. It was as if she knew he was the one she had to defend herself against. Occasionally she said something to one of the nurses, Miss Kinnell, Miss Barklund, or Miss Hughes. She developed a thing. She retained the final mouthful of liquid she was drinking, or if she didn't have that, she accumulated a mouthful of saliva. And kept it in her mouth. Sometimes vague sounds came through the liquid or flowed with difficulty out of her nostrils. Sometimes, even with nothing in her mouth, she sounded as if she did have her mouth full. He interpreted: "You need food in your mouth all the time so you won't starve." With former patients, an interpretation like this would have a good chance of eliminating a symptom. But he could see no noticeable difference in Marta. The full mouth of liquid continued, and was annoying and troubling. How a baby can trouble you if something is wrong with it! You can't explain things to it, you can't help it, you can't make it change.

Sometimes he had the feeling the liquid in her mouth was to prevent her from speaking. Or to make her speak like a baby.

Other minimal sounds. Occasional choking.

For the most part it was silence.

Or worse than that. She would sit tense, her arms in set, rigid positions. She would put her hand across her abdomen or her chest. She would form a straight line, her fingers outstretched, as if holding a bar in front of her.

Or she would do repetitive things like picking single hairs out of the sink, one after the other.

Eating too turned out not to be the easy triumph he had hoped for. He had hoped that without shock and in a new environment she might begin to eat regular meals. No. She ate what little she ate spasmodically and unpredictably. She drank some chocolate milk, but refused regular milk completely.

She'd point to her mouth and then not eat. Or start to eat and then stop.

One day Miss Kinnell told him that she had said, "I'll get Papa into trouble if I go to court tomorrow." He tried to get her to tell him what this meant. No answer. "You also told Miss Kinnell 'Tom was the face at the window.' What does that mean?"

Silence, mute.

"Who was Tom?"

Her head bent down, her hair swept over her eyes.

He phoned Fred and asked who Tom was. Several slight possibilities, but none seemed significant. "It could easily be an imagination," Dr. Marks said. He asked Fred if there had been any court case in the family, anything involving her father. "Nothing. Nothing at all," Fred said.

Just the same, the court thing stayed in his mind. It must be some kind of reality for her. What could it be? How could he use it?

OCTOBER 3, 1945

DR. ARTHUR CHANDLER
THE VANSITTART CLINIC
DEAR ARTHUR:

I'd like to have a talk with you. I've started a new case and it's like Jimmy Cady before he began to scream (for me, though he didn't know it, and maybe lucky he did because you know how many never reach that stage of despair or panic, but just sit or lie there for years).

Margaret and I are having one of our widely spaced standard parties next Friday at eight: Bill Widener and others, you know the crowd. So come and let's talk. We can even celebrate the strange state of peace in the world, one month old.

Fondly from all of us,

JOHN

He wrote Bill Widener, inviting him and Alice, adding a postscript: "Special Johns for tigers." Tigers—a couple of weeks ago, outside The Psychoanalytic Institute, he and Bill had been talking and Bill had told him something that had happened during the preceding week in a session with a patient.

The patient had reported a dream of a tiger peeing on him. "After he told this dream, he didn't say anything more. I waited a minute or two and then suggested he associate to the dream. He said, 'Once when I was in the zoo and was standing rather near a tiger's cage, the tiger peed on me.'"

Bill had a talent for deadpan humor.

"How did you go on from there?" Dr. Marks asked him.

Snickering: "Oh, there's always a way to go on."

"I don't know about that," Dr. Marks said. He was thinking about King James Bergendahl and his threat to kill, but that was not a case in point. He could have been stopped then, all right. But evidently there was always a way on. Except for Marta? What did you do when Marta never said a word, only sat there veiling herself with a stare? What was the way on with her?

He had invited Bert Lewin to the party, but the night of the party, Bert called and said that something had come up so that he couldn't get away. When Nancy heard it, she pouted because she "loved" Bert. He got cigarette ashes into the most interesting places, once into the middle of her braided hair. He had blown the ashes all around her like a snowstorm, apologizing and at last kissing her on the top of her head.

"Does it taste of cigarettes?" she had asked him.

She was growing by the minute. She now had dinner with the family regularly, and Dr. Marks often came home for lunch and to be with her and Margaret (a needed relief from Marta). There was nothing slow about Nancy's identifying this as a status thing and finding ways to convey it to her brothers. "Daddy told me at lunch—" or "Daddy read me a long story after lunch." She had begun doing water painting and had painted a picture Dr. Marks looked forward to showing "the crowd" tonight.

His cousin Ruth and Harvey arrived first. Harvey with the deep lines in his face, a regular cleft under his nose, dividing his lips, and in a side shadow, smaller clefts at the ends of his mouth. Yet they would all seem to be erased when he smiled. "Good to see you, Harvey—Ruth." Dr. Marks took them into the living room and showed them the picture Nancy had painted. "This house is pretty good, isn't it?" A large yellow house. In front of it on the green grass was a blue blob like a door mat. He pointed to it. "I asked her what this was and she said, 'If somebody walks around inside the house and gets wet paint on his feet, he can clean it off here.' "

"What a mind!"

"You can learn things from a mind like that," Dr. Marks said.

Bill Widener and his wife Alice came, still happy, still openly and obviously in love. There's a record-breaking honeymoon, Dr. Marks thought.

Margaret, I get loving looks from her too sometimes, but it isn't that continual radiance of the first days. Love. It was a little silly when you came right down to it. Like me and my damn Auburn roadster with Roy in his classy cap driving me up to call. And Margaret making like I'm a hotshot. Luring me on with gracious looks and hard-boiled eggs. Well, so it was silly and insane, but it was nice.

Ted Rutledge and Linda arrived, and right after them, Arthur Chandler. Arthur's ruddy face brought in the October cold outside. When he had ensconced himself on the sofa (his favorite place), he beckoned Dr. Marks to sit beside him. "John—now that you've graduated from the Center, can you speak freely?"

"I spoke freely before. What's there to speak freely about?"

"Well, you know I'm the one, I guess, who got you to go there."

"I'm glad you did. You probably saved my life, steering me up there."

"But I get the strong impression you were disappointed —in some way it didn't make it with you."

Watch it now, Dr. Marks thought. "Who am I to be disappointed? I mean who am I to talk about a place with the best research and psychiatric facilities perhaps in the country?"

Dr. Chandler peered over his joined fingers. "Are you being sarcastic?"

"They let me work, didn't they? You said they would and they did. I worked on enough cases to keep Margaret deprived day and night. They even let me sleep there."

"You're not coming clean, Marks."

Dr. Marks laughed. He put a cigarette in his cigarette holder and lit it. "Well, there are a couple of things. At no time did the Head come down to see what I was doing, not even after twelve cases had been 'cured'—at any rate had walked the hell out of there on two feet. He didn't have enough interest to see for himself what it was all about. I'd say that's disappointing. Maybe that's just hurt pride on my part. Maybe the great administrators of this world really have no time to go and look over Dr. Johanson's shoulder and see cell damage in the brain, or stand beside me for fifty hours and see the brain healed with words." Healed with words! He corrected himself: "Maybe not just with words. I slapped that arrogant bitch Jeannette Stone a few times, and silence has great therapeutic usefulness. My silence, that is. You get to them one way or another. You do something."

"Did you ask Dr. Carey to come and see your cases?"

"I asked him. But even suppose I hadn't."

"You have a point there."

"You'd think he could have come down once, for a single hour. Well, maybe I didn't do anything. It's against policy—nobody does anything there. Carey, Stieglitz, nobody. The philosophy of the Center is 'We only do research and teaching here, Doctor.' In that tone of condescension. You have to actually hear it to believe it. Research—like one doctor says to me, 'I've had an astonishing result from giving four electric convulsive treatments —shocks—one after another in a most recalcitrant patient who was completely wayward and nothing else could touch him, and now you should see how easily the patient responds to the commands of the nurses.' "

"And when you slapped Jeannette?"

Surprised: "If you look at slides of her brain, will you find a fine wave of hemorrhages?"

Bill and Ted were now listening to them.

"So how do you feel about the Center finally?" Dr. Chandler said.

"I find it hard to talk about it calmly. I'm a naïve bastard who thinks everybody wants to do something about sickness, physical, mental, whatever the hell it is. I can't understand it when they don't want to do something. Maybe—and I've said this to Margaret—it's just too hard for them to do the scut work of the Unconscious, and I know it's hard. You mentioned a little girl Lessie—"

"Lissie, from Alicia." This was a child Dr. Chandler had been treating for a psychic collapse following a throat operation.

"Was it hard to treat her?" Dr. Marks said.

"I admit it was terrible to see her panic, as you say, but on the other hand," smiling, "I loved her."

"My dear Arthur, you break all the rules of therapy. You mustn't have any feeling for a patient. No transference *to* the patient."

"Hah."

"I'm afraid you and I are a small handful, maybe a company of two. Well, we'd have to let in Naumann and Bert Lewin and a few others—Bill here, I hope."

Bill frowned.

"You do love your patients, don't you, Bill?"

"I'm concerned for them."

"That's already a lot," Dr. Marks said.

Now that he was in private practice, he got implicit or explicit word, both from a range of psychotic cues and from talk with colleagues, of a neat new device of the profession. It said, The patient can get well only if he wants to be cured. The corollary (and this was where it was really neat) was, If the patient doesn't get well, it's because he doesn't want to be cured.

He mentioned this to Bill Widener and said, "You know plenty of patients at New State are seen by a doctor only once in three months"—the legal requirement. To Arthur, who seemed to be paying particular attention: "I suppose this means the patient doesn't want to be cured."

Dr. Chandler said, "Shit," under his breath. He added, "I know, I've been hearing this thing too."

"How in hell can a patient like my Marta Kleinerman 'want to be cured'?" Dr. Marks said. He told Arthur and Bill about Marta in some detail. It surprised him how much he could tell them. That came from that intense preoccupation in which the minor incident becomes major and everything loses its usual proportions. He told them about saliva, arm positions, the few words she said, her very appearance: in the end he thought he had told them nothing.

Linda came and sat beside him. "I heard you," she said. "Marta. You've got yourself a rough one."

"Yes, but almost as beautiful as you are."

She laughed and repeated the remark to Ruth.

He lit another cigarette and smoked. Bill and Arthur were discussing "identification" and as in a paralogic mirror, he saw a woman patient at New State who was talking about "Christ." Christ for her was everything: man, woman, woman-man, man-woman, capable of giving every kind of love. Each patient on the ward in turn came to her and warmed her hands at this consoling id. The woman cried: "He will be the universal bridegroom. He will reach down and take us all in His arms."

"Will He marry me?" a young woman said intensely. Another said, "I'd like to raise my loaves in His oven."

"Maybe He doesn't have an oven."

"Well, if it isn't a priori, it's a posteriori."

Crazy, but with meaning.

He said to Dr. Chandler, "Do you think your little Lissie loves her mother?"

"Of course she does."

"But she needs your love."

"She looks at me like she does," Dr. Chandler said.

"Then maybe you're the mother. My patients are always after Mama. Without exception. The mother is indispensable. Mother is the breast."

Linda, who had been listening, said, "Suppose the father feeds the baby."

Dr. Marks smiled at her getting into the act. "With a bottle, you mean?" he said.

"Yes."

"Then he's the mother. Who can feed the baby but her? Does the man have any equipment to do it?"

Bill: "Then you mean the mothers are the real schizophrenogenic villains."

"Not villains. I never said that."

"But they cause the psychosis."

"They cause it. But they can't help it." Dr. Marks turned to Dr. Chandler: "You know the riddle of the Sphinx? Maybe that's the great riddle. That monster has the head of a woman, doesn't it? and the body of a lion. A woman who can tear and kill. But still all these patients yearn to love this mother."

"I think you'll find more than patients defending the mothers. This is a mother civilization."

Dr. Marks: "And I'm not going to win any popularity contest, fighting mamas."

His brother Robert had said the same thing in different words: "You're going to be unpopular." It could happen. And with Marta he might get to be worse than unpopular. What if the boys at the Center heard about her, his keeping her in a hotel apartment? It was all right to handle follow-up cases, out of psychosis, but to handle a psychotic outside a hospital? The hotel now pretended not to know what was going on, but if the word got around?

Margaret served some snacks she had made, and the talk became general. Dr. Marks asked Ted about the current poker sessions, and about Ted's and Linda's summer at Lake George. Ted said Harvey and Ruth had been up for a long weekend.

"When are you going to join the social set again?" he asked Dr. Marks. "What about a little all-night game?"

"I'm enjoying you guys right now." But he was still thinking about Marta in the hotel.

Later he talked with Arthur about it. "Am I going too far there?" he said.

"Don't let yourself get paranoid about it."

"You mean just stay with it?"

Arthur smiled: "Isn't that what you'll do anyway?"

"But it makes me nervous, knowing there's just a door between that hotel apartment and the world outside. Marta can move. You'd be surprised. Miss Barklund told me she'd undressed her for her bath and she had to go answer the phone for a minute and when she came back, there was Marta completely dressed again."

"Still, a nurse is there."

"Yes, and most of the time Marta's just rigid. Sitting or standing in some crazy position. And after the way I've been working with her, day in, day out."

"I know how you work," Dr. Chandler said.

"If there was just a little movement with her. I need encouragement."

"*You* need encouragement."

Dr. Marks held his cigarette holder in front of him and stared at it. "You'd be surprised," he said.

"You still have the best legs of anybody I know," Dr. Marks said to Margaret when the last guest had gone.

"Is that all?"

"Well, that's all I have a basis for comparing. Come here. I want you to look at the moon." The moon was shining from a great nimbus of milk-washed clouds. "You like?" he said.

"I like."

"But it means storms."

"I don't care."

"Maybe it's just as well you don't care. I love you and I care, but I don't seem to be able to do anything about storms. You can't argue with the weather."

He remembered the view from the living room in Brooklyn, the two gables of the adjacent house that at night dissolved into darkness. Sometimes he missed it, sometimes he wondered at the way he struggled, changed his life, tore up his home life, disappointed his father, his mother, and perhaps his brother, and generally exhausted and overworked himself. Why do you have to go through all that?

And then there was Marta leaning forward with her catatonic hand clutched to her breast, warding something off from her, her sightless gaze sunk into her hair. That was why. Simply that. That was what you had to help. No matter what it cost, you had to. You put your money (no money) where your mouth is.

Perhaps it was something else. Something like hate. If you see blood flowing, you can't stand it and you try to stop it. If you see the Unconscious exposed, you try to stop that. Like the brain or guts, it isn't supposed to be seen. You try to put it back where it belongs.

The only trouble now was that Marta's Unconscious wasn't being put back like Jimmy's or Jeannette's. So he had to go on seeing it. That was new. On all previous cases, some part of himself—fire, heat, energy—had been applied to the struggle in an excess of healthy passion and commitment. And that had done it. That had taken care of everything. Not now. Now there was something terribly different. He felt as if he was being asked a question to which he had no answer.

The Sphinx was a bad opponent. It (she) might look bland and beautiful, but her riddle was lethal.

22

Toward the end of October, Miss Barklund mentioned that it might be well to ask Marta's husband about her period. "She hasn't had it."

"I'd been thinking about that too," Dr. Marks said. "Of course, it's not unusual under stress. But I'll check."

He phoned Fred, and Fred verified that Marta was overdue. "Don't be concerned about it," Dr. Marks said. "It wouldn't be good if she was pregnant just now, but she doesn't show any signs. Just the same I'm going to take a test."

The test showed no pregnancy. He called Fred and told him. "How are things going at home?" he asked.

"Good. I have a colored girl, Janice, who takes care of Ruthie, and I spend most of my spare time with my daughter. It helps me. I'm glad I didn't let my parents take her. Or Marta's."

"Yes."

"I didn't want her to feel she'd lost both her parents, and she could, couldn't she? Don't kids get that feeling if you put them somewhere?"

"You're showing good judgment. Keep her with you. How is she?"

"She seems to be doing all right. A little sober sometimes."

"How are you?"

"I'm not bragging."

He had Miss Kinnell step outside the door into the hotel corridor. The apartment entrance was from an ell off the main corridor that gave them a sense of privacy, still he kept his voice down. "How long has she been taking that new position?"

"With her feet, you mean? I didn't see it until today."

"Has she eaten anything?"

354

"No, nothing. It's unusual. She said she was hungry, but then she wouldn't eat."

"Did you keep urging her?"

"For a long time, but it gets hard to keep telling her everything. Sometimes I wish I could just let her starve and then she'd eat."

Even this woman had her honest antagonisms. That wearing, endless passivity that sometimes seems like an active resistance, a sly (child's) provocation. "You say she said she was hungry?"

"She didn't actually say it, but she has a way of letting me know. She pointed to her mouth this morning."

That didn't necessarily mean she was hungry. All these multiple possibilities—

"You know I had an awful time dressing her," Miss Kinnell said. "Miss Hughes tried too, before I came on. Then after I got her dressed, she kept following me around."

"Did she watch what you were doing?"

"Yes. When I was making the bed and when I made her some juice. But then she wouldn't drink the juice."

"Was that when she took this position?"

"Yes, about then."

They went back in. Marta was on the sofa with her heels together on the floor and her feet spread toe out as far as she could get them. It must be uncomfortable, he thought. She was looking fixedly toward a corner of the room. "Marta," he said.

A firm inattention (to him) in her eyes.

"Marta, why do you have your feet like that?" He tried to sit with his own feet spread that way and it was a tremendous strain. "You know, you must be looser jointed than I am. I can't keep my feet out as far as you do. Are you a soldier? A sentinel standing guard? Maybe you're guarding yourself. Or are you that little baby hiding in there behind your eyes? Behind your lips?

"Are you a doll? Nobody hurts a doll, maybe that's what you are, a doll that everybody loves and plays with, or are you a toy soldier?" Loudly: "Where's your gun? If you're a soldier, where's your gun?"

To his delight, she puckered her lips. "Does it taste bad? Is it a bad breast? I said, Is it bad milk from a bad breast? Do you hate it?"

She resumed her blank staring.

"You pointed to your mouth this morning. Then you didn't eat your breakfast, you wouldn't even have some nice orange juice. So did you hate your mother's breast? Was it hurting you? Did it bruise your mouth?" He put his fingers gently on her lips. "I don't hurt you." Remembering his success with patients who wanted to suck, he cautiously tried to insert the tip of his little finger into her mouth, but she wouldn't accept it.

He went to the kitchen and came back with a glass of orange juice. He had learned that steady, unrelenting ordering her to do something, especially eat, would sometimes work. He held the glass to her lips. "Drink," he said.

No response. Like when she was eating, she would pause with a spoon or fork halfway to her mouth and have to be verbally prodded into action again. It was as if the hallucinatory figures captured her attention and you had to break that attention.

"Drink. There's nobody out here but me. And this isn't your mother's milk. It's just good orange juice. Drink."

Her lips opened slightly to allow the rim of the glass in, but she didn't let it go past her teeth.

"You need some liquid. Wouldn't it be nice to have this cool juice go down your throat? Mmmmmm. Take a swallow."

Still the closed teeth.

"This isn't a penis. It's just a glass of juice."

Now her feet bent forward as if she needed the leverage to help her keep control of her mouth.

"You can let go. You can drink. It's easy. You do it every day. You have to do it. It's safe. It isn't Mother." He caressed the back of her head, smoothing that lustrous, heavy hair. "I'm your new mother, your good mother. Drink."

The teeth slowly opened. He guided her hand up to the glass and she took it and drank.

Miss Kinnell gave her her breakfast and she ate the entire meal. No pausing of her hand going to her mouth.

Well, it's better than force-feeding, he thought. Slow, painful, but it was better than what they were doing at the hospital. It was something, at least.

But the energy it took out of you. The sense of that insensate resistance.

Marta resumed her position on the sofa, feet spread exactly as they had been before, but her eyes focused on a different corner of the room.

He went to that corner so that she was staring directly at him. He said, "You know, when you stare like that, you aren't quite as beautiful as when you relax, when you're more natural. And you know how beautiful you are." He thought, Suppose she should answer me just once. As casually as he could, he said, "Is it warm in here?"

No reaction.

"Miss Kinnell can always make it cooler if you want."

She stared through him. He wasn't there. He said, "I saw Ruthie yesterday. Would you like to see her?"

Silence.

Standing in front of her: "I also saw your husband. Do you know he misses you badly? Do you know you're unspeakably mean to stay in this crazy private world of yours away from your husband and your child? So maybe your damn mother mistreated you, maybe she hurt you with that awful breast of hers, but it's gone, it's gone long ago. It's all over now. Nothing to hurt you now. I won't let it. By the way, what do you hear now? What are you hearing? Do you hear my voice? If it helps you not to hear the other voice, I'll talk to you for an hour, for four hours, five hours. Stop listening for that other voice. I'm here. I'm going to be here for weeks, months, years if necessary. Do you understand that? I'm *not* going to leave you."

How insane it seemed to him that even when she was staring right at him, she wasn't seeing him! And perhaps she wasn't hearing him either. But even that was relative. One of his patients at the Center had told him: "When I'm listening to the voices, I don't hear anything you say to me." But all he had to mention was "Would you like a cigarette?" and the patient immediately said, "Yes," and took the cigarette. Strangenesses of split attention, rigidities, marathons of endurance, half-sleep, states of vigilance independent of ordinary intelligence and awareness— Marta drank and ate, bathed, dressed or was dressed (with struggles sometimes), and now she was holding her feet like a Goddamned toy soldier. Charlie Chaplin, that was what he had been trying to think of. She was Charlie Chaplin.

What did that mean if it was so? Underdog, waif, loser always apologizing for any accidental successes, always loving somebody who doesn't love him—it fit when you thought about it.

He hunted in the apartment closets and came up with a lightweight woman's umbrella. He rolled it up and came back into the living room with it and shambled around with his feet spread out, twirling his umbrella cane, hitching up his pants as he went. He disappeared sideways on one foot out the door into the kitchen, and put his head back in, smiling. "How was I?" he said to his imaginary audience.

He found Marta looking at him, apparently seeing him.

The children were fascinated when he told them what he had done. They got him a cane and made him perform for them.

Nancy said, "Did I ever see Charlie Chaplin?"

"You will, you will, kiddo," Bob said. "You'll get to see the next revival."

Johnny said to his father with professional condescension: "You should have been an actor."

"What do you mean? I am an actor."

But that reinforced an idea he had.

He finished dinner and went back to Marta's. He was curious to see how she was. To his satisfaction, she had abandoned the foot position, but now she sat with two fingers of her right hand crossed and resting on her left shoulder. He'd have to try to figure that one out.

Miss Barklund was now on duty, but Miss Kinnell hadn't left. He had begun to notice this phenomenon, that the nurses sometimes waited past the end of their tour of duty. When he asked them about it, they usually said they were "just interested."

Miss Barklund was slight but strong, and was markedly sensitive. Swedish.

He had remembered that Marta had said she'd make trouble for her father if she appeared in court. He put several books on a chair to elevate himself when he sat down (crazy, he thought), put an ironing board over the backs of two kitchen chairs to make a barrier in front of his seat, and draped the barrier with a bedcover. All this facing Marta. It had some likeness to a judge's bench. He had cued Miss Barklund to give him assistance as he improvised a court scene.

"Court will come to order." Should he use married or maiden name? He decided to take a chance and use her maiden name. "The next witness will be Marta Johns. Miss Johns, please come forward to the witness-box." A chair stood near the bench he had made.

No motion from Marta.

"The attendant will kindly help the witness to the witness-box."

Miss Barklund took hold of Marta who strongly resisted.

"Witness, come forward to the witness-box at once or you'll be in contempt of court."

Still resisting.

"Contempt of court, contempt of court—sentence is a lifetime in jail. Are you coming forward, Miss Johns?"

With something like a whimper, Marta let herself be moved from the sofa to the chair, her crossed fingers still remaining on her shoulder. Miss Barklund stepped back.

"Thank you. Now, Miss Johns, please tell the court what you've done." No answer. "We can get other witnesses if necessary who will tell the whole truth. It's no use trying to conceal anything. I'm the judge of the Supreme Court of Conscience. I look inside and know everything. I can be anything. Listen to me! I can be your father if I want to. I can bring him right here. Here he is." He shifted his voice a little, making it sound as much as he could like her father's. " 'Why did you have to come here to court when you knew it would get me into trouble?' " No answer. " 'You probably meant to do some more of your lying.' " A flicker of response from Marta. " 'Of course you have to lie like mad to try to make your mother love you. But it won't do any good. She doesn't love you. I hear her all the time telling people: "Marta probably thinks she's beautiful, but she's nothing. She ought to despise herself." Yes, that's what she says about you. And you believe it. "Marta can't do anything. She never could do anything." You believe that too. You won't listen to me or believe me. You probably came here to tell some big lies to make your mother love you. You'll tell any lies your mother wants you to.' "

The crossed fingers on Marta's shoulder were turning white.

"All right, the court will please come to order. Mr. Johns, you may step down. The criminal is incriminated.

I'm sure she knows her crimes. Miss Johns, are you beginning to know what your crimes are? You committed the crime of being born. You committed the crime of choosing a mother who didn't want you, deliberately inflicting yourself on her. You tormented her and were hateful to her. You didn't give her a single thing to make her happy, never pleased her in any way."

Now the fingers on the shoulder were definitely white.

"You don't believe me. You think you must have done something to make her glad she had you. You think she must have found some happiness with you. But you're a liar. You lie to others and you lie to yourself. She didn't love you. She wished you were dead. She even cursed the day you were born. If she dared, she would have killed you.

"Give her up. Don't go running back there after her like a fool. Don't think you can hide inside your skin and fake yourself a mother. She doesn't exist." Angrily he threw the bench and books on the floor, and said, "You're sentenced. You're sentenced to me. You're sentenced to a parent who wants you and loves you. I'm Mother now." He grasped her shoulder roughly. "You feel that? It's not those imaginations of a mother you go running to. It's me, it's real. With me you can be happy. You make me happy. I love you, I protect you." Were her fingers relaxing, was color coming back into them? He touched them. "What are your fingers crossed for? Good luck? It *is* good luck to be loved, isn't it?"

Miss Kinnell left with him and as they walked away together, she seemed disturbed. "Doctor?"

"Yes?"

"I probably shouldn't interfere because I'm sure you know what you're doing."

"What's the matter?"

"Do you really think you should say all that about her mother? I mean, mightn't it make her worse?"

"You do think I have some effect on her?" he said.

"Don't you?"

"Maybe to this extent. She must know I want her to get well. Don't you think she must realize this if she sees me struggle with her hour after hour, with no encouragement from her, saying maybe dumb things, maybe wrong things

—but trying very hard? Doesn't she know I'm fighting for her?"

"I'm sure she does—"

"Doesn't she know I love her if she knows anything at all?" He thought, Do I have to work with the psychiatric nurse too? He said, "You know this isn't my first patient. I've found from my experience that you have to somehow detach patients from the mother who seems to them to be poisoning them, hurting them, making them feel worthless. Who never gave them enough love. There can be mothers like that. It isn't the mother's fault. It's what's in the mother's Unconscious that does it. Nobody, and that means no mother, is responsible for what's in her Unconscious anymore than she's responsible for what she dreams. But I do have to detach the child from such a mother and attach him or her to me."

"It just seems so harsh."

"Don't you think life is harsh? Why is Marta like this if life isn't harsh?"

"But now you're being hard on her too."

"It's different. It's what I've told you. I'm hard on the insanity, not her. That's the difference. And I have to believe she knows the difference. My other patients did and I have to believe that she will. I have to believe that, if I'm to keep on working. I may seem confident, but inside sometimes I'm discouraged. I work sometimes by main force. You don't think it's easy, do you?"

"No, I don't." She said, "I guess I'm not bright. I appreciate your trying to explain this to me."

At his next session with Dr. Naumann, he told him what he had done with Marta. He also mentioned Miss Kinnell's reaction. He said, "I'm afraid this would be the reaction of most normal people if even a nurse who is used to caring for psychotics reacts this way."

"Does this make you feel unsure?"

"No. I guess the only thing that makes me feel unsure is that I *don't* get a reaction from Marta."

"Would you say there is no reaction whatever?"

Dr. Marks thought about that. "The reactions are slight, and it's hard to convince yourself that they're reactions to you and not some kind of inward shift that's irrelevant. How do I know these things? When she gives up a certain rigid position, she may do it when I'm not there or for some reason of her own, not right after I've attacked and interpreted it. So how do I know it's because of me? But sometimes I seem to sense something. A direct look. An increase of tension or an easing of tension even if she doesn't move or respond openly. Sometimes there even is a reaction. What I have to believe is that in spite of the defenses, she isn't different from my other cases."

Silence.

"She could be worse," Dr. Marks said. "I think of the patients in the back wards who are in the fetal position, who have no controls whatever—they're maybe the ultimate catatonia. Maybe they're what I should be trying to treat and then I'd know what discouragement is. They fill me with dread and I think of them for another reason. Could Marta become worse? Is there danger in this attack that I make? Always before I've been able to believe it can't become worse. How could Jimmy become worse? And even Nora or Jeannette? You felt them on the way to psychic self-destruction and you had to intervene. But what about Marta?"

Still silence.

"But if I don't intervene with her, she may go on this way indefinitely. I've seen it where it's gone on for years, for a lifetime. If anything, I feel the need to do more."

"I believe that I should tell you something," Dr. Naumann said. "I've talked about you with my friend Paul Federn, who is much interested in your work. He has read my copy of your paper. By the way, when is it to come out?"

"Next spring, I believe. At any rate, next year."

"Dr. Federn knows more in this field than I do and has done more work. He tells me that so far as he knows, nobody before you has used your method of direct psychoanalytic approach to the psychotic Unconscious. Jung was convinced that morbid complexes caused the schizophrenic state, but he never tried to attack the complexes directly. Since you're feeling at least some element of doubt, I'd like you to know that you have this expression of support. Dr. Federn is naturally cautious in his estimate, but he told me he thought your method might have a wider application than to the types of cases you've had so far. I mentioned your Marta case."

Dr. Marks said, "I'm glad to hear all this, but you yourself know something Dr. Federn can't know. You know, if anybody can, what my own Unconscious is. Is it capable of giving enough love to Marta?"

"You've surely shown a great capacity for such love so far. If you were able to give it to Jimmy at a relatively early stage of your own analysis and insight, I believe you should be better able to give it now. But there is such a thing as insight coming when it's needed. You're still in analysis, you're still working. Isn't it reasonable to believe that this will help you?"

Naumann, Dr. Marks thought, he never lets up.

"Perhaps now," Dr. Naumann said, "we may return to the work of the session?"

23

When he came home from his session with Dr. Naumann, Margaret said, "You had a phone call from Jeannette. She'd like you to call her back."

What could that be? He hoped there were no complications in *her* life. "I'll call her from the bedroom," he said and hurried down the long hall.

"Hi, darling," he said when he got her on the phone. "I hope you just want to hear my friendly, fatherly voice."

"Well, I do," she said, laughing a little. "But it's more than that or I wouldn't have called you at home."

"You call me anywhere you want."

"Thank you. This is what it is. Somebody I know is in bad trouble, I mean is sick, you know."

"Psychotic?"

"She's really bad."

"Is this a first breakdown?" he asked.

"Yes and she hasn't been hospitalized. No shock treatment. I told her parents about you."

"Well, that's fine."

"You'd be wonderful for her. She's so frightened, and I don't think it would be hard for you."

"Never mind if it's hard or not."

Quickly: "You were willing to take some cases, weren't you?"

"Yes, but not too many. You know how I work. But I do need a few. I'm just beginning practice and a doctor has to live."

Amused: "You'll live."

"Tell me about this girl."

"She's twenty. She thinks there's something the matter with her shoulder, but I don't think there is. I think it's a way to get attention."

"Why do you say that?"

She said hesitantly: "Well, she'll forget all about it for

364

awhile and then if like nothing's going on, no attention being paid her, she'll start complaining."

"What else is the matter with her? That's not very serious."

"Well, she can't think straight. Goes off into blanks. And she thinks there's a conspiracy to pour water on her head and she thinks her hair is wet."

Being born?

"Could that be being born?" she said.

My God, he thought. Be careful around these recovered patients. He said, "Does that frighten her?"

"Yes, terribly. That's funny, isn't it? Why should she be afraid to be born?"

"I can imagine several reasons." But the astonishing insight Jeannette had: compare it with this Miss Kinnell with all her goodwill. "Say, sweetie," he said. "I'm having a thought."

"Yes, Doctor," she said, kidding it.

"Listen, how's it with you at home just now? I mean, are you especially busy?"

"Not busy at all."

"Do you think you might conceivably want to work as a psychiatric aide? For me?"

"Hey! Why, it would be wonderful. You mean with a patient?"

"I mean with this girl, if I decide to treat her. What's her name?"

"Betty Neil."

"You think maybe?" he said.

"I'll talk to the family about it. You think I could do it?"

"I'd be there."

"Yes. Gee."

"Think about it," he said.

The next day Betty Neil came to his office with her mother. He left the mother out in the waiting room with Mr. Freud and took Betty into his treatment room. She was attractive, with a flushed, full face and pouting lips. So many psychotics he had known pouted. The next stage was to scream.

"I understand you have a pain in your shoulder," he said.

"I do, I do have. Oh, it hurts!" She clasped her shoulder.

"Take off your sweater." She was wearing a thin green sweater and a green skirt of some hard, stylish cloth. The skirt had a sheen.

She started to lift the sweater, she disengaged it from her skirt and started to pull it up, but stopped in embarrassment.

"Come now, I'm a doctor," he said. "Take it off."

She drew the sweater up over her head and swung it around, it was a mere handful of material, and dropped it on a chair. She wore a white net bra through which the nipples of her breasts showed. She shrugged, glanced down at the bra, moved her arms distractedly, and began to undo the fastener in back. "That's enough," he said. "You can leave that on."

She waited, writhing as many of them did and turning her head away. He started to examine her shoulder and as he manipulated it, she managed to come close to him. Her breathing deepened. "All right," he said, "I'm just interested in your shoulder."

Immediately she became embarrassed and put her arms in front of her breasts. Then with an uncertain movement she grabbed her sweater and put it on.

"Thank you for dressing," he said. "There's nothing wrong with your shoulder."

"Oh, yes," she said. "Oh, yes, it hurts. I can't stand it." She gave a childish wail, and held her shoulder again.

"It isn't your shoulder that hurts," he said.

"Oh, yes it is."

She lowered her hand uncertainly. She opened the zipper of her skirt in order to put her sweater inside and revealed a bit of white panty. She tucked in her sweater and kept moving her leg nervously and fumbling with the zipper.

"All right, zip it up," he said sharply.

She quickly closed the skirt up. Vacantly she said, "It's lucky I'm not married."

"Yes?"

"What would my husband think if he saw me here."

"Where are you?"

Her eyes seemed to blur. Pouting: "It's some kind of house."

"Not that kind of house. Where are you?"

"I'm sure you don't want to stab me."

Stab. Did they always have to say that? There was a certain monotony in this business. "Listen," he said. "What's this I hear about your wanting to be reborn?"

She put her hand up to her hair. "I don't—I'm wet. I want my mother," she said, beginning to cry. "I want my mother, I want my mommy."

He took her outside, guiding her firmly. With his handkerchief he wiped her eyes. He said to her mother, "I'll speak with you on the phone."

"But you'll help her, Doctor. Jeannette's told me—"

"I'll speak with you on the phone," he said.

The two shapes disappeared through the closing door.

He felt again that body quivering against him. What had she really wanted—not him, and not her mommy. Not her actual mother. Just love itself. This case would be relatively easy.

Of course he would accept her as a patient.

And he would bring her out.

Her sulky, oversinuous movements. He had seen it so often in the hospital. At New State a girl would try to leave him with a graceful movement and would bump into another girl in the corridor. And underneath that effort to be graceful, you felt disorientation and panic. Lack of love. They all wanted love, in bewilderment and ineptly (or hungrily) they asked or hinted their need. Ethel: *'Somebody's robbing my clothes.'*

When he was already worrying about how he would keep up with follow-up patients from the Center and with Betty, King James sent him a patient, a tough one, not a first breakdown, a thirty-one-year-old obsessive-compulsive who had the tone (naïveté) of a teen-ager and who had been in and out of institutions since he was twelve years old. He could communicate, he sounded sane outside of his compulsions and obsessions (saner than most people), but he was so sick he was recently found kneeling in the hospital lavatory praying to God to "go completely insane" (to relieve him of his present sufferings).

Fortunately he had had little shock.

Unfortunately he had a lifetime of carefully erected defenses.

Jeffrey was the patient's name. Dr. Marks told his father, "Your son is filled with hate."

"He *is* filled with hate, but there's gentleness and idealism in him, too."

"I know this phony idealism."

But Dr. Marks accepted the case and worked out a plan for handling it. Jeffrey was in an Astoria hospital and that simplified matters. Perhaps he could put Betty Neil there too, for obviously she had to be away from her parents during treatment, and she didn't promise to be a quiet case like Marta. He even thought of moving Marta there, but better let well enough alone. Marta was close to him and close to her nurses, and she at least accepted where she was (if you could speak of her "accepting" anything).

But he thought, The start of a case requires long hours of listening to the patient, and with Jeffrey it would mean trying to find the sources of that fine negative passion obsessive-compulsives have—he had seen it at New State in all its glory. He remembered one boy who had to protect himself with a piece of tissue paper when he touched a doorknob—he never failed, you couldn't stop him.

How would he be able to keep putting the pressure on Marta? Well, there was just one answer—he wouldn't sleep. He'd go back temporarily to that five-hour-a-night sleeping, or four hours.

His part-time secretary couldn't work full time, so he got himself a full-time one, a tall, thin Negro girl, Rosalie Barns. She was a skillful stenographer, so he told her he would dictate notes to her on his cases. "You can take down patients' productions, too," he said.

"Productions, is that what patients say?"

"Yes, well, everything's a production," he said, laughing.

"But can I be there when you're with a patient?"

"They won't even know you're there. It won't make a bit of difference."

"Really?"

"You've heard this thing about 'the privacy of the patient'? Forget it. This isn't that kind of patient. Anybody can come around and watch what you're doing."

"All right."

"You're going to help me, Rosalie."

"I hope so," she said.

He arrived early for his session with Dr. Naumann and took a seat in the waiting room. How he needed Naumann! How he needed him now, with Marta! He found that he didn't just discuss Marta with him; she became part of the whole working session.

He had just come from her. He thought, Naumann, who only has to listen—he should have Marta. No listening at all! Well, yes, you listen to nonverbal sounds, to variations in her frightened monotony—arm out rigid, arm across the breast. He sometimes felt a monotony in his own unrelenting verbal or dramatic onslaught, being (as actor) her good and bad parents, interpreting anything interpretable, anything the nurses had told him, anything he heard from Fred or Ginnie. Was he right in being so active? Why not let up? What might it do just to be quiet, listening, attentive for four hours? He might try that next.

That feeling that he had to beat out the voices, jam them like an enemy radio broadcast. So much was the same thing (the same therapeutic approach) over and over.

He was getting increasingly tired.

He looked at his watch. Still a few minutes to wait. He wondered if the great man would open the door on time, for of course you had to wait till he was ready. He closed his eyes. It might be possible to sleep a little before the door opened, if some miracle permitted it. But instead of sleep, a scene reenacted itself before his eyes. When you were tired, you always thought of scenes that bothered you, probably something connected with Freud's principle of "binding the trauma."

He was again in his office at the Center the day he left. He was to meet the resident who was replacing him, just as Dr. Belos had met him on his own first day. The new resident, Dr. Gregory LeMay, arrived punctually, knocked, and entered with an air of assurance.

First he gave Dr. Marks his credentials. Then he said, "You're older than I thought you'd be."

"I went into psychiatry late. Could I ask why you're going in for it?"

"I want to help people."

"That's good. And that's what you're here to learn?"

"Isn't it?" Dr. LeMay said.

"You'll learn that insulin is 'to balance the emotions.'"

And you'll learn just how to get the syringe in the artery and how to get the feeding tube down the nose."

"You don't seem to like this place very much."

"When you're here, notice one thing. Ask yourself, If staff doctors are interested in helping people, helping patients, why isn't that what they're using their time for?"

LeMay looked troubled but said nothing.

"You will come in, please."

Dr. Marks opened his eyes, startled. The small, delicate man in front of him looked as if he had no interest in anybody in the world but his present analysand.

As soon as Dr. Marks lay down, Dr. Naumann said, "What are you thinking?"

"I fell asleep in the waiting room—that means I'm tired, but that isn't important. What I'm thinking actually is that I'm nervous and that it's like the nervousness—not like me —that I have at night lately before I go to sleep. Why should I be nervous going to sleep? Bert Lewin thinks people aren't, or not normally. But he has that thing about satiation with good milk. I don't know too much about good milk. As a kid I was allergic to milk—raw milk. If I drank it, I'd get diarrhea. Uncle John prescribed acidophilous milk for me. That's my good milk—as far from the breast as possible. So Bert Lewin thinks when you go to sleep, you should suck the good tit of memory and go right to the dream screen. Enjoy sleep—welcome sleep. Not me. I take two more tough cases to treat so I'll sleep less. No, that isn't fair. I've taken these cases because they both appeal to me, and I need the income. And Jeffrey is in The Island Consolidated Hospital and that's going to give me an entrée there so I can probably put Betty in there too—

"To go back to sleeping. When I was a kid, they used to make me sleep outdoors when I was at the seashore or in the country. Oh, I had a dream last night."

"Yes?"

"I was going in the wrong direction in a train—that's a common dream, I know—then I was taking a baby out for a walk, and this one's weird—this baby was a small grasshopper, not much more than a slug. But it was a baby too. I had a concerned feeling about it as a baby. It began to grow right before my eyes and I was worried it would get to be a full-grown grasshopper and jump into the air and fly away—you know how they do—and get lost. But then I didn't think it would or I didn't worry about that anymore. It had rather high wings, and I held the top or tips of these wings and guided it along, and kept it from flying away too, I guess. I loved it. I was also somewhat worried somebody might step on it and kill it, not knowing it was a baby."

"What about the train?"

I knew he'd ask me about the train because I resisted telling about it, Dr. Marks thought. "I've almost forgotten that. I got on a railroad train to go from Philadelphia to New York and then found I was going to Washington. Also I had left something in Philadelphia I ought to have taken with me, but I can't remember now what it was. I think there were two things, one a small thing and one a large thing."

That detail smelled of symbolism, Dr. Naumann thought. But I won't ask him about it now. "About the grasshopper dream—"

"I think Marta's the baby. I love her and have this concerned feeling about her—this exact feeling of the dream. It wasn't a bad worry, you know that would be hostile. It was a loving worry. Well, I believe it was. I know only too well how actual mothers can say they love their babies and then want them dead."

Dr. Naumann said, "Do you need to be afraid if there's an element of hostility? We all have hostility."

Dr. Marks felt himself sinking into the couch. This hypnogogic thing of the couch, and then his fatigue. He seemed again to be in the dream, holding the grasshopper's wings. He said, repeating a refrain, "I was afraid somebody would step on the baby grasshopper." The cow! Stunned, he said, "Oh."

"Yes?"

"I was reading yesterday that there's what's called a 'poor breeder' among cows. Once in a while there will be a cow that steps on her calf and kills it. I even meant to tell you about it, that such a thing can happen in the animal world. So do you wonder I accuse these human mothers of wanting to kill? They do kill. And that thought must have been behind my dream. I was trying to protect Marta. Or protect Betty or some other patient. But I think it was Marta." That love he had felt, touching those delicate wings.

Now he thought, The whole dream was only the fragment of a longer dream. It worried him, this insane dreaming. And a terrible thing—

"What are you thinking now?"

"I was thinking that lately I've had a tendency to accumulate saliva in my mouth, I'll notice a little saliva there and I'll swallow it. Sometimes I'll even swallow it the wrong way and choke. Tension, I think. But don't think I haven't thought too that it could be an identification with Marta. This thing of unconsciously identifying with the patient, it can frighten you sometimes. I know I can't go crazy—I believe I can't—but it drifts through my mind that I'm not all that normal. And then there's conscious identification—participation in the psychosis." In the breathing at the head of the couch, did he sense a satisfaction? "This thing of worrying about the baby grasshopper growing up and flying away. I sometimes hate to think that Nancy will grow up. Of course that's just a passing thought, from loving her, but don't the mothers of these schizos I take care of—don't they want their children to stay babies? And don't they arrange for them to stay babies? And here I am in the dream holding the baby's wing tips and not wanting her to fly away.

"And I'm protecting this baby grasshopper just like the mothers protect *their* babies only they're really hurting them, making them crazy." Did this dream then mean he was functioning like a damn schizophrenogenic mother? But obviously he wasn't. He said it aloud to Naumann: "With me the patient does fly away, but still loves me and needs me. Here's Jeannette who's going to work for me, and Jimmy called me, and Nora now and then will call me up or drop me a card. Say, Nora, there's one who had great insights. Maybe she'd work for me too."

"Why do you suppose this 'baby' was a grasshopper in your dream?" Dr. Naumann asked.

Yes, that was something he hadn't given attention to. "Well, when I was in the country—I mentioned sleeping outdoors there—when I used to spend some of my vacation there, I'd see these flying grasshoppers in the late summer, kind of brown color as if their color had faded, and I'd catch one sometimes and it would secrete a disgusting fluid all over my fingers." He became silent. At last he said, "A penis." Damn, could it actually be? Obnoxious how you always found the same things behind the dream. And now he remembered the sluglike look of the grasshopper when it was first with him. He mentioned that to Dr. Naumann.

Silence.

"Talking about fluid," Dr. Marks said, "it can also be a breast. A breast secretes fluid and I guess Marta and I both think that's a pretty disgusting fluid. But I loved the baby grasshopper, or the grasshopper baby."

"You remember how I said before you should not over-weigh your hostility in this dream. Neither should you ov-erweigh your hostility to milk." With which you began the session, Dr. Naumann thought. "You're a sane man. You can love babies and you can now drink milk. One reason we are sane is that the ravaged mind has great powers of restoring itself, usually." But fascinating how tinges of hostility formed the dream. And how the dream associa-tions hunted through psychic obstructions for the breast! But what about Freud's rule: the various parts of the dream repeat each other? "Could we return to the train? What could it have meant that you left two things in Phil-adelphia, one small thing and one large thing?"

"I can't remember what the small thing was, but I think the large thing was a briefcase. Case records? Letters? No, it was kind of bumpy as if it had something else in it. 'Small thing and large thing'—that could be the grasshop-per baby that was small and then large, almost full-grown." A long hesitation.

"What are you thinking?"

Something bumpy—"A penis is small, then full-grown."

"When it's full-grown, what does it do?"

"Fucks, jerks off—you mean, gives milk. So I was dreaming about the same thing as the grasshopper."

"It has happened before, such repetition."

"Yes, but in the first dream I had left the breast behind and in the second dream—"

"You recovered it," Dr. Naumann said.

Reacting: "But I was afraid I'd lose it again."

Silence.

He was annoyed with Naumann for finding the pattern (meaning?) of the two dreams. "You think it's quite a thing, finding the breast all over. Just because I'm working at the oral stage with patients—"

"I didn't find it. You found it."

"You think I like to think or dream about my mother's

breast or remember that damn second-hand wet nurse I had? You think I like to see Marta staring at who knows what phantom in the air, hiding from it in her catatonic cave? If I have a few oral fears churning around inside me, what do you think she has? Or Betty?" In a lower tone: "Probably it's the same with Marta as it was with me in the dream as I trotted along with the breast. She fakes a good feeling about it. It makes her happy. It has to. And it has to make me happy too."

An emotion reawoke here. Dr. Naumann thought back over this long analysis and recalled crucial moments when Dr. Marks had identified with patients. Had shared their experience. The *pavor nocturnus*. The urine smell of the matriarch. Dreams and productions that came from overwork and exhaustion and the giving way of defenses. All his most meaningful insight, all this eruption from the breach of the Unconscious. It all seemed indirectly yet persistently to be moving toward oral understanding.

Part of that understanding was to get insight into his own hostility, evident here. As he did, he would recognize his patients' hostility where it remained hidden, spreading behind some make-believe of love.

'I love my mother' (the constant refrain of patients).

Was there ever any end to this reality of unreality? He glanced at his watch. Half the hour had passed. He said, "Your mother is not Marta's mother."

"I'm aware of that." Afterthought: "But I've seen Marta's old man and talked to him, and he's a rugged character. Tough. Climbed out of poverty like my old man."

Pa.

Somewhere outside Dr. Naumann's office a child was calling, just loud enough for Dr. Marks to identify the sound, which was immediately lost in traffic noise.

Bushwick Avenue. He said, "I just had a thought about my father. He has me by the hand. I'm about seven and I'm asking him to take me across the street. There's a street carnival down past the brewery, I don't know where it is. I'm not even sure there is one. It's one of those rumors that go through a neighborhood when you're a kid, when the world gives you the glad eye, tells you there's a good thing somewhere around the corner. So I want him to take me. He has to take me. 'Take me across the street, Pa. Take me.' He won't. So I kick him in the shins and at the same time I'm holding his hand and pleading with him. You know he hauled me into the house and beat me till I fainted."

Dr. Naumann said a surprising thing: "When do you feel faint now?"

"I don't. Haven't I told you? I never give in, never faint. When I see too much Unconscious, I put my head down, but I don't faint."

"I didn't say you fainted. I asked when you feel faint."

"I don't feel faint." I'm a doctor. But now he remembered something, something that had made a vivid impression on him when it happened, but immediately had faded from consciousness. And only two weeks ago.

Two weeks ago he had eaten badly, and at night, in bed in the dark, bile had come up into his throat and he had lost his breath. It was bad for a moment. He had tried to pull air in and had made a horrifying moaning sound in his throat. Then his throat opened. But just before it did, he had had a dreamlike moment of thinking, Suppose I can't clear my throat, and I die. He now told the incident to Dr. Naumann and said, "How terrible it would be to die accidentally, with no warning, in the middle of your work—"

"You felt faint."

"I felt faint. But it's different. It was physical." He tried to be honest. "It was also part of that whole strangling thing of my childhood. There must be nothing around your throat. You must always protect your breathing. Get your milk but breathe. Eat but be careful. No s-mothering. Once I had a hell of a cold when I was a kid and could hardly breathe, and my Uncle Herschel—another brother of my grandmother and no smart performer like my Uncle John—he brought me some cough medicine and gave it to me with a spoon so I could breathe. I never forgot him. Years later, one hot summer when he had asthma, I saved my pennies and bought an electric fan and carried it three miles to him so I could give him a little air."

And now you are bringing this grateful air to your patients, Dr. Naumann thought. Dr. Marks immediately echoed him, saying, "I must have some streak in me that wants to do things for people. But it's always people who are children. Of course Uncle Herschel was me when I took him the fan. And my patients are me too, I suppose." But worse, worse. That was what had been ringing through this session from the beginning on, the depth of the childlike, or prechildlike, suffering. Concealed in his dream-work. Concealed in Betty's awkwardness. Concealed in Marta's silence. If he had been shaken once or twice, how shaken must they all be as phantoms and dreams gave them not mere hints of death (the baby will be stepped on, your throat will close), but such open confrontations with it that they fled into a paralytic immobility. His dialoguist of the mind said: But some of them are happy. Jeannette with her haughty striding around.

No, they're not happy. They're haughty, not happy. It's all a pretense. When you take a close look (muscle, skin), you find them trembling. Betty who can hardly coordinate any action, her body is so distraught.

He said: "I'm thinking about my Psychiatric Research Center patients, all my patients. You think *I* fear death. Everything about them is mad with fear. It's like, I'll tell you what it's like—it's like they're breathing hard standing still. Dreaming while they talk."

Now there was a silence. Dr. Marks sank into it as into sleep. He had done his work, he'd rest. Images went disjointedly across his mind. Color. Could you dream color? He had sometimes. Then all thought left him.

Dr. Naumann could tell from Dr. Marks's breathing that he had gone to sleep. From one moment to the next. And he had spoken about his nervousness at going to sleep. Well, the session had had that usefulness. And more. Let him rest the last few minutes. He can even rest while I make notes.

But while Dr. Naumann was writing, Dr. Marks woke up and was embarrassed. He apologized.

"Don't apologize. It was one of your better sessions. I think your fatigue released something. You've done your work."

"But sleeping—"

"Once when I was lecturing in Berlin, one of the doctors in the audience fell asleep. He snored. The Berlin Psychoanalytic Society met then in the home of Erich Reiss's mother. Reiss was a prominent publisher. His mother had converted three rooms of her large apartment into one to have concerts, and later we used this room for a meeting hall. And that's where I gave the lecture I mentioned. During that lecture I could hear the lions roaring from the zoo. We were near the zoo and the Catholic Hospital, the Franciscus Krankenhaus. I'll tell you something else. In front of the Reisses' house grew an oak tree right in the middle of the pavement, that gave us a nice shade. The city cared for it because it was hundreds of years old. It must have survived from when this was farming land, and it was so large it took four men to reach around it. The neighborhood—the neighborhood? the whole city—was proud of it.

"This tree the Nazis later cut down because it had 'nothing to do on a pavement.' "

That night, in his living room, Dr. Marks went back over the day's treatment session, particularly the fear of not getting enough air that had made up so much of the session. There's a time when the baby doesn't need air at all, when it's in the womb. A fetus. The "closed room." He thought again of the patients in the back wards who took the fetal position.

I ought to get over to New State and look at them again. I have to go anyway to check on my cases if I'm to do a decent new paper. A new paper, and here I am loading myself up with more work. You went on before you had fully assimilated what you had done. Naumann wouldn't get behind like that. He'd write. Once he had said: "I didn't work around the clock the way you do. I apportioned myself. I liked to write. It gave me a feeling of control, of stability, that maybe I needed to offset the stresses of treatment." He accepted the limitations on his time and wrote, fortunately, even about his first psychotic cases. Wrote better than I do, Dr. Marks thought.

What was this schizophrenia? If he was to write, he had better try to get a firmer definition in his mind. You treat it, but can you put it into words? There was Betty with her wet hair, wanting to be born. When you were born, you were separated from your mother. Was that a prototype of later psychic splitting? Was all of life a separation and a longing to be reunited?

But death was a splitting too, the ultimate separation from the race. So life, and death were both schizoid. Well, perhaps that was just playing with words, kidding around. Not clinical. All right, so what was clinical?

He got out his copy of Bleuler's *Demetia Praecox oder die Gruppe der Schizophrenien* (still untranslated), with which he was thoroughly familiar. Bleuler was at least descriptively useful. Unmarried, he spent all his time in the hospitals, and spent it not treating, but observing (something of The Psychiatric Research Center there—only a few pages of his long book were about treatment). He observed what he called "dissociation"—the "schizo" part of schizophrenia. Different "complexes" or strivings got separated off so they could no longer influence one another as they did in a healthy person.

Nora had wanted to be what her parents—her mother, let's face it—had wanted, a boy. So being beautiful and attracting love from boys continued, but it continued somehow outside of this part of her that wanted to be a boy. She got married, but she also was convinced that she was ugly.

The old rule: in neurosis, you repressed the Unconscious, the id. In psychosis, you repressed reality, or—more handsomely—you reformed it, made yourself ugly.

He thought, But what Bleuler does is describe what exists at any one moment. But that isn't the point (I'm telling *him*). The point is, Where and why did the neurotic defenses break down, and where is the illness going? This was the important thing to know: the dynamics, the course of pathology, the changes; only then could you know the meaning of any particular stage of illness.

(Just the same, give Bleuler A for effort, for recognizing what Freud called "the advantage of turning away from the grayness of theory back to the ever-green realm of observation.")

But if you were after this process thing, this dynamic, how did you become aware of it? Know it? How did you live into that most secret of personal events? He leaned back in his chair and closed his eyes.

Jimmy, his first "case." Jimmy, the one he probably knew best of all the cases he had treated, not only because of the intensity of work, but because that journey of discovery had gone on longer after the initial recovery.

Suppose you begin when Jimmy is "all right" (before breakdown). Anybody who knows him figures he's a bright kid. He's doing well in school, all A's. But something is going on: *'my mother's hand.'* He has incestuous wishes for Mama—all his productions showed it. Defend yourself by becoming a girl, then you don't have to do it. Or be a girl to Papa, so Papa will love you—that's a way out too. So he's passive and submissive, like a girl. And this is in accord with his parents' unconscious needs too (didn't they want a girl?). This is all right for a while, but then he gets lanced near the eye and this threat to the eye (still unconsciously) reminds him of castration and shakes him up. He becomes irritable and aggressive, he asserts himself, he's mean with his mother and father. He doesn't know why, he just has to be. But now he's a boy and now his incest temptation is greater, if he lets himself be a boy. His conflict gets worse. He wants Mama, and now look— Mama's pregnant. Screams of fear. What will happen to me? Then his baby sister Frances is born, and all his mother's love goes to her: the girl she wanted. *'I'm a baby. I drank a drop.'* But he isn't going to get any drop of that milk because it isn't him Mama loves, but her. To be a girl he has to be castrated, pay with biological death. The death threat is constant—starvation, castration—he's struggling with both at once.

As this struggle goes on, he becomes physically ener- vated. He becomes just plain tired. He's had enough of it and he begins to leave reality as you do in sleep. Freud had a hell of a term for it, "affective hebetude." The schizophrenic loses "all interest in the outer world." But this is just the condition where the Unconscious can break through. It does break through in sleep. And now with this fatigue and hebetude, it breaks through without sleep. And this is a more terrible breaking through. What he needs now he gets by hallucinations and delusions, by a dream. But a waking dream. Frances doesn't exist. There's no Frances, there's no baby sister. He himself is the baby loved and wanted by his mother.

This is the nearest I can come, Dr. Marks thought, to following that terrible career. It still was hard to believe. Hard to admit those unconscious needs and wishes, hard to believe what they could do and how they could do it.

How does the organization of the mind shift around? There were hints in normal life (was anything completely abnormal?).

"The voices." If you got tired enough, and he sure did get tired, there could come a moment just before sleep when actual voices sounded in the mind or you even heard an actual piano or violin playing.

What he was particularly likely to hear was Margaret saying, "John." He would hear it when she wasn't there, simply wasn't there. Her voice, so actual you wanted to turn around and answer.

It was frightening, in a way. But he knew what was happening so it was no actual delusion. The mind was still in control. But it made you realize what could happen with a patient, under enough stress and with enough panic.

In most of the literature he had seen, Freud, Abraham, Ferenczi, the emphasis was on sexual wishes and deprivations, unconscious homosexuality (Freud on paranoia), the clamoring of the id. Not much on oral deprivation or torments, not much if anything on the hazardous frailty of the baby. For example, he could not remember anywhere seeing a dream at all like the one he had had of the grasshopper baby, that binary drama of love and death in the simple thing of holding those wing tips, guiding and protecting Marta's (and his own) fragile life.

He closed Bleuler and put it back on the shelf of books. He went over to the pack-plant donkey. It seemed a little dry. He got a glass of water and watered it, letting the drops slowly soak in, go down to the roots.

24

For the next several days, he just plain felt good. It was from the session with Naumann, he was sure, the session that had given him more understanding of himself and the processes of his patients (identification) than he had ever had before. That night he had slept well (a good six hours), and several times since, he had gone over the session again in his mind, wanting to pin down its insights. The fine line between distrusting and needing the breast. The identification of any source of love with the breast (Marta is potentially a breast, and from that the tinge of ambivalence toward her that had appeared in his associations). How much more he must be needed and feared by patients! That struggle for sanity, and every dream image, toned with longing, leading persistently back to the breast. Pa and Ma, the same distrust and need.

Insights, particularly from such a dreamlike session, could get away from you. And these were insights he must strengthen and use.

It was noon Saturday. He was walking home from Marta's hotel and he felt good just walking. His body felt good. If only Marta could know the ordinary simple happiness of being alive (but there she sat, in a new position, with one finger raised). The air was cold and bracing. The sun was out. It might be a good day to take Nancy for a walk in the park.

The park, as they approached it after lunch, was saturated with a raw fall light. Nancy pulled him, she wanted to hurry.

"Take it easy. I'm not as young as you are."

"No. You can't run as fast as me, can you, Daddy?"

"No," he said, "I can't."

"Let's run."

He trotted after her as she rushed ahead. Automatically

invigorated, he had to be careful not to overtake her. "I'm winning," she cried, a tassel of her soft hair spinning and glittering.

"You win." He thought, She knows I let her win, but how much it means to her! How much she loves it! She glanced at him and in that glance of her young eyes, he felt purified and at ease—distanced from the psychotic dream, the incessant demands of the id. Incest and desire, guilt and oral deprivation faded away as if they had never existed.

"Where do you want to go?" he said.

"To the swings."

To the swings. But why that sly look now? She pulled him again, urgently.

This must be some routine of the park he didn't know about. Out of touch. He was out of touch with some every-day part of his child's life. All right, let's see what it is. He held her hand and followed.

And they came to the swings. Here she nodded at two boys who looked like brothers and said, "That's Tommy and William." The older one (Tommy) had an urchin look to him. This must be a replacement for Murray, he thought. Nancy put her hands slowly into her coat pockets and stepped away, leaving him. (Here's where the loving parent becomes a liability.) She approached Tommy and now she and Tommy and William ran to the swings. William got the only empty one. "Let Tommy, let Tommy," Nancy cried. Then, "He can rough-tough you off of it."

Where did she get that language? But William looked determined, not to be budged.

Standing with Tommy, Nancy put out her tongue for his inspection. "See it?" she said, pointing with her finger. "It's bit! I've got a turtle and he bit me on the tongue, he just went and bit me and it hurt. It bled. He's the only turtle who ever bit anybody on the tongue."

I'm definitely working too hard, Dr. Marks thought. I never heard a thing about that tongue-biting.

Tommy leaned against a swing pole. "My father's getting me a birthday present," he said. "It's coming in the mail. It's a bullwhip."

"What's a bullwhip for?" Nancy asked. "To whip bulls?"

Very superior: "No, to use on other cowboys."

"How?"

"You use it to rip them and jerk the gun right out of their hand."

The day darkened.

Castration. Incest and desire, guilt and oral deprivation swept heavily back.

When they returned from the park, Nancy ran into the living room to tell Bob and Johnny about the bullwhip. "It's to rip a cowboy and jerk the gun right out of his hand." They laughed and she began to laugh too—as often happened, hardly knowing what she was laughing about. At last she said to Bob, gazing at him entreatingly, "There was Adam and Eve and Pinch Me. Adam and Eve fell in the water. Who was left?"

"Pinch."

"Pinch who?"

"Pinch You."

The boys laughed wildly again, and fought her off as she tried to pinch them.

Now she was coming toward him, her father, with that female "please" look in her eyes. "Can Tommy come and visit us?" she said.

Us, not *me,* he took note. "Of course," he said.

"Can he stay all night?"

"It might be arranged. But we don't have a guest room."

"Yes, we do," she said and immediately he realized his mistake. Her room was the "guessed room—because Daddy guessed right that I was to be a girl." This private misunderstanding had pleased him—and Margaret too—so much that they hadn't yet had a firm session with Nancy to explain what "guest" really meant.

And even if he did explain it, he suspected that her room would go on being the "guessed room."

"So can he? Can he, Daddy?"

"We'll see," he said, the universal stall.

When he had acted the scene of Marta in the witness-box, he had told her her mother had said, "Marta can't do anything. She never could do anything." He asked Ginnie to come to his office one evening and when she was comfortably seated in the treatment room, he said, "You grew up with Marta. You played with her. You must know cer-

tain things that went on with her better than anybody else.
I'm going to ask you to be very frank with me. I'm going
to ask you to tell me about her mother and never mind
so-called family loyalty—"

"You don't need to give me a pitch. I'd do anything to
help Marta."

"Your mother and Marta's mother were sisters."

"That's right."

"That makes them pretty close."

"Close but different," she said.

"One difference is your mother has a sane daughter."

"That's a rough thing to say, but I will say I never
cared much for Aunt Fanya, and I don't think my mother
did, either. Mother was a younger sister, she was softer,
men liked her. It took a tough one like Meyer to handle
Aunt Fanya—if he did."

"You surely saw a lot of Marta with her mother. What
was the quality of the relationship?"

"Well, I guess Aunt Fanya loved Marta. But, you know,
she gave you the feeling she thought Marta was a lunk."

"Give me an example." Maybe I can use this with
Marta.

"She never let Marta go alone to buy her own clothing.
She went along and supervised everything, even small
things. I mean not just a dress or coat. If Marta even
wanted stockings, Aunt Fanya picked them out, what
color, what would go with what, sheer or not, how much
she should pay—it drove me nuts. One time when Marta
needed something and her mother wasn't there, she asked
me to go with her."

He picked up the phone and dialed: "Fred? This is Dr.
Marks. Did Marta ever ask you to go with her when she
wanted to buy a dress or something?"

"Often. Yes, that's what she usually did—she wanted
me along. She said she wanted my 'judgment.' I was kind
of touched, and—yes, we always shopped that way."

"Thanks, that helps me. That's all."

He turned back to Ginnie. "What else—what other ex-
amples?"

"Well, cooking. Marta sometimes wanted to do some
cooking, you know, work in the kitchen. Her mother
never let her. Just never. It's a wonder she can do any
cooking now and, the fact is, she isn't much of a cook.
Fred put up with a lot."

"But that's fairly common."

"Not the way Aunt Fanya did it. She did it like, You're an idiot to think you can cook."

Cooking, food. It was elemental. It was no accident depreciation came through food. She was depreciating Marta right back to the breast. I despise you, Marta, when you think about food, but the place where you thought about it most, and most essentially (and even desperately), was when you were nursing.

Not that it was conscious. No, it could all have been done with attitudes and even with an appearance of love.

But as therapist you can't admit any maternal love. You have to go all the way to clean that murderous remnant of Mother out of her. You say that so easily to yourself, but was any of this endless attack on Mother getting through to Marta? Or did she just stay, nicely defending herself, staring him and reality down?

"Ginnie, thank you for coming and helping me this way. And I can't tell you how I appreciate the way you help out with the nurses when they need time off."

"They're so interested in Marta. They seem to be fond of her."

"They are. They're good girls."

The probable line of attack (on Marta) at the moment was appropriately concerned with food. After Ginnie had left, he phoned Miss Barklund.

"Hello."

"Dr. Marks. I want to ask you something. Are you where you can talk?"

"She's in the living room. Yes, I can talk."

"Have you been noticing lately the way Marta eats?"

"Yes, Miss Kinnell and I were going to speak to you about it, to see if you'd noticed. You mean, how she arranges her food?"

"That's exactly what I mean. But you were going to tell me about it. Why don't you tell me what you've noticed and I'll see if it checks with what I've noticed."

"Well, one thing now, she makes a circle of her vegetables before she eats them. Then she always has a spoon in her milk. And she clenches her left hand every time she drinks milk. It's more than clenching—she kind of works her hand."

"Yes, that's what I've noticed. You know what this is?"

"No."

"Well, in my experience it's a kind of magic control of the food, to make it safe to eat. Actually it's control of the breast, to make the breast safe or to make the breast want to feed you."

"But—" Miss Barklund sounded dubious.

"What's bothering you?"

"The milk—chocolate milk—maybe, but vegetables?"

"You think the psychotic mind can't rearrange a little outside reality like that? Turn spaghetti and tomato sauce into mother's milk?"

No warm reaction to this.

"Let me ask you." He had just had this thought. "You've seen babies nurse. They push at the breast and work it, to get the flow of milk going, to help it along. Ever see a kitten pushing its paws on each side of the tit, back and forth, back and forth?"

"Yes."

"Marta working her hand, the hand she isn't eating with. How about that?"

Miss Barklund: "You're right. You mean all that is like nursing?"

Now she had it.

"But then—what are you going to do?" she said.

That was a good question. What *could* he do with Marta? And at least she *was* eating. Did he want to take a chance on disturbing that?

He wondered why she had developed these rituals just now. Was it even just now? She might have had rituals before, that he wasn't aware of. They fool you. They have this sense that somebody may be watching, and they conceal things, do things secretly. Touching their side, rubbing a certain area of skin slightly—anything can be a ritual.

Isn't that crazy, that they can have a secret ritual? But the whole thing is crazy. Craziness is crazy. It's also rational. That was what was so hard for Miss Barklund to take, that the craziness was rational, that it had a meaning, and that he knew what it meant. (If he did.)

The next night, he came home early (for him) and found Margaret still up. He kissed her. "How come you're up?"

"Oh, I just wasn't sleepy. It isn't that late."

He sat down beside her on the living-room sofa. "I was working with Betty. She's developed a thing. She takes an elastic, a rubber band, and holds it against her cheek and then with her other hand she'll pull it out and let it snap back." Sometimes just a little snap, but sometimes she'd give herself a real bang. What did it mean? "I also went out to see Jeffrey for a while—he's just as tough as I expected he'd be; in the john he compulsively unwinds long strips of toilet paper, drips water all over, and has to be cleaned up after. Of course obsessive-compulsives always spend hours in the toilet—one I had at the Center practically lived there. If you ask them why, they doubletalk. And of course it has nothing to do with regression to childhood. Or infancy."

"How's Marta?" She took off his shoes and started rubbing his feet.

"Oh, that feels good. I don't realize how much time I spend on my feet. Marta? Something new with her. She's started rituals with her food, makes nice rings with her vegetables or rice or potatoes—especially potatotes. Then she's afraid to dip her fork in unless she touches the ring with the flat of the fork two or three times first. And other things. Raises her finger. Well, I felt I had to do something so I started interpreting—she was controlling the breast, purifying the breast, eating the breast—and then she wouldn't eat. I more or less figured that. It's some reaction anyway, maybe I should be glad."

"But if she doesn't eat now—"

"She'll eat. She may eat better. And she'll think about me."

"Why?"

"Because I attacked her, attacked her morbid complex about eating." Brooding: "Hey, I've got an idea. I'll have Miss Kinnell pretend she's her mother in the kitchen, fixing her food, and I'll come in and say, 'No, Mrs. Johns, I want you to get out of the kitchen. You fix such terrible food for Marta. I'm going to fix the food for her myself.' "

"John, you really will have to join Actors' Equity."

Disregarding her: "Do you know Marta sleeps now holding her head up off the pillow? Stiff, like this. Miss Hughes watches how long she does it—hours at a time, then the next day she has a stiff neck and is dead tired. But she does it. You know the thing that gets me is that there's no end to what they think up to do. It goes on and on. Marta said something to Miss Kinnell about 'seashells' and then something about a 'seclusion room.' And what does that raised finger mean? And she still holds saliva in her mouth. Oh, God!"

"You better get to bed and get yourself a long night's four-hour sleep. If I was smart, I'd turn off your alarm."

"I'm sleeping late anyway. I'm going to New State Hospital tomorrow—"

"Come along." She pulled him up.

"You know, Jeannette is making a great psychiatric aide, just great?"

"Keep moving."

"Has more insights with Betty than I have."

Her hand pressed against his back. "On your way," she said.

The next morning as he was shaving, he heard a child calling in the street, under his apartment-house windows. She called "Catherine" or sometimes "Cath" and kept calling. Nobody answered. To an adult, there was no sense in keeping on calling if there was no answer. But that wasn't a child's logic. No, a child kept trying. Or, for a child, the calling became an end in itself, an echopraxia, a *cerea flexibilitas* of the larynx.

When he got to New State Hospital and was going through the corridors and day wards, there was that "please" again. "Please, Doctor . . . Please, Nurse." They wanted to tell their stories about hallucinations or illusionary telephone calls or ladders to heaven. "Please, Doctor."

Like the child in the street, on and on. "Cath" "Catherine." "Please" "Please."

He knew that Dr. Rossman had gone to work in a private sanitarium. Dr. Harmon was gone. Mrs. Blumstein was still in a back ward—Ward K, Building Eight. Rose had recovered and had been discharged.

He wanted to see one of the back wards, but not Ward K. He wasn't up to that.

He checked the present status of all the patients he had treated. Only three had returned to the hospital, and these were patients he hadn't been able to keep on seeing. Tommy Kupfer was still making it outside—Lugano, Fischer. All the others he had fully treated.

He looked up Miss Davis. Her white cap gleamed like a

beacon and she was delighted to see him. "I hear you're in private practice. You don't need a good nurse, do you?"

"You won't leave here."

She said, "But if I did?"

"I could use you."

It was lunchtime and they decided to have lunch together. They walked through a long corridor, and a peculiar kind of depression came over him. That this whole enormous tract of grounds and buildings still existed, solid, unchanged, institutionalized, a kind of fatal home place to which you could return and notice little difference. Joe Huber, he heard, was still here. Steiner, of course. Wellman, Parker, all the old standbys.

He and Miss Davis came out into a dayroom and in the light there he saw a short, heavy woman carrying two shopping bags by their strap handles. They seemed filled. It was unbelievable sometimes how patients managed to get what they wanted, from inside or outside the hospital. The woman's lips were thin, her eyes hard. She wore some kind of soiled vest. Stopping in front of him, she said, fixing him with her hard eyes: "I come like a fish peddler to see a doctor, is that nice? I'm going to talk, if I may. I haven't studied, I'm not good in the intelligence department." She put down her bags and gestured with both arms, her tone deepening: "I accuse myself, my soul looks down, I didn't want to do it, but when things was stamped on me, tramped, everything crushed, something inside you—" Deep emphasis, expression: "You've got to do it for people who love you, for there are those who love you, who truly love you—just as there are those who don't love you. Yes, there are those who betray you, doublecross you, all of a sudden you get hurt, break a leg, get killed . . . I can see in your face you're a doctor. I'm not giving you compliments, I don't know you enough to give you compliments." With emotion: "You help people? Help somebody? Is that statement correct or am I . . . ? I'm going to ask you one question if I may. I want that pleasure. I speak very truthfully, I say this from the heart. Grief kills—is that right? Your own father and mother, they do something, say something. Grief . . ." Leaning forward, she shook her head and gestured with her hands. "I'm not well educated, haven't had opportunities. They can call me mental, they can call me no good, they can call me no good. I walked into you like a storm comes and you don't know where it comes from—you can check me with Coney Island, they check me for glands and change of life. Of course it's very foolish and childish, but I've got to get well. I've got work to do. When I was ten years old, I was and I wasn't, I was and I wasn't. Am I talking too much, Doctor? I saw my mother so disturbed, that's what hurt me—proper medicine, Doctor, not too much . . . I want to live and carry on." In a change of tone, in an almost normal voice: "Do you give shock treatment for heart, for blood pressure? No. Then how can you give it for the mind?" Quick back to oratory: "I'm willing to live, I won't cut my throat. The candle will burn out by itself . . ." With gestures: "I grieved. I was sick and worried. I'm artistic, sometimes I have a temper, but I control it. I don't behave myself just right." A large gesture: "My mind is on one thought, that there's a God who controls me . . . You saw yourself crushed, thrown down, smashed—and you didn't die. You walked for days and days and found one person, good and bad." Whispering: "May I speak further? I have no reason for living. I remember the boy I was in love with, twelve years of age—imagine that—I was never in love again. If you see tears in my eyes . . . you'll bring the smile here," touching her heart, "not here," touching her lips. "That's acting. My mother, she was the only one could understand me. I'll take more than medicine, these bags are food. If I don't take this, I take that," and she lifted one bag after the other. "Without enough medicine, God could forgive me if I gave up. A generation ago a policeman was a soldier of the law, but no more—now it's killings, murder. . . ."

He walked on, knowing that the rhetoric, the large gestures of arms and head, of eyes and lips, would continue automatically without him, the pressure of an endless torment keeping it going. And was it difficult to understand? Grief and terror kill. *'There's a God who controls me.'*

"She's been here a long time," Miss Davis said. "I'm sorry for her."

"Does she eat the food she carries around?"

"She doesn't have food in those bags. Just old papers and junk."

Now from the far side of the dayroom, a patient he recognized glided by: "What's the word about the crops?"

At lunch Miss Davis told him about a new treatment called BEST—Blitz Electric Shock Therapy. "It's strong charges—overdoses. They bite their tongues and lips and have their teeth loosened. They lose their teeth. They hemorrhage. But it's supposed to have prevented three suicides so far. Except that one of them did kill herself later."

He asked her about the Medical Ward. "Any exhaust status cases there now?"

"Yes, two. Sometimes we have more."

"They don't do anything for them?"

"Well, only what Dr. Linscomb orders."

Almost unwilling to say it, he said, "So they die."

"They die," she said.

He told her he had a special reason for wanting to visit a back ward. She arranged the visit for him and she also arranged for him to see Ethel.

He went first to Ethel's ward and the nurse there took him to a bed on which the wasted body lay, hardly disarranging the drapes of the sheets. Ethel was completely still, her eyes open but nonseeing. She was subnormal in weight. "She gained a little while she was on heavy insulin," the nurse said, "but now she stays like this. It's hard even to make her maintain this much weight."

"How much insulin did she have?"

"They gave her several very heavy series. They tried very hard with her."

They tried very hard with her. He passed his hand in front of her eyes. Nothing. When she was in the acute excitement, she had had that proud give-and-take even if she was dying. Marta was withdrawn, but not like this; it wasn't the same as this. He had seen on Johanson's slides what must be in this brain—massive replacement of live ganglion cells by ridges and corrugations of scar tissue. Life replaced by death. And wasn't this whole damn hospital just such a continuous replacing of life by death? No care, no love, no will to help these suffering human beings, nothing but evasions and beatings (when one patient had "acted up," she had been given several consecutive electric shocks—he knew this).

How could you want to discipline Ethel? So much evident life there when it showed. So much spirit. Even the imaginations were ardent and remained in his mind.

He tried to take her hand, it was rigid.

And she could have recovered, like Jimmy.

He went to Building Seven and found the nurse to whom Miss Davis had referred him there. She said, "This way, Doctor."

Screams let him know what ward they were approaching before the nurse unlocked the door—screams of limitless hate. Was it hate? He could go behind the hate now and hear fear.

Several women were completely naked. A slit of cunt showed through the hair of one like a ragged scar centering the flesh. Another woman was urinating. Two women stood like a catatonic frieze in a corner, and others brushed past them, going nowhere in a frenzy.

Only one woman lay in the fetal position, huddled against a radiator.

"May I go across to her?" he said to the nurse.

"Certainly, Doctor."

He went to the woman and touched her mouth. No response. He put his hand on her naked navel, but that was no more than a symbolic feeding place. The mother was long since severed away. "Where are you?" he whispered.

No sound.

Hardly even a sound of breathing.

Was it a wish for nonbreathing (for that safety)?

"Where are you?" he said again.

Not the slightest motion, and it even seemed to him that the breathing stopped.

Then, with a quiver of ribs, it went on.

Two nights later he said to Margaret, "Have you heard of a town in Belgium called Gheel?"

"No, I haven't. Why?"

"Since the Middle Ages, the people of that town have taken insane patients into their homes and taken care of them. They still do. And they produce many more cures than hospitals do."

"You're still angry from going to New State."

"Do you blame me?"

"No," she said, "but still it must be pretty difficult to have the insane in your home."

"Difficult, but not impossible. They seem to do it."

"But just how sick are they?"

"Pretty sick cases, from what I hear."

"That takes courage."

"From what I've heard, they get a feeling for them."
She made no further comment.

He worked now four hours a day with Marta. The rest of the time he worked with Betty and Jeffrey. He was working especially hard with Betty. This looked like one you could get through to quickly by exerting maximum pressure.

Two nights later he phoned Margaret from The Island Consolidated Hospital. He said, "Betty's coming out."

"How wonderful, John!"

"I had the feeling it was going to be today."

"Is Jeannette there?"

"No, I sent her home hours ago. But she knew something was happening. She knew before I did. Well, I've got to get back. But let me tell you one thing. You know that elastic band Betty used to snap against her cheek? She doesn't know what it is now. How's that?"

Margaret laughed. "You sound happy."

"I really am."

The next night he came home early for dinner and found Margaret alone in the kitchen. He told her Betty was completely out of psychosis. They talked awhile and he went down to the boys' room. Both boys were there and Nancy was lying on the floor beside Bob, looking at a book—at a picture, actually, of a vestal virgin!

"Hi, Dad," Bob said. That rumpled hair of his and definitely non-Marks face—handsome.

Dr. Marks said, "What's this I heard about you disgracing yourself in school today?"

"Oh, that. It was this dare—"

"Yes?"

"Jugsy and me—you know my friend Jugsy—we had this dare that we wouldn't go into Miss Merton's class with jockey caps on, corncob pipes in our mouth, and our coats inside out. But we did it. Miss Merton spotted us, of course, in the back row, and she made us stand up and 'show yourselves.' So we did. Then she asks us if we'd go to the Saturday social dance like that and we said we wouldn't mind, and she asked how many girls would want to go with us if we were dressed like that." He smiled modestly. "Every girl's hand went up."

"Did she leave herself open!" Johnny said.

Dr. Marks frankly envied Bob. He recognized that at Bob's age, he would have chickened out on what Bob had done, and he regretted it. Bob wasn't haunted by a thousand pennies given to the shoemaker's older son.

Nancy said, "I'll go to the dance with him."

"Enough from you, Miss."

From the kitchen: "John?"

He went back to Margaret, Nancy tagging along. "Do you want to take the roast in to the table and start carving?" Margaret said.

"Yes. Say, I was thinking about Betty. You know her shoulder's cured too? You know that's what made me go in for psychiatry in the first place, I couldn't cure things like that with the old homeopathic prescriptions. Now here I am curing Betty's shoulder."

He gave Betty her rubber band. He said, "Take it. Snap it against your cheek."

She held it awkwardly.

"Go ahead, snap it."

"I don't understand," she said.

"You know, like this." He took it from her and demonstrated. He gave his cheek a smart flick, pulling out the band and letting go. "Now you do it."

She tried, but was unable to. He thought she was going to cry.

"Do it," he said.

"I can't, I can't."

A new technique. Ask them to do something crazy or something they were doing while they were crazy, and it embarrasses them. Could it be a means of distancing them from the psychosis?

In early December, Betty went home. She had been living with her parents, her father and her "mommy," so now she was going back to them. Dr. Marks had a moment of misgiving, but then he thought, What can I do? She'll be all right. I'll see her right along.

Disastrously, it wasn't all right. By the end of the week she stepped out of a shower holding her wet hair in her hands and shrieking in a catatonic uproar.

You learn, you always have something to learn. He should have kept her in the hospital until he had given her a much longer period of postpsychotic treatment. Never mind what she wants or what her parents want, or what the expense is. Insist. Now look what he was up against.

Her mother came to the office and raved: "And we thought you were going to cure her. A fine cure—look at her. Is this what we paid you for?"

"Do you want a refund," he said, "or do you want your daughter well? You kept at me to have her go home."

She immediately became calmer. "You'll continue with her, Doctor? I always believed you could cure her—I guess you can cure her again? It was so wonderful to have her like herself—"

"I'm not sure like herself is good. Let me decide what's good. It might be better if she's different, say strong enough to stay well when she goes home."

"What you mean is that we're responsible. From what I hear about your method of treatment, you mean I am."

"Let's not use a term like 'responsible.' You have certain needs, I have certain needs, we all have certain needs. Do you think we created ourselves? What we are goes back a thousand years."

Her voice softened. "You're trying to be kind to me." Abruptly: "Oh, Doctor, I love my daughter."

"I know you do. You and your husband will have her again, just be guided by my advice meantime."

Naumann would give me A for that one, Dr. Marks thought. I was really considering my patient this time.

So now he'd have Betty back with her phony aching shoulder and her wet hair. And the staff at the hospital, who had been so pleased at his "cure"—

Well, what could he do? It would simply take more time. With her, he knew where he was at, he knew he could bring her out again. But then he'd be careful. Three months in the hospital or away from her "folks" outside—

*   *   *

"Look at me," he said.

Betty stared past him, the way lions can do or Indians. Or crazy women.

"Look at me."

"Whose eyes are they?"

"You know whose eyes they are. My eyes," he said.

"If you empty my life out and empty my love out, what the hell is there left?"

"My love. And you know who I am."

"I'm afraid."

"I know," he said.

"I'm afraid of emptying my mind psychically and someone will give me amnesia and there won't be anything left at all."

"You have plenty left. Intelligence—"

"Oh!" She grabbed her shoulder.

"Beauty."

"Ow!" she screamed. "It hurts, it hurts."

"Love."

Desperate screams.

"And you're going to get well. Nothing can stop it, you hear?"

Her screaming went on and on. But then it gradually stopped. He waited, saying nothing, and at last she said quietly, "There is a good place in the mountains that cures TB, isn't there?"

"Everybody knows the mountain air cures you and you'll get your weight and strength back again."

Later he told Dr. Naumann about this and said, "I guess a snow-covered mountain is really a full breast and a feeding mother." Dr. Naumann said, in a remarkably gentle voice: "And what about your own mountains?"

Two days later Betty was about out of psychosis again. No more shoulder pain. She knew her name, his name, the hospital's name, and she was generally in reality. She handed him the rubber band she had found during her neoinsanity and which she had a few times listlessly snapped against her cheek. "So what is this?" he said.

"I don't know."

"Oh, come, make an effort. You can go back enough to tell me what this is."

She looked at it dubiously. "I don't like it."

"You don't like it now, but you liked it then. You looked as if you liked pulling it out—"

"Pulling it out, but then it always got short again."

He waited.

"It was a bridge," she said.

"Yes?"

"When it stretched out, I looked over it. But then it always got too short again."

"When you looked over it, what were you looking at?"

"I don't know."

"What were you looking at?"

Shyly: "You?"

The next day she gave him a folded sheet of paper. "Don't read it now," she said.

Outside in his car, he unfolded the small sheet.

SONNET TO NOREEN—MY MOTHER

When you thought I was sleeping, I just had my eyes
    closed,
Feeling conscious through every obstruction—
So you the unhappy truth exposed,
That I was not the wanted one.
I found you saying I was bad.
I found you putting me
In the constellations of the sad,
Shutting me up in my revery.
I was definitely no good,
I know. There is no excuse.
In my awful solitude
You put me where I knew abuse.
I will suffer for all eternity—
Villain who should have been the other me.

The girl who wrote this is what I sent home to her mother, he thought. Well, I won't do it again. Not until she's as strong as steel.

25

Since Marta wasn't eating either the nurses' food or his (alas, back to force-feeding), she had transferred her rituals to voiding. She held her abdomen as if in great pain, her hands girding the slightly natural swelling there while she moaned and let go just a few drops of urine at intervals. Did that mean that she had to preserve her necessary liquids, essences? Did it have any connection with her holding saliva in her mouth? Could it mean her not losing an imaginary fetus?

He asked the nurses to keep a check, to try to see whether Marta was putting a strain on her bladder.

That was the pathology extemporizing for you. Never stopped.

Then Marta would have an uncontrollable drowsiness. And then (the other extreme—everything extremes) she would remain standing in one spot most of the night. The first night she did it, Miss Barklund—knowing how exhausted Dr. Marks was but worried about Marta—telephoned Fred and while she was talking with him, Marta left her catatonic position and came to the bedroom door to listen. She changed from one foot to the other, trembling. "A white jacket, the great pity of it," she said.

"Fred wants to talk to you."

Changing from foot to foot.

"Will you come?"

Of course she wouldn't come, but after this call, as if psychically scolded, she allowed herself to be put to bed and seemed to sleep.

After two days she voided partially, but her retention continued.

Dr. Marks told Ginnie it would be a help if she came to be with Marta more often, even while the other nurses were on duty. He asked her to read to Marta. He also had

Fred come, but Fred was not of much use. Curious that being in love (as against loving) could be such a handicap, but it was—when you're in love, you lose your controls, you suffer. Hard to keep controlled in the presence of a body sitting rigid on the edge of the couch, looking through you at somebody or something else.

At times Marta showed a generalized body tremor, and once Miss Kinnell told Dr. Marks that Marta took hold of her from behind and moved her here and there as if putting her between herself and somebody else. As Marta did so, she began breathing fast, her pulse raced, and her pupils dilated widely. Miss Kinnell said, "Nobody will hurt you. Dr. Marks and I will protect you. You know we won't let anybody hurt you. Absolutely nobody. You remember being with Dr. Marks this afternoon?"

Marta nodded and pointed to her forehead. Then she sat on the arm of a chair, resting one foot out on the floor.

"You haven't voided for fourteen hours," Dr. Marks said. "I want you to go in the bathroom with Miss Kinnell, and I want you to relieve yourself. You'll get this good chocolate drink as soon as you do, and that'll replace whatever liquid you lose. Now get in there—"

Five minutes later, Miss Kinnell reported to him that "a few drops" had come out.

He groaned.

Miss Kinnell brought her a bowl of soup. She wouldn't eat. She clenched her teeth. After he had run through a whole gamut of antimagic and visceral-oral incantations, including "You're biting the breast. That's good—" he managed to get her to swallow one mouthful.

Then she sat rigid just the way she had before.

He stared at her, baffled. What had he been doing wrong? Irritated, he asked himself if he must start a whole role-taking production again, work himself up into a sweat of transference fury when he was the only one doing any transference. When she simply sat there.

He might as well be with Betty where his work would do some good. No, that was a negative thought. He must never be negative. Yet if Marta won't void, won't drink, won't eat, won't move—what's negative? In a sudden rush of anger, he thought, I'll fix you.

You'll void and you'll eat.

He had resisted having recourse to sodium amytal. Even if it worked (and it didn't always), it would bring her out for only two or three hours and in what you knew was a drugged state. If you were familiar with it, you had the sense of its artificiality, of all the defenses continuing. It was an illusion, something he disliked. But in the crisis now, he felt turning to it was justified.

He told Fred what he was going to do and warned him that it might not work at all. But on the chance that it would, he asked him to be present. He also warned him that this was strictly a temporary thing, a matter of hours, and he explained why he was having recourse to it. Fred said that he understood. When Fred arrived, Dr. Marks gave Miss Barklund orders for preparing Marta's arm, and he injected seven and a half grains.

He stood back. Marta was drooped over forward, her hair (as often when she was completely rejecting) covering her face. For a good forty seconds she remained in this rigid catatonic position and he thought the drug would have no effect. But her breathing deepened, she pulled in air in gasps as if she had been choking, and slowly she raised her head.

"Fred."

She reached her hand out to him and he drew her into his arms. "Darling. Darling," he said.

She smiled and said, "Something must have happened."

His eyes were set. She rubbed her arm, she glanced down and saw the slight mark left by the syringe. "Where am I?"

"This is the Hotel St. Emory where Dr. Marks is treating you. And this is his aide, Miss Barklund."

Now a dreamlike look of recognition in her eyes. "Dr. Marks. I know him."

"Yes, you know me."

"Oh." With a terrible look of embarrassment and a "Please excuse me a moment," she hurried out of the room and they heard the bathroom door close.

"Well, she's relieving herself," Dr. Marks said. To Fred, "She's been holding that back for nearly two days."

Fred frowned. Dr. Marks thought, He doesn't want to hear his wife is having a psychotic symptom now. Even if I've warned him that this whole "recovery" is a dream—a dream within a dream—he needs this moment of being with her as a wife, not a patient.

And when Marta came back, smiling again, it was hard not to agree with him. Except that Dr. Marks recognized that slightly diffuse look in her eyes, the presence of the drug. He said, "You know I'm your doctor. Do you have some memory of what's been happening?"

"Do we have to talk about that?" She had been happy, now she had a look of the furtive sadness Fred had described to him.

"No," he said.

"Why isn't Ruth here?" she asked.

"She's well and staying at home with Fred. Fred, you tell her."

"She saw a squirrel crossing the street outside the house, down toward the river. It stopped to look at her and she was frightened that it would get run over. She shooed it on across the street."

"She did? She took care of the squirrel?"

"She has a feeling for everything. Janice says—" Fred stopped abruptly, sorry he had mentioned Janice. Marta said at once, "Janice's the one taking care of her?"

"Yes, she takes good care of her."

"I'm glad. Good you didn't give her to Mother."

Dr. Marks said, "That's right. What she needs is her own mother."

Again a look of sadness. Seeing it, Dr. Marks admitted that from now on all that all three of them said would have to be meaningless, would be a deliberate not speaking to the point, a deference to the special situation.

As if Marta sensed this agreement, she became happy again. They had dinner. Miss Barklund had prepared a special meal, she cooked well in the Swedish style, and Marta enjoyed it. She ate with no trace of ritual, and ate well.

What they talked about somehow managed, by their unspoken agreement, never to intrude on the area of her problems. At least he saw now the normality he was trying to bring her back to. He saw certain movements and moments of unusual beauty, covered until now by pathology. A half-smile. A breaking of dimples at the sides of her mouth. Phrases: "You mean it?" and "You can't mean it." A noticeable irresistible confidence in her attractiveness that perhaps for many years had helped her ward off the onset of her panic.

Yet an hour or so away now was the lapse into catatonia. Watching her, he thought, How many "normal" people all over the city, the country, are at this moment eating and talking (yes, and voiding) and with such fright in them that they will soon give up all contact with reality? Marta didn't remember her psychosis now, or didn't want to—when she returned to it, would she remember this brief visit to life? Would it encourage her? Would she remember how she had done all these natural things that she ordinarily fought doing almost as if she were intent on psychic suicide? Could he get the two parts of her together, mend the destroying split?

After dinner, he said to Fred, "It's time for you to go now. I'd like to discuss some things with Marta."

When Fred embraced Marta, she said, "Do you love me?"

"I want you back so much."

She said, smiling, "No, you must be disgusted with me. I *am* disgusting." Very softly she said, "I despise myself so much."

Fred glanced at Dr. Marks. Dr. Marks signaled him to say nothing.

After Fred had left, Dr. Marks said, "I wish you'd stop wasting your time and my time with this talk about despising yourself. You evidently think you have to be the greatest or nobody will love you. That isn't true. You can relax and be something in-between that's really you and that's lovely and good, good enough to endear you to me or to Fred, who's in love with you, or to any normal man. But let's not talk about that when you know how Fred loves you. In the short time we have left, I need you to tell me some things. What's very important—tell me when you first remember your mother."

A puzzled look came over her face. "But I remember my father first, not my mother."

"You do!"

"Yes, the first thing I can remember is I was in some big room alone, in a little bed. I don't know if it was a crib. There seemed to be a low, slanting roof. My father came in and put a little potty under me and I wee-weed. It was night and I was so glad he'd come and known I had to go, and let me go."

A nurse was always with her in the toilet. Could it be

she wanted to wee-wee for Father, not Mother? Or could it be she had some unconscious feelings of guilt about wee-weeing for her father.

"What do you remember first about your mother?"

"Oh, I guess I remember her feeding me in the high chair."

That was a more general memory, not a specific memory like the one of her father.

"She let my food get cold." Marta made a face.

"Ginnie tells me you drove your mother slightly crazy with your eating. You'd wait just twenty minutes before you'd eat anything at a meal, just long enough to have your mother frantic."

"I don't remember that." After a pause: "What else can I tell you?" That question indicated a remarkable amount of poise. But it was the dream, the drug. The power we have over the body with our recent chemicals. He could remember when there was no sodium amytal. Hell, he could remember when there was no insulin and what a great thing it was when Collip found a way to make it pure enough for injection. But that was for diabetics, that was before doctors found themselves able, like gods, to kill people and raise them up again— "Wake up, Erna! Wake up, Ethel! We are curing you with sugar."

"Tell me why you despise yourself."

"I'm a woman. I'm incompetent, not even a good woman, not good in bed. I'm not a good mother—"

"Just a minute. Tell me, what is a good mother?"

In anguish: "I don't know. It's all a mystery. Your baby —it's such a delicate life to handle, and you hurt it."

Mother hurt me, that was what she was trying to say. So she was frightened. She generalized: All mothers hurt all children. "That's why you despise yourself?" he said.

"I can't even cook."

"Did you ever want to learn?"

"Oh, so much. Even now I want to learn. It's just— nothing ever seems to turn out right."

That means, I'm being what Mother wanted me to be.

"Come with me." He put his arm around her and drew her to the window. "You see all that life down there?" Cars passed, people walked by, there was a distant confusion of pleasant human voices. "You see how nice it looks? All those people? Don't they look nice?"

"I guess they're happy?"

"Oh, they have their troubles, serious ones maybe, but they manage to have good moments too. They even laugh." (Important to speak of laughing.)

Staring down.

"You're going to be like that again."

"No," she said.

"Yes."

Sadly: "I feel sleepy."

"You've been having some trouble sleeping. You've been having some trouble doing a lot of things. At least now you're going to have a quiet, good sleep. Miss Barklund will take you into the bedroom and put you to bed. And you'll sleep a long time and be rested. And afterward—"

"Yes?"

"Remember that I'm doing all I can to help you. Help me."

"Of course, Doctor."

Of course, Doctor. Well, she'd had a taste of pseudo-normality. She'd had a little dream of waking, of coming "alive," of being what she had been. She'd come partway up the cellar stairs.

He thought, Now she has to go back, and when she wakes up, it may be bad. He thought, I'd better be here when she wakes up.

He felt a little shame, that he had used this hour or two to comfort himself, to see this woman for once like herself, though sad. But he thought, Not entirely sad. For the first time since he had known her, in spite of the dreamlike quality of the drug state, he had felt something countervailing, a reversal of sadness, even a sense of happiness. He remembered what Fred had told him about her laughing. Perhaps make her laugh?

He told her about his walk in the park with Nancy and described how Nancy came home and tried her joke out on Bob: " 'There was Adam and Eve and Pinch Me. Adam and Eve fell in the water. Who was left?' She wanted him to say, 'Pinch Me,' but he said, 'Pinch You.' "

And there came the laugh, rippling out beautifully. He deliberately worked to increase it, as you incite children who want to laugh anyway.

"Yes, 'Pinch You,' and she wanted him to say, 'Pinch Me.' "

Now the laughter soared. Beautifully giving up its controls, aching to give itself, to obliterate everything except itself.

But after laughing, she yawned. He said, "Time you turned in. Do you want to go to bed by yourself, or do you want Miss Barklund to help you?"

"I want to go by myself," she said.

He stayed in the apartment after she went to sleep. He took advantage of it and curled up on the sofa and went to sleep himself. When he woke up, it was dark. "She still sleeping?" he asked Miss Barklund.

"Like a baby."

The way a baby should, he thought.

He thought about his talk with her. He had been tempted to discuss her voiding. But this would have confronted her, during the sodium-amytal dream, or truce, with a psychotic symptom. It would have been treatment and he had promised himself not to use the drug state for treatment, but let her have only its relief. Let her see "life" as something to return to.

At about nine o'clock, she came to the door in her nightgown. He thought for a moment she was going to speak. Her lips opened as if about to form words. It was a flutter of imminence, an "almost," but she said nothing and merely looked at him.

"I stayed to be here when you woke up," he said. "You *are* awake?"

Silence.

"You will wake up," he said. "You and I may have important work to do before it happens and it may not be easy. But you will wake up."

Now she seemed to look beyond him. Her face resumed its withdrawn, not very appealing look, its inanimate look. Sharply he said, "If you think I'm going to leave you alone in there, you're mistaken."

Rigid. Staring.

Betrayed? Given a glimpse of freedom, of happiness, and abandoned again?

"I won't leave you there, Marta."

"Uncle Robert!" the children cried. He had come alone and they asked after "Aunt Lisa." "She'll come next time." He swung Nancy up and gave her a hug, and she tried not to seem to expect a present. He slipped a small fan into her hand.

"I love it."

He said to Bob, "Where's my brother?"

"Probably shaving. He only shaves for company, not patients."

Margaret called from the kitchen: "A fine thing to say about your father."

When Dr. Marks came out, he was clean-shaven. He greeted Robert. Robert would have no idea why this was a memorable evening: later Dr. Marks was going to give his brother a five-hundred-dollar check. While they had been drawing money from him, Margaret had noted down each payment carefully, and to begin paying him back now gave her unspeakable satisfaction. Debt was frightful and unnatural.

"John, how's this Marta case coming?" Robert said.

"Not too good, I guess. I certainly don't see any outward signs that I'm making any progress."

"Has she had a period yet?"

Heartwarming that Robert kept the details of the case in mind. "No, she hasn't, and it looks as if she's missed at least three periods. It can happen."

"You're sure she isn't pregnant?"

"Can't be. By now it would be evident."

"Odd."

"What's pregnant?" Nancy said.

Dr. Marks: "It means a mama is going to have a baby."

Robert: "By the way, it's Ma's birthday next week. I have an idea. Let's have a party for her at my dining room at the factory."

At his chemical plant on Long Island, he had a private dining room and a private chef. He and the top staff ate there, and he used it as a showplace to give customer parties.

"Well, that would be wonderful," Margaret said. Dr. Marks thought, Ma will just love it. That she'll understand. A son taking care of psychotics, no, that's incomprehensible. But a private dining room, part of a big factory, even Pa with his large distribution apparatus had nothing to match that.

Nancy pulled Margaret's skirt. She said, "Are you pregnant?"

"No, I'm not. I have enough children."

Dr. Marks said, "This conversation is getting out of my class. Robert, come in the front with me." Seeing the children follow: "No, the rest of you stay here. I want to talk privately with Robert."

When they entered the living room, Dr. Marks carefully closed the doors after them and handed Robert the check. "This is the first installment on what we owe you—"

"Nonsense," Robert said, "I was happy to help you. There's no need to do this."

Dr. Marks smiled, then he began to laugh. "Uncle John," he said.

Embarrassment on Robert's part. He remembered. Uncle John, when their father wanted to pay him for a medical visit, used to say, "Now, now, brother, don't do that. That's not necessary—" but he would walk away only just fast enough so that their father, walking behind him, would not be prevented from putting the fee into his pocket. Once it was in his pocket, he'd leave it there, but he wanted that little scene every time he made a house call.

"Don't be an Uncle John," Dr. Marks said. "I can spare it and you'd be surprised what this means to Margaret."

Slowly Robert folded the check and put it carefully in his alligator-skin wallet. "Thank you," he said. "Uncle John, what a character! You remember the shoeshines he used to get us?"

"Do I!" In striped morning pants and tailcoat Uncle John would take one of them down to a shoeshine parlor on Bushwick Avenue, and saying, "Never go out without your shoes brilliantly shined," would spend ten cents on a shoeshine for him. And ten cents meant a lot to Uncle John. "I still look at my shoes every time I go out the door," Dr. Marks said. "I'm guilty if there's any dust on them."

Robert looked down at his shoes. They were perfectly shined.

As the brothers came out into the hallway, Margaret gave her husband a questioning look and he nodded. The nod said, Robert has the check. All is well.

He was having trouble with Jeffrey. He had the feeling that Jeffrey resisted to the death any suggestion meant to be helpful to him (about how he conducted himself). His Unconscious interpreted it as a slur on his normality, any implication that he wasn't completely "bright," that he needed "to be told something." It was almost impossible to avoid this kind of situation. Dr. Marks found him reading a book in a poor light. "If you move your chair a couple of feet, you'll have better light on your book," he said.

"All right." Jeffrey got awkwardly to his feet and made an attempt to move the chair. He was naturally strong and could have moved it with one hand, but he seemed paralyzed. He pulled and struggled, not moving the chair.

"Here." Dr. Marks moved the chair over.

Suffused with embarrassment and anger, Jeffrey now tried to reseat himself in the chair. He was unable to. It was as if he had frozen into a position out of the chair, a pseudocatatonia.

"Why do you suppose you can't take a simple suggestion from me?" Dr. Marks asked him.

"I'm doing it, I'm doing it."

"Good. Please do it."

"I will, I will." More agony, more struggle.

"Stop that and try to understand what's happening to you. Why are you angry?"

"I'm not angry." His face contorted with anger.

"You should see yourself. Well, do as you please. I don't care."

Jeffrey sat down and Dr. Marks waited till his breathing slowed and then said, "Now are you willing to help with your therapy? We can make a great deal more progress if you'll help."

Silence.

"Why do you suppose you have to read without good light on your book?"

Silence.

"Maybe you're not worth having good light. Maybe you have to stay out of the light so you can keep certain things secret."

A slight redness in Jeffrey's face.

"Perhaps we can talk about it?"

"Always some meaning, meaning. I just didn't think about the light," Jeffrey said.

"Then why were you so upset?"

"I wasn't, I wasn't."

Like a child, Dr. Marks thought. "All right, let's talk about something else. You're in your cradle. You're standing up, holding the railing. Your mother comes in. What do you remember that she did?"

He had been trying for days to get Jeffrey to finish the recollection of this childhood scene. Jeffrey would tell all kinds of harmless things. Dr. Marks was sure he was inventing, furnishing what he thought would satisfy him. But the truth?

Here was a patient in full verbal communication, and the treatment hardly moved any faster than with Marta. Jeffrey had his own ingenious withdrawal. Dr. Marks remembered the theory that the patient must "want to be cured." There was truth to that with Jeffrey. His Unconscious was only partly exposed. If he could conceivably cooperate, open the content of his mind verbally, the case could move. Part of him must want to do it, but how do you reach that part?

You just keep trying. You try the difficult modulation of authority and love. As for love, he was more and more drawn to Jeffrey, fond of him as he would be of a son, and a son who needed his care. But would Jeffrey understand this—separate the love out from the previous authority figures he had hated—his father, police, hospital guards, attendants, even psychiatrists. Maybe especially psychiatrists who had done nothing for him.

He told Dr. Naumann about the case and said, "If Jeffrey would just cooperate, I could try something like an ordinary analytic session." Excited, Dr. Naumann said, "There's a Dr. James Revlin who published a terribly interesting case report in nineteen forty-two about how he did just that with a manic-depressive girl. Well, it's like your Ruth Mack Brunswick, but this was a hospitalized girl." He increased Dr. Marks's curiosity by telling him it was a girl in a State Hospital—

Dr. Marks read the paper at the Medical Library. It was about a girl named (or who called herself) Harriet Demuth. She had had a fixation on a brother who had been killed in a car accident, for which she blamed her parents. The pathology was that she identified with the brother at the moment of his death—she had been with him—and considered herself dead. (My parents killed me too, that meant.) She even had thoughts of suicide, to join her brother completely.

Dr. Revlin gave a verbatim, or near-verbatim, record of one of her terminal analytic sessions, during which he had suggested to her incestuous involvement with her brother without stating it openly. The account of this session was moving. It was remarkable that he had brought the girl, with her obvious resistances, to accept the orthodox Freudian procedures. She free-associated, though with some evidence of more than normal defenses (and in other ways more open); she remembered a dream, her mother and father and their relationship (as far as she could understand it), and when Dr. Revlin had exhausted the meanings of the dream with her, he went further than one usually does—he interpreted. The interpretations were tentative and they were Oedipal—always this massive emphasis on Oedipal material. But, Dr. Marks wondered, could Dr. Revlin's clearly parental feeling for his patient have unconsciously given her reassurance at an oral level?

He read through the whole session again. One detail struck him. Dr. Revlin had darkened the treatment room. That was interesting technically. Had it suggested sleep? Had it suggested a darkness of night feeding, conceivably? It seemed in this instance to have helped the mood that led to interpretation.

"The patient," the article ended, "escaped from the hospital shortly after this session and effected a recovery in the outside world, a recovery possibly helped by insights she received in analysis. Her therapist has had recent word that she is still well."

Dr. Marks was glad he had read the article. It was relevant to Jeffrey. This world of the hurt, all fighting help because the only help they could imagine came from a threatening mother. How could you get them to cooperate with you in the face of that fear? How did you get them to trust you? Was there any conscious way or didn't you just have to believe that at some cataclysmic moment the patient would unconsciously replace Mother with you, and so open the way ahead for you?

Wasn't that really what Revlin had been doing?

"I liked this Revlin," he said to Dr. Naumann. "He had some feeling for his patient."

"I thought you'd like him."

"Jeffrey. He's been tricked into hospitals time and time again and he thinks the whole thing is a frame-up. He has a code that validates lying to doctors under certain 'special circumstances' of treatment, of 'mistreatment' as he calls it. But I'll get to him."

Now Dr. Naumann was silent. Dr. Marks felt tired. The treatment sessions were becoming painful in a way, imitating rest (lying down) but without rest. He had so much work. Fatigue followed him everywhere. At the Medical Library, reading the Revlin article, he got in a fog of fatigue and to keep awake, he kept switching his reading light off and on.

He said to Naumann: "I'm tired." He described the light switching. "A blinking eye. That's me blinking with exhaustion. I had a patient at New State who had a tic of the right eye, and I was always feeling particularly tender about her, wanting her to rest. I couldn't stop believing the tic was lack of rest. Maybe it was, but not that kind of rest—"

"Possibly not. The other rest is more important."

Psychic rest.

"You yourself have given this rest to many patients," Dr. Naumann said.

Dr. Marks thought of that first deep sleep of Jimmy's. The basic relief of that sleep—it had been so moving. "Then why can't I give it to myself?" he said.

Silence.

"What am I afraid of?"

Silence.

"When Robert asked me to come out to the factory for a birthday dinner for Ma, I didn't want to go. I knew I couldn't say I was too busy, you can't say you're too busy to go to your mother's birthday party, but I didn't want to go—I don't want to go. There's still some hostility there. You said not to overweigh my hostility, that I'm sane. But if I'm so sane, why do I fight sleep? Why does the innocent (ha, innocent) unconsciousness of sleep seem threatening to me? Why do I have this feeling of unsureness about myself?"

Silence.

"Ma. I get mad. She'll say something even now and that old childhood mad will come back—come back strong. I'll have all I can do to control it."

"When you were a child and got mad, what did you do?"

Refused the tit. "I didn't speak to her."

"Tell me more about your not speaking to her."

Dr. Marks thought, Naumann's technique of going over the same ground. "I hated her, worse than I did the old matriarch. All that anger about her not nursing me and leaving me to the leftover breast of my wet nurse. All the woman fuss. Yak yak yak. I got tired of it, tired of hearing it. So I wouldn't speak to her—" Shocked: "Lewin would give me zero for identification. Marta hasn't been speaking to me. And Marta is me. Me not speaking to my mother. You know Marta makes a point of not speaking to me. Defies me. And I never saw it all this time. Never saw it that way. Saw that that way too I'm Marta. And I'm feeling for myself. What makes me so blind about a simple thing like this? Is it that I'm also my mother? And angry at my child for not speaking to me, not answering my questions?" Now he was silent, thinking.

"What are you thinking?"

"I'm feeling closer to Marta. You want me to get insight, but I fight it. I fight you and Marta fights me. Why is it so necessary to stay the way we are, to fight—"

"What?"

"Health."

"Why were you afraid of that word?" Dr. Naumann asked him.

"I suppose because I don't consider myself unhealthy or sick. But I suppose my health is the percentages. If I had had a few percentages the other way, I could be permanently refusing to speak to Mama. I could even be sitting rigid or picking hairs one by one out of the washbasin."

Silence.

"Maybe that's the fear, that narrow escape. And maybe I'm not entirely sure of my escape. I had that one invasion of the Unconscious. And I have to face the Unconscious again every night. And face it all day long too with Marta, with Betty, Jeffrey, and all my postpsychotic patients . . . I don't know what I'd do without the work here. The insight. Except it gets away."

"And it returns when needed. It exists and it can exert itself at necessary moments." A slight pause: "I'm afraid now we must stop. By the way, when is this birthday party for your mother?"

"The day after tomorrow."

"And how old will she be?"

"Sixty-seven."

They reached the door, and Dr. Naumann touched his shoulder and said good-by.

*   *   *

He drove, with Margaret at his side, across the East River, his car tires humming over the treads of the bridge. Winter. Behind him was that diorama of the city skyline glimpsed through the bridge's whirling struts. Going to Brooklyn, going to the Island, going back, going home.

His sisters would be there. Babe was picking Ma and Pa up. *He* could just as well have done it, but let Babe and her husband. Among any set of kids, one is likely to be the close one, and often it's the youngest, the one the mother finished with after working out on the others—the one she babied and made things up to. Let Babe take her.

Not that Pa couldn't have driven out to the plant himself.

"Say hello to Brooklyn," he said as they swept off the bridge in early darkness onto the wide eastern ramp.

"It feels good to be here," Margaret said.

They drove out the South Shore to the plant. Hand it to Robert, it had his mark on it. The proportions of the wide brick buildings with two-story windows, the concealed tanks and banded chimneys, the carefully landscaped sod gleaming a fine winter green in the headlights, everything said that this was top industrial design. Even the parking lot was attractive. And hierarchically laid out. Dr. Marks parked next to Babe's car. So Ma and Pa were here.

The executive wing, including Robert's office, was as handsome inside as a private home, mabe handsomer. There was something liberating about seeing a business building in which an early American grandfather clock stood on a landing beside an early Jackson Pollock. Robert's office was twenty feet square, sparely furnished, but the details were in character and included an Alice Neel portrait of Lisa, and old pulleys, quarry wedges, eighteenth-century house deeds, and other artifacts of the Island. He even had a small display of Indian arrowheads—doesn't every child dream of arrowheads?

Ma and Pa of course were foregathering in the office with Robert and Lisa and with Babe and Dora and their husbands. Ma was small beside Pa, and aging. Her forehead was surprisingly clear, but deepening lines by her eyes and in her cheeks and jaw had the look of women who have known poverty. Pa easily ruled the room. He had made it now, he had outlasted his mother. The sweep of his graying hair was confident. He was a man who had literally and steadily imposed his will. You felt it. The gray eyes still had the whip in them.

'Maybe that's the fear, that narrow escape.'

"Happy birthday," Dr. Marks said to his mother.

"Thank you."

Margaret too wished her a happy birthday and they said hello all around. "How does it go in the new office?" his mother said to Dr. Marks, taking him aside.

"You could come and see it."

"No! See crazy people?"

"They're not so bad. You probably wouldn't even meet any. All you'd meet is my secretary."

Puzzled: "And Babe says she's a black. In an office you should have a black?"

Yak yak yak, he thought. He said, "Why should I discriminate? Rosalie took the best dictation of anybody who applied. Should I care what color her skin is?"

His mother looked baffled.

"Come and meet Rosalie. You'll like her," he said.

"Colored working for you in the house, all right. In the office, no."

That persistent talent of his mother's for woman fussing. For not understanding, not wanting to understand—the old mad lit up in him.

But what about her problems with me? A son who puts a *black* in his office. Has crazy people for clients, and he's insane himself. (All her friends will console with her.) You can't even visit his office.

Pa came over. "How does it go?" he said.

"I have three steady patients and seven on an out-patient basis."

In Pa's eyes the memory of thirty patients in and out of his son's waiting room of a Saturday morning. And the finest families. Pa made no comment. "I hear you're paying Robert back," he said.

"I'm starting to."

"So there's a living in these crazy people?"

You'll fail. You will never come to anything. Up to now Dr. Marks had remained silent when his father started in on him. He had kept his anger inside as he had had to as a child. But it was time to do what Naumann said, use some kind of persuasion, try, at least—make some decent effort to get through to Father. Ma took her cue from Pa. If he even began to win Pa, she would follow along.

You can't any longer assume that anybody is unchangeable, particularly somebody meaningful to you. The moments of the analysis when his love for his father betrayed itself, these came up strongly in him. His love for Ma too, for that matter. (Why do you always try to forget that?)

Dr. Marks said, "The work's hard. But it's what I want to do. I've made two or three dozen of these people well, so they can go back to their families, be wives again, daughters, sons—be happy. Is this so much worse than taking out appendixes?"

In his father's eyes the whip: "I've heard these crazy ones get well by themselves. The appendix you see, you know what you did. What do you know about these cases?"

It was the whip with thongs. And he felt again the flesh that Ma had had to rub with salve. But wasn't I resisting Pa for himself, keeping my own will just as he did? Defending him? He said, "So far I've had twenty-nine recovered cases. No case hasn't recovered where I've had all the time I needed. And without shock treatment—"

"You attack shock. Everybody says shock is good."

"If you'll just listen, Pa. Twenty-nine cases have recovered. What is it? Is it a coincidence?"

His father stared at him. The internist who sold all his equipment, the internist who had to do something nobody else did. Who defied his father's wishes.

"But who does this kind of work?" his father said.

"I do it."

Robert had heard them. He came over. He said, "It's Ma's birthday. Keep the arguments for some other time —you have a long life ahead, you two. Today let's be happy." Glancing at his watch: "It's exactly eight. The chef's waiting. Downstairs, everybody." He took Pa on one arm and Ma on the other and, talking pleasantly, headed them for the door.

*   *   *

When a salad was served that had hard-boiled eggs in it, Dr. Marks picked one up in his fingers and began eating it, nudging Margaret.

His mother noticed him. "Eat salt on it," she said, frowning. "Who eats without salt?"

He carefully poured salt on his plate and dipped the egg in it. At least you have a son who eats his egg properly.

26

On the first day of spring, he went up to The Vansittart Clinic and had lunch with Arthur Chandler. It was good to be across the table from that face full of sardonic goodwill.

"How's Lissie?" Dr. Marks said.

"Oh, she's herself again. Doing wonderfully."

"Betty too. But Marta. She's back to normal voiding, but all her other problems, God! If you could know how my heart goes out to that girl, how I want her to recover. It seems insane that any human being with her loveliness and quality should *not* be sane, and not only sane but happy."

"Ha! but it doesn't work that way. You see so many beautiful girls who don't marry, who have serious problems. Rivals to their mothers. Full of fear."

After a moment Dr. Marks said, "It's not that simple for Marta. Her trouble began before her mother was jealous of her. No, it's another kind of maternal rejection—perversion, actually—"

"I know your theory about that."

"Theory?"

Dr. Chandler: "I won't say it isn't plausible."

"At New State Hospital in the back wards, women lie on the floor in the fetal position. If they go back to that, can't patients go back to the breast?"

"I don't say no."

"They want love with their milk. They're trying to find it. But I'm getting desperate. How am I to make Marta feel she's really loved? I have to do something I'm not doing now. Something more. What if I brought her into my home? What if I took her there and treated her? Gave her that evidence of love?"

Dr. Chandler was silent for a moment, then he said, "That's a pretty drastic step. I can see what you mean—"

"I'll do anything that has the least chance of helping her. This is what they do in Gheel——"

"I've heard of it. But there's no such tradition in this country and it's taking a chance, isn't it? There are the other families in your house, you have children——"

"Don't tell me, I've thought about it, I've thought about nothing else, but what am I to do—if this seems the one thing that might help Marta?"

"What does Margaret think about it?"

Now Dr. Marks stared steadily at Dr. Chandler.

"I haven't told her," he said.

That night Dr. Marks came home early, and Margaret fixed him some hot chocolate in the kitchen. It felt a little like the old days of courtship as he sipped and, gazing over the rim of the big cup, watched the play of her expression. That little cleft under her nose. She doesn't change. He put down the big cup and folded his hands on the table. "Do you feel strong-minded? I have something to talk to you about."

"What's coming now?"

"I'd like to bring Marta to the apartment to live with us."

"John——!"

"Let me explain. I've thought about it, a long time. And day after day, hours at a time, I work with Marta. And nothing happens. On and on. Something has to be done. It just has to be done. I tell you there's no least sign of movement with her. Nothing. And I think about Gheel——"

"So that's what that was."

"I think, if that could get her moving. Why not? If she's a psychic baby or child, my child, why not have her in my home? What could be more convincing to her——"

"John, she's not a baby."

"She's like one, quiet most of the time. Hardly says anything. The nurses would be here——"

"You've thought it all out."

"Darling, let her grow up. Let her grow up all over again in our home."

"You put it very well, but what about the children? What would this do to them? You'd be treating her——"

"Then you could see treatment."

"I don't want to see treatment *here*. I know it would be

a privilege, but not in our home. No. Not in front of the children—"

"It could give the children something."

"Are you out of your mind? You know what the content of a psychosis is. You've told me. You've told me the horrors—"

"Her Unconscious isn't exposed."

"But you're trying to expose it. This woman is insane. She hears voices. You told me her attention seems to be on the voices, you believe she hears them. They could tell her to kill. They could tell her anything."

"She's not like that. She simply isn't like that. I know the quality of the girl even if she's catatonic. She isn't dangerous."

"You can't know she isn't."

"I do know."

"That girl isn't coming here."

Now he tightened. "She is coming here—"

Suddenly violent: "She isn't. I won't stand it. I've done everything else. I've let you do everything else. I never stood in your way. But not this."

"I'll talk with you again, but I warn you. She is coming here."

Dr. Naumann had strong reservations about Dr. Marks's taking Marta into his home. He felt it was unreal. He cited a dream Dr. Marks had had recently, of getting into and out of an automobile (why this obsession in his dreams with driving a car?), and recalled to him his associating the dream to his father and to the stairway in the Bushwick Avenue house, and to the narrow, closed-in feeling of his child's life there—its resented tyrannies.

"Is a home necessarily a good place?" he said.

Dr. Marks: "This isn't the same home I'm bringing Marta into."

"You will think about it."

Dr. Marks was thinking. Was he going against reality? Margaret had at last, and most unwillingly, accepted his ultimatum. But do you do such a thing with an ultimatum?

But Marta. He had to get her moving. He had to.

He thought now only of how Marta might move.

The piano was put in the living room, and the extension

of the foyer between the dining room and the living room was converted into a bedroom for Marta. The time was set when she was to come. Fred had accepted the new arrangement.

Dr. Marks debated whether to use sodium amytal for transferring her and decided against it. She would come as she had come to the hotel, undrugged. He would work with or in spite of the catatonic defenses since this was what he would have to do anyway, day in and day out.

Fred and Miss Kinnell were to accompany Marta when he drove her to his apartment. It was a Saturday in early April and they planned to arrive just after lunch. The children were to stay in the back of the apartment till they were called. Margaret would open the door.

They left the hotel without incident. Marta sat in the back of the car with Fred, who held her hand. He continued holding her hand as they reached the house and as they came up, all four of them together, in the leather-seated elevator.

When Margaret opened the door, Marta looked at her —was it looking? Her eyes had their usual unfocused appearance. "Marta," Dr. Marks said, "this is my wife, Margaret. I'd like you to shake hands with her, please." He cued Margaret, who put out her hand. Fred released his wife's hand and guided it to Margaret's, and Margaret took it. When she released it, it stayed unmoving in the air.

"This is Fred Kleinerman, Margaret. You know Miss Kinnell. Marta, this is my home. You're now going to be part of my family, close to me. You'll be my child just like my other children, I'll love you just the same as I do them. I couldn't love you more. Look here, this will be your room." He showed her her small room with its single bed, its bureau with a large hanging mirror, and two chairs.

"It's not a large room, but it's nice."

She showed no interest in it, just stood where she had been placed in the doorway.

He called, "Hey, kids." They were waiting.

Nancy arrived first and eagerly held out her hand to Marta. To Dr. Marks's astonishment, Marta took her hand and shook it, but right afterward she looked through Bob and Johnny as if they weren't there and as Dr. Marks began to introduce them, she seemed distracted.

"What's bothering you?" he said.

She stood rigid, then ran to a chair and looked under it and looked under the radiator in the foyer. He said sharply, "Marta!" She stopped, not turning to him, but evidently acknowledging she had heard him.

"This is my home, this isn't a hospital or even a furnished hotel apartment like the one where you've been living—you know that. Do you think there could be anything here in my home to be afraid of? I love and protect you. Everything here is safe. Come, I'll show you the whole place." He took her hand and led her to the kitchen. "Your meals will be cooked here, wonderful meals, and if you yourself should want to cook anytime, of course you'd be welcome to." Marta stared at the stove and leaned down and touched its white door. "That's not your mother's stomach," he said. "Come." He showed her the bathroom and then his and Margaret's bedroom: "And now come here—this is Nancy's room." Nancy's room was cheerful, with Mother Goose stencils on the walls and plenty of morning light. Marta wanted to linger here. "Come, I want you to see the boys' room." But she pulled away and went back to Nancy's room.

"Do you like this room?" he said.

She sat down on Nancy's bed.

Margaret caught his eye. She was not happy.

Marta was pushing her shoes off and getting ready to lie down.

"I'm sorry, I'm going to have to ask you to get up," Dr. Marks said. "Each child in this house has his own bed—or her own bed. This is Nancy's bed."

"She can have my bed," Nancy said. "She can be in it if she wants to. Do you want to sleep with me?" she said to Marta.

Now an unusual response in Marta's eyes, the faintest impression of a smile—at least of goodwill. Dr. Marks thought she was going to speak, but saying nothing, she slowly got up and pushed on her shoes.

She seemed to accept her own room. Dr. Marks called it the "made room" (*maid room,* another bad pun after the *guessed room*)—and when he took her into it, she stood in front of the bureau mirror, staring into it. He said, "What do you see in there? Do you see yourself? Do you see a beautiful baby with black hair who can be loved? My baby. Nobody else's."

Silence.

"I want you to be very sure I love you."

No reaction.

But after a few more minutes of staring into the mirror (into its imaginary distances?), she sat down on the bed. He spoke to her quietly, he stayed with her for several hours. During that time she remained silent, but not rigid. She seemed to be aware of the apartment outside her room. It was like a cat taken into a new place. Cautious, her haunches tense: Is there danger here?

He left at quarter to five for his session at Dr. Naumann's. When he returned, Miss Barklund was on duty and told him Marta had spent two hours looking into the mirror. "Not all the time, but most of the time. I said, 'Why don't you talk?' She said, 'I can't talk.' I asked her why, but she wouldn't say anything."

Dr. Marks went to Marta and said, "Miss Barklund tells me you looked a long time into the mirror. Why?" A pause for the non-answer. "What do you see in here? I wish you could tell me." He waited, uselessly. "You see yourself. You see the outside of yourself." Almost to himself: "Or perhaps you see the inside of yourself, that child inside. That baby. Maybe it's just the visions you see in there. But if it's visions, it's not real. It's just a hallucination. This is just a mirror, just glass. Come on, touch it." He made her touch the glass of the mirror. "That's all it is, a reflection. Nothing more in there than there is in the room. Look." He waved his arms through the air in every part of the room. "Nothing here. No dream stuff. Just air, empty air."

He thought of removing the mirror, but decided not to. Better to remove the need for the mirror. That was the principle of treatment. But easier said than done.

There was one thing to explain: "Your nurses aren't going to sleep here. There isn't room for them. But anyway you don't need them. You have us now. You're part of my family and we'll be with you at night."

No show of interest. But he thought she was less frightened. Not rigid, at least. For the time being.

At dinner he had hoped to have her eat with the family. It was completely impracticable. She refused to eat at all, and after a little while, she got up and walked quickly from the table. After he had brought her back three times, and made a number of interpretations, he gave up on it. Self-consciousness about the rituals? Need to continue being the only child? Who knew what psychic mechanism was involved? He had Miss Barklund feed her in the kitchen (her previous routine) and this seemed to help. Part of the time, then, she ate.

One night Nancy said to him, "It's like I was when I had my little table, isn't it, before I could eat with you."

He said, "Yes, but now you're older."

"She's older too, isn't she, but she's crazy."

"She's crazy now."

Happily: "But you're going to make her not crazy."

"I hope so. I'm trying hard."

"Can I help?" she said.

"You can help, you can be my assistant therapist. Would you like to be?"

"Mmmmmmm."

"Okay. You are."

He took Nancy to the kitchen where at the moment Miss Barklund was having trouble getting Marta to eat. He was aware of Margaret behind him. "Eat, eat," Miss Barklund said. "This is some nice chicken soup I made you. Look at this beautiful soup." She held up a spoonful.

Marta kept her mouth closed.

"*You* take the spoon," Miss Barklund said, trying to put the spoon in Marta's hand. Marta disregarded it.

Dr. Marks went over to Miss Barklund and said, "Let me have the spoon." He spooned up a mouthful of the beaded liquid. "Marta, you're obviously afraid to use your mouth," he said. "You're afraid you might eat poison. Look." He put the spoonful of soup into his own mouth and swallowed it. "I'm not afraid of it. Anything cooked in this house or given to you in this house is healthy. Your mean mother didn't make this. She couldn't make soup as good as this. Come, try it." He spooned up another mouthful and held it out to her. "You're afraid it's garbage. You're afraid it's dope, you might get doped. You might eat something bad. But you saw me eat it, didn't you? Do you think I'd eat it if it wasn't good? It's delicious. Take a taste." Rigid, unmoving. Mouth closed tight. There was no magic in interpretations. He reached forward with his left hand and pressed on her cheeks at the tooth line until he forced her mouth open. He tipped the spoonful of soup into her mouth. Quickly she closed her mouth and kept it closed without swallowing.

"Swallow."

Motionless.

"Swallow."

Motionless, rigid-eyed.

He pressed her nostrils closed and, agonized, gulping, she swallowed and breathed air through her mouth.

"You see, it's not so bad. It's good. Doesn't it taste good?"

Motionless, mouth shut, she stared over his shoulder.

He had a thought, he had that charged, passionately sure feeling: "You're afraid to open your mouth. You'll let Mama out. You're keeping her inside, it's the only way to stay alive. But you can let her out. I'm here now. I can love you and protect you and feed you. I'll be your food. I'll be Mama."

Casually she opened her mouth and began to let him feed her, and at last she took the spoon and fed herself. He remained quiet, watching her. Margaret went away somewhere, but Nancy stayed.

The next day, Nancy had a chocolate bar for dessert after her lunch. She hunted up Marta. She found her sitting on the edge of her bed, rigid and stiffly erect.

She offered her a piece of chocolate.

No response.

She tried to put the chocolate in Marta's mouth. Marta kept her mouth closed tight.

"It isn't garbage."

Rigid resistance.

Gently Nancy tried to get Marta to open her mouth. "It isn't your mummy, it's yummy," she said. "It's good." She kissed Marta and whispered in her ear, "Eat, eat it. It's good."

No change in the rigid position.

When Dr. Marks returned from seeing a follow-up patient at his office, Miss Kinnell took him aside and told him that Marta had urinated in the bath water. She had had to change the water before Marta could take her bath. Marta had also screamed twice.

"Well, that's good," he said. "That's some sound out of her."

"I'm afraid it was rather disturbing to Mrs. Marks. What if the neighbors heard?"

"The walls are thick."

"I noticed another thing."

"What's that?" he said.

"Well, Marta was looking at a picture of her daughter, Ruth, and then she looked at Nancy. It wasn't a very pleasant look. Then after she looked in the mirror a long time, she said, 'I'm cursed. Do I have a family?' Do you think that's good?"

"What are you worried about?"

"I don't know. It's hard to define."

At least there's movement in the case, he thought.

He took Marta into her room and closed the door and said to her, "What does this mean, you saying, 'Do I have a family?' You maybe miss Fred and Ruthie more since you're here. Is that it? Is that what you mean? If it is, good. I hope you do miss them. I want you to miss them terribly and get the thought into your head that you could have them. You can, you know. They love you and need you so much, and you love them. Maybe not as much as you will love them when you get through with me. But you love them."

Lately he had been thinking of all useful psychotherapy as a medicine of "love instead of wrath."

Casually: "I suppose being here with my family troubles you. You maybe wonder if you should have this family, if you're worthy of it. You are." After a contemplative silence: "But maybe something else is what's bothering you. You're saying, 'Do I have a family?' because you're not sure if you have a mother or father. Well, you don't. But is that bad? Is it bad to give up a mother and father who hurt you—who wouldn't let you grow up—and accept a new mother and father who want you to grow up? Isn't that a better family?" He took her hand and ran his fingers softly over her knuckles. "I love you, girl. I protect you and love you all the time. What's this I heard that you said the other day, 'I'm part of an airplane and my body isn't here.' An airplane floats around maybe like a fetus and you don't know you have a body, you think you're part of Mama, safe inside there. You touched the kitchen stove. Maybe you want to be safe inside that. But that's not the answer. You're safe with me. I keep you warm and feed you and love you and I keep you safe all the time. How can you be safer than you are with me?"

She remained rigid.

"You don't have to stay inside the womb, inside the stove, behind that white door. I'll open the door and you'll step out, all new and lovely. You'll find out how nice it is out here. You hear?"

Silence.

"You hear me?"

Still unmoving, staring.

After an early dinner he went to Astoria and treated Jeffrey for two hours, the usual wearing nonsense of why Jeffrey dribbled on the floor when he washed or urinated. He came home in not too good a mood and found Marta with her face to the side, in her nice familiar rigid position. "Have you thought about who gives you life and food?" he said. "Have you thought about joining me out here in the real world?" He put his head directly in front of her, to make her look at him (if she did). "I hope you did give some thought to that after I talked to you this afternoon. I hope you thought about this being your better family. Right here. Come, you have your dinner now with Miss Barklund and then come to the living room. I want you to get better acquainted here."

A half hour after dinner, he went back and found Bob and Johnny in their room, doing homework. "I'm glad to see you both at work," he said, "but I have some other work for you—" Great interest. "Do you think we might have a session at the piano? I'd like Marta to be part of it, show her what the advantages of family life are. Come on, let's gather up Mama and Nancy and go in there. Johnny, grab your trumpet."

As they passed through the foyer, he asked Miss Barklund to bring Marta into the living room. By the time Marta came in, staring far in front of her, he was playing the melody of "Walk into Jerusalem just like John" with his left hand and spreading all kinds of pseudo glitter with his right hand, Johnny warming it up with his trumpet and all of them singing for once actually in key. He swung into "Alexander's Ragtime Band" and noticed Marta doing what he saw her do once in a great while, and what the nurses reported to him, she was moving from foot to foot —left, right—as if participating. The playing and singing continued and Marta stared and shifted feet through the moans and glissandi of the trumpet and through Nancy's highly audible alto. At last he said, "Thank you, children. Back to your homework. Thank you, Margaret. Thank you, Nancy. Marta, I want to thank you for joining us. I wanted you to hear Louis John Armstrong here and Billie Nancy Holiday. Come on, sweet," he said to Nancy, "let's us walk Marta back to her room." And with Nancy holding one of Marta's hands and he the other, Marta was again going from foot to foot, but this time walking awkwardly back to her room.

Late that night—if he could guess, it was between two and three in the morning—he became conscious of a creaking sound. Margaret was still asleep, breathing with a soft agreeable rhythm, her body interposed between him and the door. The door moved. It slowly opened and he was aware of a pale figure standing in it. Once in a great while, maybe twice a year, Nancy would come to the door. But this was not Nancy.

"Marta?"

No motion from the door. Now Margaret was waking up. "What is it?"

"It's all right. It's Marta."

He snapped on a lamp. Marta's hair was halfway around her face, protecting her. She was barefooted. Her nightgown swept down loosely over her breasts and widened around her hips.

Getting up, he said, "It's all right. Did you have a bad dream?" Bad dream—all her silence, all her life now was a bad dream. But it was the thing that brought a child to her parents in the night. "Did you need me?"

It seemed to him that she was looking at Margaret in bed. He touched Marta's shoulder. "Come." She turned obediently and followed him on her soft, silent bare feet back to her own bed and lay down on it. But she didn't take a comfortable position; she held her body partly up from the bed. He said, "You're raising yourself to Mother's breast. You're trying to eat and be happy." He interpreted insistently and gently, and at last she relaxed and lay at full length on the bed.

A full-length baby. That strange sense of her unreal infancy. "I'll leave you now," he said, but she immediately began to get up to follow him. "No, no, stay here," he said. "You have to stay in your own bed and sleep." But if you're afraid? He remembered how sometimes he had been afraid as a small boy, or how Nancy was. He took Marta's hand. There was no answering pressure, but again the body under the covers relaxed.

"You were gone rather long," Margaret said.

He described to her his lifting-to-the-breast interpretation and his conviction that it had worked.

"You know, there's a latch on our bedroom door," she said. "If you don't mind, I'd like to lock the door."

"What for?" He felt a beginning of irritation.

"I should think you'd want the door latched. What if she came in and found us——"

"Would that be so bad?"

"Wouldn't it? Didn't Freud have a whole case about a child who saw his parents moving the sheets?"

"I'm familiar with this Freud thing. But what about savage tribes, do they have a separate tent for the children? A separate cave?"

"This isn't savage tribes, darling." After a moment: "I thought you were a pure Freudian."

He moved restlessly. "Some of these things are a matter of emphasis. I'm Freudian, yes, but if you deal with a bunch of orally deprived and orally assaulted patients, you don't worry so much about the Oedipus complex. Little Hans. He wasn't a baby, he was past babyhood. He wasn't Marta."

"Well, if you don't care about Marta, I care about us. I want privacy for us."

Funny, he thought. She didn't lock the door on Nancy. Only on Marta.

He said, "How will Marta feel if she comes here and finds the door locked?"

"Let her knock."

"Let *her* knock. She can't knock." He said, "What is it with you? I thought by now you'd love Marta." And now he was aware of a quickening, and twice she seemed about to speak.

"I think it's something about me," she said at last. "It's hard for me to understand. I mean understand myself. I'll try to explain. When I was ten or eleven—I've never told you this—I was at the Warrington Summer Camp and there was to be some camp program at which the children would perform. Well, there was this retarded little girl, and I wanted her to have the fun of being in the show. So I drilled and drilled her in a short poem and she learned it, got it line by line, only at the actual performance she froze and couldn't say a word. Well, I lost sympathy for that child and I didn't feel encouraged to do things like that again."

He was amazed. "That doesn't sound like you."

"I love my family. But I have to admit, I don't love patients. You love them. I'm glad you do because they're not easy to love, and it's lucky somebody cares about them." She pressed back her chestnut hair, exposing her clear forehead in the lamplight. "And, John, you care about something else. You care about proving a psychotic can be cured."

"I did begin working with Marta that way—just as you say, wanting to prove something. But that isn't what matters now. I care about her now for herself."

"It's not all that simple."

"What do you mean?"

"I have a feeling about her as a woman even if perhaps you don't. You say, to you she's a patient—a child—but she's also a woman. In my home. Her coming here to the room just now, maybe that gives me the feeling. She's also insane. I told you my feelings about that when you first spoke about wanting to bring her here, but you insisted. I mentioned treatment. You don't always watch what you say in front of Nancy: there are things she shouldn't be hearing. All this disturbs me. It disturbs me more than you think."

He said, "I'm sorry it does. To Marta this is life or death. I don't worry about Nancy. What a child can understand won't hurt her. And what she *can't* understand won't hurt her. She understands the love involved."

Margaret said nothing.

He thought, Psychotics are like babies are to some mothers. Babies that arrive raw, bloody, and ugly and they're damn well unconscious twenty hours of the day.

They have shit all over them. They're nothing but a long instinctual cry. That's all some mothers see in babies.

(Unfair, unfair: Margaret's not one of those mothers.) Still:

"I wish you were different," he said.

"I wish I was different too. But you could be wrong. You have this theory, but you could be wrong about it, John. This girl is too sick."

The next morning Miss Kinnell discovered Marta lying in a wet, urine-soaked bed. She got Marta up and helped her out of her cold nightgown. "Whatever did you do? My goodness, you know where the bathroom is. Just because I wasn't here—or Miss Barklund. You could go to *some-body!*"

The bed—there was no rubber mat on it and the urine was through to the mattress.

"Well, the mattress will have to be thrown out," Margaret said.

"So it's thrown out. We'll get another. And put a rubber mat on it. I should have thought about that, I had a sense this was coming."

"How do you mean?" she asked him.

"All that time Marta held in her urine, we had a rubber mat on the hotel mattress."

"So why didn't you bring it over here?"

"I thought she was over that."

After Miss Kinnell bathed Marta, she wrapped her in a heavy robe—the spring air was still cool and the heat was slow coming up in the morning—and she brought her a glass of grape juice. It was always difficult to get her to drink grape juice, but, Miss Kinnell thought, it's good for her. She tried every possible persuasion and at last used Dr. Marks's trick of pressing in Marta's cheeks against her teeth. Marta opened her mouth and accepted a large mouthful of the juice, then deliberately opened her robe and spit it on her right breast.

"Marta, what possessed you!" Miss Kinnell rushed to get a washcloth to wipe the juice off. The juice stain refused to come off. She took Marta to the bathroom and soaped her breast and cleaned it. Still an ugly purple splotch remained. "I'm going to have to tell Dr. Marks about this. He just has to know. I don't know what he's going to say." Marta began to sob. She covered her breast and leaned against Miss Kinnell. "There, there," Miss Kinnell said, "it doesn't matter. You know he won't do anything to you. You know he loves you."

When Dr. Marks returned from an appointment, Miss Kinnell told him what had happened. "I never saw her act like that. It's not like her at all."

He went to Marta and said, "Miss Kinnell told me what you did, spit juice on your breast. But I'm glad. Why are you frightened to have me know? Tell me." As she continued faintly sobbing, he said, "Does it mean you don't like your breast? But this is a good breast. This has nothing but good milk in it, good, sweet, nourishing milk. Wonderful milk. This is the milk you fed to Ruthie. I wish you could have had some milk like this yourself when you were a baby. I'm trying to give you milk like this now, do you understand?" Still some sobbing. He took her in his arms and rocked her back and forth. "Bye baby bunting, Daddy's gone a hunting, to catch a little rabbit skin to wrap his baby bunting in." Her sobbing stopped. She put her head against his shoulder and breathed slowly and gently through his shirt. With a chiding tone: "Do you think I mind if you wet the bed? You're a baby just now, but I'll love you till you grow up. I'll wash your nightgown the way I'd wash your diapers." Tenderly: "Miss Kinnell told you not to worry, didn't she? Didn't she tell you I love you and I wouldn't punish you? There, there now." He hummed to her and made just the suggestion of rocking.

He heard the phone ringing and Margaret called, "It's Bill Widener."

He set Marta carefully in the chair, arranging her robe around her. "Everything's all right now. Just wait here now and I'll be right back."

"Hi, Bill," he said on the phone. "What's doing?"

"I hear you have one of your patients in your apartment."

"Yeah. Where'd you hear that?"

"Margaret mentioned it to Alice."

"Margaret isn't enthusiastic."

"I don't blame her."

"You're saying what Naumann says, or seems to say. I get no support. What is this—no love for the psychotic?"

"Isn't it generally agreed to keep them off the streets?"

"You know I could dislike you for that remark. I mean it."

"All right, I take it back. Could you and Margaret come for dinner some evening?"

"No."

"Please. It will do you both good."

"Not just now. Maybe a little later. This Marta case is moving. Something's going on and when something's going on, I have to stay with it. You wouldn't know."

"Stop being mad at me."

"I'm interpreting like mad. This thing of interpretations. You know, Bill, they don't necessarily work, but now and then they do—and how! I was feeding Marta the other day—trying to—and I told her she was keeping her mouth closed because she had Mother inside her. I suddenly knew you can confuse being a fetus with being a mother, being in the womb with being pregnant. Being inside and being outside. She sure hasn't had her period now in seven months—"

"You can go too far with this," Bill said.

"You can't. You should know what the Unconscious is capable of."

"So did she eat?"

"She ate."

"Okay, have fun. I have to go to the office."

To the office. It isn't so long since *he* didn't have an office, either.

Would Rosalie be at *his* office? He wanted her to come over and take notes. This might be the day. It was only five to nine, but he phoned on the chance she'd be there.

"Dr. Marks's office."

"Hi, chick. You get your thin self to the office pretty early. In about an hour, will you put the office on answering service and hike yourself over here?"

"Yes, sir."

"Did you have breakfast?"

"No."

"Don't you ever eat? You're as bad as Marta."

"Oh, I eat."

"Half an egg sandwich, that's eating. If you don't look out, I'll do an interpretation on you."

"Please, *Doc*-tor—"

"You come and bring your notebook and you'll get a glass of milk."

He went back to Marta, aware of feeling well. Betty was consolidating, other patients were settling back to life and living. Jeffrey—even Jeffrey was changing a little.

And now Marta was moving. He spoke to Miss Kinnell in the living room, telling her what had been going on, and went back to Marta.

Marta wasn't in the chair where he had left her, she was standing in front of the mirror, but no longer was she staring vacantly into it. She had a lipstick in her hand and in her other hand she had her right breast, the one that had still some pale blue stain of grape juice. She was inscribing a circle around the nipple. Hearing him, she let the lipstick fall and turned toward him. He saw that her mouth also was smeared with the lipstick.

She had put lipstick on her mouth and then on her breast. Was this symbolically putting her mouth to her breast?

He had identified her breast—that she had spit on—as a good breast, with good milk. He had insisted it was good.

"Your beautiful mouth—" he spoke as if the thought was rushing out of his heart to her "—that you wanted to nurse with, you put it on that breast. You nursed, you nursed. You fed yourself good milk."

Then an afterthought: *Was* it good that she had done that? Was this symbolic autism good? This self-feeding? But did it matter if it *was* good? His immediate reaction had been right: You had to let her know you understood her, you loved her no matter what she did—hadn't he accepted Jimmy's thoughts and desires and fears? "You needed that milk, daughter. It's warm. It's safe. It's good. You can be there nursing as long as you want." Self-feeding is better than no feeding. It's taking a step away from death, from fear of death.

There was still another possibility. She wanted to keep Mother inside her, the interpretation he had used before when she wouldn't open her mouth. All this careful preservation of body fluids, this holding in. Safety in staying inside, keeping everything inside.

No, he rejected that interpretation. It didn't feel true, the way the case was moving. This was feeding at least from a breast that seemed good to her. He had called it a good breast. He had often told her he would feed her, as the good mother, the foster mother, the feeding mother. Was it beyond possibility that this was what she meant? Every kind of transference and cross-identification was possible.

"You want to eat. You want love. You want to be loved. I'm glad. I've always wanted you to have milk that means love."

She closed her robe and put her arms across her breasts. There was something natural about her doing it, but slowly she seemed to become rigid, her eyes became unfocused again, and he sensed that she was frightened. Why? Had the relief been too quick? Had there been some warning from the voices? Some rage "out there"? He continued interpreting, but she had definitely slipped back behind her defenses.

He phoned upstairs on the chance that Bert Lewin had not left for his office. "Is there a chance you could stop down here?" he said.

"I could, yes."

"Can I tell you what's been happening?"

"Please do."

He told Bert what had happened. "You and your good milk," he said to Bert. "I sure took a chance on it just now. But I might be wrong. She went right back into her damn stupor. I thought it might be fright, that she was coming out and took fright, but who knows these things?"

"You have a difficult thing here. No associations, nothing to check out what you do, or almost nothing. It takes courage—"

"At least there was movement."

"Yes. I'll be down."

When Dr. Lewin arrived, they went together to Marta. "Marta," Dr. Marks said, "are you still frightened? What's happened must be frightening. But it's also good. It means you can trust yourself more, having feelings you haven't had in a long time."

She continued rigid. She stared into the right-hand corner of the room.

Dr. Marks introduced Dr. Lewin to her, and Dr. Lewin spoke to her. Then he said, "I don't understand what you're looking at. You don't seem to be looking at me. Isn't it usual to look at the person who's talking to you?"

No reaction.

"Do you confuse my voice with other voices, perhaps? I've heard that you do that. But now notice something." He picked up her hand. "I'm speaking and now look what happens. You—" He clapped her hand over his mouth so that her hand silenced him. He took her hand away and his voice resumed: "—you can't do that to the voices out there, can you? You can't silence them. Because those voices aren't real. But my voice is real so you can stop it."

Dr. Marks told Miss Kinnell to stay with Marta, and he took Dr. Lewin to the kitchen for coffee.

"That thing of her hand over your mouth," he said. "Have you done that before?"

"I don't have this kind of case. No, I haven't done it before."

"I ought to turn this case over to you. Do you know she looked better after you spoke to her?"

"This oral thing— Thank you," Dr. Lewin said as Dr. Marks gave him coffee from the pot kept heating on the stove. "This thing of the breast—she could be looking for a way out of her dream—what you call the permanent dream of the psychosis in your paper. If she could nurse from a good breast."

"But look at the strange contradiction. Your theoretic baby devours the mother, is devoured, goes to sleep, and experiences the white screen that supports all his dreams. He uses the breast as a gateway to dream. Now you want Marta to use the breast to leave her dream."

Dr. Lewin laughed. "It's a different dream, opposites are the essence of dream."

"And of insanity."

"That's a plain statement. Yes."

Dr. Marks had been looking at the white oven door on the stove. He began to laugh. "You want to know where your dream screen is?" he said.

"Where is it?"

"There, that oven door. Marta's been fascinated by it. It's been a real 'thing' with her. At first I thought it was the womb (the oven). But I give you the dream screen. Who knows? All this interpretation is part art. I don't think it can ever be entirely science. Anyway where is the science in the love you give a patient, like you just did with Marta? You helped her. I believe everything helps, every shove toward reality, toward understanding. You keep thinking some one thing will get through to her—like your business with the hand—but it doesn't. No matter how good it is."

"But sometimes a single thing has an effect."

"You give me hope."

Dr. Marks became aware of a small figure half visible around the kitchen doorframe. "Hey, your friend," he said to Dr. Lewin. To Nancy: "Come in, sweetie."

Nancy came in and Dr. Lewin took her small hand. "How are you?" he said.

"I'm fine."

"I hear you're an assistant therapist."

Laughing: "Yeah."

"You help Daddy with Marta?"

"Oh, yeah. I like her." She made a face.

"What's the face for?" Dr. Lewin asked.

"She don't—doesn't talk. Do you think she's gonna talk? She talks sometimes."

"She might talk to you."

"I guess so. Or to my turtle."

"Yes." Dr. Lewin let a long cigarette ash fall on the floor. "Remember it's important, whatever she says, to tell your father."

"I will."

"It's important. You tell him."

"I will."

"Good. Well," glancing at his watch, "I guess I have to be going."

The apartment bell rang and it was Rosalie. "You just missed Bert Lewin," Dr. Marks said. "Hey, do I have things to get down! It's lucky you're the fastest shorthand artist in the United States—"

"You're not talking to a patient, Doctor," Rosalie said.

"Come in and see the patient." He took her to Marta's room where Marta was sitting on the edge of her mattress-less bed, rigid again, still in her robe. Rosalie said, "Hello,

Miss Kinnell. Hello, Marta." Rosalie took Marta's hand as she usually did, and Marta's robe fell open, exposing the startling red ring around her right breast. When Rosalie let go of her hand, Marta slowly pulled her robe together and folded her arm over it with her hand closed as if she was holding something.

He said, "I think she's protecting that lovely breast." To Rosalie: "Come, I want to tell you about that good milk." To Miss Kinnell: "Dress her now or let her dress herself. I believe she might like to take a walk around the block."

"Yes, Doctor."

In the living room, he began to dictate notes. When he was finished with all the developments of last night and this morning, Rosalie said, satisfyingly stunned behind her curving black eyelashes, "Well, now I've heard everything."

"You better *not* believe it," he said. "Nobody's ever heard 'everything' in this business."

"No?"

Marta did take a walk around the block with Miss Kinnell who reported that she stopped and stared at a small red foreign car. "I showed her your car with its MD on the license, but she didn't seem interested. But when I told her you were going to make her well so that she could drive her own car again, she said, 'Where's the key?'"

"That's a loaded question," he said. "What did you say?"

"I said Fred was keeping it for her."

"I'd better see her."

He went to Marta's room and found her again sitting erect on the edge of her bed, her arm still across her breast and her hand closed. He touched her hair. "You know, your hair is so well combed today," he said. "You did that for me because you know I like it." He let her soft black hair run through his fingers. "Beautiful hair. Tell me, if you want to do these thoughtful things for me, why don't you talk to me? You know how terrible I feel that you don't. I think about it all the time. While I was having breakfast, I thought about it." Loudly: "Do you hear me? I command those voices to be quiet." In a normal voice again: "You must have noticed how Dr. Lewin put your hand over his mouth and you stopped his voice.

Now watch my hand." He went in front of her and raised his hand, flattened and prohibitory, in the direction in which she was staring. Her eyes flickered. I wonder what happened, he thought. Did the voices stop? Did I perform magic?

"When you were taking a walk with Miss Kinnell, you stopped and looked at some red car and Miss Kinnell showed you my car." He stood directly in front of her and, being taller, he cut off her stare from whatever disembodied figure or imagination she had been seeing. "She told you you would get well and drive your own car, I'd make you well, and then you said, 'Where's the key?' " He took her closed hand and carefully opened it. "Is it here? No. I wonder what that key could be. I'm so glad you want it. I know, of course, it isn't just a car key. It must be a key for something else. Perhaps I have it?" He looked in all his pockets and now her eyes were following him, watching as he searched each pocket. He brought out a key ring. "Oh, these keys are just the keys to my office and the apartment. I know that isn't what you want either. You want—let me see—you want a key to some difficult questions. Who are you? How can you trust people? How can you let yourself be loved?" For a moment as he said this, her eyes seemed to acknowledge his, but the unfocused stare immediately came back. He added: "You want a good parent who loves you. You want life. Is it so hard to have? It's waiting for you any time you make up your mind to accept it."

Orality. Defining the good breast. After a recent class, Bert Lewin had referred to mothers who "nurse the baby too much to compensate unconsciously for not wanting to nurse—"

"The baby feels the unconscious rejection," Dr. Marks said.

Lewin agreed. It pleased Dr. Marks because it was another evidence (and from Lewin) that not all was glorious and universally beneficent about the mother's breast.

Overfeeding. Is this why babies gag and young children dawdle over their food?

Freud. Freudianism. It was only partly science, much as Freud had approached his findings as a science, and rigorous and honest as he had been. How could the acts and wounds of the human spirit be measured? How could you measure your way into the hurt mind?

You guessed. You went by correspondences and intuitions, you guided yourself by the sense of response that you felt sometimes at an animal level.

You must do something right.

He thought, what did it mean that a case like this "moved"? What was movement? Was it something final or was it just a pause or a start? A motion that stopped again. As if the patient had an insight, but had to withdraw to unconsciously examine it and absorb it. Or reject it?

Lately he had been increasingly troubled by dreams of unfinished journeys, incomplete letters, failure symbols, symbols of not reaching the desired destination. His car would get lost in side streets. Naumann was finding humiliating things in his dreams and associations. More than half a year with Marta and nothing he could identifiably call progress. What was this so-called movement? Was there any meaning to it?

Friend Freud, had he ever felt disgusted with himself? *Analysis Terminable and Interminable.*

Nancy wandered into the living room and climbed on his lap and settled herself comfortably on his left knee. He held her against him and hummed to her. "What do you know?" he said.

"Nothing."

He laughed. "Me too."

Marta showed signs of a muted excitement toward evening. She went into the living room and stood by the piano. She began hunting under pieces of furniture, a hint (with her) of being frightened. He found her tearing a sheet of paper into small bits and breathing hard. She pushed the pile of paper over the edge of the dining-room table and it snowed down on the floor.

He thought of some of the patients at New State Hospital and how they told attendants, after they recovered, what certain actions of theirs during the insanity meant. Like Joe Huber and the man with the "bad body." And like some of his own patients. What could this tearing-up-of-paper mean? Destroying documents that would incriminate her or her father (in the court case)? No, he doubted that that was it. He was tired of guessing.

He took her by the hand and led her into her room, asking Miss Barklund to accompany him, and after closing the door, he said to Miss Barklund, "I see the new mattress is on the bed."

"Yes, Doctor."

"Is the rubber sheet under the pad?"

"Yes, everything is ready."

"Marta," he said, "you have a rubber sheet over your mattress now. If you should want to wee-wee in bed again, it's all right. And I want you to know that I personally washed your sheets and nightgown for you. I'll do that for you whenever you need me to, until you grow up. I'm sorry your mother didn't love you enough to do these things for you."

There was a knock on the door. He opened it and Nancy beckoned to him. He walked with her into the dining room. "Yes, what is it?" he said.

"Marta said something."

"Good. What did she say?"

"She had the telephone—"

"You mean she picked it up?"

"Yes."

"Did she dial?" he asked.

"No, she didn't dial."

"What did she say?"

"She said, 'I want, I want.' "

"What could that mean?" Half to himself: "What could she want?"

Without hesitation: "She wants her mummy to look for her."

He remembered the famous story. "You mean like Mixmaster?"

Smiling: "Yes."

"Maybe you have something there. Could be. Thank you very much for telling me what she said."

When he was back with Marta, he said, "I'm looking for a child I love very much."

Marta stood stiff and rigid. He pushed awkwardly around her and looked under the bureau. "She's not under the bureau." Still bumping against Marta: "And not under this chair. I wonder where she could be." Now he pulled open a bureau drawer: "Not in there." Another one: "Not in there. Could she be behind this picture?" And he looked behind a picture of Ruth. "Or behind this picture?" He looked behind a picture of Fred. "No, I don't see her anywhere. Where could she be?" Now he turned his gaze directly on Marta. He acted astonished. "There she is, right there." He touched her shoulder and smiled at her. "You tried to get away from me," he said, "but I hunted and hunted until I found you. You don't think I'd ever give up until I did, do you?"

But no recognition, no change. She might as well not have heard him. Perhaps she hadn't heard him. "She" hadn't heard him. But there was a *she,* the listener in a corner of the brain, that had heard.

In the late evening he took Miss Barklund into the living room and said, "Do you notice any change in Marta?"

"How do you mean?"

"If you ask that, maybe you don't. Maybe I'm deluding myself."

She hesitated. "She *is* less rigid. But it could be she's resisting more too. I get one feeling—"

"Yes?" he said.

"I think she knows you're really after her."

Remarkable, that she could sense that. "I am. When I brought her here, I was determined it should be meaningful, that she should recognize it as that. I sometimes get discouraged and tired, but that doesn't matter." Thinking: "I've been gentler with her today. I thought if she's conceivably more accessible, I'd try being loving to draw her out. But that isn't enough. I'm thinking of something else."

"Yes?"

"You can watch. But of course leave her to me unless I call on you."

"Yes, Doctor."

He went to Marta, who was in her room, and said, "Come."

He led her out into the hallway and down to where the archways, on either side, opened to the dining room and kitchen. This was the stage, the place of eating. He had put an apple on the dining-room table, a large pale-yellow disk that sat in the dim light like a moon or like a breast. He had chosen the light flesh color, the tint of cream-colored flesh, deliberately. Possibly it might be the culmination of this breast-cycle, this orality that was now so central.

The tree of the knowledge of good and evil. Knowledge of reality. It had been a part of his own dreams and was part of every unconsciousness. You eat to be like God. To lose Eden but to gain the world (come up out of that cellar).

It was no accident that the apple was like a breast. Bert Lewin should take note: You devour the breast and you lose Eden. You lose the refuge of the womb, the cellar, the cave, the catatonic stupor where nothing can touch you.

He casually sat down in a kitchen chair and said, "Marta, on the dining-room table there's an apple. Do you see it?"

With her arm over her breasts, she was of course not looking there but into a corner of the room.

"Not there. On the dining-room table. Look there."

No change in the direction of her gaze.

"Marta, you will look where I tell you. Look at the dining-room table."

No response.

He got up and went to her. "Look."

Still no motion of her eyes away from the corner of the room, but he did detect a slight trembling.

"You will look now at the dining-room table."

When she didn't move, he took her head firmly in his hands and turned it until she was looking in the direction of the table. "Now, you see an apple there. I want you to get me that apple."

No response.

"I'm sorry, you will have to do it, have to obey me. You will have to do what I want you to do. Marta?"

A trembling nonmotion.

"I love you and so I'm giving you warning. Get the apple."

Still no motion.

He pushed her, but she showed an unusual rigidity. Usually she would move her feet. Somewhat to his embarrassment, she fell forward before he checked his push, and fell flat on the floor. Angered now (and seeing that she had not hurt herself), he reached down and grabbed her by her long, heavy hair and dragged her across the floor, feeling that weight of an inert body pulling against his arm. At the dining-room table, he lifted her up bodily and stood her on her feet again, her hair, that he had not let go of, falling over her shoulders. He said, "Take the apple. Take—that—apple."

Her hand moved uncertainly.

He slapped her hard on the side of the face. "Take it."

She hesitated. As he raised his arm again, she took the apple.

"Give it to me."

She gave it to him. He took a large bite of it. "Now you eat it," he said. He put one hand behind her head and with the other, put the apple to her mouth and as she opened her mouth, forced her to bite into the apple. The juice ran down her chin.

By God (God is in this), you have a loving mother and she's making you be in this world: you're going to be in this world, you're going to get well.

He put the apple in her hand and steadily she ate it until finally he said, "You don't want to eat the core, woman. Here, let me have that," and he took the core away from her.

He put his arm around her and guided her back to her room. He stood her in the middle of the room, facing him. He waited. Five minutes went by. In that time she had not lifted her arm to put it across her breasts.

"You're more in the real world," he said.

Silence.

"Doesn't it feel good to be in the real world?"

She sat down on the edge of the bed, but not in her usual rigid way. He still waited. She still continued "loose."

"I guess you must be tired. You must want to go to bed now. Do you want Miss Barklund?"

No answer.

"Suppose I leave you to undress by yourself. Miss Barklund will come in in a few minutes."

He went outside where Miss Barklund was waiting. "Well, what do you think?" he said.

"Wasn't it kind of rough?"

"But it doesn't seem to have hurt her. You spoke about her being less rigid. She still is, don't you think? Maybe even freer."

"Yes," she said, "I do. It's rather amazing."

"All day it's been like this. That's why I wanted to go this far. I wanted to keep her moving."

"I never saw this before."

He said, "Would you go in her room now?"

Miss Barklund opened the door.

Marta stood undressed, in her robe.

When he went back through the hall, he noticed Johnny eating an apple in the kitchen. "You want to get out of paradise too?" he said to him. "Where's Mama?"

"She's in the bedroom."

He went on down to their bedroom and Margaret was sitting sewing. A housewifely occupation, he thought.

"Did you hear the row?" he said.

"I heard it."

"I did something rather drastic." She knew what had been happening during the day, and although she was (he knew) disturbed by much of it, she was too intelligent not to know what it could mean to him. He said, "I just made Marta do something I told her to do—just physically made her. I made her pick up an apple and give it to me and then eat it. And she ate it. I think it could be important. I don't want to count on it. I don't know how a case like this moves or if it is moving. But I *think* it's moving. Something's going on, anyway."

"That girl is too beautiful," she said.

"Odd you should say that. Do you mean today?"

"No, I've been noticing."

"You're not jealous, are you?" he said.

"I don't know. A little."

"If I was treating her somewhere else, you wouldn't think about it. It would be like all the other cases."

"Maybe. But this *is* something special for you."

"It's a harder case. There's a countertransference and it's strong, but you wouldn't be jealous of my love for Nancy."

"Oh, yes I would. I am."

He laughed. "Good then. You can be jealous of Marta."

"You laugh, but is all this good, what you're doing?"

"I believe so."

"But you could be wrong?"

"That's what you keep telling me. I'm not sure I like it. Don't you want to encourage me?"

"Not with Marta, no." She put her sewing aside and stood up. "You call all this making the case move. But move where? Marta screamed yesterday. And the things that have been going on today are hardly what ought to be going on in a private home."

He started to undress. "I'm tired," he said. "I'm going to bed."

Drugged by excitement and fatigue, he was soon asleep. He sensed Margaret come to bed beside him and, deep in a continuing coma, he knew nothing until he was awakened at some early hour of the morning.

He found the light on and Margaret facing him in a fury.

"What's the matter?"

"I just stepped in shit, that's what's the matter."

"What are you talking about?"

Her voice breaking: "I can't stand it anymore. I just can't stand it."

"Will you please tell me what happened?"

"I heard something in the hall and you were so tired, I thought I'd better see what it was. It must have been Marta because I stepped right in her shit."

"You mean out in the hall here?"

"She deliberately got up and shit in the hallway."

"I'm really sorry. But—" Thinking: "Whereabouts? Exactly where in the hall did she do it?"

"Outside the kitchen between the kitchen and the dining room."

"That's where I dragged her to the apple before. You know—" Comprehending: "She was making me a present!"

"John—!"

"That's what it must be." Exultant: "Was it a big one?"

She screamed. "I stepped in it. Yes, it was a big one. A goddamned big stinking present for you. But I had to clean it up. And wash my feet."

"I'm sorry, darling, but it could mean so much to the case. You know how tight she's been, hoarding her body waste, not voiding, not giving anything up. And you know how babies do number two to please you—"

"John, listen to me. You're wrong. It's insane. I know what you want to do, but you can't go on with it. You can't tell what this insane woman will do next. I told you. I told you before. You can't have her here. She could hurt the children—"

"Impossible. She won't do anything—"

"She *has* done something! Exposing the boys to this. What must they think? What if Nancy had woken up? No, it has to stop. It simply has to stop."

Quietly: "I didn't expect this from you."

"I can't help whether you did or not. This just has to stop."

He saw the look in her eyes. "The case appears to be moving," he said. "I don't know what it will be tomorrow, but what's happened so far is pretty hopeful, by me. I hate to take her out of here right at this moment. But I'll go this far: If there's an improvement both of us can see, that makes you feel safer—and I know how you feel—then you might want to reconsider. You might want her to stay. But if there isn't any change, and there might not be, I'll agree to move her back to the hotel."

She began to cry.

He said, "I'm really sorry. I know it's been hard for you."

27

In the morning, he went immediately to Marta. She seemed to have slept, and there was no stiffness to indicate she had stayed for hours (as she sometimes did) in an unnatural position. She had not wet the bed. Otherwise there was no change that he could strictly define.

He determined to stay with her again all day except for his session with Naumann. He treated her immediately. He treated from every least indication, from the flow of breathing, stasis, movement (there was very little—she wasn't rigid, but she was certainly withdrawn): he interpreted from the slightest motion of her eyeballs.

It was discouraging. After the progress of the day before, back to the beginning. But, he thought, this was no time to let up. But this sense of complete stillness. Nonreaction. What was going on behind that stillness?

Just before he left for Dr. Naumann's, he made the brief statement (he had carefully planned it): "Marta, thank you for the gift you made me last night. It was very valuable."

"Come in," Dr. Naumann said.

The pastel green of the inner room enfolded him in its reminders both of peace and storm. He had become attached to it. He could ask for a justified truce in its complex weather as he began to tell Dr. Naumann about the events of the night before.

"The feces—" Dr. Naumann said (a faint trace of smile in his voice, something Dr. Marks had learned to detect as a shading just before some Socratic knifing): "Let me ask, not just your interpretation of the feces, but the whole tenor of your handling of the treatment yesterday—except for the aggression and perhaps even the aggression—was it consistent with your theory?"

"How do you mean?" Now what was Naumann going to pull on him?

"What is psychosis, according to your theory?"

"You mean, orality?"

"Yes, it's being at the orality level. And what is orality?"

"Infancy, the mouth?"

"A baby's mouth. And the feces?"

"Baby shit." Shit in a diaper, before toilet training, shit in the first months of life. "Still, does that necessarily mean it's not a gift?" Dr. Marks said. "The Unconscious can consider all secretions gifts of power and omnipotence. That psychotic who mailed gifts of snot and semen, even dandruff—"

"It is not the oral period."

"No?" He was going to contend with God here. "You say yourself there are no absolutes. Marta didn't shit in bed. She went out and deliberately did it in the hallway, at the exact spot where I dragged her to the apple."

"Then you admit anality, at least an admixture of anality. But in the interpretation of that, your wife didn't agree with you. She sensed the possibility of psychotic cruelty. The Unconscious defecating on people."

"It's my wife who was angry, not Marta. You haven't seen Marta today. She may be withdrawn, but there's no anger. I could tell if there was. There just isn't."

"I'm interested in one phase of your treatment yesterday —weren't you rather permissive?"

"You mean before she lipsticked her breast? You mean my forgiving her for peeing in bed and all that? And even the breast thing? It was deliberate. I've been thinking lately that I haven't dramatized openly enough that I love her. So yesterday I tried that way to reduce the fear. But then I felt I had to use aggression, even physical force, so I tried the apple thing." He paused, thinking. "I keep saying she's been afraid of me. It isn't me myself she's been afraid of. It's me as the therapist she sensed attacking her insanity, insanity she needs like life itself—"

"What you mean is, you controlled her for her own good."

"That's right."

"It occurs to me—how many months has she missed her period?"

"Eight months."

"Babies don't have periods," Dr. Naumann said and now there was a speculative tone in his voice.

"Neither do pregnant women," Dr. Marks said.

"She's a baby and a mother." Still thinking aloud.

"A mother. A wife. The feces could have been a sign of improvement?"

"What's in your mind now?" Dr. Naumann said.

At first nothing. Then: "My mother at the famous birthday party made an issue of my not having salt on a hard-boiled egg. I told you about that. I could be six years old again and I thought, For a mother you never grow up. Or maybe it means, you never grow up *from* Mama. All patients believe that—they all want to bathe themselves in about one inch of water and the water is Mama. So me, too. I ate salt with my egg for Mama. And I went to see her last week and we had a talk. Something's changing."

"With your father?"

"Well, there's always that whip."

"A real whip?"

"You know that in the dreams I have about him—in some of them—I've had a good feeling toward him. Even a protective feeling. I've felt I was defending him. That carries over. He doesn't get to me anymore. But I think the real problem has been Ma."

Silence.

"Hard-boiled eggs. Ma and Margaret both. Sometimes I think how Ma and Margaret both had two boys—" He had a stunned feeling. "With Marta in my home, I have two boys and two girls, just the same as Mama. Nancy and Marta. Was I trying to re-create my own family? You told me—that dream of my getting into and out of a car, that I associated to the house on Bushwick Avenue—you told me that was the home I wanted to bring Marta to. Maybe I didn't want to bring her to that home. I wanted to make that my home."

"A little tyrannizing over the family?" Dr. Naumann said.

Stunned: "Yes." Then, "Amazing what the psyche can do. Was this my own running back for love?"

"For something. Maybe it's hard to grow up?"

Who is the therapist, who the patient?

"Tell me," Dr. Naumann said, "do you possibly feel Margaret isn't motherly—as your mother didn't seem motherly to you? Because Margaret doesn't want to be a mother to an insane patient, does that justify you in feeling she isn't motherly?"

"I'm about ready to agree she doesn't have to be a therapist," Dr. Marks said. "But Marta—I'm not sorry I brought her into my home. Something happened. There must have been something good about it."

Silence.

"Maybe she needed a tyrant," Dr. Marks said.

"And your wife?"

A week later he took Marta back to the same apartment she had had before at the hotel. Fred, as before, accompanied them. On the trip there, she seemed relaxed—her eyes stared less at visions and more at objects. She turned once and looked out of the car window.

At the apartment, no hunting under bureau or radiators. Miss Kinnell reported to him later: "She took hold of my dress collar and asked me, 'Where's the linen breastworks?' "

Dr. Marks said, "That's quite a remark. Nothing dull about what she says, when she does say something."

He asked Fred to his office.

"You don't feel bad about my having taken her back to the hotel, do you?" he said.

"Not if you don't."

A good answer. "I want to discuss the case with you. I can't tell you about treatment in detail, but your wife recently, while she was in my home, did some rather dramatic things—at least, considering that it was her, it was dramatic—and this makes me feel her catatonia isn't invulnerable, that there has been some minor movement, and some encouragement. That she could take any kind of initiative."

"Yes, I see," Fred said.

"It's nothing definite or conclusive."

But Fred looked happy. Well, why not?

"What will you do now?" Fred said.

"Simply work harder than I ever have before."

When he took Fred to the door, he was aware of its being a warm, pleasant day. It was the end of May.

He phoned home. Margaret answered. "This is your insensitive husband."

"You'll do for a while." He could imagine the snicker.

"What do you want to lure me home with. Lamb chops?"

"As it happens, we're having some very mild Indian curry."

"You got a deal."

"You saw Fred?" she asked.

"He just left."

"Tell me more about Marta, at the hotel."

"She didn't look under any radiators. And she ate a good meal."

"No interpretations?"

He laughed. Margaret asked the question as if she was offering him a morsel of love.

"No." It was true, he hadn't used any interpretations from the beginning of Marta's large meal to the end. "Of course she made a circle with her potatoes. You can't win them all."

"How about taking her weight?"

"I'm ahead of you. I took her weight. She's gaining."

"But that's wonderful."

"I must be doing something right."

In the first week of June, he had the nurses keep careful check on Marta's posture. Only twice in the week did she become rigid for any length of time, and both times he came at once and with a relentless interpretative attack ended it. When he felt her resisting at one point, he yanked her hair remindingly. Once he had the thought of putting some music on and trying to dance with her. At the beginning there were some faltering and staggering steps, but midway she began following and then (why, he didn't know) she began pointing violently to her mouth. He brought her a glass of milk.

The dancing continued.

Something else significant. Miss Barklund one evening complained aloud (when alone with Marta) that it was warm. She was perspiring, there were beads of perspiration on her face. Marta took out a handkerchief and wiped her face with it, with what Miss Barklund said seemed like definite affection.

He kept saying, "Why don't you talk?" Miss Kinnell, after he left one day, repeated the question and to her amazement, Marta said, "I'm afraid I'll bring certain peo-

ple's affairs to public notice." Miss Kinnell phoned him.
He said, "Put her on the phone, let her listen to my
voice," and when Marta was on the phone, he said, "Miss
Kinnell says you said, 'I'm afraid I'll bring certain people's
affairs to public notice.' What you mean is you'll bring
your own affairs to public notice. All this misery with
your mother. I don't have to repeat it, I'm sure." He told
her to put Miss Kinnell back on the phone. "This is fine,"
he told Miss Kinnell. "She put you on the phone when I
told her to. You realize that's communication? I want you
to keep asking her, 'Why don't you talk?' Hammer away
with it, get it into her consciousness. I learned lately that
they can teach retardates, retarded children, just by saying
the same thing over and over again to them. Just keep at
her, 'Why don't you talk, why don't you talk?' And let's
see what happens."

Miss Kinnell phoned him later to tell him (again he was
astounded) that after she had asked Marta a hundred
times, "Why don't you talk?" Marta said, "It'll take away
the dream."

" 'It'll take away the dream.' How about that? And they
say they're crazy. I *will* take away her dream, she knows
it. She's thinking about it, can you imagine that?" He told
Margaret (he was home at the time) and decided to interrupt his dinner and go to Marta. Take away the dream.
Give me my coat. I don't need a coat. It's spring. Take
away the dream.

"What's so good about your dream?" he said to her. "It
never was a good dream. Give it up. You get one thou-
sandth of one percent nourishment from that dream of
yours. Enough to starve to death on in two minutes. What
you need is milk."

Two days later he had an idea. Marta had listened on
the phone. He phoned Marta's apartment from his office
and told Miss Kinnell to put Marta on. "Hello," he said.
"Marta?"

He heard her breathing. "Marta?" Sharply: "Are you
there?" Nothing but the breathing. But then harder breathing. Then a sound like a struggle, like grunting. The grunting continued and lapsed into breathing again. But it had
happened.

"Yes? What do you want to say? Say it."

Again grunting. Passionate, anguished sound. A grunt and again a grunt.

He could hardly bear it.

It was a sound of effort, of trying.

"Why don't you talk?"

Now almost a syllable, but it fell into indistinctness. Then into silence.

He cut all his other work to a bare minimum. He did everything but sleep at Marta's. Margaret screamed. He told her, "I have to do this."

Who knows when a baby begins to talk? With Marta, he could not have told anybody when it happened. A baby repeats syllables and makes sounds like talking but unintelligible and then, almost without any specific designation of time, is talking. It was even more complex with Marta. She came out of silence as if out of a labyrinth, running and losing herself back in it again and again. But there was communication. She said things to the nurses to relay to him and he picked up on them as he never had before. He said to her, "You said to Miss Barklund, 'Can somebody give me some mixed dressing?' Can you tell me what 'mixed dressing' is?" Silence but attentiveness. "I give you only pure dressing, you know that. You deserve it because you're an unmixed blessing. I'm not going to let you be mixed up anymore. You're going to grow five years in one day."

Marta's gestures, her pointing, and her pantomimes increased. He danced with her, and at least once or twice every day he stood at the window with her and commented on life in the street. When he would ask her questions, she would shake her head no or yes, a previously unheard-of vote of confidence. And she would seem to be understanding everything he said (what a distance from the unfocused staring at nothingness!).

And without his knowing the exact moment when it happened, he was aware that they were talking. The talk wasn't altogether real. It was symbolic doubletalk and nonsense-in-sense, and then it got to be sense-in-nonsense.

She said, "Several policemen came to see her, didn't they?"

She said, "Children are quite small when they're little."

She said, "Something is happening, I'm sure. Could you tell me when it will stop?"

She said, "Certain thoughts seem to be here all the time."

She said, "Did you say I was away?"

"Yes, where were you all this time?" he said.

"I was in jail—I used to have to sit on the floor—on the mattress—on the edge of the bucket."

"What bucket?"

"If you don't hold all your muscles just right, you fall."

"You fall into the toilet, Mother eats you. Tell me, why didn't you talk? Why did you stop talking all that time?"

"Did everybody go free on that trial?"

"You mean you got Papa into trouble. And then it was all right. I got you sentenced to freedom."

"Thank you. Are you Dr. Marks?"

"I'm Dr. Marks. And where are you?"

"The Hotel St. Emory."

"Right. I suppose you might want to see Fred sometime."

Now her eyes had something between joy and fright. "Everybody says he loves me."

Dr. Marks: "What kind of talk is that? You're the only woman in the world he loves. No other woman is as lovable as you are."

Now a smile: "I used to know somebody who was loved."

"It was you."

She laughed.

"I heard you laugh once before. You know, it was the best laugh I ever heard. But I'll tell you something—"

She seemed very attentive, interested. "You used to laugh to pretend you were happy. You don't have to do that anymore. You can be really happy now."

On the last day of spring she had her period. And it was a good strong flow. Nine months. He said to Margaret, "Do you think she could be giving birth to herself? Do you think just possibly the nine months is symbolic, like so much else in her mind?"

"John! Well, if you want to believe it."

"What's this wanting to believe things? Isn't it human to have symbols?"

Smiling: "John?"

"Yes?"

"You *are* wonderful. I maybe don't always remember it. Or don't always tell you."

"Are you really trying to tell me you're glad about Marta?"

With that amused look of hers: "It could be."

He asked Ginnie to spend time with Marta. They were close and Ginnie had insights, she was bright and cheerful. He was more cautious about Fred. He told Dr. Naumann about Fred's first visit: "Fred came at dinnertime, just after Marta had eaten, and he kissed her, I mean she kissed him. I thought he was going to fall over, he was so happy. Then she smiled. She knew just what was going on, the bitch. You know that woman thing, that they know they've got you? And then I could see him thinking about that smile. It was a real smile. It wasn't that reactive thing he'd told me about at the beginning of the case. I'm not sure he's ever going to get that semihysterical laugh back again, nice as it was. And much as he liked it. I think he's going to have to fall in love with a new woman."

Marta's parents, when they heard Marta was "getting well," wanted to deed Dr. Marks a large part of the Bronx or Manhattan, whichever he wanted.

He warned them he had to bring Marta completely out and would need a stretch of careful postpsychotic work with her. They would have to be patient. "If she was that sick," he told them, "I want to be damn sure she gets completely well, and stays well."

She showed all the standard signs his other patients showed, coming out. One moment she'd be paranoid, or she'd have a touch of depression. Then she'd be obsessive-compulsive, except that it wasn't that awful real obsessive-compulsive thing where you knew you'd have to fight it for months. It was more like playacting. Or she would cough or gag or catch her breath.

Fred wanted her to come home "for a visit." Dr. Marks refused that too. "When she goes home, I want it to be for keeps," he told Fred. "I don't care how good she seems. She'll have a great adjustment to make, to you and Ruthie. She'll be a real mother, a real wife. She has to be ready for it. I get hints of how difficult this is. She even said, 'I didn't give Ruthie enough food.' As plain as that."

He thought, I'm going to have to get a number of things straight with her:

What it means to be independent and still love people.

What it means to be a nourishing mother.

What it means to value yourself.

Dr. Naumann followed the course of Marta's emergence from psychosis with steady interest. He responded to what Dr. Marks told him about her, warmly and open-heartedly. He said at one point, "These conversations you're having with her seem more coherent than is usual with catatonics coming out. I wonder what that can mean." After a moment: "Do you suppose it could be like a baby who has for a long time delayed beginning to talk, but has been listening?"

Dr. Marks was hardly able to contain himself. Was this Dr. Naumann's complete surrender to "orality"? he thought. He forced himself not to make any pleased or noticing remark. He said, "I find many signs of the infancy thing. She puts a finger in her mouth now and then. She disguises it the way growing children disguise their yearning back to the breast. Obviously she doesn't suck her finger. But there's that moment of wanting to."

Dr. Naumann: "I believe that you should now get seriously to work on your second paper. This case consolidates all your work up to now. I know you yourself have felt it as a test of yourself and your method. It has been that. I can reveal to you now how much and how deeply I felt for you myself. But the point is that now that you've brought Marta out, you'll find you have a greatly increased understanding of all your previous cases, and so you should be writing your new paper."

"Give me time. I'm still treating her."

"You can start the first stages of the paper. Decide on organization and emphasis. But meantime be sure your notes on Marta are complete while all this is fresh in your mind."

He promised that he would do what Dr. Naumann asked, but said his first interest still was getting Marta well.

After three months of careful work, he decided Marta was ready to go home. He made the arrangements with Fred: just Fred and Ruthie were to be there in Riverdale waiting for her. He would bring her. He went to the hotel and went up to her apartment, and she and Miss Kinnell stood waiting, the luggage packed. "I'm all right now, Miss Kinnell, I really am, and you and the other nurses were so good to stay with me all that time. I must have been terrible."

Miss Kinnell's eyes were wet. "You never were," she said.

A porter helped them down with the luggage. Miss Kinnell said good-by and Marta got into the front seat next to him. She waved.

She was silent till they were driving up the escarpment to Riverdale, then she said, "How will I be with them?"

"Just be yourself. I don't know anything better than that."

"I guess."

"By the way, the family send their love. Nancy will miss you."

"Oh, I'll miss her." Nancy had visited her several times at the hotel, sitting on her lap and talking with her. "You know she did me so much good. What she doesn't know!"

"I know. I'm going to have her give a course for State Hospital psychiatrists."

She laughed.

When he reached Riverdale, he crossed the parkway overpass and drove down the feeder road to the apartment house and parked. "Well, here you are," he said.

He helped her out. "Never mind the luggage. Fred can come down for it. Are you ready?"

"I'm ready."

"Then go up alone."

"Alone!"

"It's better."

She seemed uncertain. "I'll see you soon? You're sure?"

"Next Wednesday. You have an office appointment."

"That's right." She smiled, touched her straw hat, and walked away.

He was working at last on his new paper, which would summarize all his cases to date. It would include Marta. Marta wasn't going to be an easy case to present, but his notes were exceptionally full, thanks to Rosalie and Margaret, and he learned more each time he saw Marta.

Margaret was helping him with the paper.

He had taken on three new cases, one very difficult. A girl who believed somebody was creeping under her skin and who was continually biting herself (though not breaking the skin). She had an obsession with the number three. She wrote several letters to Jeannette, who was on the case, complaining about "spychology." (About me.)

He felt now (perhaps falsely, but it was based on Marta) that he could handle the hardest case and bring the patient out. How about Ethel? Would it be possible, conceivably, to bring her out? But when he defined the case as a hard case, it was with a qualification of no prior shock treatment or at least a minimum of shock. Ethel had had a maximum of shock: incalculable rivers of electric shock and insulin coma had flowed through her with their physical ravage to the brain. If he did bring her out, what would she be? The Ethel who had been able to say to him: "I'm getting knife stabs all over . . . Somebody's gypping my secret things from me—"? Or another Ethel, one he might not even know.

Theory began to occupy him. Since so much of his therapy depended on Freud's conception of psychosis as a nonwaking dream, he had begun to think intently about dreams. He would formulate theory verbally in his mind as he was trying to go to sleep (not, admittedly, a very good way to get to sleep). Two premises (Freud): a dream represents a wish disguised by the dream work so that the wish will not be recognized and, second, a dream results from a repetition compulsion.

Possibly, he thought one night, dreaming that has a visual and auditory hallucinatory quality has a broader function. Let's assume it's an occupation of the mind different from waking and intended to help preserve sleep. What prevents sleep? When we are preparing to sleep (as I should be now), what stops it is ordinary waking thought. Such thought may turn to projects for the future, deeply occupying us with worry, foreboding, or hope (the wish).

We may also live over past experiences, pleasurable or otherwise (repetition compulsion), but these repetitions are not hallucinatory and are accompanied by conscious thoughts about the experiences. Evaluation, testing, efforts to understand, even theorize (as now).

This is the waking or wakeful process. This is the

thought that must be translated into hallucinatory equivalents and disguised so that we can sleep.

Why hallucinatory? Because dreams go back to more primitive mental states where dreaming and waking are closer together. As they are for children. Beyond the child's dream, why not regression phylogenetically to primitive dreaming when the dreamer often thought he was having actual experiences that he recalled. After he had slept.

What about a baby's dreaming? It is necessarily uncomplicated. His wish is to survive. To have milk. How much can you disguise this—a wish for loving arms, protection, silence, sleep?

So with a baby there would be a maximum likeness between dream and waking. In both states, the baby had milk, directly experienced or hallucinated. In this individually experienced closeness of dreaming and waking lay the possibility of the psychotic dream.

Why then (he thought) don't we all become psychotics? We don't because most of us have had good milk and enough love. We don't have to find a device for hallucinating a good mother. For escaping from unnamable terrors.

In treatment you go back as far as possible, trace everything back to its ontogenetic and even phylogenetic root. You (as god, parent, beneficent force) try to separate hallucination (disguise) from reality, and you succeed because you can persuade the patient (baby) to reject bad milk and take good milk. Give up the waking dream for an attractive reality since there is now good milk to be had.

"What were you afraid of, Marta, when you were psychotic?"

"The critics," she said. She came now once a week to the office for follow-up treatment.

"Who were the critics?"

"Oh, everybody."

"I guess that follows. You certainly kept everybody away from you. But who was the real critic?"

"Well, I guess I've learned who from you—"

"Not from me—"

"No. The real critic was my mother."

Casually: "How do you feel about her now?"

"You know, she tried to go shopping with me. You'd

think she'd realize now, and know I won't do that any-more."

"And other than that, how are you with her? What's the tone?"

"I guess I like her. She has some depth to her when you get to know her. I don't know, we get along. But I'm busy."

In another session: "You know that time you dragged me across the floor—"

It was the first time she had mentioned it. "You remember it?" he said.

"Oh, yes—"

"You remember that it was me?"

"I may have thought you were some kind of police officer, but part of me—no, wait—part of me knew it was you. And knew what you were doing, proving you could control me, that I had to give in." Her hand went up involuntarily to her hair, and she smiled and said, "My hair must have been pretty strong."

"It's beautiful hair. I'm sorry I had to use it that way."

"It didn't hurt it. I think it grew some while I was sick."

"You grew some."

Smiling: "I did, didn't I?"

In another session, she told him that when she was a child, she had once had a persistent attack of laryngitis and her mother had made her drink large quantities of grape juice. "Oh, I hated it. I used to spit it out. I guess that's why I spit out that grape juice that time on my breast."

And in another session, she told him that the white enameled door of the kitchen stove had seemed to her like a painting of a cat, and she had wanted to touch the cat and see if its fur was soft.

"Why would the fur be soft in a painting?"

"I know, it's not very logical. But I wasn't being very logical then, was I?" she said.

"I'm not sure. Maybe you were."

So what he had thought was a breast and a dream screen and even a womb was a cat. A white cat?

"Was it a white cat?" he said.

"Yes, it was."

"Was there any white cat in your life?"

A look of horror. "Yes. When I was very small, we had a white cat and she was crushed in the street by a car. She had just had kittens——" She stopped.

He waited. At last he said, "Go on."

"I don't know. I just remembered I was so sad that the kittens didn't have a mama to feed them. Of course Father got rid of them then."

You worked without knowledge. Or rather, your knowledge was merely all the awareness you had, from two or three dozen previous cases and from some source inside yourself. And maybe it was more than that, maybe your knowledge was from compassion. He thought about this thing of compassion. No cow sees another cow lying sick and brings it some of its own hay or a drink of water. Compassion is human, solely or mainly human.

He continued impressed by the general lack of emphasis on orality in the classic literature. It was true that in the *New Introductory Lectures* Freud wrote that fear of loss of love is "obviously a continuation of the fear of the infant at the breast when it misses its mother. You will understand what objective danger-situation is indicated by this kind of anxiety. If the mother is absent or has withdrawn her love from the child, it can no longer be certain that its needs will be satisfied and may be exposed to the most painful feelings of tension."

But was this insight carried over into treatment? Freud also wrote, in *The Question of Lay Analysis,* that "there are cases in which the transference, once unleashed, cannot be mastered, and the analysis must then be broken off."

And Dr. Marks himself had talked with analysts who prided themselves on the sharpness of perception with which they diagnosed the oncoming of a psychotic episode and cut the treatment off "before getting into trouble."

At least he had proved that an analysis need never be broken off.

He had proved that the doctor is part of his patient's life at its most despairing and dreadful moments. That the patient is human. That the rationale of his humanity never stops. From the time he had told Mrs. Blumstein that "they" (the followers of the Fiend) were no longer after her to the present moment, he had known he was himself the patient, that there was no difference in humanity between him and a psychotic.

Was this just another way of saying compassion?

He had sent his new paper to the same psychiatric journal that had published his first one. The editor, former head of a large upstate New York State hospital (where, until his retirement, no shock treatment had been allowed), decided that he wanted to see the cases described in the paper as "recovered"—at least see enough of them to assure himself that the term "recovered" meant the same thing to himself as to Dr. Marks. He made a special trip to New York, bringing with him an associate, Dr. James Palmer, a quiet young man given to quick acknowledgments of the potential humor of any situation.

These visitors came to Dr. Marks's office and interviewed a number of his cases including Jeannette, Betty, King James, Jimmy, and Marta. Marta was decidedly self-possessed and made a remarkable impression on the editor. He said that the paper would be published early the following year, 1947.

Dr. Palmer talked privately with Dr. Marks and indicated a practical interest in his "work." Could he perhaps study with him if he should happen to come to New York?

The publication of Dr. Marks's first paper had caused a storm. The same claims of mistaken diagnosis he had been faced with at New State Hospital were made again, and there was much hinting that he was working under a delusion. One critic rehearsed the standard objection: "When the excitement of schizophrenia has been controlled, when the accessory symptoms have disappeared and even the fundamental symptoms have lost intensity and retreated, it doesn't mean the patient isn't still schizophrenic. All that has happened is a temporary remission. Within five years, the patient will be back." Back, presumably, to the welcoming gates of the hospital.

Dr. Marks wondered himself about the durability of his cures. In his happiness at the new life his patients were enjoying (usually at a better level than before psychosis, and before his intervention) was the underlying reservation: Will it last? Not that that would keep him from treating insanity. Even a limited period of remission was a price-less gift, in his estimation, if you valued life, as he did.

But were the doubters right, that the patient would re-lapse?

He had only his own patients to go on.

DECEMBER 15, 1956

DEAR DR. MARKS:

I've been thinking about you a great deal lately and have been wanting to write. No particular news except that Ruthie is going to be in her school play. Fred is so pleased—I am too.

To think that Ruth is in high school. How the time goes!

I suppose you think the same thing about Nancy.

My folks were here for the weekend last week. I wasn't feeling too well and Mother's overconcern irri-tated me. Luckily, they went home Sunday night. I sup-pose I should be more tolerant, you'd tell me, but I'm not.

Then again, perhaps it's just as well I can stand up for myself. (Thanks to you.)

How are you and the family? I hope you're all well and happy. And I hope you'll have a chance to let me hear from you.

LOVE,
MARTA

There were many similar letters from other patients over the years. Or a patient would come to the office, or to his home, Nora Paul wearing a ribbon in her hair or Jimmy bringing his wife and two children. In 1968, Mar-ta's girl was grown and married, and Marta was frequently babysitting with her grandchildren, one of whom was named Nancy.

ABOUT THE AUTHOR

MILLEN BRAND's first novel, *The Outward Room,* was the forerunner of all the psychiatric novels in the last three decades. He has worked extensively as a psychiatric aide with severely disturbed cases and has had rare access to hospitals and professional groups. He brings to his writing not only a lifetime of fictional discipline, but years of work as a poet. It is his conviction that fiction can convey elements of truth incommunicable by factual statement.

The complete ∽ John ∽ Steinbeck

AMERICA AND AMERICANS	Q3811	$1.25
BURNING BRIGHT	S4806	75¢
CANNERY ROW	HC4001	60¢
CUP OF GOLD	S3624	75¢
EAST OF EDEN	Q4777	$1.25
THE GRAPES OF WRATH	Q4574	$1.25
IN DUBIOUS BATTLE	NC4399	95¢
THE LONG VALLEY	S3538	75¢
THE MOON IS DOWN	SP5358	75¢
OF MICE AND MEN	SC4649	75¢
ONCE THERE WAS A WAR	S4748	75¢
PASTURES OF HEAVEN	S3698	75¢
THE PEARL	HP4444	60¢
THE RED PONY	HP4499	60¢
SHORT REIGN OF PIPPIN IV	S4397	75¢
SWEET THURSDAY	SC4079	75¢
TO A GOD UNKNOWN	S3832	75¢
TORTILLA FLAT	H3019	60¢
TRAVELS WITH CHARLEY	N3956	95¢
THE WAYWARD BUS	S3501	75¢
WINTER OF OUR DISCONTENT	N3623	95¢

THE WORLD OF JOHN STEINBECK   A deluxe boxed set containing *Travels with Charley, The Grapes of Wrath, The Winter of Our Discontent, East of Eden, Of Mice and Men* and *The Pearl*.   K5101 $5.75

JOHN O'HARA

*is one of America's finest writers. His books
have sold over 20,000,000 in Bantam editions alone!
If you enjoy reading about people as they
really are—from politicians and factory workers
to bankers and movie stars— you'll enjoy
everyone of these brilliant novels and short stories.
And now you can get all the O'Haras you missed
at great savings in these handsome Bantam editions!*

If you think this book was good, wait 'til you see what *else* we've got in store for you!

Send for your FREE catalog of Bantam Bestsellers today!

This money-saving catalog lists hundreds of bestsellers originally priced from $3.75 to $15.00—yours now in Bantam paperback editions for just 50¢ to $1.95! Here is a great opportunity to read the good books you've missed and add to your private library at huge savings! The catalog is FREE! So don't delay—send for yours today!